"JULIA ROSS IS A MAGICAL STORYTELLER."
—The Romance Journal

Praise for the novels of Julia Ross

The Wicked Lover

"Master storyteller Ross delivers a spellbinding double dose of intrigue and passion in this . . . fast-paced, sensual story brimming over with unforgettable moments and memorable characters. Exquisitely romantic, utterly captivating." *—Romantic Times* "TOP PICK" (4½ stars)

"An exceptional writer who creates rich, compelling characters in tales of intrigue. When [Ross] adds passion to the mix, so much the better for fans . . . [Dove] is one of the most truly heroic men in romance . . . Fascinating, appealing, and unforgettable." *—The Oakland Press*

"An exciting story that sizzles with unbridled sensual desire. Lots of amusing twists and turns, a real keeper." *—Rendezvous*

"A stunning tale of intrigue and passion [with] some of the most beautiful and erotic imagery I have read in a long time . . . I feel very strongly about this book . . . The rewards are well worth it."
—A Romance Review

"A sensual, sophisticated tale, mysterious, elegant, and lusty . . . The pages heat up with very sensuous passages, passionate without a taint of crudity . . . For a tantalizing novel rich in atmosphere, I highly recommend *The Wicked Lover*." *—Romance Reviews Today*

continued . . .

The Seduction

"Ross's lush, evocative writing is the perfect counterpoint for her spell-binding tale of a wickedly refined, elegantly attired rake who is redeemed by one woman's love. Ross, whose combination of lyricism and sensuality is on par with Jo Beverley's, skillfully builds the simmering sexual chemistry between Alden and Juliet into an exquisitely sensual romance and luscious love story." —*Booklist*

"A gripping novel starring two wonderfully tainted romantic skeptics as lead protagonists." —*Midwest Book Review*

"Brilliant [and] scorching . . . With its fascinating characters, intriguing plot, and engrossing, rewarding romance, it is a story not to be missed . . . A beautifully woven tale of an unexpected love that succeeds against all odds. This will be ranked as one of the year's best." —*The Romance Reader*

"Rich, delicious . . . Books like this are treasures . . . Put it at the top of your summer reading list." —*The Oakland Press*

"An extraordinary story . . . A superb example of Ms. Ross's outstanding storytelling talents and exceptional writing abilities. Intense emotions and passionate, strong characters are the complement to a complex love story, replete with such dastardly villains as Shakespeare might have crafted." —*Historical Romance Reviews*

"Set in Georgian England, this well-written novel . . . deftly interweaves an exciting, fast-paced plot with romance and the development of strong characters. Readers won't want this book to end!" —*The Best Reviews*

"Magnificent . . . A wonderfully tempting tale filled with unsurpassed sensuality . . . A hot and fast-paced read . . . Completely enthralling." —*The Road to Romance*

"Wit, lust, and just enough mystery . . . The characters are charming, reckless, and endearing." —*Rendezvous*

My Dark Prince

"Brilliant! Passionate, complex, and compelling. The best book of any genre I have read in a long, long while. Don't miss this beautifully written, intensely satisfying love story. I am in awe . . . Highly recommended."
　　　　　　　　　　　　　　　　　　　　　　　—Mary Balogh

"I thoroughly enjoyed *My Dark Prince*. If you enjoy exciting, entertaining, wonderfully written romance, read this book."　　　—Jo Beverley

"A fantastic cast of characters . . . Julia Ross traps the reader from page one . . . outstanding . . . a breathtaking and mesmerizing historical romance. This is romance in its finest hour."　　—*The Romance Journal*

"Lovers of tortured heroes and intense stories will take this one to their hearts . . . *My Dark Prince* has a plot filled with complications and dangers—real dangers . . . [Nicholas] is as dark and hurting as any hero of Anne Stuart's . . . A tale that will grab you and compel you to finish it in one sitting . . . I don't think I'm going to forget this one anytime soon."　　　　　　　　　　　　　—*All About Romance*

"A powerful story of the redemptive power of love, with one of the most tortured heroes I have come across in quite a while . . . a tour de force of plotting and storytelling . . . An extremely well-crafted story that succeeds in making what should be unbelievable seem perfectly reasonable . . . *My Dark Prince* has loads of danger and adventure . . . compelling . . . poignant . . . the definition of a 'keeper.' "
　　　　　　　　　　　　　　　　　　　　—*The Romance Reader*

"Enjoyable . . . fast-paced . . . the lead couple is a divine pair."
　　　　　　　　　　　　　　　　　　　—*Midwest Book Review*

"With this thrilling adventure of the heart, Julia Ross establishes herself as a powerful, distinctive force in the evolution of the romance genre . . . A new legend in heroes, Ms. Ross's mercurial, complex prince embodies every woman's secret desire for a love beyond the ordinary. Darkly erotic and sensually stunning, this innovative and spellbinding romance will enslave your heart and fill your dreams."
　　　　　　　　　　　　　　　　—*Romantic Times* (4½ stars)

Night of Sin

Julia Ross

BERKLEY SENSATION, NEW YORK

THE BERKLEY PUBLISHING GROUP
Published by the Penguin Group
Penguin Group (USA) Inc.
375 Hudson Street, New York, New York 10014, USA
Penguin Group (Canada), 10 Alcorn Avenue, Toronto, Ontario M4V 3B2, Canada
(a division of Pearson Penguin Canada Inc.)
Penguin Books Ltd., 80 Strand, London WC2R 0RL, England
Penguin Group Ireland, 25 St. Stephen's Green, Dublin 2, Ireland (a division of Penguin Books Ltd.)
Penguin Group (Australia), 250 Camberwell Road, Camberwell, Victoria 3124, Australia
(a division of Pearson Australia Group Pty. Ltd.)
Penguin Books India Pvt. Ltd., 11 Community Centre, Panchsheel Park, New Delhi—110 017, India
Penguin Group (NZ), Cnr. Airborne and Rosedale Roads, Albany, Auckland 1310, New Zealand
(a division of Pearson New Zealand Ltd.)
Penguin Books (South Africa) (Pty.) Ltd., 24 Sturdee Avenue, Rosebank, Johannesburg 2196,
South Africa

Penguin Books Ltd., Registered Offices: 80 Strand, London WC2R 0RL, England

This book is an original publication of The Berkley Publishing Group.

This is a work of fiction. Names, characters, places, and incidents either are the product of the author's imagination or are used fictitiously, and any resemblance to actual persons, living or dead, business establishments, events, or locales is entirely coincidental.

Copyright © 2005 by Jean Ross Ewing.
Cover design by Griesbach / Martucci.
Cover art by George Long.

First edition: January 2005

Library of Congress Cataloging-in-Publication Data

Ross, Julia.
     Night of sin / Julia Ross.— 1st ed.
        p.   cm.
     ISBN 0-425-20013-2 (trade pbk.)
     1. Fossils—Collection and preservation—Fiction.   2. Aristocracy (Social class)—Fiction.
3. Attempted murder—Fiction.   4. Country homes—Fiction.   5. England—Fiction.   I. Title.

PS3618.O846N54   2005
813'.6—dc22   2004058366

PRINTED IN THE UNITED STATES OF AMERICA

10 9 8 7 6 5 4 3 2 1

ACKNOWLEDGMENTS

EVEN WHEN PIECES OF HISTORY ARE JUST A SMALL PART OF THE background of a tale, they take endless hours of research. My thanks, therefore, to everyone in Lyme Regis, both for their magnificent museum and for their delectable Dorset cream teas.

I am also very grateful to Mary Jo Putney, who suggested a superb book about the British adventurers who first dared to travel in disguise across the Himalayas: *The Great Game* by Peter Hopkirk. The true tale of their exploits is far more thrilling than fiction.

The books I read about the earliest fossil hunters are too numerous to list, but I am grateful to all of those authors and to the scientists who inspired them. Though dinosaur bones were turning up fairly regularly in England by the nineteenth century, the fossil beds of the Gobi—with their dinosaur nests and eggs—were only revealed to Western science by the expeditions of Roy Chapman Andrews. Yet perhaps we may still imagine that Jack and Toby could have seen them one hundred years earlier.

I'm also very grateful to Karin and Mary for all kinds of interesting bits and pieces, and to my agent, Nancy Yost, for her sage advice. Especial thanks go, as always, to my editor, Gail Fortune, and to my readers, who make it all possible.

Night of Sin

CHAPTER ONE

LABYRINTHS OF HENNA TRACED THE ANKLES OF THE women who haunted his dreams. Silk veiled their alluring, impersonal gaze. The memories both warmed and disturbed him: irresponsible, sensual thoughts, when he waited here in front of an English inn on watch.

Rain spattered up the street. Brine glistened on barrels and crates. Beyond the port buildings, the masts of the *Venture,* the ship he had been expecting, flung streamers of water into the sodden sky.

Someone on this ship carried sacred contraband. Someone brought treasure and trouble in equal measure. Unless Jack could intercept whoever it was, there would be merry hell to pay.

The ship's passengers strode up into the town, the wind at their backs, yet a wave of disturbance rippled through them. As if fighting a flood tide, a young woman struggled downhill. The oncoming crowd parted about her black umbrella like a river split by a rock.

The kohl-eyed women of Asia dissolved into the mist of English rain.

Why the devil didn't she just wait out the storm in an inn?

Jack grinned to himself. Perhaps the inns hereabouts weren't quite suitable for a young lady walking alone, and—though she carried a basket over one arm—she seemed to be a lady, buttressed by whalebone and burdened with all the absurdity of poke bonnet and English petticoats.

Wind gusted. The umbrella ballooned, then snapped up. Buffeted by the crowd and the wind, she clung to the handle with one outstretched hand. Her bonnet slipped. Rain dashed into her face. Something there arrested Jack for a moment, something that surprised him, though he wasn't quite sure what it was. The raw day had whipped color into her lips and cheeks, but she looked cold: a cold, pinched English girl with a thin nose, as plain and virtuous as a Sunday sermon.

Yet something in her expression, something bright and valiant and eager for life, seemed oddly intriguing, unexpected. Jack forced his attention back to the crowd—just as someone cannoned into her.

Burdened by her basket, she lurched forward. Carrying his seaman's bag, his face stark, a sailor had plunged up through the passengers and knocked her aside. The young lady stumbled, almost falling. Glancing back convulsively over his shoulder, the man elbowed on through the throng.

The umbrella soared away like a raven.

Awareness flooded, pulsing through Jack's blood—that deep flow through the muscles and extraordinary clarity of the senses—plumbing the essence of survival by preparing, if necessary, to deal death. The reaction was automatic now. Automatic and dangerous. Leavened only by the glory of feeling so absolutely alive—

He thrust into the crowd.

The lady with the basket gazed after her umbrella for a moment, then shrugged and hurried on.

A horn blast echoed. Ducking their heads, the ship's passengers scurried. People streamed out of the Rose and Crown. Carriages, carts, and saddle horses jostled for position. With the worst possible timing, the mail coach arrived and the rain became a deluge.

The sailor's eyes cast about wildly as he was swallowed up in the confusion.

Jack strode forward. The throng parted in front of him as if split by a sword.

People surged back. A woman screamed.

The sailor sprawled facedown on the cobbles. With quiet authority a gentleman in a many-caped driving cloak turned him over, while the crowd milled, wide-eyed, like wet ewes pinned by a dog.

Jack walked up, his heart hammering as his brain assessed details: *poor devil, poor devil, poor devil!*

His hyperacute attention pinned every element of the scene as if captured in a painting. The crowd, the body, the brown-eyed gentleman with his fashionable hat and cane, half bent over the corpse. All movement slowed, even his own hand, as Jack crouched and closed the sailor's eyes.

So it was the towheaded man from Bristol, after all! He was too late. Two of the cruelest words in the English language: *too late!*

The sailor had been garroted. Felled by a wire cast about the throat. His bag had disappeared.

"Don't let anyone know that you recognize me," Jack said quietly, still crouching. The passengers wavered and gawked, but they were all out of earshot. "Though I'm damned glad to see you, Guy."

The gentleman in the driving cloak froze. Rain streamed from his hem to pool about his boots.

"*Jack,* by all that's holy? Or should I say, by all that's unholy? God, I should have guessed! Who else can part a crowd like the Red Sea before Moses—even when dressed as a ruffian?"

"I don't wish to advertise my identity to the world at the moment. You'd be amazed by how invisible I can become when I want to. Forgive me if we don't embrace or shake hands?"

"What the hell are you doing arriving back in England like this?"

Jack straightened up, keeping his expression a little sulky but still respectful, like any sailor accosted by a gentleman. "Reveling in the splendid workings of chance, of course: I need help and here you are, Cousin Guy Devoran—"

"Not chance. I came to meet you." Guy nodded at the body. "A friend of yours?"

"No, though I admit I'm a little disconcerted by his death."

"Because no Englishman ever garroted, whereas the assassins of . . . wherever it is you've been traveling to recently . . . kill in just this manner?"

A wiry man in a green jacket was easing away, melting into the crowd.

Jack stepped back and tugged at his cap. "Guy, will you please take charge of our inopportune mob and this poor clay?"

"Only if you'll explain later over brandy."

The milling passengers blocked his view of the green jacket for a moment. "The brandy is assured, the explanation a little less so."

Guy raised a brow. "If you can survive long enough to make it to Wyldshay, the rest of your family will also be made very happy."

"I'll no doubt darken the doors of the ancestral pile in due course," Jack replied. "But not until I've changed my coat.

Mother wouldn't like this one. Meanwhile, just make sure that no one gains access to this dead man's pockets until I get back."

Guy hesitated for only a moment before he spun about and shouted, "You there! Carry this man into the Rose and Crown! There's been an accident—"

Two workmen touched their hats and stepped forward. The crowd began to break apart. The green jacket had disappeared.

Jack's pistol slipped like a lover into his hand as he was swallowed by the throng. He followed nothing but instinct now: instinct and the ghostly scent of sandalwood, almost imaginary in the driving rain.

He caught up just as the man in green dodged into a deserted side alley. Jack followed silently. His quarry scurried past a pile of barrels, then glanced to one side and stopped: a Malay probably, though now a person without conscience or country, one of the multitude of uprooted seamen in Britain's far-flung empire.

Another figure stepped out from beneath the shelter of the overhanging upper story: a man in a blue turban.

Jack pulled back behind a stack of crates and watched.

The Malay pulled the murdered sailor's bag from beneath his green coat. The other man tore it from his hand and tipped the contents onto the cobbles. He sorted through them, then hissed a question. The Malay shrugged and threw up both hands in a universal gesture.

Nothing!

The man in the turban flung aside the empty bag and stepped closer to the Malay as if to press his interrogation. The sailor shook his head. Deft as a cobra, an open hand gripped his throat. The Malay rolled his eyes, choking. Another brief exchange followed, before his assailant lowered his fingers and tossed a handful of coins to the cobbles.

The Malay bent to gather the money. The man in the blue turban stalked away, turned a corner, and disappeared.

Coins clinked against stone. Jack moved silently. Yet his quarry turned his head, teeth bared. His hands moved fast.

Faster, Jack cracked the edge of his hand against the man's neck, felling him.

The blue turban had disappeared into an alley that led to a warren of warehouses, workshops, and tenements. Where several lanes intersected, the man's footprints disappeared into a mire of tracks. Their owner had vanished. Not that it mattered. Another lackey, though probably an even more dangerous one. No doubt he'd be several streets away by now, and he'd have nothing to report to his employer but disappointment.

Jack walked back to the unconscious Malay and dragged him beneath the shelter of the overhang. The bag was shabby, a typical seaman's pouch. The canvas smelled of brine, tar, sweat, tobacco. No sandalwood. No wild, alien scent of the East. Nothing at all.

Without much hope, he turned out the man's pockets, examining every seam and inch of padding. The lethal wire was folded into his sash. Nothing else was hidden. The sailor's bare feet curled on the wet stones, oddly vulnerable. Jack stared down at the brown face and wondered why the devil he should feel pity for a murderer.

He glanced again at the scattering of belongings, then—like any petty thief—he gathered up everything of the remotest value: the coins, the Bristol sailor's pipe and knife, leaving only his cloth handkerchief.

On second thought, Jack took that as well.

The mail coach had disgorged travelers, taken up new ones, and left. The ship's passengers had dispersed into various inns or conveyances. The street was abandoned to the downpour, gusting in sprays as if flung from buckets.

A twist of black fabric bowled along the shop fronts. Jack dodged puddles and dung, and caught the broken umbrella by the handle.

Then, in the absurd face of his failure, he laughed.

"MY DEAR CHILD, YOU'RE SOAKED TO THE SKIN," AUNT Sayle said as she opened the door. "You must have had such a journey from Lyme! We tried to watch for you from the window, but what with this terrible rain and the crowds— Were the roads all mud?"

Miss Anne Marsh set down her basket, untied her pattens, and leaned forward to kiss her aunt's cheek. Ridiculous to still feel this shadow of nerves, as if of a peril, narrowly escaped.

"A veritable mire! So we mistimed our arrival rather thoroughly, I'm afraid." She pulled off her soaked bonnet and tried to bury any lingering discomfort. "I'd no more than stepped down from Mr. Trent's carriage and started down the hill than I was being buffeted and crushed like an apple in a cider press. A ship just came in?"

"The *Venture* has arrived from the Orient. And the family? Is everyone well?"

"Everyone sends their love. I have some of Papa's latest sermons for you, and Mama sends this basket with some fresh things from our garden, plus a nice fat hen."

Aunt Sayle beamed. "But my brother has sent me my favorite

niece, which is even better. Now let's get you out of those wet things before you catch your death."

Water ran from the bonnet. Anne shook it and handed it to Aunt Sayle's maid. As much friend and companion as servant, Edith grinned beside her mistress as if still ready to coddle a little girl with a bruised knee. There was a moment of fussing, the setting down of the bonnet and the disentangling of Anne's reticule, hanging by a strap from her wrist, before she could be helped out of her pelisse.

"Lord bless us," Edith said. "It's wet through and as heavy as lead."

Anne gave her a quick hug. "When the heavens opened, everyone had their heads down. I bumped into someone and lost my umbrella."

There, it was out! She felt better, as if she hadn't caught a glimpse of that sailor's face, distorted by terror. The world began to slip back into its everyday orbit, where life was safe and ordinary again.

Edith bustled away into the kitchen, but Aunt Sayle's mouth was set in reproof. "Mr. Trent should have escorted you."

"He wished to, Aunt. Indeed, he tried to insist, but he had the horses to see to, and we were so very late already that I didn't want to wait. His man will bring my bag down later, and Arthur will come himself to say good-bye before he leaves for London to see his father."

"About the settlements? Well, well!" Mrs. Sayle led the way into the parlor and settled herself into a chair by the fire. "You're engaged to be married to a very eligible young man, my dear, even if it was such a whirlwind courtship. Living quietly in the country as you do, not meeting many new folk, you had me worried you might never marry."

Anne sat down. Little tendrils of steam rose from her damp hem. The incident in the street had been an uncomfortable moment, that was all. How could life be any better than this? She had been courted. She had accepted. She would be wed in a few months.

"I know I'm not generally good with strangers," she said, "but Mr. Trent feels almost like one of the family. Even though his faith is stricter than ours, he and I were comfortable together from our very first meeting. Meanwhile, there's nothing like a fire crackling merrily in the grate, especially when rain sheets down the windowpanes and wind rattles the chimneys!"

"I still don't like to think of your struggling through such a throng without the escort of a gentleman."

"It was only a few steps along a street that I know very well— such a very tiny transgression."

Mrs. Sayle forced a snort through her nostrils. "This neighborhood is not at all what it was when Captain Sayle was alive. All that press of sailors and riffraff! Even if the passengers from the *Venture* were all the most respectable people in the world, anything could have happened. Mr. Trent was very wrong to allow it, and I shall tell him so tonight."

"I do beg you will not, Aunt! You would embarrass him to no end." Anne began to unlace her wet boots. "What possible harm could have come to me, other than the loss of my umbrella and the gain of a little damp in my clothes—"

The door opened and Edith walked in. She was not carrying the tea tray. Her face looked oddly aghast, as if jostling alien legions threatened to invade the gentle world of her mistress's family.

"This was in your basket beneath the chicken, Miss Marsh," Edith said. "Such an outlandish thing! I don't know what to do with it."

The maid deposited her problem into Anne's hands.

"Good heavens!" Anne said. "No wonder my basket felt so heavy!"

She turned the object over, running one fingertip across the surface, noticing the traces of red, like rust long dried in the earth, the length of the ferocious cutting edge, serrated like a leaf: a tooth that must have belonged to a creature larger and more dangerous than anything that existed in the world, turned by the pressure of the ages into stone.

A shiver ran through her at the strangeness of it.

"Beneath Mama's chicken, you say?" She met Aunt Sayle's gaze, then looked up at Edith's worried face. "But I've never seen this before in my life!"

JACK STROLLED INTO THE ROSE AND CROWN. THE DEAD sailor had been laid out on a table in a back parlor, a cloth draped over his face. Guy sprawled in a nearby chair, feet kicked out in front of him, both arms folded over his chest. A brandy decanter sat by the corpse's feet, two empty glasses beside it.

Guy sat up as if to reach out for a handshake, but his smile faded as he met Jack's gaze and he leaned back instead. Pain undermined Jack's resolve for a moment. He ignored it, tossed the umbrella into a corner, and walked up to the corpse.

"Poor fellow!" Jack pulled back the cloth to stare at the man's face. "A quarrel over a woman, do you think?"

"No, I don't," Guy said. "You're far too interested in his death. When the devil did you get back to England?"

The sailor's expression was oddly bland. "Three days ago."

"But I thought you traveled on the *Venture*?"

"I did, but I left her in Portugal. She was delayed by bad weather. I hired a fishing boat."

"This rain is the tail end of a gale. If you traveled through that in a small boat, you risked your bloody life and that of any crew crazy enough to bring you—"

"Not crazy enough: greedy enough." Jack draped the cloth back over the ivory face. "My gold spoke louder than their fear."

"Can you tell me why you did it?"

"No, but I can tell you that this man's assassin is to be found lying in a nearby alley."

There was a small pause before Guy spoke again. "He's dead?"

Jack turned his back on the sailor and smiled down at his cousin. "I didn't kill him, if that's what you fear, just knocked him out."

"Can the man be questioned?"

"He wouldn't answer. I'd wager my life he speaks very little English anyway. But sadly for him, the murder weapon is still looped around his waist. So he'll be hanged and die among strangers half a world away from his home—"

"And even though he deserves his fate, you rather hate the thought of that?" Guy poured from the decanter. "I don't blame you. Have some brandy."

Jack took the proffered glass and drained it. "I have every intention, when my time comes, of using my corner of the family burial plot here in England. I don't intend to be sent home pickled in a barrel."

"Your mother will be very glad to hear it," Guy said. "So what now?"

"This, apart from the wire, is the extent of the assassin's worldly wealth, along with the contents of a bag our poor Bristol sailor here carried with him."

He tipped the hail of small objects onto the seat of an empty chair, then strode to the window to stare out at the blank wall of an alley. Rain streamed down the panes.

"You turned thief and risked the gallows just to steal this worthless junk?" Guy asked.

"They can't hang me and you know it."

"If you continue to dress like that," Guy replied dryly, "you might be strung up for the crows from the nearest tree just for sneezing."

Jack laughed—not the ironic distraction he had allowed himself in the street, but a burst of genuine mirth. The tension, the hyperacute awareness, began to melt away. He spun about, still grinning.

"Damnation, Guy, I am damned glad to see you! No one else would have such infinite self-control. Yes, I'm involved in something underhanded. No, I cannot tell you what it is. I've just robbed one man. Pray, close your virtuous eyes, sir, while I rob the carcass of another."

"Close my eyes? Are you mad? I wouldn't miss this for the world. So what might our sailor carry in his pockets that his assassin failed to steal?"

Jack poured himself another glass of brandy, then turned back to his cousin. "You don't want to know. Really. Here, take this decanter, there's a good chap, and ask the landlord for a refill."

"Can you at least tell me why you stole all this rubbish to begin with?"

"Certainly. If anyone was watching, I was just another thief, interested only in money. To fell a man and not rob him would have been far too suspicious."

"Damn it, Jack!" Guy grinned as he stood up and grabbed the empty decanter. "Did anyone ever get the better of you? Oh, don't answer that—I just thank God you're home at last, though no one would believe that such a disreputable rogue has any honorable connections. You'll survive long enough to darken the doors of Wyldshay soon, I trust?"

"I'll probably return to the ancestral pile sometime next week, demanding fatted calves and rejoicing."

"Which you'll get in full measure. You'll stay for good this time?"

"I return to Asia on the next ship out."

Guy stopped in the doorway. "You'll break your mother's and sisters' hearts, if you do."

Jack stared into his drink and hoped his distress did not show in his voice. "And how's my fearsome father these days?"

"His Grace does well enough in the circumstances," Guy replied. "He misses you."

"I miss him. I miss all of them." A fragrant lens of amber swirled in the bottom of his glass. "God, I thought for a moment—when you didn't mention him first—that the duke might have died while I was away."

"He was ill. He is, I think, still ailing. You knew that, surely? Hasn't Ryder been sending the news?"

The last drops of brandy eased down Jack's throat. "Liza writes, while Ryder nods his approval from a distance, but anything I hear from them is months out of date by the time I receive it—"

It was there, a slight tremor, betraying the depth of his feelings. Jack took a deep breath to control it.

"I'll fetch more brandy," Guy said.

Jack watched him leave the room. They were the same age and the same height, taller than most men, and closer perhaps than either was to any of their siblings. Jack would trust his cousin with his life. He wouldn't hesitate to embroil him in this adventure, however dangerous, because he had absolute faith that Guy could take care of himself. Yet it was as if the vast emptiness of the Gobi had entered his soul.

Had restraint closed about him like a prison—even with Guy—simply because the grim habits of solitude and self-reliance had become impossible to change?

Jack searched the dead sailor's pockets, then searched again, checking seams and shoes, ignoring his instinctive distaste for the task. A few more ordinary, sad items soon ranked along the edge of the table. Jack stared at them for several minutes. The Bristol sailor must have carried the fossil from the *Venture*—or the Malay wouldn't have been hired to rob him—yet he no longer had it on him when he was killed?

He closed his eyes and tried to replay every detail of the scene: the crowd, the frantic sailor, a young lady with a basket—

Guy stepped back into the room. "Did you find what you wanted?"

Jack looked up. "No."

"Then come to Wyldshay with me now. My phaeton is here, with the nicest pair of matched chestnuts Tattersall's ever had to offer."

"I can't."

"The duke has been ill, Jack." The liquor gleamed as Guy refilled the glasses. "Not dangerously so, I think, yet everyone is desperate to see you. If they'd had their way, your sisters would have been here mobbing you as we speak."

"Who stopped them?"

"The duchess didn't think it very dignified to allow her daughters to wait like a gaggle of hussies at a common inn."

"So the task was delegated to you?" Jack gave his cousin a wry smile. "God bless Mother! She's a wise lady—and thank you, Guy."

"What the devil shall I tell them?"

"That I wasn't on the *Venture,* after all, and you didn't see me." The hot glow of the brandy burned. He set down the empty glass. Time to stop, before he got drunk. "Say you discovered that I disembarked in Portugal and am now traveling home overland, but left a message with another passenger: With Napoleon gone, it's my chance to see Europe."

Silence invaded. Guy strode away, his shoulders stiff.

"I'm well aware that such a message will only wound the people who love me the best," Jack added quietly. "I can't help that."

Guy spun about. "You're asking me to lie for you."

"Yes."

"It's that important?"

"It's that important."

"And you leave this poor creature"—Guy gestured toward the corpse—"and his murderer to me?"

"Yes."

"You've become a damned cold-blooded bastard, Jack."

It was said entirely without malice, yet the words followed the brandy to his heart. He and Guy had never before met after such a long separation and not shaken hands, at least—

"I trust you to soften the message in any way that you can, Guy. I'm sorry that I can't explain. When I can, you'll be the first to know."

"I think perhaps you'll owe that explanation first to your mother," Guy said. "What will you really do now?"

Jack bent to pick up the umbrella. A small puddle was staining the floor where water had run from the fabric. Memories shimmered like reflections in a pool: the lady, her attention distracted as she fought to hold on against the wind; her valiant face, wet with rain beneath her English straw bonnet; her basket clutched in one hand as she was jostled in the crowd by this very sailor—

Anyone else watching had also seen it happen. Sooner or later they would come to the same conclusion. Dread pooled about his heart.

He shook moisture from the black fabric and closed the umbrella.

"Return this to the lady who lost it," he said.

CHAPTER TWO

S OME LITTLE RUSTLE OR CLINK WOKE HER.

Anne roused herself from sleep. A faint light glimmered through the window, throwing the corners of the attic room into an impenetrable void. She listened for a moment, reluctant to move. The tick of a clock dropped into absolute silence, colored only by the underlying heartbeat of the night. The rain had stopped.

The fire had burned away to a dull glow. Beams and dressers bulked in dark distortions, but her petticoat foamed in a frozen white waterfall over the back of a chair. Other shapes reflected dimly in the polished coal scuttle at the grate. The moon must have risen—or perhaps the glimmer was just starlight, shining coldly onto the town, the distant ocean, the cluster of ships lying in the harbor—

There was a figure at the window.

Anne closed her eyes and opened them again. Every hair had risen on the back of her neck. No one was there.

Holding her breath, she reached for the tinderbox beside the bed.

Something clinked again. She slowly turned her head. Someone was lifting the sash.

Her heart thundered. She thought she might be sick.

Damp air streamed into the room. The intruder already had one foot over the sill.

Anne's mind flattened into a blank screen, yet her thoughts raced, like flocks of crows swooping and scattering over white sand.

Not at all what it was when Captain Sayle was alive. All that press of sailors and riffraff—

A scream might wake Edith and Aunt Sayle, but not bring them in time—

Arthur and she would never marry . . . Aunt Sayle and Edith would find her mutilated body . . . her mother and father would receive the message . . . everyone would be shattered—

As the crows jabbered in her mind, Anne rolled out of bed to crouch on the floor against the wall. Hugging the shadows, she crawled toward the fireplace.

The intruder padded deeper into the room. Eyes and teeth gleamed. And something else: a shimmer, like moonlight on wire. Soft footfalls crept toward the bed. The figure halted, head tipped, then the man's face began to turn. God help her—her nightgown was white!

Anne lunged for the poker and screamed at the top of her lungs. Flailing like a madwoman, still shouting, she swung the heavy iron in a wide arc. With a resounding crash, it caught on the corner of the dresser and almost wrenched her arms from their sockets. Wood splintered.

Shadows leaped into life.

The intruder flung himself back to the window, swung over the sill, and disappeared.

Anne dropped the poker, spun about, and collided with something tall and warm. Hands closed on her upper arms. Her scream choked into a terrified sob.

"Hush!" a man's voice said. "You're very brave, ma'am, and display a most impressive prowess. It's all right now, though I think you may have demolished some furniture."

The hands pushed her back until she sat on the bed. The mad crows in her head burst into flight.

Footsteps pounded in the hallway. The door burst open. In nightcap and gown, Aunt Sayle stood in the doorway with a lantern in one hand and Edith at her shoulder. Light flooded into the room.

The maid brandished a blunderbuss. "Stay right where you are! Don't move! Put your hands up!"

"Which do you want, ma'am?" the man asked. "I cannot obey both of those commands at the same time."

"Let her go, or I'll fire!"

"Then I surrender." He released Anne's arms, lifted his hands, and turned around.

He was dressed entirely in black: black coat, black shirt, black trousers, black boots. His hair and eyes swallowed the night. His head brushed the ceiling. His shoulders filled the spaces between the rafters.

A dark giant stood in the center of her bedroom, holding his hands up.

"Pray, don't shoot, ma'am," he said with a hint of humor. "The room is already damaged enough. This lady attacked the dresser with a poker."

"Keep your hands where I can see them!" Edith snapped. "Kneel down!"

He immediately dropped to both knees. It was the pose of a man waiting for his execution. Yet in spite of his submissive posture—or perhaps because of it—power crackled about him, as if he carried his own thunderstorm in each empty palm.

Anne clung to her bedspread, wondering if she'd ever have the nerve to sleep in here again. The attic room still looked innocent enough, though the corner of the dresser showed white shards where she'd clobbered it. Someone had tried to murder her. There was a strange man kneeling on her bedroom floor. She felt ill.

"There were two of them," she whispered. "His accomplice had a weapon . . . a knife, I think. He escaped."

"Not my accomplice. My quarry—if you hadn't interfered, ma'am."

The man turned his head to look at her. A swift impression of gilt and brown beneath thick black lashes—beautiful eyes. Eyes bright with reflected lantern light. And that face! Authority imbued with an absolute calm: the face of the archangel about to spread his great swan's wings to shatter the sanity of mortal men—and finding unholy mirth in it.

"I have a brace of pistols," he said, glancing back at Edith and Aunt Sayle. "You must either allow me to lay down my guns, or disarm me yourselves. Perhaps there's a more comfortable room where we might discuss it, somewhere more suitable than this lady's bedchamber?"

The women at the door wavered. The blunderbuss barrel clattered against the jamb.

"Or you may tie my hands, if you like," he continued. "If that would make you feel safer. Though I pray you will first close the window and bar the shutters."

Anne wanted to stand up. The blood was flooding back into

her veins, but it seemed to be made of ice water and wine. She was sitting here in her nightgown in front of a dangerous angel. Her feet were freezing. Somewhere she had slippers. She really must find her slippers!

"This isn't funny," Anne said.

He looked back at her and smiled. Warm shivers raced up her spine.

"I am your prisoner, ma'am. You may do as you wish with me."

Heat flooded her cheeks. "I don't understand." Her voice sounded husky, as if she heard herself from very far away. She swallowed and started again. "Your speech is that of a gentleman. You obviously don't care whether we disarm you or not. You're not in the least afraid, are you?"

"No," he said. "You're perfectly safe now. We should close the shutters only to avoid the possibility of any further unpleasantness."

"Is this some ridiculous wager?" She gathered courage, though her heart hammered like a steam engine. "My brothers are fond of such things, though not, I think, of terrifying strangers out of their wits at night."

"Neither ridiculous, nor a wager," he said. "The shutters, if you please."

The sky outside loomed, a rectangle of darkness. Huddled in the doorway, Aunt Sayle and Edith stared at the window.

"There were two ruffians?" Edith asked at last. "The other one is still out there?"

"I'll close the shutters myself," the man said, "if you promise not to shoot?"

The blunderbuss wobbled. Aunt Sayle clung to the lantern with both hands. Neither woman moved.

"I'll do it," Anne said.

She tried to stand. Her bare feet touched the floor. The skirts of her nightgown flowed about her legs. Her knees folded like carriage steps.

In two strides the archangel caught her. She didn't see how he rose to his feet, or if he used invisible wings to fly the two strides. He scooped her up as soon as she began to fall, and tugged the quilt from the bed with the other hand. She clutched the coverlet as he carried her back to the center of the room, her giddy head pillowed against one shoulder, her bare feet dangling helplessly.

"Miss Marsh is unwell," he said. "Edith, you will set down that weapon. You will close and bar the window. You will do it now. Then you will make sure that all the rest of the doors and windows are similarly secure. Mrs. Sayle? I must apologize, ma'am, for startling you, but I must see to Miss Marsh."

Aunt Sayle sat with a thump on a chair by the door. "Oh, this is too dreadful! How do you know our names?"

"Your neighbors told me when I asked. They also told me that this lady is your brother's child. Now, Edith, the windows?"

As if mesmerized, Edith set down the blunderbuss and bobbed a curtsy. "Yes, sir."

"Mrs. Sayle?" He bowed, Anne still cradled like a child against his chest. The end of her long plait hung over his arm. "I pray you will forgive me if I take your niece downstairs? She is cold. She has suffered a shock. Once Edith has secured the house, we may all meet in your parlor for tea." He smiled again. "A strong cup of tea will, I think, put all to rights."

Aunt Sayle stared as the man strode through the doorway. Anne looked back to see Edith hurrying to the window, while her aunt remained on the hall chair as if struck by lightning.

The giant ducked his head and began to carry his burden down the stairs. Anne quaked against the steady beat of his heart. This, surely, couldn't really be happening?

She had woken to an intruder. She had been snatched up by another. Instead of coming to her rescue, Aunt Sayle and Edith had leaped to obey him. In her terror she had spoken out more boldly than she ever remembered speaking to anyone.

It was as if a dream or a fairy tale had invaded the ordered routine of her life.

Above the collar of his black shirt, his throat glowed as if he were lit with his own inner flame. Heat enveloped her. Anne closed her eyes, yet her blood blazed with awareness: his quick breath, the strength of his arms, the fascinating, rain-washed scent of his skin. This stranger was *carrying* her. In her nightgown. In his arms. It was overwhelmingly improper. Scandalous. Yet to struggle or beg to be set down would only make matters worse, so Anne clung to the coverlet and her dignity, while her face burned.

The parlor was warm. The grate glowed with the remains of the previous evening's fire. The archangel set Anne down on the sofa. He tucked the quilt around her bare feet as if she were fragile, like an ivory fan, and smiled at her.

"Better now, Miss Marsh? I would ask for forgiveness from you, also, but I'm not sure there are enough apologies available in the language. You must think me a ruffian. You have my word that I mean you no harm."

Anne curled back against the horsehair, tugging the quilt up to her chin, while the man walked to the grate and began to poke life into the fire. In spite of her discomfort with strangers, she knew herself to be a sensible, practical person, not given to vapors or panic. When reason failed, her father had taught her to try to find her way by listening to the still, quiet voice everyone carried in their heart. Yet her pulse hammered and her mouth seemed filled with dry glue.

"It's not my intention to give offense," the man continued. "But this is a rather irregular introduction, isn't it?" His back flexed as he added coal, then lit a taper to light candles. Brightness bloomed about the room. "Pretend that we've been properly introduced at your local Assembly Rooms, if you like. If that would make things easier."

"I don't think that I can, sir," Anne said. "Pretend such a thing. My father is an independent minister. We're Dissenters. Though we're not as strict as some, I don't attend local dances. But who are you? Why did you ask our neighbors for our names? What do you want here?"

He turned. Every movement seemed to flow—balanced. That was it: *balanced.* As if strength came from somewhere deep at the core, as if suppleness streamed without effort. But she had not been wrong about his eyes, colored like winter forest shadows dappled with sunlight.

"If I told you, you'd not believe it."

"Not believe what?"

His face, too, had been burnished, darkened to a tan acquired nowhere in England. The smooth skin was unbearably exotic, though she was certain from his accent that he was English—and a gentleman.

"You may not believe what my purpose is and who I am," he said. "I discovered your names simply because I wished to find the young lady who lost her umbrella in the street this afternoon."

"My *umbrella?*"

She was floating in some detached lunacy while holding inane conversations about umbrellas with the Archangel Michael.

Though of course he wasn't really an angel, nor a giant: just a tall gentleman with a peculiarly graceful power.

He nodded toward the table at the window. A crumple of black fabric lay next to the glass model of a ship that Captain Sayle had brought long ago from Bristol. "That umbrella."

Anne clasped the quilt with both fists. Her stomach had tied itself in knots.

He was lithe and strong and young. His eyes were certainly remarkable: as if humor and intelligence shimmered over unknown depths of experience. Yet now that she saw him clearly, she wasn't sure that he was handsome. Not as Arthur Trent, with his brown curls and blue eyes, was handsome. This man was too intense, too unorthodox, for mere good looks.

"You broke into a stranger's house during the night simply to return her umbrella?"

He walked across the room to gaze down at the glass model. "Not quite. I wouldn't so insult your intelligence, Miss Marsh. I had other motives also, of course."

Light and shadows caressed his cheek, outlined a stunning purity of profile. The small shock sank in as Anne stared at him: No, he was not handsome, but only because he was beautiful—with the concentrated, passionate beauty she imagined in a tiger or a demon. A beauty in firm, full lips and carved bones that seemed as alien as that of a wild beast—and thus safely removed from her world.

"Why couldn't it wait until morning?" she asked.

"So you're no longer afraid," he said, glancing back at her.

Was that true? Yes, perhaps it was. Her sense of unreality had deepened, as if she might wake at any moment to laugh about her odd dream, but she no longer felt that first unreasoning terror, and he, too, seemed a little more relaxed.

Anne pointed to the table. "When did you set it there?"

He ignored the umbrella and bent to examine the ship: masts, rigging, sails all delicately spun in perfect detail from Bristol glass. "Earlier tonight. I had reason to search the house. I did so as soon as you were all asleep."

"You searched the *house*? While we *slept*? How long were you in my bedroom without my knowing?"

"Two hours, perhaps."

"*Two hours?*"

"You snore very prettily," he said.

"I do not—" She took a deep breath. "I do *not* snore. My sisters have never complained of it. If I snored, they would have let me know. Without question!"

"That's better," he said. "You're beginning to get a little color back."

The heat began again in her neck to flood slowly across her face, not like her earlier blush of embarrassment, but a sudden flush of awareness, as if something deep at her core responded involuntarily to his gaze. As if the intensity of that calm concentration betrayed a profound and very personal concern—which was ridiculous, of course.

"I would ask, sir," she said, "that you do not fix your gaze on me in quite that way."

He glanced up at the picture clock on the wall, where the sails of a windmill turned and turned in a painted landscape, while the clock face smiled in the disk of a yellow sun.

"You're uncomfortable. Of course. Any young lady would be."

Yes, uncomfortable, but only because in some strange way that concentration had been flattering, like the gaze of a man in love. The intensity of a man suddenly aware that this one woman was powerfully attractive, more than any other female he had ever met or was ever likely to meet.

All of which was absurd.

Anne knew that she was perfectly ordinary: mousy hair, gray-blue eyes, an overlong nose that dipped a little at the tip when she smiled. Someone whom gentlemen easily overlooked. Someone who knew that she ought not to care about such frivolous vanity, yet still felt the pain of being ignored while prettier girls were noticed first.

Yet that one moment had produced the most disconcerting, unsettling sensation of this most disconcerting night.

She looked back at him. The shape of his back and legs formed lithe, dangerous shadows in the busy room.

"You said, upstairs in my bedroom, that I was safe. How could you be sure? What if we had disarmed you, and that other man had come back?"

"You are always safe as long as I am here, whether I am armed or not."

"You want me to believe that you could have prevented his attacking me?"

His voice was rich, as if flavored by hidden mirth. "Believe it, though your valiant efforts with the poker did get a little in the way."

"I didn't know anyone else was there," Anne said. "If I had known, I'd have attacked you, too."

"Try to take deep breaths and reassure yourself that I'm harmless," he said, still with a hint of a smile.

"No, sir," she replied quietly. "I cannot believe that."

To Anne's relief, Aunt Sayle stepped into the room. She had stopped to dress, though hastily. Her stockings didn't match. She was nervous, yet she was glowing, as if—in spite of her crooked cap, mismatched stockings, and graying hair—she were a girl in her first flirtation.

"My poor, dear lamb!" Aunt Sayle exclaimed. "That such a thing should happen in my house! But the window is barred tight now, and Edith and I have set the dresser in front of it."

Edith hovered in the doorway, also dressed. The maid seemed torn between excitement and servility. She might, if this man had not been careful, have made an unholy mess with the blunderbuss, but now she seemed only too ready to do his bidding.

He bowed to Aunt Sayle, then stood quietly, hands clasped behind his back, like a tiger settling down to wait beside a waterhole.

Aunt Sayle curtsied, dipping her head. "I'm sure there's a very good explanation for all this, sir. It's too strange otherwise. Goodness, I have nothing in the house worth stealing, I'm sure. And if you were a thief— Well, it makes no sense at all."

"Tea before explanations." He smiled at Edith. "And perhaps some breakfast? It will be morning soon."

Edith bobbed a curtsy and disappeared into the kitchen.

Aunt Sayle sat down next to Anne to take her fingers in her lap and pat them. It was admittedly comforting.

"I have intruded into the home of a sea captain, it would seem," the man said. "Your husband, Mrs. Sayle? This glass model was one of his ships?"

"That was the *Gannet,* sir, all done in Bristol glass."

"A fine ship. Captain Sayle was not a Dissenter like your brother?"

"No, sir. I embraced the Established Church myself when we married. My brother doesn't hold it against me."

"I have no doubt your husband was a fine captain?"

Aunt Sayle bloomed like a rose and launched into an account of her late husband's adventures.

He took a chair, booted legs crossed at the knee, and listened. He even asked an occasional question, as if this were just a social call and the captain's widow were a countess. Anne thought he might still be faintly amused, though not at them, only at himself. He was so entirely at his ease and had put Aunt Sayle so completely at hers, which meant that he was either a charlatan or a member of a very privileged class.

The door swung open and Edith set down the tea tray.

"I'll have hot scones ready in no time," she said, before she bustled out again.

Mrs. Sayle poured. Fine gold rimmed the teacups. Edith had used Aunt Sayle's best china—her wedding china. Anne didn't know whether she ought to feel amused or resentful at that.

Jack watched the color creep back into Anne's cheeks as she sipped at her tea: the gift of the forbidden realms of China. It wasn't the frantic color of her earlier embarrassment, nor the flush he had seen in the street from fresh air and cold. Just a warm blush over the cheekbones, like fine porcelain stained with a rose-colored wash.

He felt something catch at his heart. She had extraordinary skin: so white as to be almost translucent, as if she might bruise at a glance. The light eyes and nondescript hair were also very English. A light-skinned, fine-boned creature, muffled in layers of cotton nightdress and outraged propriety, she had weighed almost nothing in his arms.

Yet he had been searingly aware that she was female: a softness of thighs, the sweet pressure of a small breast. Her hair smelled of lavender water and roses, the fragrance of a Dorset summer garden basking in the sun—underlain with the more disturbing perfumes of woman and sleep, scents confusingly suggestive of both tousled beds and innocence.

A moment's distraction, obviously, when the beds of his dreams were aromatic with spices and musk.

Miss Anne Marsh was English and a gentlewoman, enclosed in fragility and a delicate shyness, and she had gone through several moments of real terror. Worse, she was a member of one of those sober dissenting cults with their earnest meetinghouses and rational beliefs. He wished he could offer protection and reassurance, as a hunter might soothe a trapped bird, stroking its feathers.

He had nothing to offer her but trouble.

Jack glanced back at her aunt. "Thank you, ma'am," he said, setting down his cup. "Now, perhaps I may answer your concerns, though first I must ask Miss Marsh a question."

To his surprise Anne looked up with a little quirk at the corner of her mouth, as if her tea—or the presence of her aunt—had driven out the remains of her trepidation and replaced it with defiance.

"I think perhaps the world has gone mad," she said. "Edith is baking breakfast for you, sir, though you broke into the house and rousted us from our beds. Since then you have ordered us all about as if we were servants to a sultan. I really don't see why I should answer any of your questions, until you answer some of mine." She dropped her head, as if shocked at her own temerity, though still calling on every reserve of determination. "Who are you?"

"I'm not a sultan. I'm a traveler."

"And your name, sir?"

"I'll tell you when you answer this, Miss Marsh: Did you find anything odd in your basket when you arrived here this afternoon?"

"Oh, my!" Mrs. Sayle exclaimed.

"No," Anne said, looking up.

Mrs. Sayle turned her head to stare at her niece. Enveloped in the scent of fresh baking, Edith walked in and set down a plate of hot scones.

"No," Anne said again. Her hands were clenched into fists. She stared at Jack with eyes like silver coins. "You must first explain who you are and why you are here, before I answer anything."

Jack stood and held out his hands to the warmth of the fire. "Very well. I came across some unfortunate events on the other side of the world. Something important was stolen and brought back to England. It's essential that I recover it, but I believe it was slipped into your basket when you lost your umbrella in the street. That is why I am here."

"And who was that other man, the man who I thought had a knife?"

"Someone hired to find this treasure before I do."

"Why did you wait in my bedroom?"

"I hoped no one would come. I hoped my rival had no idea that you might have it. I hoped I would first find it myself. All three hopes were unfortunately misplaced. Now an enemy obviously believes—for the same reasons that I do—that the lost item was passed to you this afternoon. He is desperate to find it, which puts you all in considerable danger."

Mrs. Sayle clutched Anne's palm. Edith dropped a butter knife.

"It's too fantastic," Anne said. "I'm not sure I can believe any of this."

Time now to fling this frail bird into the perilous skies, much as the hunter might regret the necessity of it.

"You must believe it, Miss Marsh," Jack said. "One man has already been killed since this object arrived in England, a sailor from Bristol who carried it with him from the *Venture*. He bumped into you in the crowd, then was slain immediately afterward."

"A man was *murdered*?" Mrs. Sayle said. "Right out there in the High Street?"

"Yes."

Edith sat down with a thump.

"How do I know you're telling us the truth?" Anne persisted. "Perhaps you're the villain, and the other man broke in merely to rescue us from you?"

Jack slipped out his pistols and laid them on the carpet. He followed with the nicely lethal knife from his boot. That he could have killed her just as easily with his bare hands was less easy to demonstrate. It was a skill he would anyway rather not advertise.

He held out his empty palms. "If I had wanted to harm you, I had plenty of opportunity, Miss Marsh."

The gray eyes glanced at his weapons, then up into his face. He thought she was hanging on to her composure now by a thread. The other two women had become very still, as if on the verge of tears.

"While you waited—" She shuddered. "What if that other man had never come?"

"Then I'd have left just as silently. You'd never have known I was there."

"Because that would have meant that this rival didn't know that I'd received such an unwelcome gift?"

"Exactly. Then I could have called casually in a few days to return your umbrella and ask after the missing object. Unfortunately, it's too late for that now. Though I admit I found nothing when I searched, you did discover it, didn't you?"

"Yes," Anne said. "It was in my basket. I think I even caught a glimpse of that Bristol sailor. His face was dreadful, as if he'd seen a ghost." She hugged the blanket about her shoulders. "Who are you, sir?"

"He's a St. George," Edith blurted.

Everyone turned their heads to look at the maid.

Edith clutched her apron in both hands. "My sister was in service at Wyldshay. I visited once and I saw Lord Ryderbourne striding through the stableyard, calling for his horse. When you ordered me to close the window—begging your pardon, my lord, but you all have that same manner about you."

"So if I planned to give you a false name, it wouldn't do, would it?" Jack said.

The maid shook her head. "Then just now when Your Lordship took out those pistols all set with silver . . . Well, I wasn't sure at first, but I am now."

Mrs. Sayle, obviously speechless, struggled to her feet and bobbed a curtsy. Jack bowed with the exactly correct degree of grace to reassure her.

"Lord Jonathan Devoran St. George, at your service, ma'am. I'm the younger son of the Duke of Blackdown. Ryderbourne is my brother."

Anne Marsh thrust both hands over her mouth. For a moment she looked aghast, but hilarity built in her eyes like water filling a tub. Jack bowed to her with a deliberately exaggerated flourish, and she burst out laughing.

"Oh, goodness!" Her cheeks were on fire and tears of mirth

stood in her eyes. "I am sorry! The Duke of Blackdown? You must see, my lord, that this really is enough to discompose anyone!"

"Of course," Jack replied. "It discomposes me upon occasion."

And suddenly they were both laughing, as if there were no peril outside this cozy parlor, no world of open oceans beyond rural England. Jack even thought he might rather like this shy, plain girl with her pale English skin and sudden flashes of courage, which only made what he was going to have to do next that much worse.

Mrs. Sayle turned to pat Anne on the shoulder. "Oh, my dear! Pray compose yourself! What will His Lordship think?"

"That Miss Marsh has been through an ordeal," Jack replied. "That she is feeling more the thing now. And that it is time to eat some of Edith's splendid scones."

"But that story you told us, my lord," Anne said when she caught her breath. "All that stuff about a treasure. Yes, that sailor did thrust something into my basket. Edith discovered it beneath a chicken my mother sent for tomorrow's supper. But it wasn't a treasure, just a curiosity."

"Though you said Mr. Trent would like it very much, Anne," Mrs. Sayle said.

"Mr. Trent?" Jack asked.

The gray eyes turned back to him. A faint blush stole over her cheeks. "Mr. Trent and I are engaged to be married. He came here to dinner. Arthur must have left again—oh, goodness, I hope he left in time, before either you or your rival discovered who I was, or where I lived!"

"You showed him what you'd found?"

"Yes. But as I said, it was just a curiosity—a fossil. Though I never saw anything like it in my life before. Quite an extraordinary thing, really."

Jack strode away across the room. *"The Dragon's Fang—"*

"Oh, no," Anne interrupted. Her skin was still flushed, making her eyes seem pure blue. "It's a tooth from an ancient giant lizard, isn't it? Surely there were never dragons?"

"Of course not." Jack turned back to her and smiled. "You gave this object to Mr. Arthur Trent?"

"Well, yes. I live near Lyme, you see. That's how we met. Our area is famous for fossils. Arthur came there to study our cliffs and beaches. He's a naturalist with an interest in such things." She frayed the end of her long plait between nervous fingers. "But I don't see why anyone would commit murder over a fossil. Does this single tooth have such value?"

"In gold? No. Yet a sailor lies dead."

She shivered. "Will it put Arthur in danger?"

"Our enemy cannot know that he exists. It took time to track you down. He'd not have been faster than I was, and your Mr. Trent must have left here long before that. Do any of the neighbors know that you and he are engaged, or that there is any connection between you?"

"No one knows except our immediate families. Our engagement is quite recent."

"Where is he now?"

"Mr. Trent has gone to London, my lord," Mrs. Sayle said. "He has gone and taken that nasty stone with him. So we may all relax. Edith, pray give His Lordship another scone—"

Perhaps it was the tea. Perhaps no one could maintain strong emotions indefinitely in the face of the pretty china cups and saucers, all the ritual with pot and spoons. Anne ate a buttered scone and almost forgot that she was still in her nightgown, threatened with death over that odd fossil, while her aunt entertained a duke's son in her humble parlor.

You all have that same manner about you. Anne had no idea if that was true. She had never met a real aristocrat before. The Duke and Duchess of Blackdown did not attend the Meeting House, or walk out on the Cobb to feel the breeze on their faces. Though her father was a gentleman with a perfectly respectable home in Hawthorn Axbury, the St. Georges did not socialize with country families named Marsh.

Yet Lord Jonathan Devoran St. George stood calmly drinking another cup of tea. He had been born into one of the families that ruled England, and thus the world. Wyldshay, his family home, spread its fields over twenty thousand acres of Dorset countryside and innumerable acres in other counties. She had often enough passed along roads that bordered Blackdown land beyond both hedgerows, eaten meals at inns owned by the duke, bought cheese produced on farms leased from His Grace.

Yet the duke and duchess were as remote to her family and friends as the king. She had never expected their worlds to cross.

"What happens now, my lord?" Anne asked at last. "You will go after Mr. Trent to retrieve the fossil?"

He turned to gaze at her. "Eventually." Then he smiled and the shadows fled. "He's not a garrulous man, I trust?"

"Arthur? Goodness, no! Not at all!"

"Then I pray you will write a letter to ask him to keep the fossil safe and mention it to no one, until you can send for it yourself. I shall ensure that the letter is delivered. In the meantime, I must see to your safety."

Anne's stomach tied itself in knots again, making her wish she hadn't eaten that scone. "Then it doesn't end here?"

"Fortunately I believe you have courage, Miss Marsh. And though it's the last thing I would have chosen, that courage is going to be important in the next few days."

"You think that other man will come back?"

"Until we give my rival reason to believe otherwise, he still thinks you might have the fossil. He's already proved that he'll hire killers to get to it. That man—or his friends—will come back."

Aunt Sayle pushed aside her cup. Her mouth trembled. "My brother's house in Hawthorn Axbury," she said. "Anne's father. We can all go there."

"I'm afraid that wouldn't answer, Mrs. Sayle." Lord Jonathan seemed merely kind and patient now, filled with the calm of a summer sky, though his words carried dread. "You would only draw the pursuit after you and put your brother's family in danger, also. If, on the other hand, Miss Marsh is seen to leave here in the morning with me, you may remain here quite safely."

"My niece cannot possibly leave with a gentleman that she doesn't know, my lord," Aunt Sayle said.

"She must," he replied. "If she does not, she will imperil several innocent people as well as herself: you, Edith, even your neighbors. I promise to keep her safe."

Aunt Sayle clung stubbornly to Anne's arm. "I'm sorry, my lord, it's quite out of the question. It would offend every rule of modesty. Anyway, I must stay with her. If she's in danger, then Edith and I will share it."

"And as you love her, you must put her in my hands," he said. "As for propriety, we'll be seen to take an outing as if I'm an old friend of the family, come to drive Miss Marsh out for an hour. Nothing could be more respectable."

Aunt Sayle looked him up and down. "Yes, my lord, but the neighbors—"

He smiled with genuine humor. "You haven't yet seen me dressed as my father's son, ma'am, at the ribbons of a fashionable phaeton. I promise to favorably impress the neighbors."

"Your intent is that we draw the pursuit after us?" Anne held herself upright with a rigid determination.

"Yes," Lord Jonathan said. "But they won't catch us."

"You cannot think to do this!" Aunt Sayle exclaimed. "Oh, Anne! There must be another way."

He sat down in the chair opposite Anne and leaned forward. "Do you doubt that I can protect you?" he asked quietly.

"It's not that." Anne closed her eyes, searching for certainty, trying to speak whatever truth she might find in her heart. "I'm sure you're very competent with those pistols, my lord, and I'm prepared to believe your reassurances. Indeed, earlier in my bedchamber for a moment I thought you might be the Archangel Michael ready to wield your fiery sword in our defense."

"Good God!" He sat back and laughed.

That laughter would have been all the reassurance Anne needed, if she had been only physically afraid. To protect her family, she would leave on a headless horse with the devil himself. But it wasn't that. Not that at all.

Yes, she was usually uncomfortable with strangers. She was, often enough, absurdly tongue-tied. Really, of everyone she'd met—other than her immediate family—only Arthur Trent had allowed her to feel natural and relaxed.

She was quite certain now that if she was with this man, this duke's son, this traveler, no murderous villains would dare to approach them. She had no fears for herself. Yet some strange new apprehension lay deeper than that, a fear she couldn't name, that perhaps didn't even exist.

Shaking her head, she tried to dismiss her odd doubts.

"You have a plan, Lord Jonathan?" she asked. "Why is it best that I leave with you?"

"At the moment my rival doesn't know that I'm here. I arrived under cover of night, and his lackey didn't see me in your bedroom. That's our first advantage."

"But if you appear openly at the door in the morning and carry me off with you in a phaeton, won't they be certain we have the fossil?"

"Not quite. They'll certainly know that Mrs. Sayle doesn't have it and they'll surmise she knows nothing about it. Otherwise, they would expect me to enter the house to question her and Edith. That will make this home safe from further invasion—though it might still be wise if you were to visit your brother in a few days, Mrs. Sayle, just to put your niece's mind at rest."

"What can our safety matter, my lord," Aunt Sayle said, "if Anne is in danger?"

Anne turned to her aunt and tried to smile. "You should visit Father to take him news of where I am, Aunt, but I'm afraid I am the hind. The hunters are only after me."

"At the moment, yes," Lord Jonathan said. "But as soon as I put in a public appearance, they'll no longer be sure of their immediate purpose, especially when I take you out in a carriage."

"I cannot like it," Aunt Sayle said. "I'm sure I don't know what the world is coming to!"

"The world is entering a new age, ma'am," he replied, "but you need not be uncomfortable in it. If I were to enter the house, then leave here openly and alone, they might think I have the fossil. But the moment I didn't produce it, Miss Marsh would once again be the focus of attack."

"Yet as long as we leave together," Anne asked, "the implication will be that you're not sure whether I really received it or not?"

"They will think that I'm merely trying to gather information—the same information that they want. We shall create uncertainty, which will buy us time."

"Time for my letter to reach Arthur?"

"Exactly. Meanwhile, we will undoubtedly be followed, but we will not be attacked. They will expect me to bring you back here. Before betraying their own hand, they'll want to see what moves I make next."

"But where will you really take her?" Aunt Sayle asked.

Anne held her breath. Did any of his argument make sense? Was she putting herself into the hands of a madman? If he suggested anything too improper or strange, she could still refuse, of course.

Yet as his smile spread—creasing the mahogany cheeks, showing white, white teeth—her heart beat hard, robbing her of judgment and making her doubt that her decision had anything to do with either reason or finding wisdom in the quiet place in her heart. Anything at all.

For one wild moment she thought she would happily go with him anywhere—

"I shall take Miss Marsh to Wyldshay," he said.

CHAPTER THREE

GUY WOKE AS IF SHAKEN. HE REACHED FOR THE PISTOL lying on the nightstand, only to have his wrist pinned in a strong grip.

"Sorry," Jack whispered. "For the second time in a night, I must creep about in other folk's bedrooms—except that it's almost morning. An orchestra of songbirds is tuning up outside."

Guy focused on his cousin's face and grinned. "What the hell are you about now? Why not knock at the door or wait until breakfast, like a normal person?"

Jack released Guy's wrist and dropped into a chair. A faintly pink light washed into the room. "I couldn't be certain you'd be alone."

"You thought I might be sharing my bed?"

"Why not? This isn't that bad an establishment, far better than the Rose and Crown. If I recall correctly, we frequented worse upon occasion when we were younger."

"And less wise?" Guy rubbed a hand over his hair and wished he had hot coffee to hand. "The ladies of a dockside inn are hardly to my taste any longer, Jack, though they might still be to yours—"

"No. My tastes have changed entirely."

"Since you've been traveling in the voluptuous East?"

"The virtuous East, Guy. But the more virtuous a culture, the more sensuous its women."

"Except England, obviously."

"Except England. No tea or coffee available yet, of course. Brandy?"

"At this hour? You've really become that dissolute?"

Jack smiled. "No, just in a propitiatory mood. I came to ask if I might borrow a suit of clothes."

"Clothes?"

"And your phaeton. I have no truly fashionable carriage here and it would take too long to acquire one."

Guy shrugged into a dressing gown and splashed cold water on his face from the pitcher on the washstand. "You should know I never lend a team of mine to anyone—"

"Except me." Jack held out a towel.

The towel wasn't as clean as it might have been. "Except you, of course. And why the devil do you want my clothes? I'm sure you have perfectly good garments of your own."

"I do, but not with me. There's been a change of plan. I'm going straight to Wyldshay, after all."

"So while you drive home in my Sunday suit with my pretty chestnuts, what am I supposed to do?"

Jack leaned back as if to examine the ceiling. "You'll spend a delightful morning with one of those young ladies who wasn't quite good enough to grace your bed. I found her in the kitchen, contemplating a bucket. For a large sum of money, she's agreed to do anything we want."

Guy looked up over the towel and raised both brows. "This young woman is skilled at hosting orgies?"

"She might be. I didn't ask. She did not demur, however, from the prospect of a short sea voyage."

"A sea voyage?"

"I'm about to collect a certain respectable female in your phaeton. Her father is a Dissenting minister and a gentleman. I intend to deliver this young lady safely to my mother, but my enemies will watch when I fetch her from her aunt's house."

"And they'll follow you?"

Jack nodded. "Therefore I shall bring her here, where we'll all switch identities. I hired a yacht yesterday in case I needed it. You and the kitchen wench, disguised as me and the minister's daughter, will take it for a short sail. Then my pursuers may cool their heels waiting for you both to return, while the real quarry and I make our escape."

The dawn light cast an exotic glow over his cousin's darkened skin. Guy tossed down the towel and poured himself a brandy, after all. "Why not send to Wyldshay for a contingent of armed men, then take your Dissenter there under adequate protection?"

"Because there isn't time, and because I would rather she simply disappeared."

The drink eased down Guy's throat. "It might work, but for God's sake! Who the devil are you running from, Jack?"

"Friends of that nasty fellow who killed the Bristol sailor, of course. You took care of that?"

"There was nothing much more I could do. Your murderer was killed trying to escape arrest. The authorities, anyway, believe it was just a private quarrel between seamen."

If Jack was disturbed by the death of the Malay, it didn't show in his face. "Over a woman, no doubt."

"The idea was mentioned."

"Thank you. The truth is that the assassin was one of a gang of Asian thugs hired by an Englishman named Thornton, who ought to know better. Thornton and I have cause for disagreement, but he does not have adequate cause to murder anybody. Unfortunately, the men he has hired do not share such impractical scruples—as Thornton is beginning to realize."

"He cannot control them?"

Jack reached for the brandy and drained what was left in the bottle. "Such men are like wrack washed up on a beach, Guy. Men without faith or culture or country, knocking about from port to port, discards of the world. Once offered enough gold and given a sacred quest, no one can control them."

"Sacred?"

"They believe the missing item has holy power."

"How many are there?"

"I don't know."

"It's impossible to communicate with them?"

"I speak one or two of their languages, so it is possible to communicate. It's not possible to change their minds. Right now they'd only do their best to kill me, if I tried. Thornton began it, but he's out of his depth."

"This is why you left the *Venture* in Portugal?"

"This is why I traveled all the way from Asia in disguise." Jack glanced at the window, now framing daylight, and stood up. "The rest of my explanations can wait. God, I could eat a horse! Please allow me to treat you to breakfast, sir. After which—"

Guy laughed. "My best clothes and my phaeton. And a nice little adventure with a kitchen girl on a yacht. How can I possibly refuse?"

$\mathcal{A}$NNE SAT BY THE FIRE AND STARED AT HER LAP. HER pelisse fell open to reveal shiny peach cotton stretched over several layers of petticoats. A band of white pleats around each wrist was matched by the same trim at the hem. It was the very best dress she had with her. She was sure it was hideously provincial and out-of-date.

Her hands lay on the peach fabric, one clutching a pair of gloves, the other her straw bonnet, a little battered from its soaking the previous afternoon. Aunt Sayle had stayed up the rest of the night sewing. The bonnet bravely sported new cherry ribbons and some glass fruit.

The decoration was definitely provincial and out-of-date, but Anne hadn't had the heart to crush her aunt's kindness. She would wear the bonnet proudly. Yet her heart beat heavily, and beneath the peach cotton and petticoats, her stomach fluttered as if filled with small birds.

Edith peered from the parlor window, Aunt Sayle at her side.

They were waiting for Lord Jonathan to arrive.

"You are absolutely certain of his identity, Edith?" Aunt Sayle's fingers moved together in fretful little embraces.

"As sure as I am of my own! All the St. Georges have that arrogant manner, but what can you expect from a duke's family? They can do whatever they like, and who's to gainsay them?"

Anne tightened her grip on her gloves. She had tried to pray, to find the small still voice, but her pulse had refused to slow down and her thoughts had circled and circled like sparrowhawks. Lord

Jonathan had announced his plans with such cavalier certainty! *They can do whatever they like—*

"And it's a drive of only a few hours in an open carriage on the public highway," Aunt Sayle said. "No need to be afraid—"

"None at all! My sister says that the duchess herself is the soul of kindness." Edith patted her mistress's shoulder. "Lord Jonathan will have his mother to answer to, won't he? He'll see that no harm comes to our Anne."

"And just think!" Aunt Sayle said as if reaching for courage. "Wyldshay! They say it's the grandest place in England—all built up from the original castle!"

"Well, I never saw very far inside, but it has turrets and battlements, sure enough, and walls high as the clouds, and my sister told me—"

Anne only half listened as Edith chattered away about spiral stairs and suits of armor; gardens and lakes and trees a thousand years old; the array of silver and glassware and plate in the grand dining room; crystal chandeliers and mirrors and paintings and marble statues; the fabulous silks and jewels worn by the ladies; the power wielded by the duke—

"What do you say, Anne?" It was Aunt Sayle, turned expectantly from the window. "Just think! That my niece, Miss Anne Marsh of simple Hawthorn Axbury, should be a guest of a duke and duchess—!"

"He's coming!" Edith said. "Oh, my!"

Anne stood up and jammed the ugly bonnet on her head. The birds in her stomach soared into flight.

"Please don't worry about me," she said. "Of course I'll be safe!"

Aunt Sayle clutched her in a fierce hug. Edith turned back to the window and dabbed at her eyes.

Anne swallowed hard and made herself smile. "After all, I'm to travel with a gentleman armed with pistols, and I'm sure that he knows how to use them."

"Oh, my!" Edith exclaimed again, staring down into the street. "Oh, my! A duke's son, Miss Anne!"

NEIGHBORS CRANED THEIR HEADS. SOME SAILORS LOOKED up from a broken wagon, where they'd been unloading barrels to lighten the load. Someone whistled as the horses trotted past, the universal workingmen's code for admiration. Anne stood in the street doorway as he pulled up his team and smiled down at her—Lord Jonathan Devoran St. George.

"Oh, goodness!" she breathed to herself. "I was wrong. I can't do this!"

The phaeton was the very latest style, wheels and trim picked out in black and gold. Two glossy chestnuts tossed their heads, eager to be off, protesting the hands of the groom who had swung down to hold them.

The gentleman who sat on the box took her breath away.

His gloved fingers displayed leather that seemed finer than silk. His blue coat fit as if his broad shoulders had been painted with woad. A cravat of pristine whiteness glowed against his tanned chin in a contrast more shocking than his black shirt of the previous night. A high-crowned hat shadowed his face, creating an impenetrable veil of aloofness and mystery. A vision of aristocratic masculine perfection, and she, plain Miss Anne Marsh of Hawthorn Axbury—dressed in peach cotton with cherry ribbons and glass grapes—was putting herself entirely into those elegantly gloved hands!

She glanced down to hide real panic. Those hands had touched her last night, carried her dressed in nothing but her night attire, tried to reassure her when she had almost been murdered in her bed. He had hooked one strong arm under her knees, and the other—

Lord Jonathan stepped down from his carriage and lifted his hat. Anne dropped a curtsy and hoped her weak knees would not betray her. The glass grapes tinkled together.

"We're being watched," he said softly. "We should leave right away."

He took her hand to help her into the carriage. Anne stared at her fingers lying on his kidskin glove. Alarm beat through her blood.

"It's all right," he said. "You're quite safe. Our groom carries two quite terrifying blunderbuss pistols, and my father's home is a fortress manned by a large and faithful staff, with a stalwart footman in every hallway."

It must be that! Just nerves about being the guest of a duchess. Anne tried to ignore her rapid pulse and lifted her chin. Yet she did not feel safe. She felt light-headed and oddly excited, as if she were spiraling into some new and terrifying awareness.

"Yes," she said. "Of course. Thank you."

The glass grapes tinkled again as she climbed up to sit on the high seat. Springs dipped as Lord Jonathan stepped beside her and took up the whip and reins. The groom swung up behind as the chestnuts sprang forward.

"I trust you're suitably impressed?" Lord Jonathan asked. "The neighbors are, certainly. But alas, the phaeton isn't mine, nor the horses. I borrowed them."

Anne folded her hands in her lap and concentrated on the one thing that mattered.

"Who is watching us?" she asked.

"Possibly only your very genuine admirers."

"Admirers! I feel like a daisy in the presence of an orchid!"

Gracious! What a stupid thing to say! She stared doggedly at the toes of her half-boots.

"I like daisies," he said gently, "but as it happens, these clothes aren't mine, either."

Anne took a deep breath. She was behaving like a ninny. Better to bury the memory of foreigners with knives climbing in windows and pretend that this duke's son really was just an old friend intent on a short outing.

"Are you trying to tell me that you're an impostor, after all, Lord Jonathan?"

"No. However, my family would be most relieved to see me thus attired."

She stared straight ahead, barely focusing on the succession of shop signs. "You don't generally dress as a gentleman?"

"There are places in the world where I'm known as Wild Lord Jack, the duke's son who went native with swamis and magicians. My mother might be expecting me to appear in face paint and feathers."

She glanced up. The brim of his hat cast deep shadows across the feral beauty of his face, the sensuous curve of lip and nostril. He seemed to be concentrating only on driving the team.

"You're teasing me," she said.

"I would never tease about something so important." He tooled the carriage around a corner. "A thorough knowledge of magic is essential when one lives in the East."

"You lived in India for some years?" There! That was quite sensible.

"I've passed through India many times, a land where holy men walk on hot coals or lie stretched on a bed of nails—"

Anne shuddered. "Surely that's more torture than magic?"

"Not at all! The practitioner remains entirely uninjured. It's a demonstration of religious faith. I've also seen men charm snakes, though why the snakes should like such discordant music is beyond me, and I've witnessed the Indian rope trick several times. It's perhaps the most mysterious illusion of all."

"The rope trick?"

"A man throws what seems to be an ordinary rope up into the air, but the rope stiffens as if hanging from an invisible hook. Then a little boy climbs up to the top and—*poof!*—he disappears. I have no idea how it's done."

"He cannot really disappear, surely? No one can."

Lord Jonathan glanced down at her and smiled. "You think not? But that's exactly what I intend us to do."

The cherry ribbons seem to get tighter under her chin. "What do you mean?"

"I regret it, but we have snakes after us, Miss Marsh, and we must elude them. You must surely have guessed by now: In spite of our armed groom, we cannot really travel all the way to Wyld-shay like this."

"So you lied last night?"

"Only by inference."

Anne tried to avoid looking at his gloved fingers on the reins. The unsteady beat of agitation flared in her blood. She had almost relaxed! She hadn't quite noticed it, but when he'd started talking about magic and India, she'd begun to breathe normally, to listen to what he'd been saying and forget her anxieties. Boys disappearing into thin air? Holy men lying down on beds of nails?

"You lied to Aunt Sayle and me and Edith?" she continued. "Then, if you don't put me down right away, I'll scream."

"I pray you'll do no such thing. Glance casually over your shoulder as we turn into the next street. Let your eyes sweep, without focusing on any one person."

Anne stared into her lap. "Someone is following us right now?"

"One of the sailors from that wagon so fortuitously damaged near your front door. It's all right. They won't attack us here."

Hooves drummed as the chestnuts trotted around another corner. Anne glanced back. A man with a blue cloth wrapped about his head rode a donkey at a smart trot behind them.

Fear leaped into her throat. "Then where are we going, if we're not going to Wyldshay?"

"We are going to Wyldshay. However, first we shall stop at a perfectly respectable inn, where you may meet my cousin, Guy Devoran. Guy is, unlike me, a perfect gentleman. This is his carriage, by the way."

"Your cousin loaned you his carriage?"

"And these clothes."

"What about your luggage? If you just arrived from the East, didn't you have luggage?"

"I sent most of it on ahead to Wyldshay."

Breath seemed to be getting harder and harder to find, as if her corset were being steadily laced in. "May I ask why?"

"Certainly. I didn't want to be encumbered with anything that didn't match my disguise, so everything else is now with my brother. I can trust Ryder not to question why I sent it."

"Does no one ever question anything you do?"

"Rarely."

Anne forced her spine upright. "Then I think I must start to do so now, my lord. You will agree, surely, that I have the right, when you have carried me off like this under false pretenses."

"Of course, but we've arrived." He turned the carriage into the courtyard of an inn. "This is a fashionable enough establishment and we shall retreat to a private room."

The horses stopped.

"However fashionable, sir, I cannot think that this is quite proper."

"Proper? I suppose not, but our friend on the donkey won't be able to follow us inside, which is what counts."

Their groom jumped down to run to the horses' heads.

"Walk them, will you?" Lord Jonathan said. "We'll be on our way again in a few minutes, once the lady has refreshed herself."

The groom nodded and touched his cap.

SHE WAS JUST AS PRICKLY AS HE'D FEARED: A PRICKLY, PRIM Dissenter. He had distracted her from her fears for a moment with his talk of India, but there was no avoiding reality now that they had arrived at the inn.

Jack reached up to help her down from Guy's phaeton. With a silly little defiance, she tried to avoid taking his hand and instead half fell against him, so that he had to use both hands to steady her. She was all whalebone. Whalebone and petticoats.

He felt a small, absurd spurt of anger.

A wonder of the deep had been butchered so that Englishwomen could pretend there was no soft female flesh beneath their clothes. So that a man's hand on a woman's waist would remind him of carapaces and shells, instead of firing him with thoughts of musk and bedrooms. Innumerable men and women had slaved to grow cotton to make all those petticoats, so that an Englishman shouldn't know that a woman had legs. So that he shouldn't be reminded that her thighs curved, that the backs of her knees hid delectable female secrets, that her calves would feel slim and smooth on a man's back.

Miss Anne Marsh could hide from him all she liked, but he had carried her dressed only in her nightdress. He already knew that she was soft and female beneath the unflattering peach dress—and that her skin was perfumed with lavender and woman.

She put up one hand to adjust her bonnet with its hideously clashing ribbons and glass grapes.

"Thank you." She watched the phaeton being led away. "I will not go inside with you, my lord, unless you can clarify what's happening. You mentioned a private parlor and your cousin. I think you must explain, or else I shall ask the innkeeper to send me straight back to my aunt."

There was no time for niceties. Jack remembered exactly who he was and spoke as his father might speak.

"Do you think I mean to ravish you, Miss Marsh?"

She blushed scarlet and her eyes filled with tears. Yet she raised her chin and shook her head. "No, my lord. Of course not."

"My cousin is waiting for us." He took a deep breath and softened his tone. "I've hired a maid who is waiting there, also. You and I shall leave for Wyldshay shortly, but in disguise. Meanwhile, the man in the blue turban is hovering just outside that arched entryway. His friends are already arriving to join him. I will explain as soon as we're inside, but we absolutely cannot linger here."

"No," she said. "I'm sorry. I must seem very foolish to you."

She straightened her spine and walked decorously across the yard to the inn door. Guiding her by one elbow, Jack ushered her upstairs to Guy's room.

The woman from the kitchen was standing beside the window. She looked pale, but determined. Jack made rapid introductions—the maid's name was Rachel Wren—and Anne Marsh sat down on a chair that Guy pulled out for her.

"Very well," Anne said, her face like chalk. "What is the plan?"

"We'll exchange clothes here, Miss Marsh," Jack said. "Then we'll begin our journey again in a different conveyance, while Mr. Devoran and Miss Wren, disguised as us, leave together in the phaeton to draw the pursuit after them instead."

"But I have no change of clothes," she said.

"When we reach Wyldshay, my sisters will be happy to lend you anything you need. For now, I have provided everything necessary."

He indicated a box sitting beside the fireplace. Anne stared at it. Rachel Wren gazed from the window as if she barely understood English.

"I'm sorry to so offend your modesty, Miss Marsh," Jack continued, "by mentioning such a thing, but you may retain your own undergarments, of course. However, I pray you will remove your bonnet, pelisse, and dress, and allow Miss Wren to put them on." He grinned. "Fortunately, that's a most distinctive bonnet."

Anne looked back at him with a certain defiance. "My aunt trimmed it for me last night."

"Then we must thank Mrs. Sayle for her kindness. Once Miss Wren is wearing that, no one will know that she's not Miss Anne Marsh, whose aunt stayed up all night sewing for her. Meanwhile,

I've provided another costume for you. You and I shall leave here as Farmer Osgood and his wife, in a nice little farm gig acquired for the occasion."

"You've been busy," she said.

The sudden brave humor in it surprised him. "Yes, I suppose so, though I can recall times when I've been busier."

She said nothing for a moment, then she glanced up at Guy. "Mr. Devoran and Miss Wren won't be in danger?"

"None at all. They're to sail about all day within view of the shore. Our pursuers will watch and wait. When Mr. Devoran and Miss Wren finally return, they'll reappear as themselves. The snakes may search the yacht for us and realize they've been duped, but we shall be safely at Wyldshay by then."

She closed her eyes and sat in absolute silence for a moment, while the others waited. At last she lifted her head and looked straight at Jack.

"It is, I suppose, a good plan," she said.

"It's a madman's plan," Guy said with a grin. "Which is why it will probably work. Are you content, Miss Marsh? Miss Wren and I should be on our way."

She nodded. Jack caught Guy's eye and the two men left the room.

"It is a madman's plan," Guy repeated as they stripped off their jackets.

Jack laughed. "Yes, of course, but not perhaps for the reasons you think."

Guy raised a brow. "Why, then?"

"Because for all her air of fragile decorum, Miss Anne Marsh is a lady with the fortitude to wear scarlet ribbons with glass grapes rather than hurt the feelings of an aunt who loves her."

"Then you don't think that bonnet was to her own taste?"

Jack laughed. "I'm damned certain it was not!"

N OW THAT SHE HAD COMMITTED HERSELF, SHE WOULD SEE it through. That was the one message she had found buried in her heart, a message carried in her father's voice: *See it through, Annie!*

Anne pulled off her hat and pelisse and the peach cotton dress, then stood in half-boots and petticoats as the maid dressed in her clothes. They were about the same size, but the maid's hair was gilt blond and her eyes as blue as periwinkles: a true English beauty. Without the bonnet, no one would ever confuse them.

Looked at objectively, the red ribbons and grapes were more than distinctive, of course, they were hideous. The deep brim completely hid Rachel's face. To her immense surprise, Anne felt a little rush of glee. This mad ruse of Lord Jonathan's just might work!

She began to feel almost merry, as if she were playing at dress-up with her brothers and sisters. Anne reached into the box and found a serviceable blue gown, poke bonnet, and brown cloak, exactly what any farmer's wife might wear to town for a little shopping. Rachel helped her into the dress.

"Oh," the maid said. "Oh, dear!"

The hem swept the floor and the waist had been cut for a far bulkier woman. Anne was as swamped in blue cotton as a baby in swaddling.

"It's too big," Anne said unnecessarily. "His Lordship could have fit both of us inside this!"

Rachel's eyes sparkled as she grinned back, then both of them burst into laughter—a glorious release from such a tense morning. Someone knocked. Rachel went to the door, peered out, then threw it open to reveal Guy Devoran and—Farmer Osgood? Mr. Devoran now wore his own blue coat, with the snowy cravat and high hat that his cousin had worn earlier, but Lord Jonathan was unrecognizable.

His clothes were that of any farmer, as she'd expected. He'd dusted something white, flour perhaps, into his hair to dull the rich color. But he'd also done something to his face. He sported a pipe and a vestige of whiskers, but even his eyes and mouth had changed. Anne tried to gulp down her giggles, but they insisted on welling up.

"Oh," she said. "Oh, my!"

"Soot," he replied, meeting her gaze. "Not a beard exactly, but a slightly unkempt failure at a close shave." Waving the pipe in one hand, he glanced at Rachel and spoke in a broad West Country accent. "Miss Wren, you look charming. No one would know that you aren't Miss Marsh."

Guy bowed over the maid's hand. She curtsied and walked with him to the door.

"See you at Wyldshay," Lord Jonathan said. "Good luck!"

Guy Devoran winked. "Same to you, Cousin! I think you're going to need it a little more than we will—I just saw the spavined jade and gig you've hired to take you home."

With the blue dress swamping her ankles, Anne was left standing alone with Farmer Osgood. He looked decidedly rustic and several years older. She could almost believe that he was a sheepman from Hawthorn Axbury, which felt a great deal safer than being alone with a duke's son.

He turned back to her and smiled.

"So the daisy becomes a cornflower," he said. "I'm sorry there wasn't time to find the right size."

"You really do look like a farmer. It's more than just the clothes and the soot. How did you do it?"

"An appropriately cheap tobacco, along with a sincere attempt to have absolute faith in my pigs and sheep. The secret to any disguise is to believe in it yourself, heart and soul."

"Add a slight slouch and a frown, and the duke's son has disappeared?"

"Exactly." He chewed on the pipe for a moment as he gazed at her. "Though your disguise may take a little more work, alas. You can't even walk, can you?"

Anne glanced down. "There's no reason a gentleman should know how to size a lady's dress."

He put away the pipe and pulled over a stool. "Stand on this."

"What are you going to do?"

"Trim the hem, ma'am. In another life, I'm sure I was a mantua maker."

She hesitated for only a moment before she climbed onto the stool. *See it through, Annie!*

The blue dress was decorated around the hem with three rows of black piping topping short ruffles. Lord Jonathan rifled through the box and pulled out a pair of scissors. He dropped to one knee and began to cut away the bottom tier of the skirt, just below the last ruffle.

Anne held her breath. He seemed merely intent on the task. So he might catch a glimpse of petticoat, but he'd already seen her in her nightgown. Her ankles were safely covered by her half-boots, of course. He surely wouldn't be able to see anything of her limbs.

Even if he did, he was a gentleman. He wouldn't be swept away by lust.

She suppressed an oddly painful little giggle. No man, ever, would be swept away by lust at the sight of Miss Anne Marsh. Not that she quite understood what that meant. Arthur Trent had fallen in love and offered to marry her, but he had never tried to kiss her—

"Turn a little more to the right," Farmer Osgood said.

Anne turned. Her petticoats rubbed against her bare thighs. His hands at the hem sent a slight tugging sensation all the way up to her shoulders. She tried to ignore the little trickle of warmth and sweet embarrassment. Were her stockings perfectly clean? She had put on fresh ones that morning. And these were her very best petticoats, so if he did catch a glimpse, he would not think the worst of her.

Yet she began to feel wicked. Wanton. Plain Anne Marsh was transformed, just for an instant, into a female who would allow a gentleman to kneel at her feet and see sinful glimpses of her undergarments!

"Turn again," he said.

She looked down. In spite of the flour, his hair was rich and thick, hair any woman would die for. His deft hands wielded the scissors like a sword. This was the way a knight errant might kneel at his lady's feet, his heart filled only with chivalry and pure adoration. She grinned to herself.

"There!" He gathered the discarded ruffle in one fist. "Done. Allow me to help you step down."

Anne set her fingers on his. Her heels clicked as they met the floor. The new length of the skirt was perfect, though it was still too bulky in the waist.

"We could use that extra fabric for a cummerbund," she said.

"An excellent idea, Miss Marsh." He held out the scissors and the discarded ruffle. His voice was rich and warm, as if it carried spiced undercurrents directly from the Orient. "Do you need me to help you?"

"I can do it," she said. "It will only take a moment."

Lord Jonathan stepped back and bowed. A little smile lurked at the corners of his lips, a smile Anne knew she had never seen on a gentleman's face in her life. She didn't know why, but she rather liked it. It felt flattering. It made her feel breathless and important and alive.

In spite of the disguise, when he smiled like that he looked every inch a duke's son—as if he had never once entertained thoughts of sheep and pigs, as if he were thinking of something quite different, something delicious and wicked and disturbing.

"Thank God for that." He spun on one heel to stride away.

Anne stared after him. The flutter of this mysterious new awareness pulsed up from her boots to intoxicate every strand of hair on her head.

"Why?" she asked.

"Because," he said over his shoulder, "if I were to perform such a personal service for you again, Miss Marsh, I might ravish you on the spot, after all."

DISMAY COALESCED IN JACK'S SPINE, TEMPERED BY WRY astonishment at himself.

She was an Englishwoman and a Dissenter, shy, naive, forced into this impropriety against her better judgment. He had not hesitated to use the force of his position to browbeat her. She was embroiled in his adventure—trapped in the company of a man she didn't know—yet she had shown courage, even something of humor. The responsibility was all his: to take her safely to Wyldshay, to tease her out of any embarrassment or fear.

What the devil had possessed him to say something guaranteed to achieve just the opposite?

Jack relaxed his back, closed his eyes, and faced it: that moment of purely self-indulgent diversion, while lust raged in his blood.

While he had knelt at her feet, cutting away the hem of her dress, he had not really been surprised by the immediate, urgent pulse in the groin. Yet self-discipline had become Jack's stringent master. Deliberately he had allowed himself the pleasure, then detached his mind from the intense flare of arousal, the passionate interest of his body. He had not betrayed himself, known he would not betray himself—until that one final, offhand comment, when the entire edifice of his control tore from top to bottom.

It was not only what he had said. It was not only that he had meant it. It was that—in spite of his experience and knowledge—in that one moment his discipline had cracked. He had spoken his innermost thoughts aloud and told her the truth: He desired her with an inexplicable intensity.

Beneath the froth of white petticoats, tan leather wrapped in soft little wrinkles over her high, springing arches. Tiny black buttons ran up in a sinfully neat row opposite the curve of her instep to the top of each dainty boot. White stockings covered slim female shins, promising garters and soft, bare thighs. Thighs made to encompass a man's naked hips, while her arched feet pressed into the backs of his calves—

He had imagined it. He had reveled in the thought. He had breathed in her scent, while the promise of sensual delight fired straight to his erection.

Fair enough.

She was female. He was male. It had been a long time. As soon as he finished this mission, he would board a ship back to Asia. In the meantime, he might imagine anything he liked, even a fantasy fired by the strangely erotic allure of buttoned half-boots and virginal petticoats, as long as he did not reveal that thought in either word or deed.

He took a deep breath to allow his mind to rediscover silence. His disquiet melted unmolested away through his veins. His arousal faded. Calm certainty flowed in like a balm. It would not happen again.

I am a man, with a man's needs, but Miss Anne Marsh is off-limits and under my protection. She was also engaged to be married to some sober naturalist who unwittingly carried an object for which several men had already died. That was his only purpose: to recover the fossil and confront his enemies.

Jack opened his eyes.

She made a small sound, like a little sob breathed by a rabbit. He had probably reduced her to horrified tears. Now he must apologize, though lightly, and reweave her cocoon of security. Not difficult.

He turned, ready to coax and reassure.

"Oh," she said. Both hands were pressed to her mouth. "Oh."

The blue dress swamped her tender bones. The extra fabric trailed, trembling over one shaking elbow.

She was laughing—*laughing!*

Jack stood with his mind empty, his palms open at his sides, and allowed her laughter to wash into his heart. She was not offended. She was not weeping or wringing her fingers in indignation. She thought it was funny.

CHAPTER FOUR

"I'M SORRY IF I OFFENDED YOU, MISS MARSH," HE SAID.

She dropped her hands and stretched out the length of extra fabric, looking at it. "Pray, don't apologize! I almost forgot that we're in danger. You've brought me so very gently back to earth. Thank you for that, my lord."

Fascinated, he leaned back against the wall and crossed his arms. "You don't think that I might have meant it?"

"Oh, no! Of course not. Though this situation is most uncomfortable, isn't it? Better to have that out in the open, then we can see how absurd it is."

"You don't believe that I might in truth find you attractive?"

"Good heavens, no! I'm not generally the sort of lady that gentlemen notice and I'm engaged to be married quite soon, which puts me quite beyond consideration, doesn't it? You are kind to be gallant, Lord Jonathan, but I cannot take your nonsense very seriously."

There was no coquetry in it at all. No flirtation. Just a simple statement of the facts as she saw them—revealing a blindingly naive view of men.

She sliced the blue cotton with the scissors, then began to wrap it just above her waist, bunching up the voluminous folds of the dress. Her movements riveted his attention to her hidden breasts. The swathes of blue made them look ripe, heavy.

"Is that all right?" She wrinkled her nose as she looked up at him.

"Pull up the fabric a little more at the back," he said.

She tried to look over her shoulder. "Where?"

Holding the calm silence at the center of his thoughts, he strode up to her and tweaked the dress into place, careful not to touch her waist, the secret curve of breast and hip, keeping his mind remote, empty, while his hands worked. Yet tiny waves of heat washed over her neck, as if a curtain moved gently in a sunny window. If he held his palm there he could warm it.

"Thank you." She ducked away, picked up the bonnet, and turned to the mirror over the fireplace.

The ugly shape hid her face. Her hand patted the top, little tapping motions, settling the bonnet firmly in place. A small, slender hand with long fingers, as white and valiant as lilies.

Beneath the bonnet her curved nape gleamed with the faintest blush, vulnerable, sensitive. Though she did not know what it meant—could not recognize her own instinctive and mysterious knowledge—with aching naïveté her body had already responded to the interest in his.

His blood stirred in eddies of pleasure, then spread hot longing once again through his flesh. He wanted to set his mouth on her neck. Taste her pulse with his tongue. Taste her flesh, soft with lavender and spring water. He couldn't remember when he had last desired anything with such intensity.

But self-discipline and calm had overlaid his body's claims. Jack stepped back. When she turned she would see nothing in his eyes but indifference. She would take it for agreement that he could not possibly desire her. She would feel better. He was as certain of that as he was of his own control.

"You're a perfect Mrs. Osgood." He strode to the door. "Time to go."

Anne Marsh wrapped the brown cloak about her shoulders and walked up to him, her cheeks bright, her gaze clear and content.

Jack led her down to the inn yard, where a roan cob stood harnessed to a plain little gig.

In six hours they would arrive at Wyldshay, still strangers.

T HE MAN IN THE BLUE TURBAN HAD DISAPPEARED. THERE was no one watching. Jack guided their gig out of town, offering the occasional laconic remark in his rustic accent about the price of hogs.

"To be sure," Anne replied in the same dialect. "That's very true, Mr. Osgood. We'll not do as well with the pigs this year as last."

He swallowed laughter and winked at her.

The traffic thinned. The last of the houses dropped away behind them. They trotted for a few miles along the turnpike, then turned off onto a country lane. Best to approach Wyldshay on the byways, avoid tollgates and other travelers.

The cob's hooves splashed through the mud from yesterday's storm. The sky glimmered, washed with threads of silver-gray cloud. New leaves tousled the hedgerows, still damp. Anne Marsh reached up to adjust her bonnet, then with a small shrug took it off. A few strands of hair whipped about her cheeks.

"What a bold lady you are, Miss Marsh!" he said in his own voice. "You would face such a brisk day without a bonnet?"

She glanced up at him. She seemed calm, unworried, even merry. He liked it.

"I cannot see past the brim," she said. "And this bonnet doesn't fit very well. Anyway, no one will see us. We've left the danger behind now, haven't we?"

"I trust that our more unpleasant friends will keep watch over Mr. Devoran and Miss Wren on their yacht. So you may certainly take off your bonnet. You may even talk to me, if you like."

"About hogs?"

He laughed openly. "Devil take the hogs! No, tell me about yourself."

He needed to learn more about her and especially about her fiancé, Arthur Trent, the man who now possessed the Dragon's Fang. Yet he was also genuinely curious. Though he was certain about her innocence, he'd obviously been wrong to assume that she was entirely bound by convention.

"What do you usually do with your days?" he asked.

Looking straight ahead, she folded her hands in her lap. Her nose seemed oddly elegant, slipping down in a long line from her brow.

"Nothing of interest, certainly. Sometimes I write out my father's sermons for him. My hand is neater than his, you see. And I assist my mother. We sew, or read, or write letters, or I help Mama with the bottling or the garden, whatever needs to be done."

"Do you go out much?"

"I walk with my sisters or sometimes by myself, whenever the weather is fine." Her deft fingers absently stroked the brim of the bonnet. It was pleasantly tantalizing to watch them. "That is,

Emily and Marianne, who still live at home. Pamela is married and has gone to live in Yorkshire."

"And brothers?"

"Dan and Will are at sea. Tom is studying to become a pharmacist. Andrew still terrorizes the schoolroom." She glanced back at him, a small wrinkle creasing her brow, the gray-blue eyes open and candid. "Though we don't adhere to the Thirty-nine Articles of the Church of England, we're a very ordinary family, my lord."

Did she think he would mind? "You aren't the eldest?"

"Almost, after Pamela and Dan."

"And are you happy at the prospect of marriage, Miss Marsh? Like your sister, you'll have to leave your family as soon as you're wed."

Her hands stopped abruptly. "Oh, no! Arthur is buying us a house in Hawthorn Axbury. He wishes to live close to Lyme, so he can study the fossils there. I shall see my family every day. Nothing at all will change."

Jack let the cob drop back to a walk as they started up a small hill. Moisture rose from the fields in little wisps, like lost shreds of lambswool. Arthur Trent's name had rolled from her tongue with warmth, but entirely without passion, as if she were simply naming another brother. Had the man won her hand, yet not stirred her blood even a little?

"And that's what you want?"

"Yes, of course," she said.

"You conjure up a picture of great domestic contentment."

She looked up and smiled. "My home is very happy, Lord Jonathan. Though doubtless it would seem far too unfashionable and simple to you."

"Perhaps," he said. "Tell me more about Mr. Trent."

"Well, Arthur is very pleasant and easy to be with. We often walk together along the seashore and beaches, looking for fossils. Though his manner is a little strict, his company is most agreeable and restful. I like it."

"How did you meet?"

"We were introduced at the Meeting House by a mutual acquaintance. I think Arthur felt obliged to be courteous, so we strolled about together a little. I was able to converse with him quite easily. Then my father and I met him again at Miss Anning's fossil shop, which is why Arthur came to Lyme to begin with."

"You share an interest in geology?"

"I've been gathering fossils myself since I was a little girl. Of course, I'm only an amateur with a small collection. Arthur has traveled to Sussex and Oxfordshire and London, everywhere the new science is being done."

"So you're bound by mutual interest, a sedate meeting of minds?"

"Yes, one could say that."

Jack could clearly imagine her bent over a table strewn with rocks, her fiancé at her side—feeling more ardor for the fossils than she felt for the man?

He swallowed a smile. "Then I predict a comfortable, if uneventful, future."

"Arthur is a man of real sincerity and honor," she said, bridling a little. "Aren't a good character and comfortable companionship the most important attributes in marriage?"

"Perhaps," he said dryly. "Though I would include sharing mutual passion—and for more than natural philosophy."

"But there's more and more proof that the Earth is very old, much older than anyone thinks." Her eyes blazed, as if suddenly burnished to a bright blue. "We know now that huge lizards—animals beyond imagination—lived before the Flood. Your fossil must be one of them, and I think it's from a whole new species. Something never anticipated before. Such stunning proof of how creatures have changed over time!"

"Then you don't believe that God created fossils simply to decorate the rocks?"

"We Dissenters believe in rational inquiry and factual evidence, my lord." She seemed both vulnerable and insanely appealing. His pulse quickened, as if her excitement warmed his blood. "The truth about Creation lies in the rocks, if we study them with an open mind. You understand, I'm sure. You've traveled the world in search of fossils."

"No." He guided the cob around a stony patch where the road crested the hill. "My involvement in fossils was quite accidental."

There was a small silence. He glanced back at her. She looked genuinely puzzled.

"Then what did you go to find?"

"I didn't go to find anything. I was just traveling."

"I don't understand how anyone could do that," she said, "unless they were in truth seeking something."

The roan jerked its head and broke into a trot as they dropped into another valley. Jack brought the horse firmly back to the walk. Fields, trees, gates, all shone with a fine coating of moisture.

"Perhaps I sought adventure, experience, a new view of the world."

"And did you find them?"

"Yes," he said.

Leaves and small branches torn down by the recent gale littered the road. They splattered through a ford, the stream running swollen under a thin swirl of mist. The cob trotted up the slope on the other side, the track running away between hedgerows and trees to the gray English horizon. Red-and-white cows clustered in the corner of a field by the stream, mud to their hocks. A scattering of cottage chimneys smoked lazily farther down the valley.

"I should rather stay in Hawthorn Axbury." Anne looked away across the wet fields. "I cannot imagine what it would be like to live amongst foreigners. You must be very glad to be going home at last."

"Glad enough." It was the simplest reply. He could never explain how he really felt—maybe not even to himself.

"You were away a long time?"

"Years. Many years."

"Well, you certainly found adventure, whether you sought it or not." Her grin made the tip of her nose flatten just a little. It was so beguiling that he wanted to touch it. "And brought it back to England with you."

"Not at all," he said. "The adventure came here by itself. I just followed."

"As I just fell into it?" She pushed a strand of hair back from her forehead. The gesture seemed carefree, almost childlike, yet an adult wit colored her voice. "But the original fault was mine. I so ignored propriety that I walked alone down the High Street to my aunt's house. The next thing I know, I'm traveling unchaperoned in a gig with a stranger."

"And without a bonnet."

"Yes, and I must confess that I like the way it feels! I can see everything now." She glanced back up at him, her eyes bright, damp hair curling at her temples. "It's lovely here, isn't it? It must be wonderful for you to be back in England."

A dry wit. A sharp intelligence. A passion for science. Yet such a naive, insular view of the world! He said nothing, wondering why he wanted to tell her the truth, when he knew that she could never understand it. Yet as the silence grew, she seemed to wilt a little, as if she regretted talking so freely to a stranger.

"I do beg your pardon, my lord. I don't mean to pry."

"Not at all!" he said. "I wasn't sure quite how to answer, that's all."

"With the truth? Even if it's just to say that it's none of my business?"

He laughed, in spite of himself. "The truth? Now, that's a dangerous proposition, if ever I heard one. Do you mean that?"

She ducked her head away with a small, shy motion, filled with natural grace, like a deer's. "The alternative is just small talk, isn't it? That's all I've ever done with strangers before, and I've always hated it. I'm no good at it, you see."

"And you would like to try something different with me?"

"I don't usually speak very freely to anyone and never to gentlemen. Yet this whole situation is so odd and so temporary. I doubt we'll ever speak privately after this, and I'll never meet anyone like you again as long as I live. Someone who's traveled as you have, or knows what you must know. A new view of the world, you said. What did you mean?"

I shall never meet anyone like you again, as long as I live. That was true for him, too, wasn't it? He would leave again for the East very soon. He had spent his youth amongst the highest ranks of the English peerage, or slumming with other young lords in the company of harlots and prizefighters. Anne Marsh represented two classes of people he'd never known and was unlikely ever to get to know: the respectable English middle classes and the virtuous Dissenters, who—thanks to their honesty and rational habits—were forging ahead in banking and commerce, as well as in science.

"Very well," he said. "Though here there be dragons, we'll risk it. It's been a very long time since I talked—really talked—with a lady. Let's forget what's left of our society manners and be honest. Do you agree?"

"Yes, why not?" She looked up at him with disarming frankness. "Why shouldn't people ever be able to say what they're thinking, or explain what they really mean?"

"We may find out," he said dryly. "You asked how I felt about returning to England. It's all that you know, of course: this landscape, so tamed and pretty and productive. Once it was all that I knew, as well."

"And now?"

"Now I'm neither glad nor sorry to see it again."

"Because of other places you've seen, places that are more appealing?"

"Appealing?" He laughed. "Great stretches of our globe are only mountain or desert, Miss Marsh, or cut by great rushing rivers, or buried beneath perennial snows. Few areas are naturally hospitable to man, though we're almost everywhere, clinging to a harsh existence."

"But England is home."

"England doesn't welcome me, any more than the Takla Makan welcomed me."

"The Takla Makan?"

Emptiness seeped into his mind, defying words. Yet he searched for them anyway. Why not? She was right. This was only an interlude out of time. Whatever he told her, she could never understand it. He could as easily spin tales of Sinbad the Sailor, which meant that he might as well tell her the stories that were equally without repercussions: the truth.

"The Takla Makan is an immeasurable wasteland of sand dunes. Dunes of shifting, smothering yellow sand that give way at last to further wastelands of rock and sand and gravel. That desert divides China from everything that lies to the west. No one goes into the deep dunes, not even the natives. There's no water for hundreds of miles. The air is so dry that the sky is infinitely translucent, soaring to forever, yet you feel that if you reached up your hand, you could grasp it. At night, if you cast up a net, you'd catch millions of stars. You could wash your face in them."

"I can't really imagine it," she said.

"It's not something one *can* imagine. The vastness, the emptiness, are beyond imagination, beyond thought."

"Why did you go to such a place?"

He smiled. She had no idea, of course, that however much he described rocks and skies, painted her a picture of desolation and enormity, it would still explain nothing. She was anyway blinkered by her provincial experiences. If he told her that he'd flown to the moon, it would have as much meaning to her. Yet he felt the truth welling up and an odd longing to make her understand, however impossible that was. Since there was nothing to lose, he decided, quite consciously, to let it happen.

"For a romantic fancy, if you like," he said. "Men have traded treasure between Turkish Asia and China for centuries, though vast reaches of nothingness lie in the way. The ancient Silk Road skirted the edge of the Takla Makan. There's no other route from West to East but those thin tracks. I wanted to follow them, like Marco Polo. I wanted to pass through a place where the existence of man on this planet is revealed only by the slow plod of camels, strung together like beads on a thread of nonexistence."

"Camels?"

"Camels and sometimes asses, their harnesses caparisoned in tassels of colored silk. The journey is too harsh for horses, except perhaps the tough, tiny horses of China. The caravans trickle inexorably along the channels of the ancient tracks. No one leaves the road without paying with his life."

"Yet you went into the desert?"

"I wanted to leave the road."

"Why?"

"To hunt dragons," he said.

"And so you found fossils," she replied after a moment. "That extraordinary tooth. Why is it so important? Can you tell me?"

Of course, she had immediately returned to the mundane, the concrete—retreated from the reality of what he'd been saying—simply because she couldn't see it. He didn't mind. It was exactly what he had expected, which left him feeling as free as an eagle.

"You don't think all fossils are important?" he teased. "Your Mr. Trent would no doubt disagree."

"Arthur thinks the sun rises and sets on old bones, but he wouldn't murder for them."

"Don't be too sure," Jack said. "Now, hush! Someone's coming."

Anne jammed her bonnet back onto her head. A man rode toward them, leading a string of laden pack ponies. He touched his cap as he passed, but paid them no other attention.

Farmer Osgood sucked at his pipe and nodded in reply, then flicked his whip and the cob trotted on.

She stared at his hands on the reins. Her pulse thundered. Bronzed, lovely hands. He'd rubbed some dirt into them, but that didn't blur the shape. Cleanly modeled, with strong tendons and a hard ridge along the outer edge of each palm. She wondered how he'd acquired that. It spoke of masculine power, but they weren't the kind of calluses men acquired from manual labor, and he was anyway a gentleman.

Shyly, under cover of the bonnet, she glanced up at his face. His profile cut clear and cold, in spite of his disguise. Nothing could hide that piercing beauty of bone, the sensuous turn of his nostril and mouth.

Lovely. Lovely.

Her heart turned and plunged, like a diving kingfisher.

The simple country clothes and the flour in his hair had made her feel absurdly safe, almost buoyant. She had chattered away with an oddly giddy freedom—because he didn't seem to mind, because she'd never see him privately again—but Lord Jonathan had traveled through unimaginable wastelands, *to hunt dragons*.

She had no idea what he meant, but his words echoed in her mind, stirring a strange, half-remembered awe. From the comfort of her nurse's lap, she had thrilled at whimsical tales throughout her childhood: fabulous voyages to lands of wonder, lands of fairies, of giants, of marvelous beasts; foolish quests that resulted in treasure and victory and the hand of a princess. It was only since she'd met Arthur that she'd tried to concentrate so entirely on the rational, as one should, of course, if one followed the true precepts of one's faith.

Wild Lord Jack, he had said: Jack, the youngest son, who went forth in tale after tale in search of his fortune, and always triumphed.

So now she knew at last what he was: not an archangel; not a villain; not even simply a duke's son, though that was fantastic enough by itself. He was a hero.

Anne smiled to herself at the absurdity of her own thoughts. He was a hero—like the first St. George!

Yet he seemed so pure and remote. She had never thought a man *beautiful* before, but just looking at him was like drinking from a cool, dark well, when she hadn't even known she was thirsty. And to listen to him! She didn't understand anything he was talking about, but she could listen to his voice and let it stir these hidden, almost forgotten feelings of delight forever.

So are you to my thoughts, as food to life—

"Have I sprouted warts?" Lord Jonathan was grinning down at her.

Blood rushed to her cheeks in a wave of embarrassment.

"I've never met anyone like you before," she said. "You are . . . fascinating. You make me think of tigers."

"Tigers?"

She tried to retreat, but the truth surged, swamping her better judgment like a spring tide. "It's most improper to have such fancies, I know, and even more improper to voice them—though surely there's no harm in it?" Her blush burned, yet she plunged on. "I think you've been telling me the truth as well as you're able. So now I'm telling you my real thoughts, even at the risk that you'll think I'm a fool. Why not? If one is caught in such an irregular situation, may one not take even a little advantage of it?"

"We agreed that you might throw caution to the winds, Miss Marsh, but have you ever seen a tiger?"

"No, but I imagine they're very terrible and very lovely—"

He brought the cob to a halt and turned to face her. The clouds were settling lower over the hills. There was no breeze at all, just an absolute quiet, as if the whole world were muffled in dampness.

His glance traveled over her face, then fixed on her eyes. She gazed back, ignoring her discomfort, knowing she could drown in those winter depths. Her heart thudded beneath her corset, yet warmth spread like sunshine through her thighs and belly and breasts. A lovely warmth, making her dizzy, filling her with a strange ecstasy. Hot blood pooled in unmentionable places.

"A tiger hunts alone through the jungle. He springs on his prey from behind, without warning. A tiger never plays fair," he said. "Are you trying to tell me that you don't feel safe with me, after all?"

"No, my lord." Her heartbeat resounded like a drum. "Quite the contrary. I feel very safe with you. How else could I admit to such fancies? It's just that you're so different—"

"Different?"

The lightness in his voice made her think he must be teasing her again, though his brown-and-gilt gaze was impenetrable, filled with jungle shadows.

"Very well. I'll tell you." The giddiness soared as she closed her eyes. "Your face is as beautiful as a sculpture. Your mouth makes me think of treacle. Your hands are like the carvings on the ends of the pews in the village church, strange and fascinating and powerful. I would never act on such mad observations, of course, but I wonder what it would be like to touch you."

The bit jingled. He looked away as the roan tried to grab a mouthful of buttercups. She clutched her palms together. Why on earth had she voiced such indecorous thoughts? But he must, surely, understand what she meant?

"I'm not a figment of your imagination, Miss Marsh," he said at last. "I'm flesh and blood. Perfectly real. You—by your own description—are alone and unchaperoned on a country lane with a predatory beast from a wild, unknown place." He glanced back at her, his eyes dark, though he smiled. "Most men would take what you've just said as a direct invitation to indulge in a little misconduct. Yet you still claim to feel safe?"

The warmth flared, like paper catching fire, burning its giddy path directly to her heart. "I thought we'd agreed to share our real thoughts—"

"Yes." He smiled. "A heady adventure, isn't it?"

"You forget that I'm engaged to be married, my lord. You must know that I mean nothing improper. It was just a feeling. My regard for Arthur protects me from any other gentleman, especially when he's only joking with me."

"No, it doesn't," he said. "And he isn't. Men never joke about this."

He snapped the whip and the cob moved forward.

Anne took a deep breath, trying to quiet her surging blood. "So I've made a fool of myself, after all."

"Ah, but I don't believe for a moment that you're a fool, Miss Marsh. I may very well be a creature of the jungle, but you're correct: You may say whatever you like to me and risk nothing. Even though—whether you know it or not—you are asking for something quite different. Would you say such things to any other man?"

"No, never! But I don't think you're like other men."

"You're right," he said. "I'm not."

She stared at her boots, stupid with chagrin. He thought she was naive, ridiculous. He thought she wanted something improper, when that wasn't it, at all. But how could one spend time with a hero from a fairy tale and not try to express this incoherent, uncomfortable longing?

"You say you reject the conventional view of Creation," he continued. "You're not concerned about the moral implications of that? After all, if we're simply products of nature, the physical needs of the body have nothing to do with sin."

"I don't know," she said. "I haven't thought about it like that. I don't know much about bodies."

"So I surmise." He guided the roan around a wallow of deep ruts. "Has your Mr. Trent ever kissed you?"

Anne clutched the rail as the gig lurched. "I don't have to answer that!"

"No, you don't. It's only too obvious that he hasn't. Does he never touch you at all?"

"He's a gentleman." Heat burned in her neck. "He would never do anything unseemly."

The lane was descending into another valley, the muddy track looping and twisting between high hedges. Thick gray clouds had congealed to blot out the sun, until a shadowy, chill mist closed about the gig.

"No, of course he would not," Lord Jonathan said calmly. "You only talk together, about fossils and rocks and the age of the earth. Nothing else at all connects you, does it?"

"You think he is wrong to show me respect?"

"If I guess correctly, he'll show you a dignified respect right up to your wedding night and very likely for the rest of your life after that. Does your Arthur ever make you long to touch him?"

Steam must be rising from her face. She tore loose the ribbons on the bonnet, crumpling them beneath frantic fingers. "How dare you ask such things!"

"You suggested we indulge in honesty." The lane filled with the echo of rushing water. Lord Jonathan eased the cob back in the shafts as the slope became steeper. He looked calm, beautiful, powerful. "You're engaged to be married. Yet Mr. Trent treats you with a distant and courteous regard, and would be appalled if he knew what you secretly longed for."

Anne bit her lip in mortified silence. The uncomfortable heat pulsed through her body, making her breasts burn against her corset.

"Don't flirt with a tiger unless you mean it, Miss Marsh," Lord Jonathan added gently.

"I wasn't flirting," she said. "I thought I could trust you with my foolish, fleeting fancies. You've responded by insulting me."

Small beads of water dripped from his hat. The reins gleamed darkly in his lean fingers.

"No truth is foolish, if it's placed in the right hands. You can trust me, Miss Marsh. I don't mean to insult you. I'm only responding with honesty to what I see in your face, which is the highest compliment that I know how to give you. Would you prefer we retreated again into small talk, or chatted some more about pigs?"

"No," she said. "But I cannot understand why you must persist in embarrassing me."

"You don't need to, but thank you for sparing me more hogs. If we'd pursued that line of conversation any further, Farmer Osgood would have begun to reveal his total ignorance of good husbandry."

In spite of herself, she giggled, though her breath rattled, fast and shallow, while hot little prickles ran up and down her spine.

"That's better," he said. "Now, suppose that—instead of retreating into outraged rectitude—you take this chance to satisfy your natural curiosity. We're cocooned in mist and the oddness of our situation. I'm not going to misunderstand, or take an unfair advantage of you. We may talk like two human beings about the things that really concern us, and not give a damn whether it's proper or not. The choice is yours. Ask me anything you want to. I don't mind. I'll probably like it."

"I can't," she said.

"Yes, you can. To tell a man that you would like to touch him, then deny that you're flirting, means that you're either very foolish, or very innocent indeed. I know that you're not foolish, Miss Marsh, so you must be innocent. I shall deliver you safely to my mother. I shall protect your shining virtue with my life. However, you don't need to reach your wedding night in painful ignorance, when you have such a clear opportunity to alleviate it."

"I don't know what you mean," she said.

The cob stopped. He reached out one hand to tug loose her bonnet, then toss it aside.

"That's better," he said. "Look at me!"

His eyes were calm and dark. He seemed remote, undemanding, offering nothing but a cool, disinterested understanding. Yet a heavy, thick glow had pooled between her legs, hot and wicked.

"Don't be ashamed of the way you feel, my dear girl," he said. "It's entirely instinctive. You're alone with a stranger, a man.

Because you've allowed yourself some unaccustomed freedom, you've let down your guard a little and your body has recognized something that you don't quite understand. There's nothing about this that's like your normal daily life. So nature is asserting herself."

"Nature?"

"You love your Arthur Trent. I'm sure he loves you. That won't protect you from what I see in your eyes."

She lifted her chin and glared at him. "What is that?"

The dark shadow outlined his jaw, rimmed his sensuous mouth. He looked nothing like a farmer. "Desire. Desire for a man's body, damnably contaminated with a stalwartly English sense of shame and fear. What whispers have you overheard, Miss Marsh? Tales of embarrassing—even painful—indignities?"

"Stop," she said. "I'm not brave enough for this."

"Yes, you are. Devil take English propriety! Should I let you go to your marriage bed in profound ignorance with some well-meaning idiot who has no idea what he's about? You'll both be terrified."

"I could never be afraid with Arthur."

"Yet you have no idea what his body is like, do you? Or what your wedding night will really entail? Your mother has mentioned something vaguely poetic about surrender and marital duty. Your married sister lives in Yorkshire and would never share anything so improper in writing. Your little sisters dance through their days, sharing the same blissful lack of knowledge, while your father and brothers maintain their stoic silence. The result will probably be disaster."

She glanced away, twisting her hands together. It was true, wasn't it? All true! Why had Arthur never tried to kiss her? By what miracle could she face her wedding night without fear?

"All gentlemen expect a chaste bride," she said. "Don't you want your wife to be pure?"

"I don't want a wife. I intend to return to Asia as soon as I can."

Her eyes squeezed shut, while her lips let the words pour out in a rush. "But you're very experienced, aren't you? In all of this? You know everything about it?"

"Yes," he said.

"You will think I am wicked."

"You cannot shock me or offend me. I shan't take your questions for an inappropriate invitation. I'd be honored to help you in any way that I can."

"Oh," she said, pushing her fingers back over her hair. "I must be mad!"

"Why? If Mr. Trent maintains the typical English attitude of our age, you'll be doomed to a life of hurried fumbling, while he'll suffer and rage in pain and silence. In the end he'll assuage his real needs with a mistress or in furtive exchanges with prostitutes, before he would ever defile his innocent wife. Thus she will fade and wilt, never knowing why, and try to find solace in her children. It's a damned tragedy."

"It won't be like that."

"Yes, it will. Because you're a lady of considerable natural passion. You can't help but wonder what your bridegroom might suddenly demand of you, can you? Will he press his open mouth onto yours? Will his hands trespass over your naked skin? Will he want you to touch him? And what happens after that?"

It was the moment of decision. She ought to be outraged. She *was* outraged. Yet a deeper reality ran beneath her indignation, a certainty that she was indeed safely in the hands of a hero. Lord

Jonathan Devoran St. George would never harm her. He would not misunderstand. And he was presenting her with the only chance she might ever get.

"It's all right, Miss Marsh," he said. "Go on! Be brave!"

Brave! Her nerves felt flayed. Every inch of her skin flared with sensitivity. Her heart pounded so loudly she thought he must hear it, a drumbeat resounding in the damp lane.

"What I said earlier was true," she whispered. "Though I'm scared, I do want to find out. That's not what I meant when I said I wanted to touch you, but if I thought I could do so safely and without repercussions—if I thought it was just another lesson, like learning about rocks, or what to tell Cook when the mutton is tough—"

"It *is* just another lesson."

"But I can't!"

"Yes, you can."

She dropped her hands and glanced up into his eyes. Her heart eased at the cool detachment of his smile. She felt gawky and graceless in comparison to him.

"My mother has told me so little. We're encouraged to read and inquire about anything—except this. I do wish I could explore it, just in the spirit of scientific inquiry, you understand. I haven't any idea how a man is made!"

"And you're scared of it, aren't you?"

She nodded.

"Then I would be honored to help you find out whatever you need to know. You may do so entirely without harm or embarrassment, or any disloyalty to your beloved, but at some later time, perhaps? I refuse to disrobe even for you, my dear Miss Anne

Marsh, out here among the chill uplands of Dorset, especially while driving a gig."

She giggled. The giggles gathered and coalesced into open laughter. Uproarious, cleansing laughter. Anne clutched both arms about her waist and rocked back and forth.

"I am mad!" she exclaimed at last. "Mad as a hatter!"

"Not at all. You're simply honest enough to admit to natural human feelings. Shall we sing?"

Surprise jolted her upright. "What?"

He whipped up the cob and they trotted down toward the water. The roar grew louder. Somewhere in the mist below them a river ran fast and strong toward the sea, hidden beneath a fog like thick cotton.

Lord Jonathan threw back his head and broke into song.

> *"It was a lover and his lass, With a hey, and a ho,*
> > *and a hey nonny no,*
> *That o'er the green cornfield did pass, In the spring time,*
> > *the only pretty ring time,*
> *When birds do sing, hey ding a ding, ding,*
> > *Sweet lovers love the spring."*

It was all right. It was all right! Light-headed with relief, Anne swung her discarded bonnet in time to the tune.

"In the spring time, the only pretty ring time—"

Shadowed trees loomed on either side of the lane, great trunks wreathed in mist. The water thundered under the stone arch of a humped bridge. The cob trotted valiantly forward. As he sang, Lord Jonathan put a hand on her arm.

Her voice faltered when she saw his eyes. "What is it?"

"Keep on singing!" He grinned down at her—but with the unholy mirth of the archangel. "When birds do sing, hey ding a ding, ding . . ."

She launched back into song. Prickles ran like ants over her skin. "And therefore take the present time, With a hey and a ho, and a hey nonny no . . ."

"Good girl!" His voice whispered, soft and warm, as she sang. "I was wrong. The yacht wasn't enough. When I stop the gig, jump down and press your back against the nearest tree, then don't move till I tell you."

Her heart lurched. There was something—a branch, an uprooted tree?—across the entrance to the bridge. Water crashed and tumbled.

He picked up the tune again. "With a hey and a ho, and a hey nonny no, For love is crowned with the prime—"

The roan shied to a sudden halt. A black shape detached from a branch high above, like a huge falling leaf. Dark figures loomed from the mist, swarming toward the gig. Something blurred past her face. Anne screamed.

"The nearest tree," Lord Jonathan hissed.

She ducked and scrambled down, landing with a squelch in the mud. *The nearest tree!* Mist swirled. Moist tendrils seized her arms and skirts. Her feet felt as heavy as coal buckets. Yet she ran, slipping and skidding to a huge oak that towered beside the road. With her back pressed against the rough bark, she peered into the mist as chaos overtook the English lane.

Black shadows had thronged over Lord Jonathan like monkeys, catching at his arms and legs. Steel flashed. He had pistols. Why didn't he use them? But he wasn't there! Somehow he had disappeared in a blur of grace, while the blade sliced empty air and his jacket crumpled without him to the ground.

The attackers scattered as, in a haze of white, Lord Jonathan kicked and danced and spun into the center of them. A ghostly whirlwind, spreading mayhem. Yet the man in the turban rushed up behind him, his brown face set in a grin, both arms raised. Lord Jonathan crouched—the white shirt stretched over his back forming a harsh, lovely curve—as if, while balanced on a wire, he coiled into a spring. The blue turban was pressed into his shoulder, the grin became a grimace, the man sprawled on the ground.

The assailants flew apart, then regrouped and charged in again. No one spoke. Dull grunts and thuds resounded, while the sound of the river roared in her ears.

She had never witnessed anything like it: this fighting art. His hands sliced, the edge of his fingers as stark as a blade. A whirl. A step. A kick. A fast arc of arm and shoulder and thigh, as clean and pure as a tiger strike. A lovely, lethal dance. Men dropped to the mud, while more came screeching out of the fog.

The gig skidded backward and upended in the ditch. The cob, suddenly released, cantered away up the road.

A man turned from the tipped shafts, his face split by his white teeth, a knife in one hand, a length of chain in the other. He tossed the end to a comrade and they ran at Lord Jonathan together. He was not there. The men stopped, poised like cats, only to be cut down by that lithe white shape, spinning again out of the mist.

Yet he could not fight off a whole gang of thugs, armed with knives and wire and ruthlessness. However strange and terrible his fighting skills, these men would kill him, and then they would come for her.

Clinging to the bark she prayed silently, incoherently. She wanted to hide. She wanted to find a weapon, anything—a broken branch, a stick, a rock—but her feet remained trapped in thick mud and soft grass, and he had told her not to move until he came for her.

Her mind seemed frozen, petrified by nightmare. Thoughts raced like scattered rabbits.

She was promised to Arthur—dear, handsome Arthur, who was buying her a house in her home village. She was crazy and upset and frightened. Yet she would stand here until Wild Lord Jack came for her, because he had said so? Just as she had trusted him in that wild moment of clear longing that he had indeed understood, and had not judged, nor condemned—

Oh, God! Oh, God! She didn't know what she felt, and she loved someone else—so it couldn't be that—but this blind faith in Lord Jonathan left her feeling very much as if she were falling. Falling, tumbling headlong into a whirlwind of intense emotion. If she didn't know it to be impossible, she might think she was falling in love.

Silence fell with the suddenness of a stage curtain, though the water roared on. Fog wrapped her in feathers of moisture. But there was no human sound. Nothing at all. No thumps or hisses. Just an empty void.

Anne strained to hear a footstep, a whisper. Oh, God! Nothing!

She put both hands to her head and shrank down to crouch in the wet grass. *Don't move till I tell you! . . . I would be honored to help you find out whatever you needed to know. . . . Don't be ashamed of the way you feel, my dear girl . . . my dear girl . . . my dear girl—*

"My dear girl," his voice said in her ear. "It's all right. Put your hand in mine and come with me."

CHAPTER FIVE

NNE CLUNG TO HIS HAND AND SLIPPED WITH HIM INTO
the mist. His grip was warm and certain. They slithered
through thickets of willow and over banks of wet grass, running,
running. Water raced. Trees loomed and disappeared. Trailing
leaves whipped at her hair. Thorns tore at her skirts. Her lungs
burned as if they would burst, but his sure clasp fired her with
courage, as if strength pulsed from his blood directly into hers.

He was leading her downstream, away from danger. She was
safe, as long as he held her hand, palm to palm, his strong fingers
wrapped about hers.

Cows scattered, red-and-white shapes lumbering away into the
fog, hooves sucking in the waterlogged meadows. A heron sprang
from the reeds and beat its escape across the river.

He had laid waste to their enemies as indisputably as David
felled Goliath. *You are always safe as long as I am here, whether I am
armed or not.* So Anne ran at his side as a bird flies, giddy with freedom and abandoned to the air.

She stepped after him through a break in a hedge. His back

and arms powerful, his fingers lovely, he stopped in the shelter of the hawthorn and turned to face her.

"You're tired?"

Damp air seared her throat as she panted for breath. "I can't . . . I'm not used to running. I can't keep up."

He drew her closer, a hand on each upper arm, and studied her face. "You don't need to be afraid."

"I'm not afraid—not as long as I'm with you!"

Something changed almost imperceptibly in his eyes—something that spoke of regret or withdrawal, perhaps—but he smiled.

"You need to learn how to breathe," he said.

"I am breathing!"

He released one arm to set his palm flat against the base of her throat, his fingers cool on her hot skin. Her breath fluttered beneath his hand, as if a burden of choked thoughts and emotions constricted the air flow. Though his gaze seemed masked by distant smoke, his smile teased.

"You're fighting for each gasp of air, Miss Marsh, and panting like a basset hound." He caressed beneath her jaw. Her pulse thundered. "Your breathing is all up here in your throat." He slid his fingertips into her hair, as if to support her head on his palm. "Relax. Close your eyes. Take a deep breath."

She closed her eyes. Her heart hammered in her chest. Her ribs struggled. Every nerve twittered with awareness: of his nearness, of his scent, of the power that crackled like lightning from his fingertips.

"Let it flow," he said. "Deeply. Deeply. Hold the breath as quietly as you'd hold a bubble of soap. Then release it as gently as you'd open your hands. That one exhalation will clear away all of your fatigue."

Her blood coursed through her veins, hot and hard, dizzying her. Her senses burned at the cool, sweet touch of his fingers. *A bubble of soap.* She felt fragile, insubstantial. If he took away his hand, she might fall. But her breath still battled, fast and shallow, choking her.

"I can't," she said, opening her eyes as heat and embarrassment flooded her face. "My lacing—"

Shadows of mist moved in his eyes, but his palm dropped to her elbow and he laughed.

"Ah, of course! Your damned corset!"

As she wavered, still giddy, he pulled her within the circle of one strong arm to cradle her head against his chest. His heartbeat thudded, slow and powerful, beneath her cheek. His voice whispered against her hair, his breathing unhurried.

"I forgot that you were encased in a shell of English propriety, and so you can't breathe. Not to worry. We may move more decorously now. We're almost there."

Hard muscle lay beneath the thin fabric of his shirt, warming her until her heart eased and her breathing slowed, as if trying to match the dreaming rhythm of his. "Where?"

He set her carefully away, holding her by both elbows, and gazed down at her. "At our destination. Did you think we were running randomly along this riverbank?"

She glanced about. There was nothing but mist and rain, spattering droplets into a wet world. "You know this place?"

"All of the land on the other side of this troublesome water belongs to Wyldshay. Ten miles beyond those woods lies my father's house, where in a few hours you may drink tea in the decorous aridity of the gold salon. We need only to cross the river."

Lord Jonathan seized her hand again and led her through

another stand of willows. Moisture splashed onto her face and soaked the hem of her skirt.

They emerged into a small clearing. A dark structure bulked in their way: a ferry house, apparently long abandoned, the track leading to it overgrown with weeds and young trees. A small jetty jutted into the river, the wood half rotted and slimy with age.

"There's no boat," Anne said, swallowing disappointment. "But how could there be, out here in the middle of nowhere?"

"Then perhaps we should take to the water like ducks?" A wry amusement hovered at the corners of his mouth. "Hush! We're about to have company."

He spun her with him into another stand of willows. Tall green stems, the leaves jutting like arrows, blocked her vision. The river roared.

His nostrils flared like a stag's scenting hunters, but he smiled down at her and winked.

"A cob," he murmured in her ear, "carrying an unfortunate burden."

Anne bent against him like a withy, his arm about her waist, and thought she could face down demons—*as long as I'm with you!* The hoofbeats sounded closer. Between the waving stems, she caught a glimpse of leather hat. Her breath stopped, leaving her nothing but her own heartbeat. The leather hat moved, revealing a thin face, narrow through the chin.

The man scanned the riverbank. He was pale-eyed, the color surprising against his tanned skin, like that of a blue-eyed dog. The horse moved again and the man was lost to view. Anne listened to the rustle and the sucking of the cob's hooves in the mud. The arm at her waist was strong, secure, yet hot little shivers ran down into her belly, as if she were afraid after all.

"We're safe now," Lord Jonathan said.

Anne filled her lungs with damp air and honest relief. "Who was that?"

"The man who'd like to find me. I'm not ready to meet him just yet."

"He won't come back?"

"He'll have gone on to watch the ford and guard the roads, farther downriver."

Lord Jonathan walked away to gaze down at the rushing water. Rain glistened on his dark hair and powerful shoulders, silhouetting him against the trees on the other side of the river. He stood like a statue, as if lost in concentration.

"So we're trapped here?" Anne asked at last.

He looked around. For a split second she thought she saw absolute indifference in his gaze, before he smiled. Was she just another tiresome, petty duty to be suffered, when he was engaged in events that might shatter the world? Why on earth should that observation sting? Of course she wasn't important to him. Nor— in the end—was he important to her. She would soon be going home to Hawthorn Axbury, where she was going to marry Arthur. Yet here, beside this rushing river with this one man, that was a strangely dismal thought, especially when that wild mirth began to flicker over his face.

"On the contrary. A boat is hidden about a hundred yards farther along the bank to our right."

"How on earth do you know that?"

"By observation and deduction, Miss Marsh, the methods of science. A bent reed, a slick of disturbed mud, the shape of the landscape, and a knowledge of human nature." He held out one hand. "Come!"

The boat lay tied to a willow stump hidden among the sedge and tall grasses in an eddy at the side of the river. Anne clasped his fingers, splashed after him, and let him help her climb in.

Awareness pulsed through her blood, firing her senses with a new fervor.

In moments he had freed the oars and headed the boat into the center of the river. Anne clung to the slippery seat and watched the play of fabric across the front of his shirt. The changing shapes filled her with yearning.

The boat tossed. Water churned and swirled among thickets of reeds. Logs and mats of debris raced with the current.

Her single thought was for the beauty of a man's chest, lithe and strange. A tiger.

Jack allowed the craft to be carried along with the current. Their only immediate danger was the floating rubbish, remnants of the gale. Otherwise the river could carry them downstream, safe as in a baby's cradle, to where the swollen water must already have spread beyond its banks at Smile's Bottom.

He worked the oars casually, his bones flooded with certainty.

"The ferry house," she said. "And that overgrown track. It was abandoned a long time ago?"

Thick with muck about the hem, the blue dress swamped her fine bones in a waste of fabric and dragged heavily about her ankles. A nest of tendrils and wayward curls, her hair had sagged onto her neck. Yet her face was misted and bright with exertion, and her throat gleamed like white porcelain.

He gazed at it. Her pulse had quaked beneath his fingers, as shallow and fragile as a bird's. The scent of freshness, wild and vivid, suffused her skin. She was brave and vibrant. Yet she couldn't breathe, because she wore corsets. Even the air necessary for life was restricted, rationed, as if licentiousness must necessarily follow a free breath.

Jack recognized something of anger, but he let the emotion flow away with the river, emptying his heart.

"When my mother suggested a new road and a new bridge," he said, "the ferry became obsolete. Twenty years ago, give or take a few winters and summers."

"Yet someone still keeps this boat?"

"Poachers. Boys. The ne'er-do-well barnacles that cluster about any river."

"Oh!" Her lashes were long and surprisingly dark, fanning over her cheeks as she looked down at the water sloshing about her feet. "But not recent ones?"

"You would prefer recent ones, Miss Marsh?"

"I don't swim." She glanced up at him and smiled with open bravado. The drizzle trickled down her face. "I believe that this craft was designed for a clear day and calm waters. And some years ago, at that, with very little maintenance since."

He leaned back on the oars, pulling against the rush of the flood, and felt his heart lift. She was extraordinary!

"It'll do. Even running in spate, English rivers are tame enough creatures."

"Unlike those violent waterways you've traversed in wilder parts of the world?"

Muscles flexed agreeably as he bent his back, steadying the boat. "We shan't come to grief on rapids or plunge over a precipice, certainly. Our craft is seaworthy enough for our purposes." He nodded toward a leather bucket tossing about in the bottom of the boat. "Though it might help if you bailed."

Her color deepened, but she grabbed the bucket and began to

scoop water. "Though you've known rapids and precipices all across Asia. And conquered them all!"

"You're thinking of Alexander the Great, Miss Marsh, not Wild Lord Jack. I've conquered nothing. We'll just allow this flood to carry us away from our obstreperous friends for a while, that's all."

Her head rose and sank as she bent with the bucket, then tossed its contents over the side. "You expected that ambush at the bridge?"

"Expected? No. Anticipated the possibility—certainly."

"But you knew when the attack was imminent, didn't you? How?"

"Always watch a horse's ears, Miss Marsh. His senses are invariably better than ours."

"The roan heard something? Right before we started singing?"

Jack grinned and corrected the boat as it wallowed into a bend.

"How did you fight off all those men by yourself?" She stopped bailing for a moment. "I never saw anything like it in my life."

She was disheveled and wet, her breath coming too fast, her hair an unholy mess of mousy tangles. Though she claimed to be dedicated to science, a bright, imaginative soul shone from her blue eyes.

Jack forced himself to concentrate on her question. "You have witnessed men fighting before?"

"No, though my brothers practice boxing sometimes. Their sport always seemed very upright and brutal to me, with a great deal of potential damage to the knuckles, but you—"

"I wasn't boxing," he said.

"No. You looked as if you were dancing."

"I wasn't dancing, Miss Marsh. Neither were our assailants."

Her cheeks flushed pink like the curved petals of a dog rose, as lovely as a sunrise.

"Yet your eyes held such . . . calm elation. I don't know how to describe it." She bent to scoop again with the bucket. "They want the fossil, of course, and don't know whether we have it. If you had not . . ." Her voice died away, then she sat up straight and faced him. "They would have murdered us?"

"Not without the answers to a few questions first." He pushed away from a threatening log. The boat swirled and dipped, then bobbed back into the center of the river. "Their employer wants to know where the fossil is, and since his hired men don't speak much English, I assumed they intended capture rather than assassination."

"Oh," she said. "I see. The man who is hiring them would have wished only to question us. The man who came by the ferry house?"

Jack bent his back to the oars, sending a wave of water past the front of the boat. "He doesn't like to soil his own hands."

She bailed in silence for a few minutes. "So you didn't use your pistols, because you surmised they had instructions not to hurt us." Her forehead wrinkled as she looked up. "You thought it wouldn't be very sporting to shoot at men who did *not* intend murder?"

He choked back laughter. "I didn't use my pistols because each barrel has only one ball. Not enough to delay that motley crew very long."

"Oh," she said again.

He liked the way her mouth formed the syllable, as if kissing the air. He liked her small, tender wrists and elegant fingers. He liked her remarkable courage. He had thought she might collapse into hysterics, but instead she had run with him, climbed without hesitation into the boat with him, and now she was valiantly bailing.

She had even found the courage to trust him with her naive, heartbreaking little confidences: *I don't have any idea how a man is made.*

Her fiancé, her family, the entire society, had all conspired to keep her in ignorance. God, how typical of the English! She would go to her marriage bed like a lamb to the slaughter. Noble, God-fearing Arthur Trent would probably deflower her in an agony of conflict, despising himself and terrifying his bride as he did it. Devil take them all!

It was not his problem.

I'd be honored to help you in any way that I can. He had meant it, every word of it. Yet Jack breathed away his craving to offer her an education in deeds rather than words.

They would be at Wyldshay before nightfall. Let his mother take the matter in hand. Then Lord Jonathan Devoran St. George need play no further part in it.

A solution that was compassionate and sensible—and contrary to all of his desires.

The rush slowed as the valley widened: Smile's Bottom. The river had flooded the meadows to lap against the foot of a wood. Rain pattered audibly now, splashing on the water and soaking his back. Jack rowed for the left-hand bank.

"There's a track," he said. "Up there, through the trees. Do you see it?"

Her neck gleamed like a pearl beneath her wet hair as she peered over his shoulder and nodded.

"When the river's not in flood, there's a ford. That path leads to a cottage inhabited by one of my father's gamekeepers. Mr. Kenyon will stand guard with a blunderbuss, while his wife wraps you in respectability and warm blankets. You're safe now."

"The men who attacked us won't follow us here?"

"They may follow our tracks, but they won't find another boat. Nor will they know where we abandoned ours. I intend them to find the wreckage far downstream. Then I'll borrow the Kenyons' horse to ride the ten miles to Wyldshay to fetch a carriage and armed servants. Your adventure is over, Miss Marsh."

"Yes." Her shoulders were stiff, brittle as glass.

His heart sank, with a bitter little twist of self-condemnation. "What's the matter?"

She ducked her head away, then glanced back at him. Her lashes had begun to stick together, ringing her eyes in tiny spikes. As if aware of her own vulnerability, she quickly looked away again, but he knew that she blinked back tears as well as rain.

"Oh, it's nothing," she said. "I'm not quite accustomed to having such shining faith in a stranger. It's a little disconcerting."

"You regret the end of our journey?"

"I think that, entirely for your own reasons, you've deliberately invited my blind adoration. You shouldn't be surprised if you've achieved at least part of that." She rubbed the heel of one hand over her cheek. "Perhaps I seem a little like a rabbit with a snake. Fortunately, I'm confident that the affliction is only temporary— one cup of strong tea and I shall be sensible Miss Anne Marsh again."

Damnation! He had needed to charm her to convince her to obey him, but he had not intended to do more than that. Yet—as if she had unwittingly undermined his resolve—he had been careless and self-indulgent, taken risks, allowed himself to revel without restraint in her company. With her innocent courage, she had not rejected it or retreated into outrage.

And so he had caught her, like a shining fish in a net. If he reached out his hand, she would fall into his arms in a paroxysm of confused longing and sacrifice her maidenhead without a murmur.

Desire fired, hot and urgent. Devil take it! Part of him wanted to do it. It would be stunningly poignant to educate that pretty innocence. Wonderful to initiate her long limbs and limber spine and white neck. His fingers ached to unlace the restricting corsets, free her chaste breasts to his mouth, to his hands. He yearned to give her an education in rapture. It would be so very easy.

As if his fingertips trawled over naked female flesh, arousal flared in intensity, demanding and imperious. *Pleasure!*

She had no idea that she, too, longed for it. She didn't even know what it meant.

She was an Englishwoman, engaged to be married.

The boat spun, scraping over roots as Jack thrust the prow into the bank. He sprang from the boat and tugged it closer, holding out one hand to help her. She set her fingers on his and scrambled up next to him. The empty boat turned slowly in the eddying current to be carried away downstream.

"A shared adventure often tends to forge temporary bonds," he said. "I feel them, too, but they'll disappear when I deliver you into the bosom of my family. My sisters will regale you with tales of my less dignified exploits. My elder brother will immediately outshine me in every gentlemanly aspect and reveal my feet of clay. You'll forget all of this immediately when you see me for what I really am."

Anne dropped his fingers as if he burned her, clambered over the tree roots to the track, then stood still for a moment, staring away into the trees, while raindrops spattered down over her hair.

"What are you?" she asked.

"Just a man." The rain thickened, chill on his shoulders.

She gathered her skirts in both hands. "No, I think you're exactly what I see and that I'm right to be impressed. You're extraordinary. Different. Like no one I've ever met, or am ever likely to meet again. I saw no harm in being honest, as we agreed, and a certain naive hero worship is only natural in the circumstances, don't you think? Don't try to negate my feelings."

"I'm not a hero, Miss Marsh."

Anne bit back the pain that seemed to have settled beneath her ribs. "Yes, you are. But it doesn't matter. After all, I'm safely in love with my fiancé."

Leaving him gazing after her, she strode away up the track. Torn leaves and twigs littered the path. Branches scraped where one great tree had toppled and crashed into its neighbors. The upturned roots twisted, leaving a gaping scar. Her heart burned at the bitter knowledge that she and Lord Jonathan could never be equals, that they moved—and would forever move—in separate worlds. He outclassed her, in rank, in experience, in natural power.

She might be safe from thinking that she was really falling in love, however wildly her heart beat. She was not safe from the heady fascination inevitably felt by the rabbit.

Even running in spate, English rivers are tame enough creatures. . . . I don't want a wife. I intend to return to Asia.

How could she be in love with Lord Jonathan? She loved Arthur. She was going to marry him. Arthur would make her happy, give her the future she had always wanted. Yet now she had risked a glimpse of something quite different, only to discover that it glittered like gold.

Miss Anne Marsh would never forget this day as long as she lived. To Wild Lord Jack it meant nothing.

He had traveled across deserts where the sky leaned down to kiss the earth, survived unimaginable adventures in places more exotic than she could imagine. He was going back there as soon as he could. She was English and provincial and plain. Once he retrieved his precious fossil, Lord Jonathan wouldn't even remember her name.

The rain began coming down harder. The path was muddy and slick with leaves. She tripped over a root, almost falling, and stopped, overwhelmed by a surge of angry tears. She was such a fool! Why not just live the day for what it was and think no more about it?

"Move!"

Anne whirled around. Lord Jonathan was bounding up from the river, his eyes focused somewhere above her head.

"Move!" he shouted. *"Now!"*

A rending echoed through the woods. Anne stared about wildly, took a step, and slipped again, her skirts bunched in both hands.

The noise screeched like the tearing open of the earth. Lord Jonathan cannoned into her. With one sweep of his arm, he knocked her from the path. She slid, caught her foot in her hem, and fell against the foot of a stout beech. Ripping down through the other branches, the broken top of a tree crashed onto the exact spot where she had been standing.

Lord Jonathan was leaping away as it fell, but a tangle of limbs thudded onto his shoulder. In a shower of splinters and twigs, he ducked beneath the blow and rolled. Yet the ricochet of whipping boughs bounced over his body, and a broken stub leaped up to strike him hard on the temple.

Anne struggled to her feet. The woods crowded in, thick and quiet, spattering the leaf litter with droplets. Nothing moved except the gathering rivulets of rainwater, skeining through the mud and racing down to the river. Lord Jonathan Devoran St. George sprawled silently on the path, facedown. He had fought off a gang of assassins in a mad dance of defiance, then been felled by a tree.

Rain drummed as she yanked away the shattered branch and knelt beside him. Gulping back panic, she brushed away leaves and twigs, staring at his white face. Blood and dirt smeared above his ear. The gash ripped into his hair.

"God," he said thickly. "Devil take that bloody gale!"

Relief flooded in with one gasping breath. "You're alive!"

He raised his head, but dropped his face into both hands, his elbows half-buried in the mud. "I would seem to be, Miss Marsh."

"You're bleeding! I should make you a bandage."

"It doesn't matter. Just let me have a minute."

His face hardened, white as stone, as he turned and sat up. Rain pounded over his shoulders, sticking his shirt to his back, while he cradled his head, supporting his arms on both knees. Anne pulled up her skirt and tried to rip a strip from her petticoat, her sensible, hard-wearing cotton petticoat. It wouldn't tear.

"Shall I go for aid? I don't know what's best! I don't think I should leave you."

"No, stay! You're not safe by yourself." He reached out and grasped her wrist. "I can walk, if you'll help me. I can't quite—"

Leaning heavily on her hand, he rose to his feet, then stood swaying for a moment. Anne put both arms about his waist. Cold and damp beneath his soaked shirt. His eyes seemed oddly blank, feral.

"You're losing a lot of blood," she said.

"Rain always makes bleeding seem worse than it is." He draped one arm over her shoulders. "Let us limp together through the woods to the cottage. It's all right. Mrs. Kenyon will have bandages. Mr. Kenyon will take care of you and get help."

"It's my fault," she said. "If I'd moved more quickly—"

"No one's fault, unless it's mine. When I shouted, you looked as if you expected the hordes of Genghis Khan to come crashing through the woods. I wasn't clear enough— Damn!"

He shuddered like a ship in full sail. His eyes closed.

"Here, lean against this tree," Anne said. "Are you going to be sick? It's all right. I don't mind."

He smiled and shook his head, but she clung to him as he quivered against her. Lean, hard muscle filled her arms. An intense focus smoothed over his features, as if he concentrated only on breathing. Something in it terrified her, as if he were already lost to the world, each breath so deep and even and controlled, while the blood trickled down over his cheek and the woods shivered in the rain.

She tried to keep her voice light. "I thought for a moment that you were about to cast up your accounts."

His mouth was wry, almost mocking. "Did you?"

"It wouldn't have mattered," she said.

"I'm all right now." He looked down at her, still smiling, and brushed his fingertips over her cheek. "We're almost there."

She helped him, taking his solid weight on her shoulders. The trees thinned. A bright splash of bluebells spilled over the slopes. The path ran down into a small clearing where a stone cottage was tucked snugly into the hillside. Step by step they walked through the downpour, wading ankle-deep past the wellhouse and into the shelter of the front porch.

Anne hammered at the knocker and called out. Rain sheeted down off the thatch and pummeled a pair of fruit trees. The door remained locked.

"No one's home," she said. "Would they have hidden a key somewhere?"

Lord Jonathan slid down to sit on his haunches, head tipped back, eyes closed. "Perhaps. I don't know."

Anne plunged back into the deluge to turn over stone after stone, anywhere that seemed likely: the little rock border that edged the path, a crumbled piece of garden wall. A snail pulled its horns back into its shell. Young potato plants drooped in the rain.

The stable was dim and dusty. Though dung littered the floor of one of the stalls and fresh hay filled the manger, there was no horse. No halter on the wall. No harness on the hooks. Yet it was better shelter than the porch. Anne ducked her head to race back through the deluge and saw it: hanging on a nail beneath a cracked board, like an answer to prayer.

She seized the cold metal and splashed back to the cottage. Lord Jonathan was curled up, his head pillowed on his arms, apparently asleep. Her hands shook with cold, with alarm, as she fitted the key. The door swung open to reveal a simple parlor and the welcome glow of coals in the grate.

"Well done," he said. "Persistence is an underrated virtue. Was there a horse?"

Anne shook her head as she bent to help him stand. "There were fresh droppings and quite recent tracks. The cart was taken out early this morning, I'd think. Perhaps the Kenyons have gone to town?"

His face might have been carved from stone, yet his eyes shone with secret amusement, as if he calculated odds and found hilarity in the indifferent tumble of dice. She held out her fingers. His gaze locked with hers: winter-forest depths, sparkling with misted brilliance. He seized her hand in one of his, but with the other he reached up to cradle the back of her neck. His lean fingers spread into her hair. The mirth spread from his eyes to his mouth. Warmth leaped like a wildfire through her blood.

"Then it must be market day," he said. "So I am jousting with fate and losing."

Anne stared into his eyes as he pulled her face down to his and pressed his cold mouth onto hers.

Her mouth yielded softly, shaping to the dulcet, cool pressure. It rooted her, paralyzed her. Her bones melted at the pliant intensity, sweet and chill, as his lips eased against hers. Firm. Soft. Flexible. Firing confusion and pleasure. His tongue touched, once—a shock of lithe fire. Her lips parted, welcoming the heat, trembling at the pure wickedness of it. He slid the tip inside her mouth. Tendrils of flame raced, launching her pulse into wild new rhythms. Suppleness and firmness and heat.

Sinful, baffling sensations.

Wonderful sensations.

Improper, marvelous sensations, spreading like molten gold through her thighs and groin and belly.

With one last teasing flick of his tongue, he dropped his palm from her neck and released her. Anne pressed her free hand to her mouth. A confused jumble of yearning tumbled through her mind. She felt enthralled. She felt lost. She wanted him to do it again. Just one touch, one moment of chilled naked lips to naked lips, and she wanted to give him the world?

"In thanks," he said, gripping her fingers. "Now let's get inside and get dry."

With concentrated determination, he pushed himself to his feet and she helped him over the threshold.

The scent of woods and rain, cool and fresh, spiraled up from her skin. Her arm wrapped firmly about his waist. Her fragile, determined shoulders flexed beneath his hand.

The world spun, giddy and light as dandelion down. His head throbbed. He was almost entirely blind.

"Here," she said. "Sit here."

Jack sprawled onto a wooden settle and dropped his head against the back. His vision filled with the blurred image of her face, surprised, shocked, flushed with color after he had kissed her. That gentle, teasing little kiss! Her lips had softened in such artless surrender, her innocent mouth opening in a natural, untutored response. Piercingly lovely—lovelier than he could possibly have imagined!

He wanted to do it again. At the madness of the thought, he laughed aloud.

"Are you all right?" A nimbus of colored lights flared about her hair, as if she walked through rainbows.

"Yes. Yes. I'm witless, Miss Marsh, and you're an angel."

"I think I must see to the fire." Her voice sounded stiff, awkward.

Her boots squelched as she left the room. A few moments later she was back, rattling about at the grate. Flames scattered like broken stars.

She straightened and faced him, draped in blue-and-golden radiance like a Madonna. "Can I use other things, too? Maybe some dry clothes?"

"Clothes, food, drink, whatever you need. My father owns this cottage."

He surrendered to the warmth as the fire took hold. Rain drummed. Flames crackled. Camels trod steadily, *pace, pace, pace,* tassels swaying in rhythm. Scorched boulders stretched to the horizon. Planets wheeled overhead. In the cold darkness of a silk tent, a woman smiled at him. Opened to him. An exotic, musky scent perfumed her soft arms and supple hips, lingered in the crevices of her body—

"Are you awake?"

Jack tried to focus. A wool blanket was tucked about his chest and shoulders, though his shirt stuck to his back. The golden-haloed Madonna stood over him, frowning a little, but she was no longer wearing the soaked blue dress. Her new gown was white muslin, simply cut. The virgin.

"You've changed your clothes," he said. "And combed your hair."

She glanced down, plucking at her skirt with nervous fingers. Her hair lay, damp and straight and shining, over a dark paisley shawl she had wrapped about her shoulders.

"Mrs. Kenyon must be close to my size. Her things are quite a good fit, even her shoes. I hope she won't mind."

"She won't mind."

"I found some clothes for you, too." She pointed to a pile of fabric draped over a wooden chair near the grate. "You'll catch cold unless you take off your wet things." Her face seemed hazy beneath the cloud of drying hair, though her cheeks bloomed like wild roses. "If you cannot manage, I can help you. I can at least take off your boots. And I can clean that cut on your temple. I've brought some warm water." She nodded toward a side table. "In that basin. It was in the kettle in the kitchen."

"You still wish to make me a bandage from your petticoats?"

The pink roses deepened to crimson. "I found some clean cloths. My petticoat is all mud."

Jack leaned back and allowed his lids to drift shut. "Dab away, if you want to. Do whatever you like. I shan't stop you."

Her fingers touched tentatively as she sponged at his temple. The water stung like a snakebite and left a new damp patch in his hair. He supposed it must be an improvement.

"There," she said. "Except for some bruising, it doesn't look so bad now. I'm not even sure that you need a bandage, after all."

Jack opened one eye. It helped to look at things indirectly. The edges were more clearly defined than the centers. Rimmed in gilt, with fuzzy, imprecise movements, she put down the basin and bent to tug off his boots.

"No," he said. "I may be a little light-headed, but I believe I can still dress myself."

"Then I'll go back to the kitchen. I would make us some tea, but the caddy is locked. The door to what I think is the scullery is locked, too, and the water from the pump is muddy, not fit to drink. The well must be flooded. But I found some homemade plum wine in there." She indicated a cupboard in the corner. "Would you like some? It's very good. I'm not sure what else to do, except wait until the Kenyons get home."

He tried to keep his voice gentle—quite a feat when all he felt was this sardonic mirth. "Alas, Miss Marsh, they aren't coming home."

Her brow wrinkled. "They're not?"

"They must have gone to Blackdown Abbas this morning. Thanks to the wretched contrariness of fate, the river has now trapped them on the wrong side of the ford, and we stole the only boat for several miles. I imagine the Kenyons are sitting snugly in the Royal Oak in the market square by now, planning to spend a few days."

"Then no one will come at all?" She sat down with a thump. "We're trapped here for the night?"

"Unless you wish me to walk the ten miles to Wyldshay now. I will, if you like. There's nowhere else to get help this side of spreading waters."

He could—though it would take a passionate concentration—make it to Wyldshay, if he wished. However, he could not leave her here alone. He would not drag her back out into the storm so that she could try to lead him, half-blind, through the dark. And he had already surrendered to the new path that was unfolding like the Silk Road before him.

" 'Take therefore no thought for the morrow,' " he added almost to himself. " 'For the morrow shall take thought for the things of itself. Sufficient unto the day is the evil thereof.' "

"We face social disaster and all you can do is quote St. Matthew in jest?"

"In jest? I may be a heathen, Miss Marsh, but I don't take these holy words in vain. I live by them."

"No, you don't," she said dryly. "You take all kinds of thought for the morrow, just as I do. That's how people are."

He laughed, though it hurt. "Then I stand corrected."

"When you can barely stand by yourself?" She glanced at the

rain beating steadily on the leaded windows, then bit her lip as if making up her mind to something.

"You cannot go alone," Jack said. "You don't know the way."

"No." She swallowed, then smiled like a sunrise. "And I can't swim."

He leaned back, delighted by her brave humor, and rubbed one hand over his treacherous eyes.

"So how about that wine, Miss Marsh? I was this thirsty once before, if I remember correctly, when a promised well turned out to be dry and we had another day's journey to the next one—"

She stood, rocking as she turned, as if she were a boat floating gently on the uneven stone floor. The white dress glimmered. Two bottles and two glasses, one already used, stood on the table beside the fireplace.

Jack managed to take his glass without flailing pitifully at empty air. The flavor of plums eased sweetly down his throat, only to kick through his gut in a scorching glow. He almost choked. This wasn't wine. It was country-brewed brandy, the honeyed taste cloaking the strapping sting of pure alcohol.

"You've been drinking this?" he asked. "How much?"

"Two glasses." She poured more for herself, spilling a little on the table, creating rings of shattered brightness. "I was thirsty. It *is* good, isn't it?"

"Very good indeed. And not at all suitable for young ladies."

Her giggle made the tip of her nose flatten just a little, as charming—when seen from the corner of one's eye—as a dormouse with a nut.

"It's just plums," she said. "My mother makes wine like this and all of us drink it. And I found bread and cheese in the kitchen. I'll make us toasted cheese, though that's not a very elegant dinner for a duke's son, is it?"

He thrust aside the blanket. Steam rose from his boots. The fire danced brightly. His feet seemed to have disappeared into a dark tunnel.

"None of this was quite what I had in mind, either," he said. "We're at the mercy of the wild hand of destiny, Miss Marsh."

She swallowed more brandy as if it were lemonade. "Only because the woods wanted it this way. Do trees have plans of their own, do you suppose?"

"Ancient woods like these? They've been plotting their survival since the Norman Conquest, though I'm not sure that they care very much about puny creatures like us."

"Then they should," she said. "We have axes."

His gathering appreciation for her wicked sense of humor caught him out. Though it sent shooting lights across his vision, he laughed aloud. She was amazing, more remarkable than she knew. He cherished her courage and dry wit like water in the desert.

"Toasted cheese will also take you decorously to the kitchen, while I wrestle with my damp linen and unfortunate footwear."

She wavered, holding the half-empty bottle and her glass. Her hair streamed sinfully, shimmering over her shawl. Her body trembled like a lily in a spring breeze, but she turned and disappeared, so he stood and pulled off his shirt. Heat from the fire flowed over his cold skin. He pushed his hands back through his damp hair and stared at the flames. Wild Lord Jack with a void in the center of his vision and dizzy in the brain!

The cut on his temple burned. Another painful lump swelled at the back of his head. With a shrug, he began to unbutton his breeches. Then he remembered: He was still wearing his damned boots. He bent to work them off.

A little rustle whispered from the doorway. Jack glanced over his shoulder. The Madonna glimmered there like a wraith, though her cheeks glowed like coals.

"I thought . . . Well, I don't think you need to change into those clothes, not if it's too difficult," she said. "I can fetch you a nightshirt or just another blanket, if you like. I don't mind. Perhaps, once we've eaten, it would be better if you simply went to bed?"

He swallowed the impulse to a dark laughter that she would never understand. Unless he looked at her obliquely, her hair streamed like sunlight. His entire being yearned for that brightness, as if he could negate his solitary self-reliance in the pure radiance of this one Englishwoman.

"Nothing about going to bed is very simple under the circumstances," he said.

CHAPTER SIX

S HE KNEW SHE OUGHT TO LEAVE, YET ANNE STOOD IN THE doorway, fired with bravado.

His hair curled darkly. His brown skin shone: naked and damp and carved from mahogany. Sleek and strong and firm, marked with sliding knots of muscle. A man's arms. A man's back.

Everything else in the parlor shone wobbly and hazy bright, making her dizzy. Only Lord Jonathan seemed to be clearly in focus. She gazed at him, struggling with curiosity and fear and a confusion of unfamiliar emotions.

He gleamed with beauty, like a carving of sin, of a tiger, of a fallen angel.

Her blood pooled, heavy and hot, in unmentionable places.

Nothing about going to bed is very simple under the circumstances.

"Although," he added, almost as if to himself, "it sounds like a promise of heaven to a man long abandoned to the primrose path of iniquity: something very much longed for, but completely out of the question."

Her hands clutched the wine bottle. The kitchen beckoned behind her, the safe retreat. "Why?"

Firelight cast fascinating patterns over striated ribs as he reached for a towel. "I cannot possibly retreat into bed with a young lady in the house."

"You're concerned for my *reputation*? When we're trapped here together for the night? I'm already ruined. My reputation will be in shreds. I may even have to cry off—"

"No, you won't. Whatever happens here, my mother's influence in society will ensure that your name remains spotless. However, there's only one bed, isn't there?"

Of the two rooms she had explored upstairs, one was a small workroom with tables and tools and strips of leather, a place for repairing and making things: traps or harnesses, perhaps. The other was a tiny bedroom, with one bed and two dressers.

She nodded. "With a quilted coverlet."

"Then you may have the bed, Miss Marsh, quilted coverlet and all. I'll sleep down here."

"Whatever the power of a duchess," she said, "it's too late to pretend that all of this never happened."

He glanced around beneath his lashes, his eyes glinting with gold and shadows. "Of course this has happened and is happening. However, you may do as you like without fear of any consequences."

His naked skin gleamed, rich and brown. The bones of his hands gleamed beneath his tanned skin. His shoulders flexed, as she imagined a tiger's shoulders might flex on the return from a hunt. Her pulse hammered, making her feel wicked and restless. *I wonder what it would be like to touch you!*

"I don't understand how I feel," she whispered.

Shadows slipped lovingly into the indent of his spine as he reached for the dry shirt, shrugged into it, and turned to face her. His dark gaze seemed reassuringly grave, as if her befuddled feelings were all that mattered to him.

"It's all right. Nothing will harm you. You're just beginning to glimpse the heady hazards of freedom—from social strictures, from all of your life's prior assumptions—but nothing will happen between us unless you wish it."

"I don't know." The room began to turn lazily, like a slow wheel. "I don't know what I want."

He tipped his head and smiled. "Yes, you do, or your body does, but you may not have it, though that's not—in spite of our earlier conversation in the gig—why we shan't share a bed tonight. Though either way, your virtue will be safe. Yet you're tired and a little foxed and more distressed than you know. You need to eat and sleep—and not with me."

Anne turned and stumbled into the kitchen. The walls glowered darkly. Rain sheeted down the windows. Though the fire had been banked that morning, it had gone out. The bedroom was just a space beneath the roof, the ceiling diving down over the single tiny window. She didn't want to go to bed up there, alone and dizzy and filled with nameless yearning. Only the parlor, warm and inviting, beckoned, because of the man who said he would sleep there: this duke's son who seemed to understand the mysteries of her heart and offered her glimpses of wonder.

The small ache blossomed into something close to pain.

So this was what came of ignoring propriety! Caught up in the ferment of strangeness, she had shed caution and discretion—and this was what came of it. Not the obvious threat to virtue and reputation, but the inevitable loss of contentment that came from glimpsing something new, this painful realization that she had sacrificed her complacency forever.

"My lord," she said aloud to the empty kitchen. "I've already come to worse harm than you know. Whatever happens next, I'll be different for the rest of my life, because I've been alone with a stranger who once hunted dragons."

She caught her lip between her teeth. *Hunted dragons?* Amusement welled, drowning the pain. What was she afraid of? This was only an episode, a dream, as if she had been carried away on a magic carpet. She could do anything she liked, without consequences. He had promised.

She poured herself another glass of plum wine, as sweet and potent as his kiss. *His kiss!* Anne touched her fingertips to her mouth.

The memory had been drifting like perfume, coloring all her potential misery and turning it into something precious and bright. Fleeing along the riverbank, wet shoes, wet dress, mud thick on her petticoat; the worry about Lord Jonathan's being hurt; the fear of a gang of foreign assassins loose in the English countryside: It had all been as nothing, because he had kissed her and the lingering loveliness of that had made every discomfort seem irrelevant.

It was as certain as death that a duke's family would never let any hint of scandal tarnish their son. Her commitment to Arthur was not in question and neither, of course, was her virtue. She could do anything, anything at all, and tomorrow the duchess would wave her magic wand to make all come right again.

The wine spread its heady glow. The cold grate gleamed and rippled. The little bosses on the fire irons winked at her. It really was a very funny room, this kitchen full of locks. The back door, the tea caddy, the scullery—were they locking out mice? If they wanted to lock out the determined daughters of Hawthorn Axbury: the determined, damp, dizzy daughters—

Anne giggled and fetched plates and food from the dresser by the hearth.

The bread was coarse, a mix of wheat and rye, but the cheese smelled nutty and delicious. She nibbled a small piece, then found a breadboard and knife. She piled several slices of cheddar and bread on a plate, then looked about for a toasting fork.

She could do anything and no one would ever know. She could eat toasted cheese with her fingers. She could drink this lovely sweet wine that tasted like sugarplums. She could dance like an angel or sing like a frog, and no one would ever know, or judge, or remember, except the dragon hunter—who didn't care!

Arms laden, she marched back into the parlor, her heart capering.

He stood beside the fireplace, tall and lean. A splatter of purple bruise marked his temple, but the cut barely showed. His dry hair had curled over the wound, hiding it. He looked splendid—not ill at all!

She stopped and grinned at him. Everything had begun to feel ludicrous. Her heart thumped, but she felt light with merriment.

"That shirt's too small and those breeches are too short," she said.

"Shockingly so." His mouth quirked. "You don't comment on my stockings, but then, you picked them out."

Anne surveyed the yellow stripes stretched over his muscular calves.

"You have wonderful legs." Scarlet heat flooded her cheeks. "Oh, I can't believe I said that—"

He lifted the plate from her hands. "Pray, don't try to take it back! That's the nicest compliment any lady ever paid me. God, you'd better eat!"

He speared bread and cheese on the toasting fork and knelt at the grate.

Anne collapsed onto a chair. Her thoughts seemed to have taken on a life of their own, colored by a giddy intensity of contrasting emotions. There was certainly no connection whatsoever between her wayward tongue and her will. Her gaze wandered in wanton pleasure over the shape of his hands. "You shouldn't be doing that."

"I don't want to have to carry you upstairs." He glanced up. "You're foxed, Miss Marsh. Charmingly, harmlessly foxed—at the moment."

"But I feel wonderful!" She leaned forward, resting both arms on her knees and clasping her fingers together. Otherwise she thought she might just reach out to touch him. Would he mind? Now that the rain had washed the flour away, his hair seemed so soft and dense and dark. "I've felt splendid ever since you kissed me."

He twirled the toast so the cheese wouldn't drip into the flames. "Ah!" he said. "I did kiss you, didn't I?"

It seemed a subject for very serious reflection, though her mouth filled with a sweetly vulnerable bliss at the memory.

"Why did you do it? Not from affection or . . . or intention of courtship, obviously. You know that I'm already engaged to be married."

"Then why, do you think?"

"I thought perhaps because you wanted to demonstrate that we could do something that foolish without blame."

His bronzed hands were lovely, twirling the toasting fork. "May I tell you the truth?"

"Yes! Yes, of course."

"Then you must know that my motives were nothing so noble," he said. "It was just the whim of the moment."

"Oh, I see. I know it had nothing to do with me—"

"On the contrary, it had everything to do with you."

"Only because each moment that you and I spend together is isolated, isn't it, like a cocoon spun from time, because we come from such different worlds? That's why you haven't since referred to it? Because it just happened and only because of our odd situation? A perfect, mysterious lesson and a memory to cherish— Oh, I'm burbling, aren't I?"

"Like a merry brook." He smiled and slid a slice of toast dripping with cheese onto a plate. "Here, my dear girl, be quiet and eat this."

Anne perched on the edge of her chair. Toasted cheese! Soft and crisp and salty and sharp. She closed her eyes to savor it. So very, very good. She licked her lips with her tongue.

"Very charming," he said dryly. "Though not entirely harmless, perhaps?"

She glanced up at him. Her lids felt heavy and sleepy. "What's not entirely harmless?"

Lounging once more on the settle, his stockinged feet crossed at the ankle, he was eating his own piece of toast.

"Your helplessness in the face of plum brandy and cheese," he said.

With his eyes still on hers he took a bite. Melted cheese oozed over his fingers. His gaze did not waver as he licked them clean. Her pulse surged, a sweet, heavy yearning.

"But it's not the plums and cheese," she said. "It's you."

"Not really." His throat was strong and brown, his mouth

lovely, as he swallowed. "Or not in any personal way. You've launched into an adventure, terrifying and heady, and though it scares you, you don't want it to end. Even though now you find yourself wanting to forget decorum and modesty, and break all the rules—"

"Why not?" she interrupted. "I'm doomed to discontent, either way."

"No, you're not. There's no reason why we can't part with your feeling joyful and confident."

Anne tried not to flinch away from the brave new world he seemed to be offering.

"But this is my one chance to learn something new about men and about . . . about being married. And you promised. At some later time, you said, when we weren't among the chill uplands of Dorset, when you weren't driving a gig."

A little smile hovered as he looked back at the fire. "Yes, I did, didn't I?"

"You didn't mean it?" she asked. "That's not what you want any longer?"

"My own desires are irrelevant." He glanced back at her. "Though there's probably no other man in England who could say the same and mean it."

"I thought it might be disloyal to Arthur, but it wouldn't be, would it? Any more than it was when you kissed me. It would only help."

"Nothing you and I might share would mean any disloyalty to your fiancé. I'm just a cipher in your life, Miss Marsh. Nobody. In your heart you think I'm just a dream, don't you?"

Perhaps she had simply dreamed all of this: the fossil, the intruder at her window, the mad journey, this cottage. But if so, why did she feel so very different from her usual self? As if she ran barefoot like a child over a vast open lawn, where a strange gilt horizon shimmered beyond the tall trunks of unknown trees—

"I think you're a hero," she said. "Like someone in a story."

He ran his hands back over his hair and laughed. "I'm no hero, though I admit I have little enough existence of my own."

The room moved lazily, disintegrating at the edges. "I don't know if I understand," she said. "How can you not exist?"

"It's how one survives in the desert. It's a matter of letting the self dissolve, until the wind blows through you as if you weren't there. Yet do that often enough and you begin to disappear in earnest."

She closed her eyes, trying to imagine such a wind in such a place, and saw only Dorset, trim and neat—though as she watched it, that picture of a golden England split open to spill chaos through the cracks.

"Is that what happened when you fought off all those men?" she asked. "It was almost as if you had given yourself to some other force, something deeper or greater or . . . I don't know how to explain it."

"Ah, perceptive Miss Marsh!" His laugh this time held a bitter edge that she couldn't understand. "No man can defend himself against attackers trained in the East, unless he has had the same training, which is impossible unless he has lost himself first." He reached forward to poke at the fire. "So I'm just a tool of your imagination, after all. You may take advantage of that in any way that you wish."

She glanced about. The room ought to seem ordinary enough, a gamekeeper's parlor with its simple furnishings, but her perception shifted as she tried to focus. Perhaps the walls were made of gingerbread and the doors spun from sugar? Anne squeezed her lids shut again and tried to find the still voice inside, the prompting of a higher power, but the voice wasn't still and quiet. It was singing:

And therefore take the present time, With a hey and a ho, and a hey nonny no . . .

His voice broke into her thoughts. "What would you like from me, Miss Marsh? You wish to learn about men, enough to know that there's no cause for fear?"

She gathered bravery, plucking it like daisies in a meadow, amazed that they grew in such abundance, and sat up straight, facing him.

"I'm just so entirely ignorant of such matters. And I think everything you said to me earlier is true." His steady gaze seemed to offer her more courage. "There's no one else I can ask. You must be experienced in such things."

"In teaching English maidens what to expect from the marriage bed? No, not at all."

She wrung her hands together in her lap. "But you must know."

"Yes, I know."

"But isn't it something you can show me? Simply in the spirit of scientific inquiry? Because it's all about bodies, isn't it?" She ducked her head, her cheeks flaming. "I should never have asked. I'm sorry."

"If I learned one thing from the Takla Makan, Miss Marsh, it is this: When there's no going back, you must go forward. It's too late to retreat now. You have nothing at all to lose. We're only talking. How can words harm you?"

She shook her head, renewed heat and mortification warring in her blood.

"Tell me first what you do know," he added gently. His voice was steady, reassuring. "What do you imagine will happen when you allow your husband into your bed for the first time? Be brave! It's all right. Just tell me the truth."

"I don't know. But I think it must be rather undignified and . . . and very uncomfortable and embarrassing. And that his body must be very strange. Why else does no one talk about it?"

"Do you love him?"

She glanced up. "Oh, yes."

"Then what you do together should be lovely: life-altering, life-affirming. Men and women who love each other should share passion."

"That's what you said earlier, but I don't know what you mean." White muslin cushioned her anxious fingers.

"How do you feel right now? Can you describe it?"

"Hot and woozy and my heart's beating too fast. And I feel a stream of . . . I don't know, almost as if I shared a sacred bond with you, as if the air between us might catch fire. Do you feel it, too? Is your blood too hot?"

"Yes and yes, but I can experience it, and enjoy it, and not act on it unless I wish to."

"Enjoy it?" Deeper truths began to pour through the gap in her defenses. "It does feel exciting and rather wonderful, but it frightens me. I don't want to lose myself."

He slid forward on the settle to take her hands in both of his. "Hush! You can say or feel anything you like. Sensations by themselves never hurt anyone. Now, stretch out your fingers and let them lie in my palms. Take a deep breath, in through your nose and out through your mouth. Then another. Slowly. Easily."

She began to breathe as he directed, until her hands lay relaxed in his. The anxiety dissipated, her blood cooled, her frantic yearning eased, until she felt light and open.

"There, that's better," he said. "We're only talking about making love. It all begins with touching. Have you never explored your own body? What do you know about yourself?"

Her face glowed. Her pulse fluttered. His warmth enveloped her. Yet she felt safe, as long as he held her hands like this.

"Nothing," she said.

"As you know nothing of a man's. We can remedy that, without harm to you—or to your promise to your Arthur—but I must be sure first that you know what you're asking, and sadly that's not a judgment that a foxed person can make."

"You said I might ask for anything that I wished."

"Ah, but would you wish for the same things if you were sober?"

"Yes, of course."

"In vino veritas?"

"You don't think there's truth in wine?"

"Very seldom, in my experience. But I promise, if you wake up still feeling the same way in the morning, you may ask anything you like of me then, and I'll do it."

She glanced at the dark doorway leading to the stairs. "May I ask something else now? Will you come upstairs with me? There's a window—"

Jack studied her face, the white skin and long nose. Anne Marsh no longer wore a halo of colored lights, though firelight danced over her lashes and delicate jaw. She was just an English girl, soft and confused and made vulnerable by wine, that he had dragged into his adventure.

He knew what he desired. It seemed as if he had been desiring it for a very long time now: her legs wrapped about his waist, her brave hands clinging to his shoulders, his erection buried in her body, her face flushed with passion and excitement and pleasure. A desire that he had no intention of acting on, though he knew he could fulfill hers, in any way that she liked, and keep her safe while he did it.

But not now. Not with the plum brandy racing in her veins. And so he had deliberately cooled the flare of ardor that had begun to burn between them—taken that energy and absorbed it into himself—and replaced it, to the best of his ability, with calm. His desire for her was personal, direct, knowing. Hers for him was only the vague longing of a virgin, searching for any convenient focus. She did not desire *him* at all, though she might imagine that she did.

"Our enemies can't come here," he said. "The river's busy flooding the meadows. All the tributary streams have also burst their banks by now to turn the lanes into marshes and the fields into lakes. We're safely adrift on an island, Miss Marsh, and it's still raining."

She rose unsteadily to her feet, a ruffled, long-nosed mouse with a heartbreaking smile.

"There's no bed down here." She swayed gently. Shimmering hair streamed over her shoulders. "You were hurt. You should have the bed."

Though the room spun when he stood, he caught and steadied her. "I've slept without a bed often enough."

"But you were only a visitor in those places." She folded forward into his arms. "This is England."

"Wherever I go," Jack whispered in her ear, "I'm just a visitor in my own life."

She tucked her head into his shoulder as he carried her out through the hall and up the narrow stairs. It was simply a matter of will. Just as he would have gone to Wyldshay, running and swimming where he had to, if he had thought it necessary.

The bedroom was cool and dark. Jack set Anne on the bed and lit candles. She curled up like a kitten and closed her eyes. He pulled off her shoes and tucked the quilt over her, then sat down on the bed. He left her clothes—the foolish corsets and lacing and petticoats—undisturbed, but he took one small foot in both hands. With the balls of his thumbs he began to rub the sole in little circles, working up over the arch.

"Ah!" She sighed. "That feels good!"

He rubbed the other foot, soothing away her distress. He would teach her whatever she needed to know. But now she needed sleep and she was in no state to take risks.

Her breathing soon became deep and even. Jack tugged the quilt down over her feet.

The candlelight fired flecks of amber in her hair. He smoothed it back from her face. It flowed like water beneath his fingertips, a light English silk brown—like a field mouse—that one would never see in Asia.

What a strange creature she was! More alien than any woman he had ever known. Alien and innocent and fascinating—and destined, apart from this one momentary encounter, to play no further part in his life. Why the devil did he think he desired her with such intensity, when he had known women who knew all the subtle, exotic practices that could take a man beyond ecstasy?

The downpour beat steadily on the thatch and ran in sheets over the windowpanes. Jack stood and crossed the room, ducking his head to peer out at the unfocused darkness. He had taken a blow to the head like this once before, near the Khyber Pass. His turban had saved his life, but he had been helpless, half-blind and giddy for several days, dependent for his life on his native guide.

The reaction did not seem as severe this time. He glanced back at the bed. She was sleeping soundly, one hand flung out on the pillow, her long nose buried in dreams. She might think he was a hero, the St. George who had slain dragons, but if they were attacked right now he would be lucky if he could defend her at all. Not much of a knight in shining armor!

Yet she believed in him, which was quite something for a man who wasn't sure if he believed in himself.

The candle guttered. He reached with thumb and forefinger to pinch out the flame, then stretched out beside her. After a few minutes he stripped off the ill-fitting breeches and bizarre stockings. Dressed in nothing but shirt and linen underdrawers, with hands crossed over his chest—like a stone effigy in a church, he thought wryly—Jack let consciousness slip away.

*T*HE ABSENCE OF SOUND WOKE HER: A PROFOUND NEW silence. Lost for a moment, Anne stared at the unfamiliar window, small and glimmering beneath a swoop of low ceiling.

Yet the quiet wasn't absolute. Someone was breathing gently, a rhythmic, comforting sound barely disturbing the night. She was in the upstairs bedroom at the gamekeeper's cottage with Lord Jonathan Devoran St. George, the dragon hunter. He was asleep. On the bed. Wearing underdrawers and shirt and nothing else.

Wherever I go, I'm just a visitor in my own life.

Perhaps it was the loneliest thing she had ever heard anyone say: to belong nowhere, to no one.

Moonlight cast shadows over his face—the dark lashes, the chiseled flare of nostrils, the sensuous mouth—as if he were carved from marble. Her pulse quickened. She wanted to touch his lips with her fingertips, outline the deep curves, explore the little marks etched by laughter at the corners of his mouth.

A wave of heat washed through her body.

She pushed a fold of the quilt over him and swung her feet to the floor. As if she waded through a dream, she padded to the window and peered through the glass. Moonlight gleamed on a platter of onyx. If only she could swim, she could dive down like a kingfisher into that smooth darkness.

"What do you see?"

She spun about. Lord Jonathan lay stretched on the bed, long and lean, his head propped on one elbow, gazing at her. Black hair spilled like ink over his forehead.

"The clearing's become a lake," she said. "The rain's stopped."

He dropped his head back to the pillow. "How do you feel?"

Anne wandered back toward the bed, then stopped to tug some knots out of her hair. "Quite well. Extraordinarily well, in fact. As if I had slept in heaven."

"Perhaps you have."

"Though I fear I may have behaved very improperly."

"If you think so, we may forget every word and return to our dulcet, innocent sleep."

She sat down and smoothed the tossed edge of the quilt. A wraith in the shadows, he seemed perfect, as remote as an angel or a church carving.

"I thought I had stumbled into a fairy tale," she said. "Where everything was lit with glitter and amusement. Did I make a very great fool of myself?"

"No. Not at all."

"Do you remember what I said?"

"If you'd like me to."

"Didn't you think that I meant it?"

His eyes were gilt and dark, like a stalking tiger's. "On the contrary. I thought you meant every word of it. Did you?"

A hot little shiver ran down her spine. *"In vino veritas?"* She pleated folds of white muslin, while her sense of dreamlike unreality deepened and the mysterious yearning bloomed to become all-consuming. "Yes, I think that I did. And there's no undoing that now, is there?"

"Perhaps not. But it doesn't matter."

She glanced back at him. "Yet I cannot leave things as they are. When there's no going back, you must go forward—you said that."

"It's generally better than paralysis or regret, certainly." His lashes swept down, soft and black, as he closed his eyes. "This is your opportunity, if you want it. I'm at your disposal."

So he wouldn't help her. He was going to force her to make the choice by herself.

Her pulse beat relentlessly, heavy and hot. Her voice whispered up her dry throat. "You said there would be no harm in it."

He held up one hand. Moonlight slipped over the faint shine of callus and the severe glow of bone. Darkness pooled in the cupped center of his palm.

"No harm will come to you," he said. "I promise."

"Then I do want to touch you, just a little." She bit her lip. "In the spirit of . . . of a scientific exploration. I want to know how you're made."

"Like a man," he said. "Like any man."

Her corset had closed like a vice about her ribs, stifling her breathing. Anne stood up. The white dress stuck to her hot limbs. Whalebone dug into her breasts.

His hand remained steady, absolutely still, strong and secure and carved like stone in the moonlight.

"If I don't do this now, it will indeed be from cowardice and . . . and a kind of self-pity, won't it?"

"Not really. You want to do something you've always thought totally outside of possibility, and very probably sinful and wrong, as well. Only you can decide what you want and which voices to listen to."

Her entire body trembled as she closed her eyes and sought for guidance. Why had providence presented her with this strange opportunity? It did not feel sinful or wrong. It felt heady and wonderful and entrancing. . . . *With a hey and a ho, and a hey nonny no . . .*

"Perhaps the snake is telling you to bite into the apple of knowledge," he added, "and the penalty will be banishment from Paradise?"

"No," she said as the voice murmured—*but he's an angel, not the snake!* "Because I'm not in Paradise now. Perhaps I've already bitten into the apple and am doomed to discontent unless I swallow it. All my life I've been encouraged to examine nature to uncover the truth. Why should this be any different?"

He smiled, a fleeting, generous smile. "Then do as you wish, Miss Marsh."

"You won't mind?"

His dark hair spilled on the pillow as he tipped back his head and laughed. "God, no! I'm going to love it."

Her pulse thundering, Anne set her palm on his. Long-fingered, gracefully made, his hand supported and comforted and eased the weight of hers, but the deliberately conscious contact felt shamefully intimate. Hot blood swooped and dived in her heart, sending a flood to scald her face and neck. He closed his fingers gently about hers for a moment, until the wave of panic passed.

"Don't try to understand your feelings." He opened his hand again, as if surrendering. "Just savor them. Let them happen. You may feel things you've never felt before, but you cannot do anything wrong. You're gathering empirical evidence, that's all."

Trembling like a flame in a furnace, Anne nodded. She touched his wrist, then slid her fingertips over the tender skin and prominent veins just below the base of his palm. His pulse throbbed against hers, like two halves of one secret, beating in rhythm.

"Your arm is so different from mine," she whispered. "Every bone and tendon so much larger and stronger. You feel lovely." Her wandering fingertips pushed up his shirtsleeve. "You have wiry little hairs on your arms!"

"Yes," he said.

Her face flamed. "As well as . . . as there on your chest—"

"Lesson one," he said with a small grin.

"Do all men have such hair?"

"Most of them."

"As much as you have?"

"Many men have a great deal more."

"Oh," she said. "I've never seen a man before without his cravat."

He lay absolutely still as she stroked his forearm: supple and alive just above the inside of his wrist, then firmly muscled beneath the rough sprinkle of hairs—such a fascinating contrast!

"Do you like that?" she asked. "It doesn't bother you?"

"It doesn't matter what I like. That's not our purpose."

"But you don't dislike it?"

"Not if it eases your fears, Miss Marsh."

She set his open hand back on the bed and ran her palm over his upper arm: solid flesh beneath the fabric of his shirt. The amazing contours of muscle. A bulk she could not encompass with one hand. Enthralling. Magical. The unyielding male body always hidden before by layers of clothes, or only partially glimpsed when men threw aside jackets for boxing or fencing. Never witnessed—never *experienced*—like this!

Her blush burned as her seeking fingers moved over his shoulder and collarbone, caressing every hollow and prominence, until she came to the sensitive skin at the base of his throat: a small indentation as tender and smooth as her own. It fluttered like a bird.

"Ah!" She felt hot and enchanted. "You're as vulnerable here as I am!"

"I'm as vulnerable everywhere as you are."

"But you're so much stronger and . . . and firmer than me." She smoothed her palm over his shoulder. "Do you like this?"

He opened his eyes and smiled up at her. "I like it that you're finding pleasure in it."

"But I'm not doing it right? How does a man really like to be touched?"

"You're doing nothing wrong, but men like to be caressed with real firmness. You don't need to be hesitant. I won't break."

"No," she said. "You're all hard."

He laughed, though her observation didn't seem to be so very funny. Anne grinned at him. A fine mist of madness enveloped her, hot and lovely, far more intoxicating than wine.

She wanted this. More than anything. The craving to go further, explore further, burned away all caution. Perhaps she was wicked and wanton, but she felt drunk with the need to discover everything.

When there's no going back, you must go forward!

She sat back on her heels. "Can I— Can we take off your shirt?"

"As you wish," he said.

"I saw your back in the parlor. I was . . . mesmerized. I was right to think of tigers—all that power and grace. Are all men so lovely?"

A frown chased over his features for a moment. "The thought never occurred to me. I'm glad that you think so, but—" He broke off the sentence and laughed aloud.

"Because you make those judgments only about females?"

"All the time, Miss Marsh," he said with a kind of a wry solemnity. "And I assure you that I don't find you in any way wanting."

Hot pleasure burned up her cheeks, setting her ears alight. Anne ducked her face and shook her head. "No, don't! Don't make me think about myself."

"Very well." He winked. "I'm happy enough to let you think about me."

He wrenched his shirt over his head, then lay back with his arms flung out to each side.

Anne dropped her hands and stared. "Oh," she said. "Oh, my!"

Severe bands of muscle. Ribs arcing strongly from lean, hollow flanks. Powerful shoulders. A smooth flow of energy glowing beneath his bronzed skin.

"As you see," he said. "I have a little more hair for you to discover yet."

The dark fuzz on his chest curled about two flat nipples, then ran all the way down to his waistband, marking another indent of knotted muscle.

"May I touch it?"

"Do as you like," he said. "I'll tell you when it's wiser for you to stop."

Her breath sparkled into her lungs as if she inhaled moonlight on water, though her face burned. "Wiser, Lord Jonathan?"

He grinned. "We'll cross that bridge when we get to it. In the meantime, I'm lying here half naked on a bed allowing your indecorous exploration. I think you'd better call me Jack, don't you?"

"If you think so."

"I think so."

"Very well . . . Jack. And by all means, in the circumstances I'm happy to give you permission to call me Anne."

"No, Miss Marsh," he said. "Our intimacy is all one-sided."

She hesitated, her attention riveted by the glide of muscles under his skin. She had touched him and looked at him. She wasn't in the least afraid, or even troubled by it. His body was flawless and exciting and beautiful. It was enough, wasn't it?

"Are you done?" he asked gently.

Her heart quaked as she laid her palm flat on his chest. The dark fuzz felt softer than she expected, lovely and strangely exciting. She closed her eyes, wanting to absorb the moment. Then slowly, slowly, with yearning sensitivity, she traced the even finer down that delineated the centerline of his body and circled his navel with one finger. Her pulse fired with dark agitation.

"No," she said, gathering courage again. "I want to touch you some more."

CHAPTER SEVEN

*T*HE TENTATIVE CARESSES HOVERED AND TICKLED—INEF-
fably sweet. Jack felt humbled. Amazed. Enthralled. And
strangely vulnerable.

He had sought all his life to be in charge, in control. Fate had
laughed in his face and taught him other lessons. Yet it took an
aching effort of will to lie passive now and allow her fingers to
trawl over his flesh.

Her face floated, a pale oval. Her hair gleamed in the moonlight. Long strands flowed and tangled over the hidden curves of
shoulders and breasts. He wanted to touch her. Of course, he
wanted to touch her. But he lay still, watching her face, while she
explored his body with her innocent, cautious encirclements.

Her hand turned, her wrist slender and graceful, as she spread
her fingers on his chest. His skin tingled. A sharp pulse of eroticism ricocheted to the groin. He negated it, even when his nipples rose to her touch. Light, intimate caresses that might also
touch the heart?

Jack closed his eyes to let his mind float into darkness, where
the void might safely entomb him. Though images and memories

jostled, he knew the core of his control was absolute. He lay trapped in a cave in the high Karakorams, a supplicant to the snowbound passes, where death waited. He was lost, swept by a hot, dry wind in the great yellow sand dunes, his tongue bound, his intellect silenced. Camels walked. Tassels swayed. A woman smiled from her tent—

She trailed a caress around his navel. Heat seared from her fingertips.

The images shattered. He opened his eyes. Anne was trembling, her breathing ragged.

"Oh," she said. "You are so—"

"It's all right," he said. "Take a deep breath—as well as you can. You may stop whenever you wish."

"No," she said. "I cannot. Not now!"

She set her palm on his thigh to stroke the muscle all the way down to his knee, then past the linen cuff to the naked flesh of his calf.

"More hair," he said dryly.

Her hands quivered as she choked back a small laugh, charming and silly and innocent.

Jack lay back and surrendered once again to the void. . . . If he had not been wearing a turban, the blow would have killed him. In sheer gratitude for his life, he had kissed the cold floor of the cave. Impossible then to imagine how easily he would later yearn to trade that life for oblivion—until, later still, he had been encompassed in musk and silk, and an urgent, hot impulse that tore into his soul. Beating him to his knees, this time, in the face of all-consuming desire.

Lights flickered through the darkness, distracting him. Her slim thighs were satin beneath his fingers. Her touch was maddening, erotic and sensuous, carrying musk and silk. She had enslaved him and taught him and driven him to ecstasy. His mistress, his possessor, with her black eyes and blacker hair, her neat, small body, hot and willing. He would have died to pleasure her. Instead she had died to please him—

In one long, lovely stroke, her palm moved back to rest on his hip.

He lifted his lids just enough to gaze up beneath his lashes and knew a rush of relief, as if he were saved from a torture. Miss Anne Marsh! Something contracted in his heart at the sheer, blind courage stamped on her face, in the teeth clamped onto her lower lip. He felt oddly moved, as if he suffered pain without the courage to hold back tears.

Yet in the strangely unreal jumble of emotions he didn't quite understand, desire flamed and cavorted, mocking his self-control. With the resolve of a knife blade, he blocked his incipient erection.

She hesitated, her fingers hovering. Her cheeks on fire, she set her palm directly over his penis.

The moment stretched, as Jack felt stretched—extended suddenly on a rack.

"Oh." Her trembling hand fired him with an agony of concentrated pleasure. Through the covering fabric, she stroked her fingertips from the base to the head. "Oh, my!"

Heat scorched. It was the most sweetly erotic charge he had ever experienced.

"I want to see." Her voice whispered. Choked, stiff with bravado.

His fists had clenched by themselves. Jack opened them and relaxed his hands, searching for the harsh, narrow path where he might eradicate craving and remove himself from the reality of his desire. The way opened before him, as certain and as treacherous as the Karakoram Pass.

"You may," he said. "If you like."

She slipped her fingertips beneath his waistband to snap open buttons. Her nails pressed gently into the flesh of his flank. Her knuckles worked against his belly. She opened the flap of his underdrawers.

His breath rushed, a trapped spate of water in a floodtide. He sought absolute darkness and plunged, until his breath became deep and even, like the stroke of a strong swimmer. Desire sank, purged, to the depths. Control was easy, simple. However his body might react, he was in charge.

Her fingertips outlined the hollow beside his hipbone, strayed across the fine down on his belly. She tugged his drawers down his thighs and off over his feet.

"You have hair here, too," she whispered. "All the way up your legs and around your—"

Her voice faltered, agonized, fascinated.

"My privy member. Men are made differently from women."

"Yes," she said. "It's very strange."

She was trembling like a lily: moonlit dress, moonlit hair, and shaking as if her heart thundered. Yet she put out her fingers to touch his naked flesh.

Thoughts fled. Control slipped in the face of a mass of vulnerable emotions. Perhaps he was not really in his right mind, after all? He must retreat, before she plummeted him into an unforeseen intimacy. Yet inexorably, the blood pooled and stirred beneath her seeking fingers in scalding, blissful urgency.

She snatched her hand away.

"Oh," she said. "What's happening to you?"

Jack clung to detachment, though his erection throbbed with its own delight.

"I'm aroused by your touch," he said. "More than I planned. It's all right. You're safe. I shan't act on it."

"That doesn't hurt?"

Wry amusement cavorted. "No, it feels wonderful."

She met his gaze. Suddenly she smiled back, the tip of her nose dipping. Even in the moonlight, he knew she was pink from her neck to her earlobes: pink and flushed and flustered. Yet she leaned forward to stroke one finger around the sensitive rim. Vibrant with longing, his erection leaped to meet her touch.

"Oh," she said, snatching away her hand as if he burned her. "It's so hot! And . . . and alive!"

He swallowed, searching for the knife edge between desire and detachment, allowing only mirth as a balance. "Most men would say that it has a life of its own—"

"You refer to such an amazing part of yourself in the third person?"

"All men have pet names for it," he said. "As if it belonged to someone else, someone they aren't quite responsible for."

"What kinds of names?"

He winked. "Boys' names, and other words no lady should know."

"But it feels good for it to grow like that?"

"What does it feel like to you when you touch me?"

With an intense focus, she cupped her palm over his shaft, her fingertips straying back to the head. The touch blazed as if she were on fire. The breath poured scalding from his lungs.

"So smooth and velvety, like hot satin over steel."

"That's not what I meant—" Ecstasy thrilled through his blood. He clamped a hand over her wrist. "Enough!"

He was present. Now. Here. He was naked. His erection reared against his belly. And she was a virgin.

She pulled back. "I hurt you?"

Jack sat up and took her hot fingers in his. "No, you brought me great pleasure, but perhaps you've learned enough?"

"Yes." Her gaze met his bravely. "I'm not afraid at all of your body. You're beautiful. Your . . . your privy member is lovely. I like it."

He groaned. He didn't want to, but the sound ground up from his throat as if he had been struck, then he dropped his head and laughed.

"Good," he said. "I wanted you to lose your fear, to like it and welcome it, only not mine—"

She turned her back. Her nape gleamed beneath skeins of tangled hair. Her breath rattled, in short little puffs.

"So now I know how a man is made, which makes a certain sense out of some of the things my mother hinted. Thank you, Jack. It is, really, rather remarkable. You liked being touched there?"

"Very much. Though I have more control than most, I'm not immune to the desires of the flesh, Miss Marsh."

Her neck curved, vulnerable and lovely, as she turned her head. "Neither," she whispered, "am I."

"Then you've learned something of great value," he said gently.

"But I don't know how it ends. I feel frantic, on fire—it's rather frightening!"

Jack swung his feet to the floor and knotted the discarded shirt about his waist. A wave of giddiness almost felled him. He leaned his shoulders against the wall, while his ironic mirth mutated into a kind of hidden hilarity. He was longing a little too desperately for orgasm, and he couldn't even see well enough to make it alone down the stairs?

"Don't be afraid. I can show you what you want to know. I can do it without harm to you. I just don't think that I should."

"Why not?" She slid from the bed and stood facing him. "Why didn't you warn me that I would feel like this?"

He tried in vain to control the dizziness. "I said you might feel things that you'd never felt before."

"If you did, I didn't know what that meant. I'm burning as if I had an ague and . . . and it aches. All over, but especially here." She pressed one palm over her heart, then waved her hands vaguely below her waist. "Yet it's somehow enchanting and urgent, as well!"

The dark cave where he had first begun not to exist was waiting. Blackness closed safely around him. Arousal dissolved, existence dissolved, until he was entirely empty and calm, and his swirling vision became irrelevant.

"That's only natural," he said.

"But I can't breathe!"

The cave trickled and dripped with water. Stone pushed hard beneath his head and shoulder and hip. It was not safe to light a fire and it was cold, cold. So cold that a man could survive only if he ceased to be real. And so he must remain light and amused instead, because mirth was all that was left.

He opened his eyes and smiled at her. The lights flickered, but it no longer mattered. "Thanks to those injudicious stays!"

"They feel like armor," she said.

"They're making your heart hurt."

"My corsets?"

"Your confusion is making your heart hurt. The things you don't understand."

"I'm not afraid of your body," she said. "But I am afraid of these feelings. I don't know what they mean, or what to do with them."

"They cannot harm you—your body's natural reactions."

She glimmered—clear and sparkling, like a waterfall—standing bravely beside the bed. "Then will you teach me about that, too?"

"I cannot do so without trespassing beyond what modesty should permit, Miss Marsh. You would allow that?"

"Yes. Yes, I would. After what I just . . . after what you just allowed me to do . . . if I were to hide behind modesty now, I would only prove that I'm spineless and weak. Wouldn't it give you any pleasure at all to teach me?"

"It would give me the greatest pleasure."

"But you think it's disloyal of me?"

"Your loyalty and your promises and your modesty are not at issue. Knowledge by itself admits neither virtue nor sin."

She turned away, hugging her arms about herself. "Then you will show me?"

The flashing lights faded. He began to return to his feelings and found nothing but a humble, aching desire to please her.

"Yes, if you like. After all, you're in charge. When we return to civilization, this will anyway seem no more real than a dream."

"It already feels like a dream."

As if swimming through moonlight, he walked up behind her and set both hands on her shoulders. His fingertips strayed over her nape and smoothed up her throat. She trembled beneath his touch, her skin blazing. Her woman's scent curled into his nostrils: smoke and rain and lavender and musk. Jack bent to kiss her neck, as if he were a supplicant. A gasp vibrated through her body.

"Your hair is a gilt mist," he said. "Your spine is elegant and tender, like a gazelle's. Why do you wear clothes that hurt you?"

"I don't know." Her breasts rose and fell. "It's just what's considered proper."

"If you're to breathe at all," he said, "I must free you from all this mad binding."

She trembled beneath his hands and dropped her head forward. "Yes."

He unbuttoned the fastenings on her dress. It slithered through his fingers to the floor. The sound echoed in his memory: the sound of blue or gold or ivory—silk on silk on silk—falling away beneath his seeking hands.

Her neck grew warmer, as if a furnace had been stoked. He set both palms on her waist, over the harsh whalebone. The stiff satin was wickedly appealing. A corset was more than just proper female attire. Slick and lace-trimmed and feminine, it was also fuel to the tinder of eroticism, an impious lure to the simple-minded male beast.

He swallowed his smile. "This carapace. I may remove it?"

She nodded, fiery and trembling. Beneath the corset she wore nothing but a thin shift.

Jack began to pull out the laces. Awareness blazed as his knuckles rubbed over the swell of her bottom. Warm and female beneath the linen. His thumbs hooked lacing from eyelets: the sweet depression of her spine and the soft flesh at her waist. The next set: the resilient arc of her ribs, rising and falling in broken, erotic rhythms. The next: the flushed, delicate curve between her shoulder blades.

She dropped her head forward and shivered, her nape tender and graceful. Her skin burned beneath his fingers.

A blaze of white-hot desire flamed in his groin. The male ecstasy. *Enjoy it!*

Jack reached around to untie the little bows where her shoulder straps fastened at the front. He arched his wrists, yet his fingertips must inexorably follow the valley between her breasts, his hands shadow her panting, delectable curves. The bows fell apart. She released one quick breath, like an arrow shot from a bow.

Her corset sprang open, sundered like a broken shell. He caught and held it. Her nipples rose beneath her shift to press directly into his palms.

He was erect, hard as steel, wanting her.

Night air rushed back into her lungs, as exhilarating as plum brandy. Cool moonlight flowed over her flesh as if she bathed in the Milky Way. Yet she was burning. Her skin scorched and her blood ran like liquid copper. No one had seen her without her corset before, not even her mother, since childhood.

Anne knew it ought to feel wicked. It did. Very wicked. To allow a man, a stranger, to remove that shell of satin and whalebone, to lift the cruel burden from her heart. Yet how could a dream be either bad or good? How could anything that happened here be real enough to matter?

He was a hero, her hero.

And the honeyed ache in her core had become all consuming.

He stood frozen behind her with the open corset caught in both hands. His palms tickled her nipples. Powerful pleasure plummeted to her groin. Her breasts burned with exquisite promise, the tips rising and puckering, an ineffable sweetness, wanting more. Anne stood in her stockings and chemise and stared at her feet, her heart hammering.

The room breathed silence, as if the moon, too, held its breath. The moment stretched. His steady breathing eased over her shoulder, even and controlled, though hers rushed like a river in spate. At last he inhaled once and tugged away the remaining laces. As he breathed out again, her corset clunked to the floor.

Free from constraint, her shift caressed her skin like a thousand fairy fingers, raising goose bumps. Anne closed her eyes. Hot blood seared her cheeks. Her breasts felt swollen and warm and lovely. Her blood pooled in rapturous eddies in places without names.

She had looked at him. Touched him. He had allowed her eyes and hands to feast at will on the wonder of his body, even in the most private, vulnerable places. He was so beautiful. Perfect. Yet to remove her chemise and let him see her naked, as she had seen him! A sweetly wicked shame flared at the thought, making her feel weak and helpless and—willing?

Yet nothing had ever given her courage—since this adventure had begun—except his presence and the trust she felt in it. She bit her lip and crossed her palms over her aching breasts. Her pulse hammered.

"You would take off my chemise?"

"You're more beautiful than water in the desert." His voice was husky. "But you may keep your pretty shift."

His hands caressed lightly as he collected her hair, smoothing it away from her shoulders. The breath rushed from her lungs.

The ache in her belly gathered strength, becoming fiery and heavy, threatening to peel all the strength from her knees.

His fingertips stroked up her scalp. Hot shivers raced like demons down her spine. He combed out the tangled tresses with his fingers. Light, fleeting touches over her neck, the base of her skull, her earlobes. Her breathing launched into a race with her pulse, and yet somewhere in her heart deep ripples of relaxation spread and spread, soothing the panicked rhythms. Night filled her lungs, as if she inhaled starlight directly into her blood, as if she breathed in a kind of brilliant ecstasy.

"That feels nice," she said. "Lovely."

He set both palms on her waist, his fingers burning onto the swell of her hips. "And you're almost breathing at last, Miss Marsh."

His hands stroked back up, rubbing, kneading. Her thighs trembled with a terrible weakness. Her arms dropped to her sides as his hands brushed past her breasts, up, up to her collarbones. He cupped her throat gently, turning her head just a little so that it rested in the hollow of his shoulder.

"Smile," he said. "The tip of your nose dips a little when you smile. I like it."

Anne bit her lip, helpless, overwhelmed. She was filled with moonlight, yet she was burning and trembling as he slid his arms under her knees and shoulders, and lifted her onto the bed. Moonlight slid over his features, the unfathomable shadowed eyes, the entrancing smile, then wavered like a guttering candle as moving clouds plunged them both into darkness.

The mattress gave under his weight. The lean stretch of his thighs beside hers fired an intense, mysterious awareness. Anne curled against him and thought that his heartbeat merged into her own. She was breathing freely at last, though she rested against that resilient, lovely male nakedness—and between her legs the most urgent demand of all still throbbed, honeyed and hot and profound.

He brushed lightly over her linen shift, as if to savor the curve of her waist before setting his palm over that tender, unmentionable place.

"This place is the heart of your pleasure," he said. "Safe in warm darkness, deep inside. It's the cause of all your heat and heaviness and yearning. Once you know where it ends, you'll never be afraid of your own body again. Nor will you truly be innocent. Do you want that?"

"Yes," she said. "I don't want a life of . . . of hurried fumbling. I want to understand—"

"Then keep breathing and let yourself flow with the sensations. Whatever you feel, nothing can harm you. The instinctive reactions of the body are only wonderful and natural and good. You agree, just for this one lesson?"

"Yes," she said. "I believe in you."

He was silent for a moment, as if she had just said something unutterably clumsy, but then she felt his breath warm and soft on her cheek.

"Then hush, Miss Marsh, and let it happen."

An odd sense of humility had washed through his heart. She believed him. She believed *in* him. *I think you're a hero, like someone in a story.* Naive, simple-hearted Miss Marsh, who trusted the promises of a naked man with an erection!

His body pulsed with importunate ardor, yet Jack had spent long, hard years learning every nuance of self-control. So for just this once, he thought he believed in himself. If he forgot, even for a moment, who she was—and what he owed to whatever was left of his tattered sense of honor—the cave was waiting.

He stroked her hair away from her forehead and smoothed his fingertips around her jaw. His thumb painted her portrait in the dark—her chin and the corner of her mouth. Tender and supple and warm. Her pulse fluttered.

Jack lowered his head and kissed it, the sensitive place where her skin quivered over the vein.

"Oh!" The sound, tremulous and trusting, pierced his heart like an arrow.

He trailed small kisses over her jaw and earlobe, nuzzling, inhaling the heat and lavender emanating from her flesh, while his hand strayed over her flank. Lovely, slender, female curves.

"Oh," she said again.

"Hush. Hush. Don't talk. Just breathe. They're only sensations. Fleeting and temporary. They can't harm you. Enjoy them."

Jack smoothed his palm up her bare arm, lingering for a moment on the inside of her elbow. He followed the caress of his fingers with his lips, kissing the sweet, soft flesh in the erotic little arch where the pulse hovered just beneath the surface. Meanwhile, his seeking hands filled with the wonder of her curves, moving up over her woman's belly where her skin burned like a flame beneath her thin shift. Her breathing skipped a beat, then settled into a darker, deeper rhythm. Her flank, her navel, her waist, shapes that tantalized and disturbed and filled him with delight.

He kissed the corner of her mouth. She turned her head blindly, seeking with soft lips and a hot, moist tongue. He circled, teasing, then met her open lips with his own, mobile and supple and eager.

As their tongues touched, Jack trailed his fingertips over one small breast, tracing the round, even shape. She lay back helplessly to allow his exploration, whimpering with pleasure. His hands worshipped. His lips whispered tales of adoration. His arousal nudged against her bare thigh.

With harsh determination he clung to the core of his control. This—all this—was only for her. To help her learn to find her release. Not his. Not now. Not with her.

Yet his hands roamed as if sculpting, his mouth as if feasting. First one breast with its tightly hardening little nipple, then the other. He smoothed his thumb over the shift where it hid her intimate curls. Her flesh caught fire. An answering flame scorched in his groin. Slowly he smoothed his fingertips up her thigh, knowing she was hot and moist and ready. He rubbed his palm in small circles as a yearning compassion threatened to shatter his restraint.

Her pleasure flamed and throbbed beneath his hand. She writhed beneath him and reached for his body with stunning charity, firing passion and potency and hunger.

Now! Find the empty darkness of the cave! Now, Jack!

But her palms swept from his shoulders to stroke down to his buttocks, scorching his mind with a soul-destroying, oddly vulnerable lust. Lights flickered and danced. Lavender filled his nostrils. Her fingers strayed with tentative, searing little touches to caress his rigid penis. The intensity of the pleasure blinded him, as if the doors of rapture were suddenly flung open. Bright, imperious, the sweet demands of an ineffable bliss! His heart broke open in wonder.

Jack fought like a drowning man fights the water—overwhelmed by the infinite power of the ocean, striving in heartbroken helplessness for air—and descended instead into madness.

CHAPTER EIGHT

S HE KNEW ONLY THIS DEEP TREMBLING, HER LIMBS SHAKING beneath his questing hands. His lips fired her with wondrous, burning sensations. Sparks seared all the forbidden, unknown secrets of her body. His fingertips strayed back to her nipples, circling and tugging, a pleasure so intense she cried out.

Then his palm stroked up her thigh once again to the heart of her longing.

Only sensations. Fleeting and temporary. They can't harm you . . . can't harm you . . . can't harm you. Enjoy them!

Yet it was all so profound and intense and terrifying and breathtaking. Sensations she had never imagined. Feelings that overwhelmed and negated and urged, until coherent thought fled—

Long skeins of her hair were caught in his fingers and ensnarled about their wrists. They were tangled together, caught together, in a web of hot need. She was vaguely aware that her shift was crushed up around her waist, that her most intimate self lay naked and exposed.

Yet he was so lovely! His back felt strong and hot and alive beneath her palms. His tongue thrust and licked, his mouth demanded and devastated. His silken, burning shaft rubbed against the nameless place between her legs, firing an exquisite flame that yearned only for more.

Blindly she stroked the firm arc of his buttocks and ground her hips to trap his hard male organ against her belly. His tongue danced with hers, hot and bruised and eager, only breaking away to suckle at one nipple, then the other. Helpless need plummeted its strange loveliness straight down to her groin. The scalding ecstasy between her legs built and built, until suddenly her building pleasure knew exactly what it wanted.

"Yes," she said. "Yes!"

As if seeking for themselves, her fingers found the wonder of his mysterious male organ. She rubbed the head against her own fiery center. Sensations built and shattered in rolling breakers of ecstasy, but it wasn't enough, there must be more—surely there was more? She opened her legs and lifted her hips.

"Yes," she said again. "Everything! Oh, please, please, don't stop! I want to know everything."

For a split second she felt his hesitation, but then, firm and hot and lovely, he pushed himself deep into her body.

*H*E DIVED STRAIGHT INTO BLISS. HER HANDS CLUTCHED his shoulders and she cried out, a small inarticulate cry. Every fiber of his being craved her brightness and acceptance and pure generosity. His heart seared by tenderness, he slid deeper. Hot. Silken. *Yes!*

A profound, wicked pleasure, so absolute and overwhelming he thought he might almost be falling in love.

So good! So very, very good!

Negating the cave, negating the years of harsh control and bitter humiliation, brilliance possessed him. *Yes!* As if blind, as if infatuated, intellect silenced, in one flawless, exquisite slide, he thrust all the way home. She gasped in his ear and lay quivering beneath him. Then, vibrating like a violin, she moved her hips to caress him back. Untutored and liberal and scalding in intensity. *Yes!*

His mind took flight, leaving only the body—in thrall to the sacred skills of sensual pleasure—to seek and find without restraint.

His hands stroked, his mouth suckled. Her breasts shaped round and full in his palms. Her nipples rose and hardened. Her flank ran smooth beneath his fingertips. His mouth kissed hers, their tongues soaked in honey, while her hands grasped his arms and her bare legs wrapped about his.

His penis pulsated inside her, kissing her womb. His mind lay silent and open, consumed by the pure flame of desire. His thumb tantalized. While his penis explored and thrust without restraint, his fingers slid on her moisture, a clever torment designed to fire all the wicked little places that shocked and besieged. She shuddered her rapture, deep inside, and dug her nails into his buttocks. *Yes!*

He was the Traveler of Chinese wisdom: *the mountain remains while flames rise above it.* As if he flung himself helplessly from that mountaintop only to catapult straight up into the stars, his spirit wheeled over and over in star-studded darkness. And she soared with him, open and loving and compassionate, accepting everything, judging nothing, until he plunged down at last into the rainbow tumult of their mutual release.

He felt stunned, as if something fragile and precious in his soul had just shattered.

Still buried in their shared moisture, he kissed her mouth once again.

His lips found a tiny trace of salt. In a blind trance he smoothed the hair away from her forehead and touched her cheek with his tongue. A little track of moisture.

Tears! Bravely withheld, but now leaking slowly down her face.

The stars flickered and faded, leaving him nothing but blackness, colored only by lavender and weeping.

Then he knew exactly what he'd done.

In absolute silence Jack eased himself from her body. He tugged her useless shift back down to her knees. There was nothing to say. His shame was so profound he must doubt his own sanity. *The Traveler, whose only safety is within himself. If he ever forgets, weeping and lamentation will result.* Yet whatever bitter recriminations might flood his broken mind now, it was too late.

So he enfolded her in his arms, offering whatever wordless comfort might be left, as her tears dampened his hot skin.

"I'm sorry," he said.

She turned her face into his shoulder and cried herself to sleep.

Sunlight flooded into the room, streaming warmth across the bed. Anne sensed it through her closed lids and wondered for a moment why she felt afraid. Birds chattered and trilled outside in a mad cacophony, but the lack of human sound was absolute.

She knew before she opened her eyes that he was gone, and that the fairy gold had already turned into dust.

Her eyes hurt. Her mouth tasted sour. The mysterious place between her legs ached with a dull new awareness. The quilt tangled as she sat up. The bedroom yawned, empty of life except for dust motes, dancing in the sunbeams. Her mind reeled at the memory of an ineffable sweetness.

She had sinned. She had welcomed it. She was ruined.

Her corset and Mrs. Kenyon's dress were draped over a chair. Steam rose from a jug on the washstand. Anne pushed herself from the bed and padded over to it: warm water for washing, with fresh soap and towels, and clean cold water in a basin. So he had not been gone long. He was probably downstairs.

She glanced back at the bed. Her head throbbed. A small stain marked the sheet. Using the cold water, Anne worked at obliterating the offending smudges. It was not the right time for her courses to start. This trace of blood meant something quite different.

It meant that she was hurt, violated, though it had not felt like a hurt at the time. Far from it!

Anne dropped onto a chair and buried her face in both hands.

He was *sorry*! He regretted it. Of course.

She had not understood what happened between a man and a woman in the marriage bed. Now she did.

Your loyalty and your promises and your modesty are not at issue. Knowledge by itself admits neither virtue nor sin.

There was a difference, of course, between knowledge and action. Naive, foolish, stupid, she had trusted in Lord Jonathan—*Wild Lord Jack!*—and been betrayed.

The water was getting cold. Anne forced herself to walk back to the washstand. She stripped off her crumpled chemise and scrubbed herself all over, then dressed again, layer by layer, before brushing out and securing her hair. A plain young lady with a long nose stared back at her from the mirror. She did not look different. Not different at all, except for some little frown lines between her eyebrows. With two fingers she smoothed them out.

Whether he was waiting downstairs or not, she must face the day—and the rest of her life. She was no longer a virgin. She had betrayed all of her promises to Arthur. All of her parents' expectations, her sisters' admiration. Distress beat at her, as if a dark bird were trapped in her mind. She had been ravished. But, like any wanton, she had embraced it.

A crash echoed up from the kitchen, followed by the sound of rending wood and screeching metal. Anne froze. She must think! Yet there was little reason left. Only these desperate, swooping emotions, defying her attempts at composure. The noise stopped. She forced herself to walk to the window. The morning sun shone peacefully on a watery world. Nothing seemed changed.

Silence stretched, broken only by a slight echo of footsteps and crockery clinking.

She closed her eyes and sought for the quiet voice. *See it through, Annie!*

The dark bird bated frantically, but taking three deep breaths—searching for calm and control, just as Jack had shown her—Miss Anne Marsh of Hawthorn Axbury turned from the window and marched down the stairs.

It was perhaps the bravest thing she had ever done in her life.

T HE DOOR TO THE PANTRY STOOD OPEN, BROKEN FROM ITS hinges. A jug of milk sat on the kitchen table, cooled with a wet cloth. Beside the jug several slices of bread were arranged on a plate. The fire blazed merrily in the grate, a kettle bubbling over it. A long-handled wood-cutting ax lay against the door that led outside.

Jack stood, arms folded, beside it.

He was devastating: the angel fallen, but still cloaked in desire. His hair tumbled darkly over the storybook features. His eyes still echoed the fascination of tigers, powerful, lithe, and stalking in the shadows. A gaze that seemed remote, grave, without any hint of derision, though something she could not recognize hovered at the corners of his mouth. Something that made her heart quail and robbed her of courage.

"Your washing water I gathered outside," he said. "But there was clean drinking water in a crock in the pantry. The tea caddy also offers its treasures. I pried it open with a knife."

Anne sat down at the table and felt the color rise in her face, not simply embarrassment, but a clear, cold anger. What had she expected? An apology? Reassurances? At the very least, some recognition of what they had done.

"You wrought all this destruction with that ax?"

"Destruction would seem to be my stock-in-trade."

"Please," she said. "Just leave me alone."

Perhaps he flinched. Perhaps he was anyway already turning away. "Please drink your tea and eat breakfast, Miss Marsh. You're going to need it."

He lifted the ax. His steps echoed in the hallway. Hinges squeaked, but there was no thud of a door closing.

Anne stared at the table. Her stomach churned at the thought of food, but she wanted tea. Hot and strong and sobering. Something other than despair to sustain her.

* * *

JACK WALKED OUT INTO THE GARDEN TO LET THE SUN assault him. Even the pitiful English sun, watered and delicate, was too strong. He leaned back against the porch wall and squinted out across the flooded clearing.

All the colorful warp and weave of his plans had just frayed into a heap of dry dust. He had no one to blame but himself. Yet he felt incredulous at the thought of what he'd done, as if he had just witnessed someone else, someone trusted and strong, suddenly disintegrating. As if need had simply torn him apart.

Apology was obviously absurd. Explanations even more so: *I was not in my right mind. I intended something quite different. I simply cannot fathom— And yet it only happened because it was you.*

None of that mattered. It could not be changed, and so the future—his and hers—had imploded, trapping them both in a nightmare. *Destruction would seem to be my stock-in-trade.*

He strode to the stable to put away the ax. He had destroyed an Englishwoman's innocence, taken her virginity. What the devil had possessed him?

A splash. Jack stepped back out into the sunshine. Wending slowly across the pool that cut off the cottage from the woods, the world had already arrived. A horseman was dragging a boat and leading a second saddle horse, the water up to the horses' knees.

Jack stood perfectly still and allowed the man to come, bringing reality into focus with him.

"Good morning." Guy rode up beside the garden wall. "I've come to play knight errant. Or were you planning on rescuing yourselves?"

"From this particular white space on the map? Alas, there's no escape. Here, too, there be dragons."

Guy stared at him for a moment. "What the devil happened to you?"

Jack touched a hand to his forehead, the black-and-blue skin beneath the fall of his hair. "An argument with a tree."

"Not with your nasty friends from Cathay?"

"I argued with them, too, but in that happy circumstance, most of the damage was inflicted in the other direction. You found Farmer Osgood's gig in the lane?"

Guy swung down from his horse to secure the reins to the gate. "And the pony, cropping grass half a mile away. When you didn't arrive at Wyldshay, Ryder thought you might have taken shelter here."

Jack gazed at the second horse, the empty saddle. "He didn't come with you?"

"Your mother thought it best this way."

"So as few witnesses as possible will observe for themselves that Miss Marsh and myself spent the night here unchaperoned—even my own brother? Ryder doesn't think that I've fled back to Kabul?"

"And abandoned Miss Marsh? Hardly!"

Jack walked up to the horses. He ran a hand over each dark nose.

Standing quietly in the shadows, Anne watched from the doorway. The outside world had arrived and she was going to have to face it. Not hand-in-hand with her hero. Alone. But first she must gather a little more courage.

The horses—a bay and a chestnut—sighed as if Jack were a

necromancer. She had no idea what he was thinking. He was cradled in calm sunshine, his expression remote.

"Miss Rachel Wren," he said. "The kitchen maid. So absolutely in your power. Did you ravish her?"

"Are you serious?" Guy seemed genuinely startled. "No, all your plans went like clockwork. We enjoyed our sail in the bay. Then we returned as ourselves, to the confusion of your enemies."

"Not quite enough confusion," Jack said. "They laid an ambush at the Withy Bridge. A similar trap probably waited on every approach to Wyldshay. Fortunately, the confusion you created was enough to limit both their numbers and their effectiveness. Thank you for that."

"Glad to be of service. If you'd been followed directly, an attack in full force might have been lethal."

Each horse dropped its head beneath the caressing palms. Remembrance fired in Anne's heart. Like a dumb beast she, too, had been captivated by that exquisite touch. Even now—even after what he had done—she was enthralled by the sheer beauty of the lines of his back.

"And Miss Wren?" Jack asked.

"I paid her a pretty little fortune, as we agreed, and she left."

"Not back to the kitchen, then?"

"She took the next stage for London."

"Ah," Jack said. "So we have one happy ending, at least."

Anne's body trembled as if she were being buffeted by an invisible wind. As she reached out a hand to steady herself, Guy Devoran looked up and saw her. For a moment she felt pinned. Surely he would instantly know what had happened? He would see her sin in her face and know that she had condemned herself to ignominy. Yet he bowed.

"More than that! You're safe. And I see that Miss Marsh looks none the worse for wear. So two happy endings." Guy strode up to Anne and bowed again. "Your servant, ma'am."

"As you see, Miss Marsh," Jack said, though storm clouds gathered darkly in his eyes. "We are rescued."

OUNTED ON THE CHESTNUT, JACK HAULED HER through the flooded meadows in the boat, Guy's bay splashing at his side. The men conversed in low voices, too softly for her to hear. Anne clutched at the wooden rail and tried to think. She had always enjoyed a certain autonomy, even when living at home with her family. She made the decisions about where she would walk, what she would do with her days, which rocks were worth adding to her fossil collection. Now she was being carried along helplessly behind the man who had ravished her, because no other options had presented themselves. And it was all her fault.

She knew Jack did not love her or care for her in any personal way. He'd made a mistake that he obviously regretted. A mistake that could not be undone, whatever the power of his family. Would they offer her money? Would they try to force Arthur to marry her anyway? Oh, God. Arthur! The only truly innocent victim in all this, he'd be devastated when he learned why she had to cry off.

And how could she explain? That in a moment of madness she had done something that was contrary to everything she had ever believed about herself, everything she had ever been taught?

Anxiety and shame surged and pounded like waves against the Cobb. She had invited it—though perhaps she had not quite

understood what she was inviting. She wanted to go home to beg
her father to forgive her. Instead she was being taken to Wyldshay
to face the family of a duke.

At the end of the valley they reached higher ground. A carriage
stood waiting. The coachman, tigers, and four outriders were
boastfully armed.

"Guy is the best of conspirators," Jack said as he helped her
from the boat to the carriage. "He's brought us an army. Another
hour, Miss Marsh, and you'll be safely in my mother's care."

She met his dark gaze. In spite of everything, her heart turned
over. "That's supposed to reassure me?"

"The duchess took lessons long ago from Athene—and my
mother is more reliable than I am, it would seem."

"Is what's at issue between us a matter of reliability?"

"Yes, in large part." The remorse in his eyes threatened to
break her heart. "I promised something and I broke my promise."

Anne's cheeks began to burn as the truth began to flare in her
heart. "It was as much my fault as yours."

"That's a matter for debate," he said.

"If you deny that I was an equal partner in what happened,
then there's nothing left to say."

The sun gleamed on his dark hair as he looked away into the
woods. Tight creases marked the corners of his mouth. "On the
contrary, there's everything to say. Yet you're still in shock—as I
am, I suppose. You're better without my company."

He swung back onto his mount. The coachman whipped up
the team. Jack and Guy rode out in front, leading the way.

Anne leaned back against the squabs. Regret streamed like a
drumbeat. For one night of blissful excitement, she had destroyed
her entire future—and Arthur's! Though there would never be

enough time to make sense of what she'd done, she was afraid of what would happen next. She tried to breathe deeply, to find some solace and peace in the quiet place in her heart.

See it through, Annie! What strangely bad advice that had been!

The carriage bowled along the lanes to the rhythmic beat of the horses' hooves. They left the woods. Fields of wheat and barley alternated with hedged enclosures pasturing cattle or horses. The armed outriders bunched tightly about the carriage. Her thoughts tumbled and tossed, like twigs in a stream.

It was a lover and his lass, With a hey, and a ho, and a hey nonny no,
That o'er the green cornfield did pass—

A lover? What had she ever understood that to mean? Some vague notion of a meeting of souls? Certainly not that intoxicating melding of the flesh! She tried to think calmly, but soon the words of another song began to repeat over and over in her head and refused to be silenced:

Sigh no more, ladies, sigh no more; Men were deceivers ever:
One foot in sea and one on shore, To one thing constant never:
Then sigh not so, But let them go, And be you blithe and bonny;
Converting all your sounds of woe into hey nonny, nonny.

A ditty from *Much Ado About Nothing*! Perhaps the first message she had heard—only yesterday morning!—was the only meaningful one that was left, after all: *See it through, Annie!* What else could she do?

Yet her brain still ran madly on that one refrain: *Men were deceivers ever—*

The carriage swayed into a wide turn.

Anne peered from the window. Their road had been running

for some time alongside a high stone wall, the tops of trees springing green on the other side, but now the carriage turned more sharply and stopped. Wrought-iron gates blocked their way. The gate pillars were topped with dragons, each writhing beast pinned with a stone spear in an eternal death agony. The driveway beyond disappeared into parkland.

A grizzled man had already run from the gatehouse, his face lit with excitement.

"Lord Jonathan!" Tears stood in the gatekeeper's eyes. "Welcome home, my lord! Welcome home! They say you have traveled the whole blessed world!"

One foot in sea and one on shore, To one thing constant never . . .

Jack leaned from the saddle and shook the man's eagerly extended hand. While they talked, Guy Devoran rode up to the coach window. Anne forced her attention back to Jack's cousin.

"Your servant, Miss Marsh," Guy said. "We must say good-bye, I'm afraid. I have pressing concerns of my own elsewhere, as well as one more little errand to perform for my mad cousin."

The gatekeeper had run to swing open the gates. Jack rode up beside Guy. The men shook hands.

And be you blithe and bonny . . .

Anne forced herself to smile and extended her own hand through the carriage window. "I must also thank you for your assistance, Mr. Devoran," she said. "Godspeed!"

Guy cantered off along the road. Jack sat his horse in absolute silence and watched until his cousin's mount disappeared around a bend.

The carriage horses blew and shifted. The outriders waited.

At last Jack gave a signal. The carriage sprang forward. Deer scattered as the wheels crunched on raked gravel. The country seat of the dukes of Blackdown loomed twenty minutes later. Reflections shimmered, creating rippling mirror images of every crenellation and gargoyle. Wyldshay Castle was an island, a small city of towers all contained within massive battlement-encrusted walls soaring straight from the depths of a lake.

The Blackdown coat of arms fluttered in the breeze. A scattering of modern windows softened a few of the high towers. Jack's home. A medieval fortress. For seven or eight hundred years a private sanctuary, a bastion of power and privilege—and a prison. Impregnable, defended by pooling water and accessed by a single arched bridge.

Converting all your sounds of woe into hey nonny, nonny—

The horses clattered over the bridge and beneath a stone archway, where the teeth of a portcullis still threatened. In the courtyard beyond, the carriage pulled up before another arched doorway, where two massive oak doors had been designed long ago to intimidate. Yet a livery-clad footman let down the carriage steps. The outriders disappeared. Jack swung from his mount, handed the reins to a groom, and walked up to Anne.

"Don't be afraid," he said. "You'll be safe here, and whatever it is possible to mend will be mended."

Anne folded her hands and took a deep breath. "I'm a little concerned, as you may imagine, my lord, by the reaction of your family to my arrival. I don't know any of the rules that dukes live by, except the one that we've already broken."

"The rule that I—not you—have already broken is the only one that should apply to all classes," he said. "There are two kinds of people who ignore all the rest: criminals and the families of dukes. They are upon occasion the same thing."

The heavy oak doors swung back. Flanked by more bewigged

footmen, a woman stood framed in the opening. She walked forward with both hands extended.

"I have come down to welcome you to Wyldshay myself, Miss Marsh," she said. "I am the duchess."

Jack's mother moved like a whippet, small and slender and fired with intensity. Her hair shone in tones of pale gold and wheat, a shimmering, upswept mass framing an almost unlined face. Yet the white skin and the ethereal blond hair were belied by leaf-green eyes, a stunning emerald clarity that might have gazed down from a pagan idol.

Anne dropped into a deep curtsy. "Your Grace!"

Ignoring her son, the duchess grasped Anne by both hands to pull her gently to her feet. "You have no doubt suffered quite an ordeal, my dear," she said. "It is over now. Come!"

Anne glanced back as the duchess led her inside. Remaining absolutely still, Jack stood watching them leave. As if she felt his gaze drilling into her back, the duchess stopped and turned, still holding Anne by the hand.

"Your siblings are gathered in the blue salon, Lord Jonathan," she said. "They are so anxious to see you that I had Ryderbourne corral them. As soon as Miss Marsh is safely ensconced in her room, by all means ask your brother to unlock the door and allow them to mob you."

"And the duke?" Jack asked. "Guy said he'd been ill."

The whippet slenderness quivered. "Blackdown insisted on being carried into his study in the Fortune Tower. He awaits you there. It is up to you to decide which door you wish to open first."

Though he smiled, thunder hovered about his dark hair. "Yours," Jack said.

But the duchess had already turned away to lead Anne up the stairs.

THE FOOTMEN STOOD IMPASSIVE. THE WALLS OF THE CAStle brooded in silence. Jack hesitated for only a moment, allowing the force of it all to wash over him like breaking surf, until at last the wave receded and receded, leaving him still standing. *For God's sake, Mother!*

Swallowing his emotion, he strode into the soaring Great Hall. Antique weapons and armor hung from every wall. Around the huge fireplace, stone dragons expired forever beneath the inexorable power of the St. Georges. Jack stopped to look at them. As monsters they had a certain charm, tongues wagging, eyes rolling, but the carved spears that impaled them were all too convincing.

He took a deep breath. What the hell had he expected from the duchess? Open arms? Maternal tears? In front of a stranger? A stranger whom he had just ravished?

His mother's heart had never been worn on her exquisite sleeve. Not even in her green goddess eyes. But he knew the rhythm that underlay its fast beat. Her younger son had returned. He was alive and unharmed. She did not want him to leave again. Whatever Jack had done, she would defend him like a tigress protecting its last cub. But she wouldn't hesitate to cuff him about a little first.

With one last glance at the St. George motto, the stone worn away until it was unreadable, Jack walked swiftly beneath arched doorways and through innumerable chambers and parlors. Ceilings soared, walls glittered with gilt and stucco and masterpieces of art. He ran up one great curving staircase, then another.

The final narrow spiral stair was carved into the ancient heart of the castle. The doors here were blackened with age and studded with brass. Jack rapped hard with his knuckles on oak planks nearly two inches thick.

"Come!"

The door groaned on its hinges. The round room beyond filled an entire floor in the Fortune Tower. Shafts of sunlight spilled from narrow windows to illuminate bookshelves and tables and portraits, a maroon-and-green rug, brass lamps, and the rigid figure of the single occupant.

Jack's father sat wrapped in a bathrobe, rugs tucked over his knees, in an upright wooden seat that might have belonged once to Charlemagne. So his father, too, seemed determined to intimidate! And why this room? Because it symbolized the last bastion of strength for an aging man?

"Well," the duke said. "The prodigal returns."

His Grace the Duke of Blackdown was several years older than his wife. Silver-streaked hair webbed above the fine bones of his face. Bones he had bequeathed to his sons, sharpened by a lifetime of power, though the deeply set eyes seemed to have seen a great deal of life and mostly found it wanting.

"Your Grace." Jack straightened from his bow and met his father's jaundiced gaze.

Shock sank to his gut. The duke had without question been ill and was still not strong—a frailty Jack had never seen in his father before—but any visible trace of emotion was without precedent. Something stirred in his heart, as if he had just unwittingly trespassed into some forbidden private space and accidentally witnessed a vulnerability composed entirely of pain.

Jack walked up to his father and knelt at his feet, head bowed, avoiding the dark gaze until the duke could recover.

"My boy!" Blackdown said at last. "Sit! Sit, for God's sake!"

A shaft of sunlight fell between them as Jack sat down in one of the armchairs. Perhaps he had simply imagined it, or perhaps the trace of moisture had been caused by a stab of physical pain, not feeling? Either way, the moment of weakness would go unremarked. His father was dry-eyed now.

"Devil take it, Jonathan! After this many years, you might have shown me the respect to have first bathed and changed before coming into my presence."

"Then I must apologize for my indecorous clothing, Your Grace. Mother made it quite clear that she didn't like it any better—"

"Hah! The duchess! Wouldn't speak to you, eh?" The duke laughed. "She's furious with you! Why the devil did you dawdle when you arrived back in England? What's all this nonsense Guy told us about treasure and villains?"

"An accidental and unfortunate consequence of my wanderings, Your Grace."

"Yes, yes. Trouble has always followed you like a damned flock of ravens. We've heard enough outlandish tales of your adventures, yet I hear you also did some good work for the Empire."

Jack gave his father a searching glance. "Only from the most discreet of sources, I trust?"

"A hint here and there, and only at the highest levels. We'll say no more about it. You're home now. It's bloody unfortunate about the girl, of course. She's being taken care of?"

"She's with Mother. Miss Marsh is a respectable minister's daughter from a village near Lyme Regis—"

"And a stalwart enough example of her kind, no doubt. Never mind. When Guy told us what was up and when you didn't arrive here yesterday as planned, the duchess took the necessary steps to salvage the chit's reputation. The servants and your sisters believe that the young woman spent last night as a guest of your aunt Matilda."

Jack raised both brows, though he was not surprised. "The Countess of Crowse has agreed to this falsehood?"

"Of course! It's irregular, perhaps, but at least now the girl can be said to have been properly chaperoned. What do you want? That the world should know that you spent the night alone together—"

The duke began to cough. Jack grabbed a glass and poured water, then tried to hand his father a handkerchief.

"For God's sake, don't fuss! Ring the bell for Hardy. He'll see to me. Go down to your sisters and Ryderbourne. In the blue salon. But first dress yourself like an English gentleman, devil take it—"

Another spasm of coughing shook the broad shoulders. Jack rang the brass bell, and the duke's personal servant slipped into the room. Hardy poured some white powder into the water. The duke took the proffered glass, closed his eyes, and swallowed.

Jack bowed and left the room, suppressing a strong tremor of dismay—and not only about the duke's apparent weakness. News of his exploits had arrived home ahead of him. The only question was, which ones?

"*Y*OUR BEDCHAMBER, MISS MARSH," THE DUCHESS SAID. "Your maid, Roberts, who will help to make you comfortable."

Roberts curtsied. In her black dress, white apron, and cap, she had been standing waiting, as if part of the furniture. Anne smiled at her, then looked about. The walls were painted in pale blue and ivory, with scallops of white plaster leaves and flowers. A row of three tall sash windows framed bright sky and space.

This bedroom was twice the size of her father's front parlor in Hawthorn Axbury. The embroidered bedspread, a cornucopia of intertwined blue-and-silver flowers, was exquisite. A priceless collection of paintings and vases and furniture decorated the rest of the room. A careful, delicate taste that could be achieved only when money was no object.

"Not quite what you are used to, Miss Marsh?"

Her blush burned as Anne realized she was gawking like a child. "No, Your Grace."

The duchess's mouth quirked with a certain wry tolerance. "Though your status in this household is a little ill-defined, I saw no reason to relegate you to the servants' quarters."

"At home . . . at home I share a room with my two sisters. I did not mean—"

But the duchess had already turned away. "You have prepared a bath, Roberts?"

The maid was stout and brown-haired, with a deferential tuck to her chin. "Yes, Your Grace, as soon as the hot water comes up."

"Have tea brought up, as well."

Roberts curtsied again and left through a small door disguised as part of the paneling.

The duchess walked to a window and stared out. The room settled into absolute silence, except for the loud ticking of a gilt clock on the mantel. In spite of her quiet stance, Jack's mother seemed to carry her own little breeze with her. It agitated the ribbons on her dress.

Unsure of what to do or say, Anne waited.

"Mr. Devoran told us an extraordinary tale last night," the duchess said at last. Her voice was charismatic, almost bewitching. "That my son forced you to leave your aunt's home, very probably against your better judgment, because he claimed you were in danger from a gang of ruffians from the Orient. Is that true?"

"Yes, Your Grace."

With a shushing of skirts, the duchess turned. "Yet Mr. Devoran says that you are a respectable female of good family."

Her heart seemed to be blocking her throat. Anne nodded before she found her voice. "My father is a minister. We're Dissenters—"

"Just so," the duchess said. "Thus I have created the fiction that you stayed with the duke's sister last night. She lives less than five miles from here. I refer to Matilda, the Countess of Crowse. That is her portrait."

The duchess indicated a painting on the wall beside the door. Anne turned to look at it.

Wearing the draped fashions of the turn of the century, a young lady lounged elegantly on a marble bench. Ivy climbed over the pillars of a vaguely Grecian temple behind her. A wreath of the heart-shaped leaves twined about her hair and more ivy spilled over her lap. It was a classic enough portrait, though the dark eyes stared down at Anne as if Matilda, Lady Crowse, were about to burst into laughter.

"Ivy is the symbol for fidelity," the duchess continued. "A pretty sentiment of the time. That was painted over a generation ago, of course, before my sister-in-law married and was widowed. Her hair is a little silvered now, like mine. Yet her position in society is unassailable."

Though there was a hint of humor in the duchess's voice, Anne was already drowning in an unpleasant awareness of being a misfit, as if she were a trespasser in her own life.

"Other than Mr. Devoran, only the duke, myself, and Lord Ryderbourne know the truth," the duchess went on. "The staff and the rest of the family believe what they have been told: You arrived at Crowse after dark, too late to see anything much of the house, which will explain why you cannot describe it. Your baggage was lost because of the storm. All you need to remember is that Lady Crowse fed you a meal that consisted entirely of vegetables. Matilda is an original. You may fabricate almost anything else that you like about having stayed with her, except that she does not eat meat and allows none to be consumed in her house. You understand?"

"Yes, Your Grace."

"I wish to protect my careless son, as well as your character. As for this other, more physical danger from which Guy Devoran tells us we must also safeguard you—"

The imaginary breeze blew a little stronger as the ribbons moved and fluttered. Anne stood quietly.

"Very little in this place is what it seems, Miss Marsh, except the grim reality of stone. The medieval walls of Wyldshay still lurk behind all this paneling and plaster. Your person and your reputation are equally safe in our hands."

Anne swallowed. "You are very kind, Your Grace."

"Nonsense! The ordering of correct appearances is my life's work. It only remains to explain to the world why my son brought you to Wyldshay at all—a slightly more challenging proposition."

The duchess's gaze swept over her, not unkindly. Was she

assessing the crumpled, water-stained dress? The unkempt hair? Or simply whether this odd visitor was really worth all this trouble? Surely she could never see into the dark depths of despair in Anne's heart?

Yet Anne met the green gaze with quiet dignity. "I am not the sort of person Your Grace would normally welcome to Wyldshay as a guest. I am aware of that."

The duchess laughed. "Nevertheless, your security will be assured as long as you are here, though I do not wish fear spread among my household. You will say that Lady Crowse considers you for the position of paid companion and that I have agreed that you may stay at Wyldshay while she reflects on it. My son conveyed you on your journey merely as a courtesy, after your own carriage was wrecked. Meanwhile, one of my daughters will lend you some clothes. I believe you and Lady Elizabeth are much of a size."

"I can send home for clothes," Anne said. "I would not wish to cause Lady Elizabeth any inconvenience."

"My daughter will have everything you need." The duchess opened another white-painted door. "You will find a small sitting room, with books, embroidery, a harpsichord, through here. Roberts will bring you your meals." Leaving the door open, she walked back. "And now I will leave you to your bath, Miss Marsh."

To Anne's amazement, Jack's mother reached out to brush a knuckle over her cheek. For that one moment, the leaf-green gaze seemed only wise and tolerant.

"You are a brave child! You have demonstrated a remarkable generosity of spirit toward my wayward son. He can be far too persuasive, can he not?"

At a loss for words Anne curtsied. In a rustle of silk, the duchess left the room.

Anne took a deep breath and walked to the window. She struggled for a moment, then threw up the sash. A fresh breeze wafted from the far horizon.

Whatever it is possible to mend will be mended—which did not, alas, include her maidenhead!

She was dismissed, trivialized, and would eventually be sent home as if nothing had happened. She must pretend she had spent the night with a countess who might hire a paid companion. Not with Jack the dragon hunter, who had burned her to the soul with his beauty and his passion.

I have created the fiction—

No doubt it was a fiction the duke's family would embrace heartily and Jack along with them. Yet it was not a fiction Anne could maintain to Arthur, or to her father and mother. She was ruined. All of Arthur's hopes and plans for their life together in Hawthorn Axbury were ruined, as were all of her parents' hopes and plans for her. She would take home nothing but bitter disappointment and heartbreak to everyone she loved, while Lord Jonathan Devoran St. George merrily escaped unscathed into whatever future he desired.

It was all settled. Very probably she would never see Jack again. Perhaps she did not even want to.

The bedroom looked out over woods, fields, a drift of distant downs and at last the far shoreline, where the sea pounded incessantly at the south coast of England.

Anne thought she could see forever.

Everything beyond the glass—and within it—belonged to the Duke and Duchess of Blackdown.

CHAPTER NINE

❧

*J*ACK STRODE BACK TO HIS PRIVATE SUITE OF ROOMS, THE three stories of the Docent Tower. Not a rooted trunk of the castle like the Fortune Tower, just a small turret added in the time of Charles the First to house a library acquired by the then Earl of Blackdown. The collection of books at Wyldshay had expanded long since, so the tower had been abandoned. On his sixteenth birthday Jack had taken over the empty rooms. The gothic arches and rough stone walls had rather appealed to him at the time. They still did, though not for the same reasons.

Ryder had set his boxes in a pile in one corner of his study. Only his case of clothes had been carried up to his bedroom. A formal jacket, shirt, and trousers had been laid out for him there, already cleaned and pressed.

Jack stripped and threw Farmer Osgood's clothes into a pile to be thrown away. Without ringing for a manservant, he shaved and washed his entire body in cold water, before pulling on clean underdrawers and tugging a fresh shirt over his head. He stared at himself in the mirror for a moment. The bruises marked his face like the shadow of a bird's wing. *Trouble has always followed you like a damned flock of ravens—*

Dressed as his father desired—*like an English gentleman*—Jack ran lightly down the stairs to his study. Nothing had been changed since he had left for India. Shelves were still filled floor to ceiling with his books and notebooks. A handful of brass instruments, a telescope, a sextant, sat undisturbed on their table. A riding whip, a pair of boots, a brace of pistols left to be cleaned had been neatly picked up and put away, but the entire tower had been carefully preserved as a reflection of the young man who had once lived there. Even a pot of ivy that he had dug up from the woods as a boy and watered daily.

It was unfortunate, perhaps, that the traveler who had returned from the East was no longer the son or brother that his family had once loved. Yet, because he loved them, he would hide that from them for as long as he could—at least for the next hour or two—and then, of course, he would be obliged to shatter all of their illusions.

Somewhere in this enormous pile of stone the duchess had set Anne Marsh as if she placed a daisy in a flower arrangement: somewhere suitable, without being showy. Though no doubt the daisy felt hideously out of place among the more sophisticated blossoms of the duchy!

Was Anne terrified? Had Mother already turned her into ice, or into a quivering mass of insecurity?

Jack knew perfectly well what the duchess would have observed. His father had already hinted at what Her Grace intended to do about it: a neat tying up of loose ends, so that the social fabric might remain unruffled. Though for the duchess to have been forced to enlist Aunt Matilda—!

His cases glowered at him from the corner. Jack threw back the lid of a trunk. Lengths of silk, bricks of tea, curious objects carved from jade or ivory. Gifts he had hoped would please his family.

Would Anne like something here? He ran his fingers over the folds of a rich blue silk, embroidered in silver thread with tiny flowers: a fabric he had imagined made up into a gown for Liza. Or the pale, whisper-soft jade green with the tiny golden birds? Or this pure, almost translucent white-on-white, where ghost dragons trailed their snow-burning breath beneath the fronds of ghost trees?

How would Anne look dressed in some of the most exquisite fabrics in the world? Silk sliding over her slender limbs and white skin as she moved? Would she like such a gift, or be embarrassed?

He grimaced. A man could give personal clothing to his sisters or his mistress. One did not give such an intimate gift to a young lady one barely knew. But what if the lady in question was one the man had ruined? Still, no—or at least, not until she had already agreed to the only possible solution. He lifted aside the bolts of silk and dug further.

For his father, an illustrated wooden tablet dug up in the Takla Makan, bearing writing in some unknown, ancient text. For Ryder, a perfectly carved jade horse. For his mother, a smiling ivory Buddha. Jack stared at the little effigy, the serenity and peace of the features. Would Anne think it a heathen monstrosity? Why did he care? He set the Buddha aside for further contemplation. For his mother he had already brought himself.

Carrying several bundles, Jack traced his steps back down through the castle. The occasional maidservant stood to attention, mop or duster at her side, and stared into space as he passed. A good servant was supposed to become invisible when a member of the family walked by. It would not be like that in Hawthorn Axbury, would it? The servants in small households usually became, in some sense, members of the family.

Beneath the final archway before the blue salon, Jack stopped. A painting of St. George in full armor filled one wall of the antechamber. The white steed reared over a luscious green dragon with rolling red eyes.

Growing up, Jack had taken it for granted: The whole castle reeked of power and always had. Almost every room held some motif to remind the viewer of the owners. It was as if everything you glanced at was decorated with your own name. Even if you looked away, that pedigree would be shouted into your ears for a lifetime.

When had the needs of the Anne Marshes of the world ever been more than a remote nuisance to the likes of the dukes of Blackdown?

Jack strode the remaining few yards. He nodded to a footman, who stood at attention in front of a pair of white-painted doors. The servant knocked and the doors were flung open. Ryder's dark-lashed gaze met Jack's for a second—with a hint of guarded uncertainty—before he smiled and stepped to one side. A sweet bouquet of silk dresses and flower-garden perfumes, though shrieking like banshees, Jack's sisters tumbled out to greet him.

ROBERTS HAD BROUGHT HOT ROLLS WITH BUTTER AND cheese, fresh fruit, and a selection of sweet and savory pastries. Like the room—like the whole castle—it was a demonstration of good taste with a complete disregard for waste. It spoke clearly, whether that was the intention or not, of unimaginable privilege.

"Will there be anything else, miss?"

"No, thank you. Except perhaps— May I have writing paper and quills?"

"There's a writing desk over there." The maid nodded to a small secretary set against one wall. "It'll have everything you need. If you wish to send a letter, just give it to me and the duke'll frank it."

"I must write to my father and mother," Anne said, "to let them know that I'm safe."

For a moment she was overwhelmed by a rush of homesickness so acute she felt faint. She could not write about what had happened, of course—not in a letter! She would have to wait to tell her father face-to-face. And Arthur!

Anne stared at the plate of food, so beautifully presented. If only time could be peeled back like the skin of a peach. If only she could start the week all over again.

She sat down at the desk, closed her eyes, and sought for peace, but her heart was filled with a frantic emotion that might equally well be love or hate.

It was a lover and his lass, With a hey, and a ho, and a hey nonny no—

JACK LEANED FORWARD TO ALLOW HIS BROTHER TO LIGHT his cigar. They were sitting in Ryder's private study. Ryder had an entire wing to himself, had long ago chosen a set of rooms off the Whitchurch Gallery, all remodeled in the reign of George the Second. The stone walls of the original castle seemed to have left no visible impression on its elegant simplicity.

The gathering night wrapped about the brothers as intimately as the wisps of smoke that spiraled above their heads. They were very alike. Perhaps Ryder's hair was a shade or two lighter, more like the coat of a fine blood bay, and of course he had the duchess's uncanny green eyes: eyes that were impossible to read, if he chose—as he did now—to conceal his feelings, though Jack thought hesitance still lurked there. It bothered him, that they could not simply be brothers without all these undercurrents, yet Ryder met Jack's gaze now with a light smile.

"Sorry about the pummeling earlier," he said. "The girls could hardly be restrained—"

"I wanted to see them, of course, but Mother orchestrated every element of this homecoming, didn't she?" Jack stretched out his legs. "A subtle little punishment for everyone?"

Ryder raised a brow. "You seem to have survived. You don't think that you should have spent this one day—the day you finally came home—with all of us?"

"A day carefully arranged to make sure that none of us could exchange anything except small talk? From the moment of my arrival, until we all dined formally as a family—"

"We had to limit our conversation to what was suitable for even the youngest member's ears. Yes, of course. But the girls were desperate to see you."

"It's almost painful to me that they're so excited about my return," Jack said.

"Painful? Why? Your gifts were a stroke of genius."

Jack glanced at the little jade horse prancing on Ryder's mantel.

"Yes, an easy triumph. But perhaps it's a little wearing to be seen as such a hero. However, it's not that. There are other events afoot, which Mother knows perfectly well. For a start, I might have appreciated a moment alone with you first."

Ryder watched a trail of smoke rings float up to the ceiling. "Not a moment alone with Mother?"

"That, I imagine, will come later—whenever I'm least expecting it. I did enjoy a short private audience this morning with the duke. I didn't realize how ill he'd been."

"There was nothing you could have done. I knew you'd come home as soon as you could."

Jack blew rings to intersect Ryder's, though he didn't feel in the least joyful. "Which could never have been soon enough—"

"Not for Mother, certainly. She wants you to stay home for good this time. As for Father, today was the first time in several days that he didn't dress to come down to dinner."

"Yet His Grace greeted me this morning in a bathrobe," Jack said dryly.

Ryder laughed. "He was very ill, Jack, but the doctor says if we can avoid stressing his heart for the next week or so, he'll live to be ninety. I'm in no hurry to inherit."

"You're already running Wyldshay?"

"Essentially. He's damned stubborn, but I do what I can."

"I don't envy you," Jack said. "I hope you don't resent it that I've had so much more freedom than you?"

Ryder flicked the ash into the fire and stubbed out his cigar. "I resent it like hell, but I don't resent *you,* you damned fool! I remember the day you were born."

Jack swallowed genuine surprise. "Spare me!" he said lightly. "The thought of Mother having to bow, even for a moment, to the demands of Nature rather than to her own will gives me the chills."

"What the devil makes you think the duchess didn't decide exactly when each of her children would arrive?"

"God! None of us would have dared to inconvenience Her Grace, would we?"

Ryder caught Jack's eye and they both laughed. If there were no outside world and no past for either of them, perhaps they could sit companionably together at this fireside, forever drinking brandy and blowing smoke rings in perfect camaraderie.

"You're still her favorite. And no, I don't resent that, either," Ryder said, though his eyes remained hooded. "You began to arrive in this sorry world when she was trimming her roses, as I recall. Mother scattered scented petals over my uncomprehending little head and said that she was going into the house to fetch me a brother, but that I couldn't play with him until morning."

"You must have been damned disappointed when you saw me."

"I was. You looked like a hairless puppy without a nose and you were screaming."

"Yet she specified a brother? How did she know I'd be male?"

"She wanted another boy, and of course Mother has always been confident that she'll get what she wants." Ryder's lashes hid his eyes as he lit a taper in the fire. "You could begin by offering Her Grace an apology, Jack."

"It wouldn't be enough." Jack took the taper from his brother's fingers and stood to light the candles on the mantelpiece. "Even if I crawled weeping to her bosom—"

"That might suffice," Ryder said, leaning back. "Except that she abhors unnecessary displays of vulgar emotion."

"Don't we all?" Jack paced away to the dark window. "So why the devil are you reminding me now of my helpless infancy? I'm damned if we've ever discussed anything like it before."

"Perhaps to remind you of your blood bond to this family," Ryder said.

The glass reflected a candle flame in each pane, then multiplied them, an infinity of pinprick suns.

"Or perhaps to remind me how very much I displeased the duchess when I left? And how much more I've offended her by the manner of my return? Father told me this morning about Mother's little fiction. Apart from everything else, my bringing Miss Marsh here in such irregular circumstances has put the duchess under a distressing obligation to Aunt Matilda, who will crow over it until doomsday."

"Which Mother hates, but it seemed the best plan. Fortunately, the girls have swallowed it hook, line, and sinker, and so will society." Ryder pushed himself to his feet. Jack turned to watch him. "There have been rumors about you—"

"Yes, I can imagine."

Ryder thrust one hand through his hair and dropped back into his chair. "This young lady was trapped alone with you for the night. Mother is only trying to save her reputation—"

"And she would never allow a St. George to be disturbed by something uncomfortable, would she?"

"Don't treat this lightly, Jack!" Ryder leaned forward to stare into the flames. "Who would believe that any innocent female could emerge unscathed in the circumstances?"

"I would have believed it," Jack said.

"*Would* have?" Ryder glanced up, his eyes dark. "Well, the world wouldn't have seen it that way. Half of Dorset and all of London already believe some rather unpleasant tales concerning your sexual adventures in the East."

"So this is what all the softening up was for?" Jack asked. "Unfortunately, the unpleasantness has only just begun."

"What the devil do you mean?"

It was, of course, too great to explain. He knew his brother would never understand, yet he must try. From love, if from nothing else.

"Mother's fiction is a valiant effort," Jack said. "But this time, even abject crawling won't suffice."

Ryder stared at him. "The duchess just wants you to stay, Jack. She wants your love, for God's sake."

"My love? She has that! As for the rest, you don't know what I've done."

An involuntary rigidity passed over his brother's features, as if Ryder were being turned slowly to ice. "Then tell me."

"I can't spare you this, Ryder," Jack said. "You described a pretty infant mewling in his swaddling—whether to disarm me or yourself, I'm not sure. Perhaps simply to remind us both of a safer, more innocent time. What you neglected to mention is that the infant was a changeling."

"A tiger cub?"

"Perhaps. This cat certainly cannot be put back neatly into its bag."

"Two different kinds of cat," Ryder said, his face set. "A cat-o'-nine tails and a barnyard moggy—"

"Oh, no," Jack replied softly. "The same kind of cat—in either case, one with unsheathed claws, bent on punishment. You see, those rumors you heard no doubt contained an element of truth. If what you want is my swift denial and my reassurances, I can't give them. I hope you'll understand that I'm trying to pay you a compliment by telling you first."

"Telling me what?"

Jack walked back and sat down in his chair. "What you hoped wasn't true—though you've been afraid that it was. I did more than compromise this young lady's reputation. I compromised her."

Ryder sat in absolute silence for a moment, then he thrust himself violently from his chair. His heels rapped harshly on the wooden floor as he strode away.

"I refuse to believe it! Guy said she was a minister's daughter, for God's sake!"

"She is. Furthermore, she was a virgin and affianced to some God-fearing Dissenter—"

His brother spun about. "You bloody, unconscionable rat!"

"Yes," Jack said.

Beneath his light English tan, Ryder's skin was as pale as death. "I don't know what the hell to say. Should I knock down my own brother for the sake of a young woman that I haven't even met?"

Jack stood, his hands relaxed at his sides. "If you like. Perhaps I even wish that you would, though it won't change a damn thing. So take a swing at me, by all means. I shan't stop you."

"I am of course being manipulated by a master." Ryder stalked away. "I will not give you the satisfaction of beating you within an inch of your life, even if that's what you deserve."

"No, the punishment is all mine to inflict on myself. I assure you that I shan't temper the self-flagellation. However, whatever I may feel about it now, I cannot undo what I did."

"God," Ryder said. "Am I to switch in an eye blink from maudlin reminiscences of your babyhood to this?"

The tremor was beginning deep inside. Jack took a few deep breaths to control it. "You're doing quite a bit of the manipulating yourself, Ryder. I'm not impervious to it, either. It's just that I'm the guilty party and so feel less shock at voicing a truth that you've been trying to avoid."

"*Avoid?*" Ryder spat the word.

"Why else invoke memories of a blood tie even deeper than love? Not for the first time, you've been afraid of what I might have become, haven't you?"

Ryder was completely in control now, his features congealed as if by frost. "If I was, I wish to God that my fears had been misplaced. Does Mother know?"

"You don't think that the duchess didn't immediately guess, as soon as she saw me arrive with Miss Marsh?"

"So this is why she went down alone to greet you? She needed to know exactly what she was dealing with."

"*What* she was dealing with? That's not what made her turn away from me without any greeting after all these years. No, she wanted to know *whom* she was dealing with, and one glance told her that her worst fears had come true. I'm no longer that child who tagged behind you through Wyldshay. Nor am I the man who left for India, leaving my sisters weeping and Mother stiff with dismay. She doesn't really give a damn for Miss Anne Marsh, or for my behavior. She only cares that she cannot control or even always comprehend my thoughts—"

"She never could! But perhaps if she'd been more successful, this damned tragedy might never have happened."

Jack turned away to walk softly about the room, looking up at the paintings. He felt ill, as if he had stabbed himself in the gut, yet for Ryder's sake he must keep trying, and because he in fact loved his brother too much to try to manipulate him, he had only the truth to offer—

"I don't wish to shock your sensibilities, Ryder, but I happen to believe that the loss of a lady's virginity isn't necessarily a tragedy."

"For God's sake! You've just destroyed this girl's life and written off your entire future."

"Very probably," Jack said. "However, though that precise thought is causing me considerable distress, it's not exactly a tragedy. The wrecking of a ship in a storm, or a stupid man getting control of a nation: those are tragedies. If the world were not so insane, women could give up their virginity with joy and never look back."

"I feel as if I'm talking to an absolute stranger," Ryder said. "You *are* a bloody changeling!"

"I tried to warn you as gently as I could. Mother's fears are correct. I've moved beyond her reach and become alien. I cannot live by your rules or fit neatly back into the conventions that bind English society together."

"Yet this is still England. To destroy a respectable girl's virginity has consequences, even for a duke's son."

"Of course. Believe it or not, that was not my intention. Yet why must a *respectable* girl marry in ignorance and fear—and often for reasons that have nothing to do with love or desire—while all the girls who can't afford respectability must sell their bodies for whatever they can get?"

"I don't understand you at all," Ryder said. "You're not sorry?"

"I cannot spare you the distress of this discussion. Among other things, I'm sorry for that."

Ryder dropped into his chair as if infinitely weary. "Is she some kind of old connection? Are you in love with her?"

Jack closed his eyes and swallowed. He did not love Anne. He did love his brother. He had brought nothing but pain to both of them.

"I just met her."

"Then it was uncontrollable lust? What? I'm at a complete loss, Jack. Guy says the girl is a retiring little mouse, that for looks she couldn't hold a candle even to the maid in the inn—"

"That's true."

"Then what the hell happened?"

She had set her fingers in mine and was scrambling through a hedge. She had said she believed truth lay in empirical inquiry. She was wearing an absurd dress several sizes too large for her. She was afraid and out of breath. Her pale skin glowed as she looked up at me, her brave spirit shining in her eyes. That courage robbed me of my soul. When she looked at me like that, it touched something in my heart—

I drank a viciously potent plum brandy after ramming my head into a tree. I was half blind—

I am rotten at the core, Ryder. I am damned. Perhaps in my madness I almost thought I was in love—

"What do you think?" Jack said. "There was only one bed. We shared it. I promised—as a St. George and a gentleman—not to compromise her virtue. I believed I had enough control to keep my word. I was mistaken."

His brother again pushed violently from his chair. "You shared her bed? What the hell did you think would happen?"

"I make no excuses, but I can try to offer an explanation, if you want it. There were reasons why I wasn't quite myself—"

"Not *yourself*? Then what the devil were you? The man of the rumors?" Ryder's hand chopped down as if he would divorce himself from his own words. "A rake who explored every vice that the East offers, visited every brothel, indulged in practices that are unimaginably lurid and scandalous?"

"You believed all that?"

"No! And I assure you that nothing of the kind was ever said purposely in my hearing, for if it had, the speaker would have given me satisfaction the next morning. Now I don't know what to believe. I don't even know if you still claim to be a gentleman."

It was impossible to explain. Perhaps it was better not to try. Yet Jack tried to keep his voice calm, to let reason break through his brother's distress. He strode back to sit down opposite Ryder.

"The word *brothel* conjures up images of degradation and a kind of cheap nastiness, doesn't it?" Jack said, meeting and holding Ryder's gaze. His brother's pupils were like pinpricks set in jewels of bright green, like a cat's uncomfortably blinded by sunshine. "And what the hell is *vice?* Flagellation and sadism? Boys? Some of that goes on in the East, but you'll find more of it right here in London. It's not a world that you frequent, because you no doubt keep a mistress: clean, compliant, a woman of some class, probably, who may even love you a little."

"My choices are not at issue at the moment," Ryder said. "Yours are. So what world did you explore, Jack?"

"Not *vice,* if that term is to have any real meaning. Not boys, though they were available. Not even brothels as you would imagine them. But yes, I explored the sensual wisdom of Asia at every opportunity and made a study of customs that even I would not, or could not, practice."

"And sent manuscripts guaranteed to shock back to London?"

"Yes. Mostly in the form of translations of ancient texts from India and China. My connection to those translations was supposed to be kept secret. I had no desire to embarrass the family. But such things always leak out, I suppose."

Ryder leaned back and closed his eyes. His jaw was rigid, the words bitten off like pieces of thread. "Yet I'm to assume you put at least *some* of those erotic arts into practice?"

"Absolutely. I've learned things that you cannot imagine."

"Try me!"

A log thumped in the fire. The little shower of sparks illuminated Ryder's face, the strong, handsome lines of bone and flesh, set now in anger as a bulwark against—what? Despair? Disappointment? Disgust? Or all of them?

"I can reach climax without ejaculation," Jack said bluntly. "Several times in a day, or in an hour, if I so desire. If I wish, I can lose my arousal and regain it, over and over again, without withdrawing from my lover's body—"

"Climax without ejaculation?"

"The Chinese believe that a man loses vital essence in every act of love, unless he learns not to waste himself. They have spent a thousand years perfecting such techniques—"

"Then you spent five minutes with an English virgin forgetting them!"

Metal rang on wood. Ryder had leaped up, knocked over a table, and sent a candlestick clattering to the floor. The brothers' eyes met.

"I don't give a damn about your sexual prowess or habits, Jack. I care only that my brother has divorced himself so entirely from honor."

"Yes," Jack said, standing to face him. "I was wrong. But what do you suggest I do now? Would you rather I simply abandoned Anne Marsh? Mother's plan might still work, if I make no objection. Unfortunately, I shall object. I forgot my own skills and took no precautions. There could be a child. So—in spite of whatever opposition Mother, or you, or the duke may offer—I shall marry her, if she'll let me."

His brother kicked the candlestick aside and stalked to the door.

"Unless she is with child—over my dead body," he said.

The door closed behind Ryder with a thud. Jack dropped back to his chair and tried to control the shudders that rippled down his spine. He had mishandled that badly. He needed his brother's support. Without it, Anne would be caught in the crosscurrents while a storm raged in his family. Though he had known it was a vain hope, though their love had always been splintered by misunderstanding, even rivalry, Jack had felt forced to at least try for Ryder's real empathy.

As long as he could remember, his home had been a battleground between two strong-willed individuals locked in a combat that had always been disguised as a dance. Now that delicate, seesaw balance of power between his father and mother was about to be overthrown. Now, as always, he and Ryder would be forced onto opposite sides.

"Why the hell do we try to change those we love?" he asked the empty room.

He had gone to India, though his brother and mother had tried to prevent it. He had come home and fulfilled all of their worst fears.

He had gone to India with his father's blessing, though the duke was at heart indifferent to whether his younger son lived or died. He had come home and betrayed what little faith his father had shown by allowing him to go.

Yet all this family strife paled in comparison to the chaos about to be let loose, if he did not succeed in his mission.

Jack walked back through the silent castle to the Docent Tower. He passed at least one burly footman in every corridor. Guy had done his job well, and the duke—and Ryder—had taken Jack's alert seriously. They had that much faith in him, at least. Even though his enemies must now know perfectly well where he was and that Anne was with him, they would never be able to penetrate the strong walls of Wyldshay.

Holding that small relief in the forefront of his thoughts, Jack ran up the stairs and threw open the door to his sitting room.

A woman rose from a chair beside the fireplace and turned to face him.

"I want neither apology nor explanations," she said flatly. "I only want to know what you intend to do next."

Jack's mind sizzled as if it were being pressed beneath a flat-iron, but he bowed and smiled wickedly at his mother.

"I'm not sure that's up to me," he said. "But isn't this a little late, even for duchesses, for a flaying of souls?"

Candlelight cast gilt-and-red reflections in her pale hair. "I have waited all these years for my son to come home. Am I to be disappointed?"

Jack stepped into the room and closed the door behind him. He was more than a head taller than his mother, yet she did not look up into his eyes. Instead her gaze bored into his chest, as if she looked right through him into a far distance.

"Why ask me a question for which there's no answer?" he said. "Miss Anne Marsh is safe?"

The duchess sat down. "From you? Yes. For now."

"She did not tell you, of course."

"She didn't have to. She's been laid open like an unfolded sheet. Her eyes are both terrified and ecstatic, as if she has suffered a visitation from an angel. You not only deflowered this child, you made a very thorough job of it, didn't you?"

He walked up to her, unable to completely control his distress. "If you intend to be deliberately insulting, Your Grace, I'm not sure that we're going to get very far in this conversation. May I sit? I am, believe it or not, tired to the bone. Though I may deserve your nice little flaying knife, it will do neither of us any good if I don't have my wits about me."

"You might have thought of keeping your wits about you last night, before you ruined this girl and brought disgrace to your family. I hoped to God it wasn't true, until I saw your eyes, and hers, and knew you had discarded everything I ever tried to teach you."

"You could always read me like a book," Jack said. "I will accept any punishment you think fit to hand out. You may cast me off, disinherit me, banish me, as you wish. However, you will not dismiss Miss Anne Marsh out of hand—"

"Whatever makes you think you may demand anything of me, Jonathan?"

"I demand nothing of you. But if you think to hush up what I've done for the sake of family pride, you will have me to contend with."

Ribbons fluttered as the Duchess of Blackdown stood up, graceful, precise. With a swishing of silk, she stalked to the door. Jack strode across the room to open it for her.

"You will join the duke and myself in the Fortune Tower at ten tomorrow morning. We shall decide then what's to be done." The pain of winter ice glazed her expression. "Ryder knows by now, I assume?"

Jack glanced away at the once familiar walls of the Docent Tower and nodded. "He would very much like to shoot me at dawn."

"Then he's not the only one," the duchess said.

"You cannot possibly despise me as much as I despise myself, Your Grace."

"That is—partly—what I am afraid of." The emerald eyes looked up at last. His mother's thread of control was as stretched, as fragile, as his. "What really happened on the other side of the world, Jonathan? Can't you tell me?"

Jack shook his head blindly. Impossible to answer her, whatever the consequences.

The duchess hesitated for only a moment before she walked away down the hall. Jack listened until the rap of her shoes faded to nothing. As silence invaded, he leaned his head back against the doorjamb, while a knife seemed to twist slowly in his gut and his vision misted and splintered.

The green goddess eyes had also been blurred—but in his mother's case only by tears.

THE SUMMONS CAME WITH HER BREAKFAST. ANNE WOKE TO sunshine and Roberts setting down a tray beside the bed. She had been dreaming—dreams of heaven, blindly sought by a blind woman. In spite of the bright morning, she shivered.

"The duchess wishes you to join her in the Fortune Tower, miss, at ten minutes to ten. It won't do to be late. I've brought hot water, and here are some of Lady Elizabeth's gowns. So terrible about your luggage! Such a storm!"

"Yes," Anne said, struggling awake. "I must send a note to thank Lady Elizabeth."

Roberts smoothed her hand over an elegant gown of sprigged muslin. "The young ladies have all gone, miss. They bundled into the carriage, as merry as blackbirds, and went off to visit Lady Crowse."

So Wyldshay was emptied of its innocents?

Well, there was no use in lying in bed and lamenting about what she had done, so Anne forced herself to nod to the maid and get herself ready to confront the day.

She could face any of them, perhaps, except Jack.

Chapter Ten

THE FORTUNE TOWER SANK ITS ANCIENT ROOTS AT THE heart of the island that held Wyldshay. Wearing a dress that was indeed a temptation to worldly vanity, Anne followed the footman who had been sent to fetch her. She ought to feel nervous, yet it was almost as if her trepidation had so overwhelmed her that she couldn't feel anything at all. *Hey nonny, nonny!*

The footman knocked, then thrust open a heavy oak door.

Neat, precise, radiating self-assurance, Jack's mother stood gazing from a window. As the footman closed the door behind Anne, the duchess turned to face her visitor.

"There is no need for pretence," she said. "I know what my son has done."

As if exploding into life, hammers began to strike in Anne's chest, pounding home the awareness of just how helpless she was in this place. Neither Arthur nor her father could rescue her, if the Blackdowns used their power to destroy the commoner who had so embarrassed their family.

The duchess stared as if assessing her unwanted guest. Anne gathered her dignity and waited.

"So you are ruined, Miss Marsh," the duchess said into the humming silence. "And you have barely begun to comprehend what it might mean. Yesterday I hoped that my fears about my son might be misplaced. Now I know for certain that they were not. We must all deal with the consequences."

"It was my fault," Anne blurted as if someone else spoke the words. "I began it . . . I asked him—"

"Perhaps, but Lord Jonathan knew what it meant and you didn't." The duchess walked forward, her shoes tapping lightly. "The fault is entirely my son's."

"With respect, Your Grace, if I had behaved with more propriety, Lord Jonathan would not—" Anne stopped and took a deep breath. *If you're to breathe at all, I must free you from all this mad binding.* "He didn't really want to."

"Didn't *want* to? My son?" The duchess stopped in front of Anne. "You poor, deluded child!"

The hammers redoubled. "Perhaps I really didn't know what it meant, but if I hadn't insisted, nothing indelicate would have happened. He was not . . . he was hurt. He wanted to be generous. If anyone's to be punished, it should be only me. You must not make him suffer for my mistake."

Silence descended with stunning abruptness.

See it through, Annie! She tried to focus on a tapestry where knights in armor rode in procession through a magical wood, but they wavered like spume on an ocean.

"You are a bold young woman," the duchess said at last. "I am not in the habit of being told what I *must* do."

"I'm sorry, Your Grace, but I believe I must tell you the truth."

"The truth is not always as easy to know as we might think. So you believe that you encouraged him?"

"Yes."

The goddess eyes gazed into hers with a certain compassion. "That was not the way you were raised, surely?"

Anne shook her head. "I wanted to know . . . I can't explain. It was a kind of madness. It was raining."

"It was *raining*?" The duchess lifted one elegant brow. "And now you are deeply afraid of what we will do about it? Come, sit over here. It won't do for you to faint."

Jack's mother led the way to a pair of chairs set by themselves between two bookcases. She indicated one of the chairs and Anne sat down. Was she dizzy? Or was this all just too unreal?

"My daughter's dress suits you very well," the duchess said. "That pretty muslin will remind everyone that you are the innocent party, which may help to mollify the impending passions of the rest of my family." She smiled, though there was something close to heartbreak in the tiny lines of tension around her green eyes. "In a few moments we shall be joined by the duke and my two sons. No one intends to punish you, but Ryderbourne may forget himself a little. My younger son, of course, faces a trial by fire."

"And I do not?" Anne asked. "I deserve to."

"That is a matter of opinion. You are not the intended target, but we will not spare your sensibilities. Even Lord Jonathan must resent you for what you've forced him to face about himself. It may not be pretty. If you wish, you may leave now."

The hammers had begun to resound against an anvil of steel. "If Your Grace will allow it, I think I should stay."

The duchess walked away a few paces. Her personal breeze moved with her, agitating the ribbons on her dress.

"Very well," she said. "It is your future at stake, though rest

assured that you will not be cast out into the world without support. However, whatever life you might have planned before last
night has now changed. You are aware that one of the consequences of my son's behavior is that you might be with child?"

A betraying blush crept up Anne's neck. Swallowing her panic,
she nodded and wondered why she didn't flee now, while she had
the chance. But the door was already opening.

A man with the face of a hawk walked unsteadily into the
room. The duke carried a stick, but he also leaned on the arm of a
tall young man who could only be his eldest son. Anne stood up
and dropped a deep curtsy. Lord Ryderbourne's glance seemed to
assess her from head to toe, before he nodded briefly in greeting.
The duke took no notice of her.

Like a servant, she was invisible.

Jack's brother helped his father settle into a carved wooden
chair with a high back, then he stood before the mantel with his
hands clasped behind his back. In a rustle of skirts the duchess
took a seat on the opposite side of the fireplace.

Relegated to her backwater against the wall, as irrelevant as an
unlit candle, Anne sat down.

In silence they all waited.

As the clock on the mantel began to strike the hour, the door
opened again.

Jack had to duck his head to step into the room, then he
stopped for a moment, framed by the archway. He was immacu-
late: crisp white linen, dark suit, his hair neatly barbered. The
fallen angel masquerading as a gentleman.

His gaze swept immediately to Anne, but the dark eyes
betrayed a strange blankness, like those of a man confronting a
ghost.

The blood drained from her face.

He had terrified her in her aunt's house. He had seemed intimidating at the reins of his cousin's phaeton. He had teased her into laughter in a farmer's gig. He had flattened assassins who leaped out of the fog. He had become the passionate lover of one wild night. Now he was an absolute stranger.

Why had she stayed? She could hardly leave now without creating even more embarrassment. One night. A mistake. Jack had not meant there to be consequences. Now he faced the wrath of his family and the destruction of his dreams.

Anne looked down as the hammers began thundering a rhythm of terror. Whatever the duchess thought or said, what had happened was not really his fault. It was hers.

He must be regretting that heady exchange with unimaginable bitterness.

As if she had just become invisible to him, too, Jack stalked to the center of the room and bowed from the waist.

"I am here," he said. "Ready for my chastisement."

"The duchess and I do not wish to waste time in recrimination, Jonathan," the duke said.

"Though that will, without doubt, happen at some time during this conversation," Jack replied.

"A respectable young lady has been ruined. You are the agent of that. You will not make light of it."

Jack jerked as if he'd been struck. "Make *light* of it! No one in this room is more aware than I am of the significance of my offense. However, I will not see Miss Marsh humiliated or hurt in the cross fire. Whose idea was it that she witness this discussion? Mother's?"

"Miss Marsh remains here of her own volition, Jonathan," the duchess said. "You do not think that she has an interest in the outcome?"

The morning sun broke suddenly through the window. A shaft of light washed over Jack's hair and shoulders. Ugly bruises still marked his temple and cheek, yet his profile shone pure and bright against the dark stone walls behind him.

"She is afraid," he said. "She is trying to conquer her fear with courage."

Ryder spun from the fireplace and stalked away. "If you cared a whit for her feelings, you would not have ravished her."

"But I did." Jack's tone held a deadly softness. "Which puts me under a certain obligation to her, don't you think?"

"It puts all of us under an obligation," the duchess said. "The St. Georges do not ruin the respectable daughters of the ministers of any church without providing for the consequences."

"The usual answer would be to arrange an immediate marriage," Jack said.

"You are not the usual seducer," the duke said.

The duchess was very pale, her eyes fixed on her son's. "Nevertheless, are you offering it?"

"Marriage?" Jack stood with his hands loosely clasped behind his back, his head slightly bowed as he met his mother's gaze. "There are other considerations, not least her own wishes, but I am certainly letting you know that I am willing."

The duke pursed his mouth as if exasperated, but he folded both palms on the top of his stick before he propped his chin on his hands, his eyes hooded, and said nothing.

"Are you?" the duchess said. "However, there is no need for you to offer yourself as a sacrifice just yet. If Miss Marsh proves not to be with child, we may return her with suitable compensation to her family."

"Compensation deducted from my personal fortune, of course," Jack said with clear irony. "Not a particularly severe punishment for me. I assume I shall hardly miss it."

"You will miss it," the duchess said.

If intangible strings connected mother and son, they were slowly being tuned to a higher and higher pitch. The almost visible tension sent tendrils curling into Anne's stomach. She felt ill.

"So she will possess a handsome dowry. Alas, I believe Miss Marsh may be too honest to hide the truth from her fiancé, or from her father."

"If her family will not take her back, or if in the circumstances she no longer wishes to marry her fiancé, we can find her a suitable position. Yours would be the funding for that, too. Either way, her future is secured and you will not distress her again."

"Concisely put, Your Grace," Jack said. "And if there is a child?"

"Then we shall with regret insist on a marriage. The duke and I are agreed on that." The duchess seemed brittle, spun from sugar. "However, not necessarily to you. We trust that if we offer him sufficient inducement, her fiancé will still agree to marry her."

"You obviously don't put much stock in the affection that Mr. Trent might feel for his affianced bride." Jack's voice burned. "He may still wish to marry her in spite of us, not because of us. However, if his attachment is not sufficient, or if either of them proves awkward, we can use our power and wealth to ensure their cooperation? The poor man would need a powerful pride to stand up to the Duke and Duchess of Blackdown. Miss Marsh would capitulate right away, of course, if we were to threaten ruin to either him or her family."

Ryderbourne had been listening, head bent. Now he spun about to face his brother. "For God's sake, Jack, no one is talking about ruining her family!"

"No, but that's implied, isn't it?" Jack said, glancing at him. "Mother is trying to be polite, but there's no question that iron lies beneath her velvet. If Mr. Trent does not wish to raise another man's baby, how else can we force him to do so? And if threats and inducements are still not enough, no doubt we could find a convenient stranger who will take Miss Marsh in exchange for a promise of discretion and a large part of my fortune."

Ryder's eyes blazed. "You're about to insist that the alternative is for you to marry her yourself?"

"I believe that's the usual solution offered when a gentleman—even a duke's son—ravishes a virgin, unless Miss Marsh decides otherwise of her own free will."

His father's stick pounded hard on the floor. "There's no question of your staying in England."

"Is this something that needs to be further explained?" the duchess asked.

The duke looked obliquely at his wife. "You gave birth to a wanderer, madam. Let him go!"

"I shall anyway return to the East as soon as I can," Jack said. "However, that journey may be delayed long enough for a wedding."

The duke thumped his stick again. "For God's sake, remember who you are, sir!"

Jack's stance gave him the lithe look of a dancer—or an assassin. "How could I forget, Your Grace?"

The duke matched the acid in his son's tone. "Then you will recognize that there is a certain dissonance to the idea that any son of mine would be saddled for life with a Miss Anne Marsh of Hawthorn Axbury!"

Ryder strode back to the center of the room. "What about the consequences of such an unholy alliance for the lady?"

"I shan't harm her," Jack said. "I am not quite a monster. I was, if you remember, raised as an English gentleman."

"You've already harmed her," Ryder snapped. "You could not keep your damned breeches buttoned."

Anne's blood was running alternately hot and cold, but now it burst into flame, scorching up her neck into her face. She wanted to swallow, but her tongue seemed to be filling her mouth.

"That is not the true cause of the harm," Jack said quietly.

"What the devil do you mean?" Ryder's fingers clenched into fists. "In your heart of hearts you don't even think that what you did was wrong, do you?"

Jack's steady gaze did not waver. "This is not quite the time nor place to explore my philosophy, Ryder."

The duchess smoothed one hand over her skirt. "But everything hinges on it, Jonathan. You will answer your brother, please."

"Very well. I was wrong to put Miss Marsh in such an untenable position. I was wrong to create pain for her fiancé, a man I've never even met. I was wrong to create heartbreak and confusion for her. I was wrong to misjudge my own desires. However, I don't agree that a lady should never know erotic passion simply because she's wed to a bloody English gentleman."

Ryder stalked away to a window. He thrust his hands against the folded shutters and leaned there, looking out. "You would have men behave like beasts? Prey to every base instinct?"

"Not at all. I would have us be honest about desire. I would have us embrace passion, not demonize it. Genesis had it wrong. It's not knowledge that expels us from Paradise. It's fear."

The duke stared as if his younger son had grown two heads. "You add blasphemy to your sins, sir?"

"I don't intend to offend," Jack continued softly. "But deny the body's natural needs in the name of virtue, allow the triumph of sexual Puritanism, and the outcome will only be hypocrisy, prostitution, and human misery, as one visit to London would prove."

"My son obviously finds English culture contemptible." Her skirts rustled as the duchess stood up. Ribbons fluttering, she walked up to Jack. "Yet the East offers nothing better, does it, Jonathan? Only an endless flight from yourself, while dishonor still lies like a canker at the core. Your search for the grail is empty. The prize you seek can only be found by a man with a pure heart."

"You have two sons, Mother," Jack said. "But you're right, as always. Who else can see with one glance into every hidden corner of my soul and find it wanting?"

The duchess stopped in front of him and gazed up into his eyes. "I did not raise you to cause pain to every woman who loves you, but that is what has happened."

The sunlight shimmered over mother and son as if they were alone in the room. Cast into shadow the duke sat rigidly at the fireplace, his face set. Ryder stared blankly from the window. Anne clasped her hands in her lap, knowing she understood nothing of the undercurrents beneath this passionate, private exchange.

"Because I went to India against your wishes?" Jack asked softly. "Because you could not control me and still cannot?"

"I am not such a fool as that. Yet at the time I could not bear to lose you."

"Then you're not happy that my obligation to Miss Marsh might give you a way to make me stay in England?"

The duchess set one hand on Jack's sleeve as if longing to hold on to him. "That has always been my heart's desire. However, I am now prepared to forgo it."

Jack stared down at her fingers. "You were right to resent my leaving Wyldshay all those years ago. I went to Asia without any particular purpose, simply another useless scion of the English peerage out to see the world. However, after I arrived I found that I had an unexpected gift for following a purpose, after all."

"A many-hued purpose, as I understand it," the duchess said. "A purpose that took you through deserts and mountains. But the son that I loved and wished to keep by me died, did he not, somewhere in those high passes?"

Jack stood very still, his head slightly bent. "Yes."

"And so you became the man who dedicated himself, between wild adventures and risks to his life, to the single-minded pursuit of sensual pleasure? My son is now an aficionado of the erotic arts, who despises any civilized restraint?"

"Erotic art and restraint are not mutually exclusive, Your Grace. On the contrary."

"Yet you did not hesitate to indulge your basest needs when alone for one night with an innocent girl who put her faith in you?"

"I offer no excuse for that."

The duchess dropped her hand and turned away. "I thought perhaps the tales I was hearing were not true. I hoped that my Jack would come back to me, older and wiser, perhaps, but at heart unchanged. But can you deny that you have studied esoteric techniques that would shock every idea of decency? That you have been a willing pupil of the most shameless of courtesans and concubines? That you consorted without limit with every lascivious, exotic female, from Greece to Asia, who offered you her tainted embraces?"

The eerie stillness changed almost imperceptibly, as if Jack were a tiger lurking in the shadows. "I don't expect you to understand, Your Grace, but it wasn't like that."

"I do not wish to know what it was like," the duchess said. "I have read your letters over these last years with an ever-increasing fear for you. I care nothing for your erotic entanglements, but did you think you could hide from your own mother what you were becoming? Do you deny that you can never be content with England again?"

"There are other reasons why I must return to Asia."

"Which is why Wyldshay is being patrolled and guarded against intruders as we speak?" Ryder strode up to him. "What the hell trouble really followed you home?"

Jack met his father's eyes for a moment. The duke shook his head.

"Trouble followed me when I went," Jack said with a dry smile. "Don't you think that I carried it with me?"

"Whatever your other objectives, I think that a petty English sexuality and a virginal English bride don't interest you in the least," Ryder said. "I think you've become depraved."

"*Depraved?* Neither you, nor Mother, know what the devil you're talking about," Jack said.

"Yet the facts cannot be ignored," the duchess said. "As a result, I am prepared to give up my dreams. They have anyway been ripped apart, one by one, since the day you were born. In the pursuit of decadence, you have squandered your natural power. You have eroded honor with shame, leaving nothing at the core but this brittle, clever pride. England and this young woman are both better off without you."

A *trial by fire.* Beneath the dark tan and the bruises, ash gleamed in the tense curl of his nostril, the deep lines carved like grief on each side of his mouth.

"I cannot explain," Jack said at last. "Nevertheless, I admit my fault with Miss Marsh. I am prepared to accept my punishment. The only thing that I won't do is plead."

The duchess sat down, spreading her skirts. "Is that what you think I want from you, Jonathan?"

"I think that's only a small part of what you want from me. All of this has anyway been only a game, hasn't it?"

Ryder strode back across the room. "*A game?*"

Jack gazed at his brother. "Of course. Her Grace wants me to bury my shame in her skirts and beg for a mother's forgiveness—not for what I have done, but because I have not become what she intended."

"Then you're not sorry?"

"I'm more filled with regret than I can express, but only insofar as I have damaged Miss Marsh. But that isn't what's at issue, is it? However accurate her dissection of my soul, nothing Mother says can make me stay in England. Knowing that, the duke and duchess have already agreed on the only possible solution, though for very different reasons."

Anne gripped her hands together until the knuckles shone white. Had they all forgotten her? Even Jack?

"What solution?" Ryder's voice stung like ice.

"Marriage, of course."

Ryder spun to face his father. "Your Grace cannot possibly countenance such a marriage!"

As a tiger might move from a stalking crouch, Jack stepped forward, the sunlight slipping over his back.

"For God's sake, see reason, Ryder! Whatever tales Aunt Matilda may spread, the truth is bound to leak out. Even if I dower Miss Marsh with a fortune, she'll still be the cast-off lover of the notorious Lord Jonathan Devoran St. George. If Trent won't marry her, what the hell will happen to her? She cannot return home. She has unmarried sisters. Will her father allow her disgrace to ruin their prospects, also? Or should she set up housekeeping by herself as a fallen woman, cut off from friends and family, and prey to every upright, moral Englishman who believes that any such female is fair game?"

"You think marriage to her seducer would be better?"

"Times have changed, sir," the duke snapped. "These days we retain our position only as we keep the respect of the middle classes—and their morality is stricter than ours. If the chit does not marry this Trent fellow, she marries Jonathan."

"So you no longer believe it would be too crushing to our family honor for a St. George to be 'saddled for life' with a Dissenter's daughter?" Jack asked pointedly. "I'm only a younger son, of course. Yet Your Grace is a little cavalier in your assumptions about Miss Marsh. Is she to have no autonomy in this whatsoever?"

"Devil take it, does no one in this room recognize that this young woman would be equally saddled for life with my brother?" Ryder's face was ravaged by distress. "The thought of any innocent falling into his power horrifies me, just as it horrifies

Mother. I will not stand by and allow my brother to further corrupt an innocent Englishwoman."

"She will not be in his power, or his to corrupt," the duchess said. "Your brother will give Miss Marsh the protection of his name only. As our daughter-in-law, she may enjoy wealth and consequence and live without scandal, whether there is a child or not. Jack will leave England immediately. He will never see her again."

"I intended to return to Asia," Jack said. "I had not intended to die there."

Tears gathered in the emerald eyes. "Then this is our mutual punishment."

"So you play the trump card." Jack's face set like stone. "I admit I expected more subtlety and more finesse."

The duchess was weeping! He had made his mother *weep*! Anne gulped down despair and a kind of blind horror. Clutching the side of the bookcase for support, she stood up. The room spun for a moment, before a clear, bright anger swept away her dizziness and everything sprang into focus.

"No!" she shouted. "No! I don't agree to any of this! Stop it! You can ruin me and you can ruin my family, but you can't make me marry anyone against my own wishes."

Jack immediately strode to the door, as if to allow her as much free space as possible, but the others turned to fix her with three shocked pairs of eyes.

"How dare you discuss my future as if I were part of the furniture?" Anne plunged on. "None of you understands anything about the true nature of love. Whatever I've done, whatever you do, my father will never abandon me, nor banish me—and neither will Arthur!"

Jack set one hand on the latch. "Anne! Don't! I should have insisted you leave before this. Please, come away!"

Her heart felt full enough to burst. "Leave me alone! Go back to Asia to all those exotic women, or stay in England and marry a lady who won't embarrass your family with her unsuitable connections. I don't care!"

"You cannot embarrass a St. George," Jack said. "We're shameless."

He flung open the door, then walked back to stand beside the duchess. He bent to whisper something in his mother's ear. Her green eyes became suddenly opaque, like chalcedony.

"We made a mistake," Anne said, her breathing shattered. "But it was mine as much as yours. Perhaps a person of such humble background may not quite comprehend all the niceties of the nobility, but we understand honesty. I'm not simply a victim and I shall make my own future, alone if need be."

"You would embrace poverty and disgrace rather than marry my brother?" Ryderbourne asked. "I thought so!"

"I thank you for your concern, my lord. But there's no disgrace in poverty, nor in the errors of an honorable heart. Meanwhile, I would like it very much if you and your family would recognize that I am an independent being with a mind and soul of my own."

As a clamor of confusion roared in her mind, Anne rushed for the open door and fled the room.

She ran blindly until she reached a staircase. She went up, skirts bunched in both hands, two steps at a time. Dragons curled and snarled from the newel posts, no longer comical, only beasts that she didn't understand. More stairs led upward. Footmen and the occasional maid watched her pass, but one young man in a white wig detached himself from the rest to follow her.

"What are you doing?" she asked, spinning about.

"Your pardon, miss," the man said, blushing a little. "The duke's orders. For your own protection."

"Oh," Anne said. "That's right. I'm a prisoner, aren't I? By all means, trail along, though I have no idea at all where I'm going."

JACK CLOSED THE DOOR BEHIND HER AND LEANED HIS HEAD back against the panels.

"Well," his mother said. "So the duckling grows wings. I thought she might!"

"Grows wings?" Jack asked. "I wish mine were as bright, because Miss Marsh's would put a kingfisher's to shame."

The duchess looked up, her eyes dry and bright. "What the devil do you know of shame, Jonathan?"

"Nothing learned at your knee, Your Grace. While I concentrated on playing your nice little game of discord, Anne was an unwitting casualty, after all. I will forgive you any barb you wish to plant in my flesh, but I won't forgive you for subjecting her to this, and I cannot forgive myself for not preventing it."

The duchess stood up, ribbons fluttering. "She was not seriously hurt. And it was necessary."

"That you bully her? Plant fear and confusion in her mind?"

"It is necessary that she knows how impossible it is for you to have a future together, before she falls any more deeply in love with you."

His heart seemed to stop beating for a moment, as if he had been thrown heavily and unexpectedly from a horse.

"Ah," he said. "So the barb sinks and I am to be reeled, floundering and gasping for mercy, to shore?"

Her eyes searched his face with the remote gaze of the goddess, though she trembled like an aspen hanging over a pool. "Nothing I can do will ever damage her as much as what you have already done. Though that, perhaps, can still be mended. If she allows herself to accept him, this Mr. Trent will now enjoy the patronage of a duke and duchess. They will be wealthy. Her heart will not be broken. But mine will. Knowing that you have behaved with such dishonor, that you reject me and everything I have ever taught you, I'm damned if I'll let you leave me again scot-free."

He felt torn from the currents of his life. "Oh, I'll pay, Your Grace! But only my mother would levy a tax designed to plumb to the depths my ability to pay."

Jack bowed, wrenched open the door, and raced after Anne.

S HE STOOD ON THE BATTLEMENTS, WHERE PART OF THE curtain wall met the bulk of the Fortune Tower, and stared away toward the distant coast. The footman hovered awkwardly behind her, no doubt trying to maintain the delicate balance between protection and intrusion on the privacy of a guest.

Anne did her best to ignore him. Clouds drifted, chasing light and shadow over the green countryside. Somewhere out there lay Hawthorn Axbury: her father and mother and brothers and sisters. The people who loved her. The people who would forgive her and rescue her from this—whether Arthur still wanted her or not.

She couldn't think of Arthur. If she tried to conjure his face or any of their conversations, every pleasant memory was lost in a haze of self-recrimination and guilt. Never in her life had she wronged someone so badly. It seemed terrible. A terrible sin. Arthur was entirely innocent. He loved her.

She had ruined everything.

Footsteps sounded on the stone stairs, a light, running tread coming ever closer.

Immediately her heart took flight. *I know his step! No other man ever moved like that—like a bounding tiger, like a ghost!*

"Good man, Graham," Jack's voice said. "You may return to your other duties."

Anne clutched the stone merlon with both hands. The footman's heavy shoes rattled away down the stairs.

"Will you talk to me?" Jack asked.

The small breeze whipped wisps of hair about her face and tugged at her muslin skirts. Not even her clothes were her own. She was a stranger, an impostor, in the home of a duke, and she had— She didn't even know the words. She had sinned with a duke's son.

Anne rubbed one hand over her eyes and kept her back to him. Yet she was aware of him, as a bird is aware of a cat: a quickening of an already rapid pulse, a heightened alertness in case she needed to take wing.

"I was wrong not to prevent that," he added. "I can imagine how you must feel."

"I very much doubt it," she replied.

"You're filled with anger—at yourself, at me. You're wishing you'd never laid eyes on me, that the tree of knowledge had never dropped its bittersweet fruit into your hands. Then there's grief and guilt, as well, along with a small, dark fear—that perhaps you don't have enough courage, after all, that perhaps my family will overwhelm you. Is that some of it?"

Anne spun about. He stood watching her, the door closed at his back, the battlements throwing shadows at his feet. Sunlight marched stridently over his face, his skin darkly tanned, his eyes forest shadows and gilt.

Streamers of silk ribbon unfurled in her stomach.

"How can you presume to know?" she asked.

"Perhaps because I share many of those uncomfortable emotions. Neither of us can undo what has happened." He strode up to her, the wind whipping his hair. "I need to know what you want to do."

"My life was happy until I met you. Nothing can make it right now, except Arthur taking me away."

His lips compressed a little as he looked away. "Then there's no need for further strife between us, is there? If Mr. Trent doesn't rescue you, you may still have my name and fortune without having me."

Anne turned her back, painfully, bitterly aware of him, his wild scent, his power. *Lord Jonathan is bound to resent you for what you've forced him to face about himself.* Her blood ran hot beneath her skin.

"Was that true, what the duchess said, that you've dedicated yourself to . . . to exotic sensual pleasure?"

"Yes, as far as it goes. But never fear, once things are settled, I'll remove myself from your life as quickly as I can."

"So what was all that really about just now in the Fortune Tower? I don't understand. What kind of family is this? Do you all hate each other?"

"Perhaps we St. Georges value cleverness more than kindness.

It doesn't mean that we don't love each other. It does mean that we're very good at causing each other pain."

"Even your mother wishes to hurt you?"

"I have failed her. She cannot bear it."

Anne clung to the harsh stone wall as she glanced back at him. "I've failed my father and mother, too. Papa will be devastated, but he won't wish to punish me. Nor will Arthur. Love and kindness are two sides of the same coin, aren't they? How can they be separated?"

"If the human passions commonly invoked in the name of love did not involve a great deal more than kindness, Miss Marsh, you and I would not be in our present predicament."

She was stung into silence, staring up at his forest-shadow eyes. Passion burned across his cheekbones, melting her resolve, deep in the bone. Her heart thumped heavily, torn open by her own confusion, deep in the bone. For one wild moment she hoped he would thrust her back against the stone parapet and kiss her, even force her. She wanted him overwhelmed by desire, wanted him to sweep her with him into that blissful delirium again. An absurd, humiliating weakness. She despised it.

"I want nothing more to do with you," she said. "And I imagine you cannot stand the sight of me."

"Who suggested that? The duchess? My mother is clever. She's not infallible. Though it hardly matters, of course, what my feelings may be."

"Whatever they are," she snapped, "they are shallow enough."

He looked away, his profile bright, his mouth set. "It's not so easy for dukes' families to love too simply. Our rank creates complexities. We can never escape them."

"Not even with each other?"

"Especially not with each other." He glanced back at her again with that harsh, ironic intelligence. "Let's try to find a little dry detachment and perhaps you'll understand. Come, let me show you something." Without waiting to see if she followed, Jack strode off along the battlements to an arched doorway. He flung open the door to reveal a spiral stair. "These steps will take us to the roof of the Fortune Tower."

"What for?"

"Either your righteous anger, your natural curiosity, or your sense of humor should sustain you, unless you're afraid of heights?"

I'm not afraid—not as long as I'm with you! From some deep, mysterious place, Anne found a certain sardonic mirth, though rage still stained her emotions like vinegar spilled into wine.

"No," she said. "I don't think so. I once climbed to the top of the church tower in Hawthorn Axbury."

"Then this is nothing. Wyldshay is nowhere near as close to heaven as an Establishment church."

She bit her lip, unsure if she choked back tears or laughter, and followed him.

They emerged onto the highest battlements. A maze of roofs sloped away, as if a child had chopped at a cake with a hatchet. Only some chimneys and the flag mast with its flapping standard pierced the vast bowl of the sky. Open countryside stretched beneath them.

"Just about all the land you can see belongs to Wyldshay," Jack said. "All that responsibility: farms, villages, shops, markets—the lives of hundreds, if not thousands, of people. That is what power means. That and the making of laws; that and a show of splendor; that and moral leadership. It would have seemed an odd concept to my ancestors, but a certain decorum is what the modern world demands of dukes. Ryder had to be raised so that he can take over the reins of all of it one day. He must do so with compassion and justice, but without sentiment or passion. My father was raised the same way."

"Without *passion*? What else was on display in the Fortune Tower just now, if it wasn't passion?"

"Game playing."

"With hearts as the playing pieces?"

"If you like. My family is angry not only because I disappointed them, but because they believe I have flown beyond their reach. Perhaps I was allowed too much and they think that's what made my sins possible. While Ryder always knew what he must become, I was raised only to be ready in the wings, in case I was needed to take his place. I was otherwise useless. As a result I had a great deal of freedom."

"Which made you an enemy of your own brother?"

"An *enemy*?" Jack's hair tossed wildly as he strode away. "Ryder's upset only because he cares so much and that caring makes him afraid for me. When we were boys we cavorted together like barbarians."

"You're trying to convince me that you were once human?"

"No, I was never human, of course. Not as you are. Not even as a child. Perhaps that's why I so like your company." He wrenched open a small door. "God, I'm amazed that this is still here!"

Muscles flexed as he dragged a large wooden tray out of some kind of storage closet. Anne stared at him. Her heart pounded like a drumbeat. *I so like your company?*

"How can I trust anything you say?" she insisted.

"If you have enough nerve, I shall prove it!" Jack lugged the tray to the base of a chimney and thumped the wood with his fist. Roofs sloped away in a dizzying array. "Ryder and I did this a thousand times, flew our wooden dragon over the slates to the roof of the Great Hall." He balanced the tray, sat down on it, then opened his arms to encompass the space in front of him. "Please take a seat! Unless you're afraid?"

"I'm not afraid of anything you can do."

"Then trust me!"

In a kind of blind defiance she marched up to him and sat down on the tray. He held her snugly in front of him with a powerful thigh on each side of hers.

"Now, madam, behold! The flight of the dragon!"

The tray rocketed over the shallow roof with the clamor of a thousand galloping horses. At the guttered edge their wooden chariot leaped, airborne as if it sprouted leather wings. Anne screamed and grabbed Jack's arms with both hands. Hollering like a banshee, he hugged her close while he leaned back to balance their flight.

They landed with a thump on a second stretch of slate. Her spine pressed into his belly and chest. His strong thighs embraced her hips. The muscles of his arms flexed hard beneath her hands as his male exhilaration echoed in her ears. Her blood responded, her bones melted. She felt light-headed and reckless. She was already breathless.

The tray leaped off the second roof, launching them into another split second of free flight, before it landed on a battlement-surrounded stone terrace and bumped to a halt.

Free and merry, their shared hilarity encompassed her in a heady moment of lunacy. Her dress had blown up around her knees, revealing stockings and shoes and a glimpse of tied garter.

Blushing like an idiot, Anne tugged down her skirts as she staggered to her feet.

"Oh, my!" She sat down again as her knees wobbled. Her bones had dissolved into runnels of hot copper. "I believe I just trusted you with my life!"

Jack stood as if arrested for a moment—something open and vulnerable lingering in his eyes—then he bent to offer her his hand. Anne took his fingers and scrambled upright. All of her rage had bleached away in the bright light of his merriment. For a heartbeat they stood facing each other. Laughter had etched deep lines on each side of his mouth. She knew with giddy certainty that he wanted to kiss her.

If she wavered, if she gave the slightest indication of welcome, he would press his lips once again to hers and she would melt like hot honey. Images fired like fireworks—of this man naked, of his body joined to hers, of that bliss doomed to turn into bitter regret. Marriage to her would be only a punishment to Lord Jonathan St. George. Either way, he would leave her.

Nevertheless, Anne knew she still wanted it. Wanted him. How ridiculous to be so angry with a man, simply because he had given her exactly what she'd asked for! She pulled free and escaped to the edge of the terrace. A courtyard yawned far beneath. Blossom frothed over the tree at its center.

A twittering cry sounded far above her head. The breeze had gathered strength, tumbling clouds and a ragged sweep of swallows across the sky. Jack spun about to stare after them with the wind in his gaze, as if the designs of his soul were being written in that ceaseless, swooping flight. The patterns of her future were no part of his plan. Why did that hurt so much, when she had already decided that the course of her life was better off without him?

"Why didn't you want to stay here?" she asked. "You were born into all this wealth and power and freedom. You must have had everything your heart desired."

"Not quite." The birds soared with flashing grace, a curve of feathers and long tails in the air.

"So that's what you really want? To fly away like the swallows? Where do they go every winter?"

"To Africa, Asia—who knows? They're all blank spaces on the map."

Jack dropped down to squat on his haunches, his head tipped back against the stone wall. "Would you really like to know what I have wanted all my life?"

"Travel? Pleasure?"

"I would like to have your certainty, Miss Marsh."

Anne was genuinely surprised. "But I'm not certain of anything."

"You're sure of your father and mother. You even believe that you know who you are. You're sure of your moral compass, even when you have strayed from it. Unfortunately, as I said before, it's more complicated for dukes."

She set both hands on the stone baluster, rough and damp beneath her palms. "To love a baby? To offer security and safe haven to a young child?"

"That's what any child wants, of course: a father and mother to love him or her unconditionally, without judgment or blame."

"I had that," Anne said. "I still do. Weren't you ever loved like that? Even as a little boy?"

"Perhaps I was given a lust for freedom instead."

"Yet your mother didn't think you would use it?"

A handful of swallows swooped down to perch in a row on one of the nearby roofs. Their forked tails shone blue-black in the sun.

An odd little quirk marked one corner of his mouth. "My mother thinks I abused her trust. I did."

Her face fired with color. "By ravishing me?"

"Yes, there's that. But she's more concerned that I have adopted the beliefs that made it possible. That's what she cannot forgive."

"Beliefs?" she asked. "Beliefs about . . . love?"

His moving shadow scattered the birds into flight as Jack rose and walked up to her, close enough to touch. Her blood surged in her veins as if a spring tide raced onshore, then retreated and retreated, until she felt weak and dizzy again.

"Exactly," he said, his forest eyes gazing down into hers. "Shocking, foreign beliefs. And if the duchess is to be believed, ones guaranteed to break the heart of any innocent English lady. The duchess judges correctly that I am alien at the core. Are you in love with me, Miss Marsh?"

Anne shook her head and turned away, deafened by the drumbeat in her ears.

He didn't want her. He was going back to Asia. He wanted her to marry Arthur. Yet deeper than all of that grief, a fierce, wild anger burned at herself: that she could have been so foolish; that she couldn't better control her heart. Anger at herself and a renewed rage at him: that he had engaged her ardor so carelessly; that he would see how she felt and rightfully recognize it as a passing infatuation.

Of course she was in love with him, with his glamour and mystery. In love, like a silly young girl, and suffering all the real pain and giddiness and ecstasy of those feelings. But this could not be real love, not the love on which one might build a marriage and a family, the kind of love her parents shared. It was as if she were suffering because of a dream. The suffering was real, though the dream was not—and Miss Anne Marsh was surely sensible enough to tell the difference?

"How could I be in love with you," she asked, "any more than you'd be with me? I'm in love with Arthur."

"Yes," he said. "But if he refuses to have you, we shall marry instead."

"That would have consequences for you, even if we don't live together. Why must you sacrifice your whole future for one mistake? Because you made one bad choice, you'll never be allowed to make free choices again?"

Sun and shadows flitted over his wayward hair. The swallows soared and circled over the roofs of Wyldshay. With that lean, powerful grace—the wary grace of a tiger watching prey—he turned to gaze up at them again.

"That would seem to be the situation for both of us, wouldn't it? I'm sorry. It was very far from my intent."

"And mine," she said.

To her surprise he spun to face her and lifted her fingers. His lips pressed onto the backs of her knuckles, first one hand, then the other. Though shivers of desire pulsed through her bones, she shook her head and pulled away.

"You don't want me, do you?" he asked.

"No," she lied. "I don't want you. I want my own life back, as if we'd never met."

CHAPTER ELEVEN

ALERT TO EVERY SOUND THAT SHE MADE, JACK CLOSED HIS eyes and listened to her shoes tapping away. His heart echoed the distressed cadence of her breathing, every flutter of her dress. A door creaked on its hinges. Her footsteps pattered down stairs. She was fleeing him. Pain burned, somewhere deeper than he could quite fathom.

I want my own life back, as if we'd never met.

He leaned both forearms on the baluster and dropped his forehead onto his crossed hands. That was all that he wanted, too, of course: his own life back. Instead—*alien at the core*—he had incurred a debt that could never be repaid.

To destroy a respectable girl's virginity has consequences, even for a duke's son. . . .

What the devil had possessed him? He still craved her with a kind of wild folly, an urgent longing to engender that innocent, passionate abandonment once again. An abandonment as absolute as if she had laid her soul in his hands.

That—just that—made him despise himself.

Then it was uncontrollable lust? What? I'm at a complete loss—

Uncontrollable lust? God, he must be mad! Jack tipped his head back. Clouds raced. Broken sunlight scattered across the sky, dancing with the plunging flight of the swallows.

She had been standing on the battlements with the wind tearing at her mouse-brown hair. The elegant muslin dress had tugged and flattened over the curves of her body. She had turned to look at him, her face flushed, while distress, rejection, dignity, and vulnerability made her eyes vivid.

He had felt an explosion of carnal desire so strong that he could barely control it.

You bloody, unconscionable rat!

Yet she had allowed him to take her speeding over the rooftops on a damned wooden tray. She would even have allowed him to kiss her again.

Why the hell did he desire this English Dissenter's daughter with such burning ferocity? Even when he had forced himself into a kind of amused detachment, even when he had made himself touch her without perceptible fervor—as a reassurance to her, or to himself?—he had longed to sweep caution aside and bury himself once again in her body.

Why had he even sought her out now? What difference could his apology or attempts at explanations ever make? Had he thought to test himself? If so, he had failed. He had only proved that he was still panting like a satyr for her white legs in their sensible stockings, for her pretty little garters, tied at her delectable knees.

Even if at the heart she offered nothing but simple generosity, he craved it with every fiber of his being.

Yet if what she offered was only innocence, then he hated himself for wanting it. He was not a green boy. He had known the

reality of adult passion. He did not want attachments or complications. He did not want an English bride.

Yet as Jack knew, as the duchess knew—in spite of her splendid
performance in the Fortune Tower—Arthur Trent would never
marry Anne now, because she would not be able to deceive him.
With her stubborn Dissenter's honesty, she would feel bound to
tell her fiancé the truth. She would believe she'd be trapping him
into matrimony under false pretenses if she did not.

So Jack still owed her whatever he could give her. He must at
least help her to imagine a new future that promised something
of happiness when she had to face life alone. For what Englishman would knowingly take another man's leavings to the
altar?

*A*NNE FLED BLINDLY DOWN THE STAIRS AND ALONG A
corridor. More stairs led her to the next floor, where she
was immediately lost. She stood in a large room with a soaring
ceiling and a multiplicity of doors, a room she had never seen
before. She spun around. Two staircases. She was no longer even
sure which one had brought her down here. She marched across
the expanse of polished floorboards and opened a door at random.

Sunbeams slanted down from high windows across a long, narrow room lined almost entirely with books. Glass-topped cabinets
filled the center of the space. Curious, she walked forward to look
into the first one.

"A collection," Jack said behind her, "of oddities. Among other
things, it has fossils."

Anne spun about, pressing both palms against the rim of the
case behind her. "So I see."

"You are still our guest here," he said. "So I thought, perhaps, I should come after you, in case you were lost."

"I was," she said. "I still am."

He strode forward to glance into the case next to her. "Then I'm glad you discovered this room. I should have thought of it before. You may study in here at your leisure, if you like. We St. Georges have been in the habit of unnecessarily slaying dragons for centuries, then dragging the bones back home."

So he was reaching for dispassion, even friendship? Anne swallowed and try to match his light tone, to retreat to a place that seemed safe.

"Dragons?"

"The first St. George claimed he had killed a terrible serpent to save a fair maiden from the beast's lascivious clutches. Yet in China dragons breathe clouds rather than fire. They bring life-giving rain, not destruction. The Chinese believe that dragons are creatures of good fortune."

"And you agree with the Chinese view?"

"I certainly don't think we should live in fear of what the dragon seems to symbolize. The Chinese believe so powerfully in their positive attributes that they grind up dragon bones to use as medicine."

"But none of these bones ever belonged to dragons. They were real giant lizards, lumbering through disappeared worlds."

"No doubt your more prosaic approach is the more appropriate. That door over there"—he pointed with a forefinger—"will take you back to the hallway that leads to your room. Meanwhile, come! You'll like these."

Anne glanced at a display of small marine fossils. She did not feel safe or dispassionate. She felt disturbed, breathless, full of trepidation. Why did Jack think he must offer this amity? Wouldn't it be simpler if they never spoke again?

"But they're all misnamed," she said. "How long have they been here?"

"Decades? Centuries? I've no idea."

With that lethal, lovely grace he walked the length of the cases. Anne tried to concentrate on the displays. An odd miscellany: stones, artifacts, fossils, anything dug from or found on the earth, none of it properly described, and a treasure house for any scientist.

"Fossils may be the most important things man's ever discovered," she said. "Yet here they are, languishing in a duke's library, mislabeled, not studied by scholars, and given absurd descriptions. I wish I could open a museum to study them properly."

"Then rest assured, if it becomes necessary that you marry me after all, you may still open your museum. It would shock society and the Established Church, of course, but a St. George may do as she wishes." He stopped at the last of the cases. "But if your approach is that of a scientist, why are you still struggling with the idea that you and I have sinned against the soul?"

Anne took a deep breath. So he would not allow her any safety, after all. It was simply not in his nature. "I don't know what you mean."

His profile seemed grave, his expression intent, as he studied the display. "If we're born neither inherently evil nor good, if we're truly just products of nature, we're left with a stunningly harsh version of free will, aren't we?"

"Yes," she said. "Our choices really are ours to make, as are the consequences to deal with. I'm doing my best to do so, my lord." She walked up to him and glanced at the huge fossil he was studying. "This is the end of a thigh bone, the remains of a real giant animal, a *Megalosaurus,* possibly. Arthur would know."

"Indeed, but it was first named in 1763, as it's labeled here." Genuine mirth colored his voice as he looked back at her. "The same name was published in a scientific paper in 1768 by a Frenchman. Though strangely apt, I doubt that Mr. Trent would approve of it."

His deep humor and intelligence were part of what turned her limbs into liquid. She was determined not to be seduced. "His approval wouldn't matter. By the rules of scientific nomenclature, the first Latin name coined applies to that species for all time. But I thought you knew nothing about fossils?"

"I don't. It was just that Ryder and I thought this label a great joke and read some of its history. The Frenchman believed his fossil was part of nature's effort to perfect man, so he named it from its resemblance to a certain part of male anatomy—at least, as it might be found on a giant—which reduced us both to boyish hysterics. I believe we'd better leave this one buried here at Wyldshay and say no more about it."

Whatever she thought she wanted, this melting sensation robbed her of breath. With his mouth bracketed by laughter, Jack seemed only too human, only too desirable.

"Why?"

He winked with wicked solemnity. "It's named *Scrotum humanum:* a man's stones. Should an entire species be named for such an awkward accident of history?"

She was shocked for only a moment, before a wave of cleansing giggles caught her out, bubbling up like homemade cider. In the next instant they were both laughing aloud.

Jack recovered first, still grinning. "Ah, but I love your laughter! I knew you'd never retreat into prudish indignation. Will your fiancé be able to share the joke?"

"Alas, Arthur would never think it funny." She swallowed a certain pain at the thought. "But he'll never see it, will he?"

Jack walked to the doorway, then glanced back with a bitter-sweet smile. It almost seemed that naked yearning lurked beneath the mirth in the forest-dark eyes. Her pulse began to throb in heavy rhythms, like strange currents running beneath the surface of a river.

"Guy went to London yesterday to fetch Mr. Trent," Jack said. "They'll arrive here tomorrow surrounded by a nice little army of outriders. Though when he brings the Dragon's Fang, of course, your fiancé won't know what you and I have done. Whether or not you tell him is entirely up to you."

ANNE WAITED IN A SMALL PARLOR NEAR THE BLUE SALON. She had taken a chair beside the fireplace and folded her hands in her lap. Her heart beat heavily. Jack had not spoken to her again since he had left her with the fossils the day before. She had let him charm her again, hadn't she? She had even risked the adventure on the tray, his carrying her down in a thumping rush, all the time holding her helpless and shrieking in his arms.

Why had she allowed him to do it? If he had tried to kiss her, she wouldn't have stopped him. She'd have welcomed it! The thought filled her with shame.

She had spent the rest of the day in her rooms, with her meals brought up by Roberts. Her only company had been a gray-and-white kitten that had appeared at the window, balanced precariously on a stone ledge and mewing piteously.

Anne had rescued the tiny creature by enticing it inside with some scraps of ham, then forgotten all of her troubles when the kitten had discovered that the fringed edge of one of the rugs was in dire need of killing. But Roberts had taken the kitten away.

"You'll not want to be bothered with a stray cat from the stables, ma'am," she had said, not unkindly. "This little fellow needs to be with his mother and the others."

Of course everybody needed to be with their own kind. And it was very clear that at Wyldshay Miss Anne Marsh was a stranger in a strange land. Could she really expect Arthur to rescue her from all this?

The door opened. Anne stood up, clutching her hands together over her roiling stomach.

"Miss Marsh," Arthur said, striding forward. "Anne! My dear!"

He seemed exactly the same. Slender and neat and handsome in his plain dark coat and trousers, his face open and guileless. He stopped at a respectful distance and bowed. Anne dipped a small curtsy, her pulse hammering. They each took a chair.

Familiar, safe Arthur! He seemed so uncomplicated, sitting there with his blue eyes fixed on her face. She knew him as a kind man and an agreeable companion, even though his faith was stricter than hers. She had thought he was pleasant to look at. Yet he was also young and male, fit and wiry and athletic from his excursions after fossils. She had never consciously taken note of that masculine strength before. She did so now with trepidation, not desire.

"Thou art quite well, Miss Marsh? Thou art pale. May I call for anything?"

"No," Anne said, swallowing hard. "I am quite well, thank you."

"I understand thou hast suffered some inconvenience," Arthur said. "Mr. Guy Devoran told me how thou fled thy aunt's house with Lord Jonathan St. George." He leaned forward a little in his chair, his eyes full of concern. "Thou art not ill? Please, let me call for some tea."

To her intense chagrin Anne burst into tears. She groped for a handkerchief and mopped vigorously at her eyes. Her fiancé was far too correct, of course, to sweep any weeping woman into his arms to offer comfort and kisses. Instead he bit his lip and looked down, obviously uncomfortable.

"May I call for a maidservant to come to assist thee?"

She gulped back the tears, folded the handkerchief, and tried to smile at him. "It's nothing that tea will solve, sir. Didn't Mr. Devoran tell you why he brought you here from London?"

"Because of the monstrous tooth, of course. Thy letter quite took me aback." He stood up and moved away, as if to maintain his distance from such discomforting female distress. "It's a most extraordinary find. Though we did not discuss it very much in all the hurry of my leaving for London, thou recognized how unique it was, how important it must be?"

"Yes, I did. That's why I gave it to you."

Though she recognized that he was strong enough and a man, Arthur still seemed oddly insubstantial as he paced, striking the air with one hand.

"Imagine the creature that must have possessed such a fang! Clearly a carnivore! If enough of the skeleton could be uncovered—if we could only see the skull!—it would no doubt revolutionize our understanding. I should like to see a paper presented to the Geological Society right away. Then who could deny that giant land-dwelling lizards walked the earth before the Flood?"

"Mr. Trent," Anne said. "There is something else, sir."

"Another fossil? Lord Jonathan made no mention of it."

The handkerchief was crumpled into a tiny ball in the palm of her right hand. Anne stared at it. "You've met His Lordship?"

"Yes! And what an extraordinarily interesting man! He behaved with a very fine condescension, I must say, in welcoming me to Wyldshay just now. He even apologized that circumstances had made it necessary—"

She glanced up. "What circumstances?"

"Why, the tooth, of course! I brought it with me and gave it to Lord Jonathan as I was asked. I did the right thing?"

The lump still blocked her throat, but Anne nodded. "Yes, it's his. And yes, I knew that such a thing must have great significance for our science. I do not think that Lord Jonathan really cares about that, though."

"How could he not care? There's no question that he has a brilliant mind and a searching perception. He showed a very real interest in my ideas. I believe he would not shrink from becoming a patron, if asked, for I never had such an attentive audience before. He wanted to know everything about what has been discovered in Britain in the last few years, what the latest theories are—"

As Jack had listened to Aunt Sayle rattling on about her late husband? Or as he had made plain Anne Marsh feel free enough to chatter about her family and her hobbies? Had he given Arthur that same absolute attention and made her fiancé think that His Lordship was also a passionate geologist?

"He has other motives, other interests," she said.

"Lord Jonathan is not truly interested in fossils?"

"No, I don't think so. Not as we are." The blues and reds of the carpet formed intricate patterns of intertwined plants: leaves and flowers from some faraway, exotic land. "But that's not the only reason you were asked to come here. Mr. Devoran could have fetched the fossil. There are personal reasons."

Arthur walked back to his chair and sat down. "Personal reasons?"

Only a coward would keep examining the carpet! Anne looked up to meet his gaze, so earnest and innocent.

"You were summoned so that I may release you from our engagement, sir, if you wish it."

The clock ticked into a dense silence. Arthur sat like a rock, staring at her.

"I don't understand," he said at last. "Why would I wish for such a thing? I have already spoken to my father about the settlements—"

"Arthur, I'm so very, very sorry."

His handsome face had become as pale as the plaster, his hands clenched into fists in his lap. "If it is thy wish, thou art free immediately, of course." He thrust himself to his feet and strode away across the room again. "Yet may I ask the reason? I thought we were well suited. Have I offended thee in some way?"

"No, of course not! But I am not what you thought me—"

He stopped at the window, his back to her, slender, upright, correct. "*Thou* art not?"

Anne took a deep breath and found a strange sense of calm. *I must free you from all this mad binding.* She stood up. Now that it was too late to retreat, she felt almost relaxed, as if some fresh conviction spread a balm through her blood, as if she were indeed a new person, after all, and could face even a disastrous future without fear.

"My journey here took two days, sir, not one. The duchess is prepared to tell you that I stayed with a relative of hers, a Lady Crowse, before coming to Wyldshay the next morning. The world would believe it, if we all agreed to the deception. But I cannot lie to you, Arthur, and still marry you."

He spoke without looking at her, his head bent, his spine rigid. "I don't understand. Why does this matter? Surely this Lady Crowse is perfectly respectable? So thou spent a night with her?"

"No, I did not," she said, her voice clear and quiet. "Lord Jonathan and I spent that night alone together. I am not the lady you believed you wished to marry, sir. I am someone quite different."

Arthur spun about. "Anne?"

She met his eyes without flinching, though somewhere inside her heart bled at the pain obvious in the blue gaze. "I am no longer a virgin, Arthur. I'm sorry."

His fist struck out and connected with a bookcase. "His Lordship *dishonored* thee? I cannot believe it!"

"I know this will hurt you and I don't know how to avoid that, but I'm not worthy to be your bride and must free you from any further obligation."

"Lord Jonathan St. George *ravished* thee?"

"Yes, but you must not misunderstand. I was quite willing. More than willing. It was my idea. Thus I can do nothing other than release you from our engagement."

Color eased slowly back into his face. Then, as if a floodgate opened, a rush of anguish fired a red glow over his cheeks and forehead.

"I cannot comprehend this at all. It makes me feel as if thou art a stranger. Or as if I'm going mad. Did I not know thee at all?"

"Perhaps not," Anne said.

He stalked back to her, his face ravaged. "He's a duke's son, yet he cannot behave as a gentleman for even one night? He took shameful advantage of a young lady in his power? I don't care what connections he has, or who his relatives are, I shall have to call him out."

She clutched at his sleeve. "No, please! It would be against all your principles. He would kill you!"

For the first time since their courtship began, Arthur clasped her fingers in his. Not in passion, only in distress. She gazed up into his fine-boned face. His eyes swam with tears. Arthur Trent was a good man. He had offered her respectability and a home of her own. They shared interests and ideas. He had felt almost as dear to her as a brother—

A brother? Was that a basis for marriage?

If she loved him, wouldn't she wish to beg for his forgiveness, fling herself into his arms, do anything to keep him? She glanced down at his hands holding hers. His touch felt empty, even a little uncomfortable.

"Will he marry thee?" he asked.

She pulled her fingers away and sat down. "Rather than see me publicly disgraced, the duke and duchess will require him to do so."

Arthur hammered one fist against the other. "The bastard!"

"The duchess doesn't really wish her son to marry me. I'm obliged to tell you that she will give you a fortune, if you'll still take me instead."

"So they would insult me with money and let their son off scot-free?"

"I'm so sorry, Arthur! I'm not worth this!"

He stared down at her, his blue eyes dark, as if bruised. "Wouldst thou have me do less than avenge thy honor—and my own?"

"You must not call him out, sir. I saw Jack fight off some brigands who attacked us—"

"*Jack!* Thou call him *Jack?*"

"Does it matter what I call him? He has traveled all over the world. He has trained his body to become a lethal weapon. His mind I cannot fathom, but you were right to think that he is brilliant . . . and quite ruthless, I think. You cannot fight him, sir. Promise me you will not!"

"They will make him marry thee? A man like that—he'll destroy thee! If it were just that he had dishonored thee—Heaven help me! But thou wast willing?"

"Yes," she said. "If I had not been, it wouldn't have happened."

Arthur rested both fists on the mantel. His shoulders quaked. "It's worse than the fact that he destroyed thy virtue, isn't it? Thou art in love with him."

"No," she said.

"Yes." He turned to stare down at her from red-rimmed eyes. "I can see it in thy face. Thou never felt that way for me."

"I liked you," Anne said. "I respected you. Doesn't that count far more?"

"Thou knowest I would yet marry thee, even though thou hast been dishonored, and throw the duchess's money back in her face. If thou wert ravished against thy will—and in spite of it had still wanted to become my wife—I'd have wished damnation on the man involved, but we could have wed as planned. But it isn't that, is it?"

"I don't know," she said. "I only know what has happened and that it's changed everything. It's changed me. Can you ever forgive me?"

"Forgive *thee*? The fault is entirely his. I can see that. The man is an unprincipled lecher. He has not only robbed us of our hopes, he's corrupted thy thinking, thy purity of mind. Thou wouldst rather be this man's harlot, even if he abuses thee, than live the decent, honorable life that thou and I had planned?"

"I cannot begin to explain," she said. "I never wanted to cause you pain. If I could undo what I've done, if we could go back—"

"But there's no going back. There's nothing for it now, is there, except for thee to marry him. But I'll not see that happen without . . . Not without my first demanding satisfaction! Where is he?"

His face working, Arthur stalked toward the arched doorway.

Anne ran after him. "Arthur! Stop! Don't do this! Violence solves nothing. Your faith preaches rationality and gentleness—"

The knob rattled under his hand as he wrenched open the door. "It also preaches honor and justice."

"But he'll kill you!"

His eyes were blurred. "Then I'll take the bastard with me into hell!"

"You wish to chastise me, sir?"

Anne's heart stopped, then leaped back into thunderous chaos. Looking every inch his father's son, Lord Jonathan Devoran St. George stood waiting for them in the antechamber. He bowed, his face impassive. Though he seemed to be ignoring her, a giddy craving instantly flooded her bones.

He's corrupted thy thinking, thy purity of mind.

"It is what I would do in your place," Jack added. He seemed to speak with deliberate insolence.

Arthur was very white, his shoulders thrown back. "So thou knew—in spite of all of thy family's scheming—that she would tell me the truth about thy perfidy?"

"I didn't *know* it, sir," Jack said. "That was Miss Marsh's choice to make. However, I strongly suspected that she would. Though it is not perhaps what I would have done in her place."

His mouth working, Arthur rushed up to Jack and slapped him hard across the face.

Jack's eyes flinched closed, but he made no move to defend himself or to retaliate. He simply stepped back, the marks of the other man's fingers livid on his cheek.

"If you would come with me to my study, sir, perhaps we may discuss what can be done?"

"Thy *study*? What can be *done*! I demand satisfaction. Pray name your seconds!"

"In that case, if you will follow me, Mr. Trent," Jack replied with icy politeness, "you may have your satisfaction now."

"*Now?*"

"By all means, sir. I am at your disposal."

"Then prepare to be thrashed within an inch of thy life!"

Jack spun on his heel and strode from the room. Arthur clenched his fists and marched after him.

Anne felt sick, as if she might faint, as if her courage had fled with the men. Her knees seemed to melt like ice in a spring sun. For a moment she sagged unceremoniously against the wall, then she sat down on a hall chair.

A large tapestry filled her blurred vision: St. George piercing the dragon to the heart.

If the men fought, Arthur would die and Jack would have committed cold-blooded murder. The outcome was certain. Yet if

Jack refused to fight, her fiancé—her *ex*-fiancé—would feel dishonored and shamed and belittled, and he did not deserve that.

She had created this misery. It was all her fault.

"I am to assume that you have told Mr. Trent the truth about your fall from grace?" a woman's voice asked.

Poised in her trembling ribbons, her hair pale and neat, the duchess stood framed in the opposite doorway.

Anne rose and curtsied, then faced Jack's mother with a straight back and high chin, though she knew her red eyes would betray her. "I could not do otherwise, Your Grace. I could not marry a man I had deceived in such a fundamental way."

"Just so. Thus my son and your fiancé—in defiance of his religious convictions, I imagine—have gone to settle their outraged pride like men, ignoring your more delicate feminine sensibility entirely."

In spite of the pain lodged in her throat, Anne felt her heart lift just a little. "Yes, Your Grace."

The duchess laughed. "My son will not harm Mr. Trent, Miss Marsh. Lord Jonathan may be lost to most norms of morality. He is lost to me. But take courage: Though my son may be a seducer, he is not a murderer."

Anne said nothing as the duchess walked forward, her every movement graceful, precise.

"Your fiancé did not insist on marrying you, in spite of what has transpired?"

"No, Your Grace. Mr. Trent is hurt and outraged and offended, but—"

"But you do not think that his heart is broken. You had not realized that until this moment, had you?"

Anne stared at the duchess. Arthur's pride and sense of social probity were damaged, but his heart was not. Had he never really loved her, then? Had she never really loved him? In which case, how could anyone ever know whether they could trust their feelings?

"No, Your Grace," she said, searching for another truth—one that was oddly painful. "Though I also believe that we might have married very happily. Mr. Trent is an honorable gentleman."

"No doubt. And one who was affronted at any mention of money. Such upright sons of the gentry often are." The duchess gazed up at the tapestry, her face as calm as still water, though her eyes sparkled. "Now, if you had been engaged to marry an earl's son, or the scion of a marquess, any such young lord would have jumped at the chance to still marry you, sullied or not, if the wedding would redeem his gaming debts. Indeed, he would have schemed to secure a large enough settlement to enable him to rattle away the rest of his new fortune as fast as possible."

"I don't know," Anne said. "I've never met any sons of the peerage—"

"Except mine," the duchess said. "And you cannot understand them. You cannot understand any of us. You think I am a cruel mother, Miss Marsh? Life is not always so straightforward for us, my dear, but I shall take care of you, whatever Jonathan or Mr. Trent may do."

"You are very kind, Your Grace."

The duchess ran one finger over the head of the woven dragon. The fabric moved as if the beast came alive beneath the shivering spear.

"My son is trying to fight me." The duchess turned back to her. "Though he is no doubt battling with Mr. Trent at the moment. I imagine they have gone to the rose garden."

"The rose garden?"

Ribbons fluttered, innocent and bright against the tapestry forest, though Anne thought there was nothing in the least naive about Jack's mother.

"We have planted roses in an open space within the curtain wall at the base of the Whitchurch Tower. There is a nice little patch of greensward there, suitable for punishment, even bloodletting, but far too congenial for outright slaughter. Jonathan has been longing for someone to make him hurt enough over his transgressions ever since he returned home. I have done my best to assuage that. But perhaps you should go after them and make sure that it's done more thoroughly this time?"

Anne curtsied, her heart beginning to pound like a drumbeat. "But Lord Jonathan would never allow— Mr. Trent cannot possibly hurt him!"

The duchess moved gracefully across the antechamber toward the door of the blue salon.

"The rose garden is easy to find," she said. "Any of the footmen can direct you."

THE GARDEN HAD OBVIOUSLY ONCE BEEN PART OF THE outer bailey, now tamed with topiary yews and formal rose beds. Most of the bushes were in bud, or were still unfurling leaves, but here and there, where the sun was trapped by warm stone, a flower had already opened. Yet dense hedges and an occasional spur of buildings broke the garden into several private enclaves.

Voices and a dull scuffling echoed from beyond one circle of trimmed yews. Anne broke into a run, dodged beneath an archway, and stopped dead. Stripped to open-necked shirt and trousers, Jack stood facing her fiancé on a circular patch of turf. Similarly undressed, Arthur squared up to him, breathing hard, both fists clenched.

Behind the two men a large fountain spurted water, casting tiny rainbows like moving colored fishes. The water rained continuously into a round stone basin. Tucked up against the hedges, a set of benches ringed the grass. A peaceful sanctuary. Transformed now into a boxing ring.

"I would rather we had met with pistols tomorrow at dawn," Arthur said.

"Have you ever handled a pistol, Mr. Trent?" Jack asked.

"No, but since thou cannot behave like a gentleman, perhaps a gentleman's weapons are not for thee, either, in spite of thy noble blood?"

"It will be cold in the morning, Mr. Trent," Jack replied. "I have justly earned your wrath. By all means take it out on my flesh while your blood and the day are still warm."

"Then if thou wish for more fisticuffs, thou shalt have them. But I warn you: Righteousness is on my side."

"So I have already noticed, sir."

He held himself with that strange, quiet grace—the lethal power that had made her think of tigers—but a man's muscles also moved beneath Arthur's shirt. He shrugged as if to loosen his shoulders and bounced after Jack, punching the air. It was not perhaps an entirely unequal match, except that Jack had somewhere learned to fight like the ghost of an avenging angel. Yet Jack did not kick or strike or whirl into the attack with that lightning speed. He seemed as remote as if he were pacing a delicate measure in a ballroom, a little bored, even mildly amused.

*Yet your eyes hold such . . . calm elation. I don't know how to describe
it—*

Arthur dodged and hit out with passionate determination.
With that same cool indifference, Jack blocked the blow, but
Arthur ducked and landed a solid clout to Jack's gut. Jack dou-
bled over. Immediately Arthur hammered home another strike,
then another, cutting up with ruthless force into Jack's face.

Jack staggered back toward the fountain. He smiled, though
blood oozed from a small cut on his lip.

Arthur stumbled after him and punched again, his fist landing
with sickening force on the taller man's temple. Anne grabbed
her skirts in both hands and raced out toward them.

"Stop!" she cried. "Arthur! Stop! Stop now!"

His blue eyes glazed with triumph, a red bruise flaming on his
cheek, Arthur glanced over one shoulder and shook his head. "Go
away! I'm going to wipe that smirk from his face once and for
all!"

As Arthur spun back toward him, Jack's fist landed with exact
precision against the smaller man's shoulder. Arthur grimaced,
but with two swift, hard blows, he cracked his bare knuckles
against the side of Jack's head, while the other fist connected once
again with his enemy's stomach.

"Don't you see?" Anne shouted. "He's not fighting back. Lord
Jonathan's already injured. You're attacking an injured man!"

Arthur jigged back, punching the air. "Dost thou think his
injuries anywhere near as severe as those he has inflicted on me?"

"I've already apologized for that, sir. Though I cannot make it
right, and perhaps it's the lady's discomfort we should be thinking of now?"

Anne dashed between them to grab Jack by the sleeve. "You're not fighting him," she said. "You're not even protecting your face. There's blood."

"It's all right," he whispered as he took her gently by both upper arms. "Let him do this! You don't have to watch."

"Go away, Anne!" Arthur shouted. "This is no place for a lady. Hast thou lost all sense of decorum?"

"You see?" Jack said. "If you don't leave right away, one of us will undoubtedly knock you down by mistake."

"But you could prevent all of this," she insisted. "I saw you fighting in the lane, remember? You could end this right now, if you wished."

"I've made a different decision this time."

"Very well. But if you insist on behaving like barbarians, you'll have to do it with an audience." Her back upright, her handkerchief clutched in one hand, Anne marched off toward the fountain.

"She's in love with thee." Arthur's voice quavered from exertion. "Didst thou know that? Isn't it enough that thou wouldst trifle with a lady's virtue? Didst thou need to despoil her heart as well?"

"Her *heart*?"

"Yes, her heart! The pure, innocent heart of a lady. Yet thou wouldst only defile her, whether in the marriage bed or out of it. Canst thou not find thy animal relief elsewhere?"

Jack's eyes became dark, as if night fell in a forest. He dropped his fists. "Then you would not stand in the way of Miss Marsh becoming Lady Jonathan Devoran St. George—as long as I only *defile* her once a year, while I take other women as my whores?"

Arthur swung back his fist and struck with all of his strength. Fabric ripped. Knuckles met flesh with sickening force. As

Arthur reeled back, shaking from the impact of his own blow, Jack collapsed to both knees, clutching both hands over his gut.

"That's enough!" Anne shouted. "You don't know what you're talking about, Arthur. He wants you to hurt him. He's goading you."

Though his opponent was already on his knees, Arthur ignored her and struck again. Smiling like St. Francis gazing at squirrels, Jack keeled over to lie on the grass, his breathing fast and shallow, his eyes closed.

Panting and grimacing, trembling from head to foot, Arthur stared down at him.

"He wouldn't fight a proper duel. He said . . . he said if he was to marry thee, he would like to be in possession of all of his limbs. He made clear for what purpose!" Arthur looked up to meet her gaze. "If it had been up to me, we'd have met in a meadow tomorrow with pistols and I'd have killed him."

"But it *was* up to you." Anne brushed away hot, frantic tears— of anger and fear and a kind of clear exasperation. "As if a fistfight could ever solve anything, or undo what's been done!"

Arthur wiped his face with his sleeve and stared at her as if they'd never met before. "But I did this for thee."

"You did *not* do it for me. How can you say so? You claim to be a God-fearing man, but you're no different from any of my brothers, who think fisticuffs are fun. You're all mad for blood and physical relief. Even you, sir!"

He looked away. "Very well, then, I did it for myself and now it's done. His Lordship is not that badly hurt. I'd not permanently cripple the man thou art going to have to marry, Miss Marsh, however much he might deserve it."

Without another backward glance Arthur grabbed his jacket and waistcoat from the bench where he'd thrown them and stumbled from the garden.

Jack turned over to stretch out on his back on the grass. He pushed the hair back from his forehead, then touched the side of his mouth with one fingertip. A tiny trace of blood marked the corner of his lower lip. Bruises were already blooming on his face. He was panting a little, but as he opened his eyes to meet her gaze, she knew that he was holding back not outrage or pain, but a kind of desperate, ironic amusement.

"You're possessed!" she said, clinging to the stone basin at her back with both hands. "You're mad! Why did you let him do that? If you'd wanted to, you could have disabled him without hurting him and not received a scratch yourself. That's true, isn't it?"

"Alas, I'm merrily ensnared in my own deceptions. Please don't tell Mr. Trent!"

"Why did you let him hurt you?"

Jack winced as he felt the place on his temple where the tree had first injured him and where Arthur had landed another blow. "Didn't my mother tell you?"

"She said you wanted punishment."

He sat up, his hair tossed wickedly over his battered face, his shirt hanging open from a ripped seam near the collar. "Don't you think I owe the universe some small measure of justice for what I've done?"

"Justice?"

"I had to let him do it, Anne, and I had to hit him back just enough so that he wouldn't know that I allowed him to win. Yet he's damaged me far less than I've hurt him."

A tight pressure was building in her chest. "Maybe. But you didn't have the power to really hurt him. Only I did that."

Jack rested each forearm on a bent knee, his hands relaxed. "He refused to marry you, even if my mother bribed him with a fortune, didn't he?"

She glanced away. "How can he have felt or done otherwise? You're a duke's son."

"What difference does that make?"

"None! Only it does, to men like Arthur. Of course it does. His future is bound to fall into the hands of men like you, yet he took your mother's offer as the insult that it was."

"She didn't mean it as an insult," Jack said. "Only as a test. As she tested me in the Fortune Tower."

She looked back at him, aware of nothing but scorn. "Yet what a hazard for a man like Arthur to risk offending a duchess!"

"Mr. Trent is a brave man and a man of a certain integrity. He turned down what must have looked like a golden chance to gain influence and wealth. I respect that. Yet as soon as he knew what you and I had done together, he was glad enough to be free of the engagement, wasn't he?"

"He had no choice."

Shadows haunted his eyes as if the tiger stretched and moved in the forest. "Because he puts so much value on purity? If I loved a lady, I would not give her up so easily."

"I don't deserve a man like him," she said. "Honest and upright and considerate."

"*Deserve?* God! As if any of us get what we deserve!"

"Yet you thought you deserved a beating?" She pushed away from the stone rim and paced past him. "So you indulged in this vulgar masculine display and achieved precisely nothing."

Jack rose to his feet and walked to the fountain. His torn shirt revealed glimpses of firm golden flesh, dappled now as if with rose petals. Saying nothing, he bent and pulled the ruined garment off over his head, before plunging his bruised body and face beneath the rainbows of cold water.

Anne stared at his back: the strength and dignity and wicked beauty of it, his spine sliding down from his powerful shoulders into the slim, taut loins. Something moved in her heart, that yearning, painful sensation that triggered an avalanche of hot confusion.

If I loved a lady—

She wanted to fold to protect herself, like a closed rosebud. She wanted to open like a full-blown blossom to be ravished by the sun. The insanity of her own feelings filled her with rage. She stalked back to him.

He straightened up, shook his head like a wet dog, and used his shirt to dry himself.

"Will you also try to claim that you did this for me?" she asked.

"For you?" He grinned, though his lip had to pain him, at least a little. "No. It was all for Mr. Trent. He'll feel a great deal better now. His dignity is restored and his future is back in his own hands. He may even decide to take my mother's money and marry you, after all."

As pain surged in her heart, Anne swung back her hand and pivoted with all of her strength. She wanted to damage him. For a moment she even thought he would allow it, but Jack caught her fist in one hand.

"No," he said. "I was wrong. Not you, too!"

He pulled her against his chest to cradle her in both arms, allowing her head to find safe berth in the curve of his shoulder. Angry tears spilled down her cheeks. Yet Jack held her as he might hold something infinitely fragile and precious.

So he could perjure himself even with his body, as blithely, as innocently, as an angel!

"I'm sorry. I'm sorry. You didn't deserve that. I'm a brute to want you, too, to chastise me. Yet I cannot make it right, though I am trying to the best of my wretched ability. What do you want me to do, Anne?"

"Nothing!" she said, her voice muffled and broken. "Leave me alone! I was mad to think I could learn anything from you except heartbreak."

"Hush," he said. "Don't! Don't! All of this was nothing but damaged pride—mine and his. If your Mr. Trent loves you, he'll still want you, in spite of me and my cursed family."

She pulled away and used her handkerchief to wipe her eyes. "Do you understand nothing, Lord Jonathan? Marriage to Arthur is absolutely impossible now."

"Why impossible?"

"Because I don't love him and never loved him—and he doesn't love me and never loved me—and now we both know it."

Jack propped his hips against the rim of the fountain. His hair spilled over his forehead. His jaw was mottled with growing color. The glowing skin over his ridged muscles was marked as if he had been trampled by horses, and he was obviously in pain. The thought filled her with frantic distress. Yet he seemed far too firm, too lean, to have suffered much real damage.

Why had he tried to push her, too, into striking him?

"Ah," he said. "Then it cannot be mended."

She tried to pull back, to find some dissociation, some distance. "Yet he is still a good man and he is genuinely suffering."

"Whatever I can do to make it up to him, I will do," Jack said. "Now that he has defeated me with his fists, he may even allow me to do it. He needs a patron for his work with the fossils? He may have the support of the king. He wishes to advance in London society? Mr. Arthur Trent will find doors opening, opportunities flourishing. In spite of his religion, his path will be smoothed for him in whatever he wishes to do in life and his success is guaranteed."

"Then it was a happy day for him," Anne said, "when I asked you to teach me about bodies."

"Was that what you wanted?" Jack asked gently. "Only a lesson?"

"I don't know what I wanted, but that is what happened. Yet you don't need to marry me. I can remain quietly at home, or perhaps I shall choose to live independently. No one will know why I didn't marry Arthur. I'll be seen as a jilt, that's all."

"No, you had better marry me," he said. "Though I can promise you nothing more than a ceremony."

"Oh, no!" she said. "You're bleeding again."

She dipped her handkerchief into the falling water and stepped between his spread knees to press the pad of damp fabric to the small cut on his lip.

He closed his eyes and allowed her to do it, but his entire body began to tremble very slightly, as if fever flared beneath his skin. Heat seemed to emanate from his skin in rolling waves. Anne stood arrested as the hot breakers scorched her own flesh. He was burning—the blaze burned in him like a forest fire—and she, too, was about to burst into flames, like a sapling in the path of an inferno.

Her hand dropped to her side. The handkerchief fell to the grass.

"You're ill," she said. "You must go inside."

His eyes opened, the pupils enlarged as if he were drugged, though he smiled.

"Not ill, Miss Marsh. Don't you recognize these symptoms yet?"

"Oh!" She glanced down at the front of his trousers. "Oh!"

Tears pricked at her eyelids. It was the moment to move away. She was not disinterested or uninvolved, and neither was he. She must leave now, leave him, leave the rose garden, before it was too late. Instead she stood between his spread knees and quaked like a sapling. Her leaves shriveled in the face of his intensity. Her branches quivered like plucked strings. And her roots melted.

"If you don't leave immediately, I shall kiss you," he said.

"I can't. I can't leave." With her eyes on his bruised face, she pulled off her shawl as if to wrap it about his bare shoulders. "You're in pain."

He set his hands on her corseted waist as if to hold her at arm's length. "Please, Anne, don't!"

She stared at his mouth—at the tiny cut that must sting every time he spoke—as the burning entirely consumed her heart.

"I know you don't want me," she said. "I know this is a mistake."

"I must return to Asia. You must remain here in England. Our lives will take separate paths into different futures. I cannot kiss you now and answer for the consequences."

"I don't care any longer. What difference will it make, now that I'm already a fallen woman? But won't it hurt you to kiss me?"

"Not enough to matter."

The fountain rippled behind him in a never-ending curtain of cold water. Anne's heart was seared with longing. The shawl slipped from her fingers to fall abandoned to the grass. Her hands found his naked arms, warm and smooth. Her palms slid up to his muscled shoulders. She leaned forward, ablaze as if the sun had expanded to embrace her.

Tentatively she pressed her lips onto his, careful to avoid the little cut in one corner.

Not tentative at all, Lord Jonathan Devoran St. George kissed her back.

CHAPTER TWELVE

❧

IS HANDS SLID DOWN PAST HER WAIST, CAPTURING HER bottom and pulling her into his body. Wild sensations flooded through her blood. Thoughts fled. She was consumed: by the touch of mouth to mouth; the pressure of seeking lips; the sweet entanglement of tongues. Desire throbbed and demanded, absorbing everything.

His flesh burned, hot and firm and lovely beneath her hands. His mouth burned, moist and sweet against her lips. It was worth anything, anything, to feel this wonder and pleasure and exhilaration, as if she were melting beneath a foreign sun and were being formed into a new creature.

His mouth released hers at last, and he gazed at her with drugged, hot eyes. Her eyelids felt heavy, her lashes cumbersome, as if she, too, had inhaled some intoxicating vapor.

"Not just a kiss," he said. "I can't promise that. God, I'm insane to do this! Please, Anne! Go inside now!"

She leaned forward and replied again with her lips and tongue, searching his mouth, only pulling away when the honey of his kiss hinted at a rusty trace of blood.

"Oh!" She touched the corner of his lips with one fingertip. "I hurt you."

He dropped his forehead into the curve of her shoulder and laughed unsteadily, his breath warm on her neck. "No. You cannot hurt me. Nothing about this can hurt me. But I can hurt you."

The falsehood was there in his voice. He was already hurt, physically beaten and bruised. Yet there was something else that made her think he was more vulnerable in his assurances than he knew, vulnerable to desire and love and suffering. Vulnerable to *her*? Her heart seemed to crack open at the question, swallowing all of her anger, swallowing all of her better judgment.

She stroked one hand over his hair, playing with the damp strands, smoothing it past his ears. Her palms strayed over his shoulders, marveling at his warm, resilient flesh. She pressed her lips to his neck, tasting man and cold water. His scent, as clean and chill as the rushing fountain, filled her nostrils.

Hot longing for his touch suffused every pore of her being.

"The damage is done long since," she said. "I know it means nothing to you, but what can one more time matter?"

He groaned as his hands slid down the back of ther skirt, lifting her legs. Anne closed her eyes and wrapped both arms around his shoulders. Her feet left the ground. One shoe fell to the grass, then the other. He pulled her knees up high over his legs, until she straddled his lap. Her feet found the rim of the fountain, the stone damp on her arches. Her thighs rested on his, while she clung to him and kept kissing.

His mouth ravished her jaw and neck and the little hollows of her collarbones. Shivers of fire raced in colored flames over her skin, pulsed away into her bones. She began to tremble. The hot longing streamed urgently. Down, down to pool heavily in those unmentionable, mysterious places, where it burned and ached, demanding resolution.

She arched in his arms as his mouth sought the neckline of her dress, kissed the swell of her breasts, the top of the valley between them. Her nipples rose and ached. Through his trousers she felt his arousal pulse strongly between her legs. The memory seared, of her touching that naked heat, discovering those male mysteries. The ardent demand of it felt lovely, lovely and imperious and terrifying.

Terrifying? She dismissed that whisper of panic in a rush of blind courage. No fears! She wanted this to go on forever. *Forever, Jack! Forever—*

Supporting her with one arm, he stroked the other hand down to where her dress and petticoat had fallen back to reveal her garter and the top of her stocking. His palm caressed her knee, then his fingers strayed down the back of her thigh, pushing aside fabric and lace, until his fingers wickedly cupped her bare bottom.

Anne gasped and opened her eyes.

Water cascaded from the fountain. Rainbows scattered and leaped like mackerel in the falling water. Jack leaned back, balancing her in his lap, one hand on her spine, one palm embracing her nakedness. Sunlight caressed his bruised face. His lids were closed, robbing her of the tiger-rich forest depths, yet he looked exalted.

She had done that? She had brought him that blissful oblivion?

Cold water streamed behind his back and shoulders, occasionally splashing his bare skin. He seemed entirely absorbed in his slow embrace of her flesh. His fingertips moved between her buttocks, tickling, caressing. Shame and hot excitement merged into one scorching conflagration as his palm stroked up over her flank and down again to brush over her belly, until his knuckles caressed the intimate secret between her legs.

Anne sagged into the support of his arm. Her surrender to this ecstasy was absolute. His thumb flicked over that mysterious place, the spot that filled her with rapturous madness. A rush of moisture flooded deeply within her body, as if the fountain had entered her soul.

"Yes," she said. "Yes."

His fingers persisted, gently opening the damp folds of flesh. His mouth persisted, kissing her breasts through the thin muslin of her dress. He tasted her bare neck. His tongue flicked maddeningly over the base of her ear. His thumb flicked maddeningly over the slickness between her legs. The place that was swelling and throbbing for him, until the heat and craving turned her body into liquid fire.

With his supporting arm he lifted her a little. Anne pushed with her feet against the fountain and braced herself as she clung to his shoulders. She felt him fumble with buttons to push fabric out of the way.

Searing rigid heat nudged against her bare flesh. She knew what it meant. She had touched it, been awed by its strangeness—her first lesson in sin. Now once again the smooth, naked head pushed against her hidden opening. Hot. Silken. Instantly the yearning coalesced, becoming one strident, deafening demand.

"Yes," she said. "Oh, yes, my lord, my— Oh, Jack!"

He held her hovering above him, her insteps curled over the edge of the stone basin, her bare thighs burning against his. Then slowly, slowly, while her breath wept in her lungs, he eased her down onto his erection.

Now! Oh, yes! Now! Just like that! My beloved fallen angel!

Slowly, slowly, he sank himself deep inside her, until she felt his body pressed tightly against hers. Immeasurable pleasure. Immeasurable wickedness.

"Oh," she said. "Oh, Jack!"

He caught her head in both hands then and kissed her again, tongue and lips and teeth. His bruised mouth asked no mercy and gave none. Anne kissed back as he began to move inside her. Deeply. Deeply. Unfathomable and profound and satisfying. And even more lovely than she remembered.

Jack broke the kiss and set his hands on her waist. He threw his head back and closed his eyes, rocking his hips and hers, helping her to find the rhythm. She clung to his shoulders and concentrated on the feelings.

At each stroke delight burgeoned. She was wicked. Wicked and sinful and beyond redemption. But heat and shame and bliss mingled into this one overwhelming pleasure.

Pleasure? Ah, what a weak word for this! But yes! Please me! And please may I please you as much, my lord?

Pleasure. Pleasure. Pleasure—

He filled her. Rapture filled her. Limp as trampled petals, her body swayed forward against his, her skirts bunched up about her waist and trailing down over his supporting arms. Locked safely in his embrace, she concentrated on the growing intensity that pulsed from their joining. He moved her, loved her, made love with her, until at last her absorption scattered and she was overwhelmed by those terrifying, beautiful ripples of ecstasy—

Pierced to the heart Anne collapsed against his chest. She wept inarticulate cries of relief, of pure bliss, of burning shame, into his shoulder.

"Dear God!"

It was a faint sound, barely audible. A cry from another planet. Perhaps she had imagined it.

Anne raised heavy eyelids, her lashes burdened with enchantment.

Jack's hair shone darkly against the rushing water, the damp strands mingled with devilish highlights of red and gold, as if he lived in an aura of his own flame. His eyes were still closed, but his expression was clear and bright and rapt, negating the bruised temple and mottled jaw, the tiny cut on his mouth.

Her heart could break over loving him.

Anne laid her cheek on his shoulder. Her naked thighs were still wrapped about his waist. Her cotton stockings were wet. The flesh of her calves and feet shone pinkly through the fabric. One of her garters had come undone. So had her hair. It straggled half-pinned, half-disheveled, down her back.

He did not want her. His life offered no place for a Dissenter's daughter, even if he married her. He had only made love to her because he was hurt and, for that one moment, vulnerable. She knew that. He had pretended nothing else.

"Dear God!"

She turned her head dreamily toward the sound, too clear to ignore this time, a cry of heartbreak and shock and outrage.

Cruel heat flooded her face just as Jack's spine stiffened almost imperceptibly beneath her palms. So he had opened his eyes and followed her gaze. Humiliation surged through her veins. Two men stood at the far end of the path between the roses, staring in disbelief.

Shame coalesced into a terrible mortification. To be discovered!

Like this! Anne wanted to die or disappear as if she'd never been born. Tears stung with real bitterness to scald down her red cheeks.

Yet Jack held her unmoving. He was still erect inside her body. She glanced up at his face, at the wild curl at the corner of his mouth, at the bruises darkly dappling his skin. His thoughts were unreadable. Something of annoyance? Something of that mysterious ironic amusement? Something of dread?

A violent shiver ran over her flesh.

"Hush, hush," he said, stroking her back. "It's all right. They've gone now."

"Oh!" Her voice was muffled by distress. "What have I done?"

He lifted her face to kiss her quickly on the mouth. "*We* have made love. We *are* making love. It's all right. I will marry you. This is what married people do."

"But that was your brother and Mr. Devoran! And we are— We are *outside*!"

"Guy will understand." His hands gently pushed the tangled strands back from her cheek. His voice was warm and light, reassuring. "Though for the sake of family honor, Ryder will probably now try to take his turn to kill me."

"But this wasn't what you wanted!"

"Wanted? For my brother and cousin to find me taking advantage of a respectable young lady in the rose garden? To be discovered having my wicked way with a guest of my mother's on the edge of my grandmother's fountain?"

"It's not funny!"

He kissed her again and slowly lifted her away, slipping himself from her moist body.

"Yes, it is, though it might not feel that way at the moment. It would seem very funny indeed to our grandchildren."

"But you're not— You are still—"

Jack set her on her feet and tugged down her skirts. He turned his back and leaned forward to cup cold water in one palm. He flung the water over his face and body, then glanced back to wink at her.

"Cold water is the recommended remedy, ma'am, for most male ills," he said formally. "Cold water and beatings do wonders to cool our disordered blood."

Her knees felt like boiled noodles. "You didn't finish," she said. "There was no pleasure for you."

He arranged his clothing, then faced her again, buttoned and neat, though still naked from the waist up. His mouth grinned, but she thought his eyes reflected a terrible blankness, something close to despair. Anne turned her head, not wanting to see that, not wanting to acknowledge what it might mean.

"There was very real pleasure for me, I assure you. Enough to justify several hair shirts, which I shall commission right away."

"Your brother will beat you, as well? And you'll let him?"

Supporting her with one arm about her waist, he walked her to a stone bench beneath a yew. "No. Ryder's chastisement will be far more subtle and more painful than that."

Anne sat down and gazed away across the garden. "What will he do?"

"I don't know."

The fountain streamed, its downpour endlessly cycling, forever recaptured in that wide stone pool. Anne set her feet neatly together and smoothed her skirts over her lap. She knew she must look like a prim schoolmarm who had been suddenly and unexpectedly dragged backward through a hedge. That's all she was, after all: a foolish country girl who had encouraged a duke's son to take improper liberties, and must pay the price for the rest of her life.

"You're all right?" Jack asked.

"Yes, yes, of course." She bit her lip. She knew that restlessness haunted him now. Restlessness and something of grief. "That was all my fault. I think I've gone mad."

"No. On the contrary," he said. "You're one of the sanest people I've ever met. For God's sake, don't regret what you are, or what you've done."

She gulped back the humiliating tears that threatened to scald down her cheeks. "You must go to find your brother. Please, go! I'd rather be alone."

"You should allow me to escort you to your room, at least. I can't leave you here."

"Yes, you can! Why not?"

If he didn't leave immediately, she would break into open sobs and recriminations, and her disgrace would be complete. Almost as if he understood that, he turned his back.

"Then allow me to send my mother to you. The duchess may even be able to explain what just happened."

"Yes," she said. "Go! It's all right."

Jack walked away a few paces to retrieve his waistcoat and jacket and gather up his damp shirt.

"I'll write to your father immediately," he said.

She lifted her head. "My father?"

He shrugged into the jacket. "We must marry by special license. Though I don't imagine he'll withhold his consent, you may give Mr. Marsh whatever reason you like for such irregular haste."

"No," she said, scrubbing her face with her handkerchief. "Whatever games your family may play, I have always told my father the truth and I shall do so this time."

He bent to grasp her shawl, where it had dropped onto the grass from her nerveless fingers. Anne watched as he scooped it up, his back lithe, every movement lovely and potentially lethal.

"And what's the truth, Anne?"

"That I have trapped you into marrying me," she said. "Against your will and against my own better judgment. I didn't mean to do it. You don't love me or want me."

Jack strode back to her to tuck the shawl about her shoulders.

"As for not *wanting* you," he said dryly, "I believe the rim of that fountain would give the lie to that."

Anne snuggled into the soft wrap, because his hands had just touched it, because he had thought to bring it to her. She wasn't cold. She had caught a fever, a madness, and her blood still scalded her veins. She was in love with a man who could only come to resent her more with each passing day. And the world would force them to wed.

She watched him leave, his boots soft on the grass, his breath soft on the spring air. Once she was alone, Anne pulled her feet up onto the stone bench, wrapped her arms about her knees, and lost her fight to hold back a torrent of weeping.

THE DUCHESS WAS STANDING BESIDE AN IRON GATE INTO the garden, examining the unfurled petals of an early yellow rose. As Jack strode up to her, the rose shed its golden petals, one by one, under her suddenly convulsed fingers.

"So you could not refrain from further fornication," she said, "not even for an hour?"

Jack bowed, though his bruised body complained, as it had protested dully when he'd begun to make love. Arthur Trent had landed more than one telling blow.

"Apparently not. I'm to assume that you've just met Ryder and Guy. I will marry her immediately, of course."

"It is not what I would have wished. For her sake, as much as yours."

"Because you believe I will damage her, even if I leave right away? I don't know. I never wished to hurt her."

The duchess opened her hand. Bruised yellow petals drifted one by one to the grass. "Then you need to better understand your desires. As for Ryder, I think you have broken his heart."

"Surely he didn't tell you what he witnessed?"

"No. He didn't have to. One look at his face was enough, as was the manner in which he refused to face me. He left without another word. So what was it? A rape on the grass?"

Rigidity began to seep through his bones, as if ice turned the reeds by a cold pond into stone. He closed his eyes. "No, on the edge of Grandmother's fountain."

"Guy had to drag your brother away bodily. I made your cousin tell me that much, at least. Otherwise you might not be standing here facing me now."

"I regret it," Jack said.

"Regret what? That you allowed Mr. Trent to punish you a little first, before you reasserted your manhood on his affianced bride?"

"Believe what you will, Mother." Jack looked back at her face, and knew that all of his rage was for himself. "I cannot begin to explain it, but I assure you that I feel as mortified by this latest development as you could possibly desire."

His mother's troubled gaze searched his face. She quivered in her own aura of distress: a deep anguish that he had caused. "You did not even allow him to give you a particularly thorough beating, did you? Yet I am sure you held back nothing from the ravishment that followed."

Yet he had! He had tried to hold back. Why had he not done so earlier, better?

"You would rather I had allowed him to inflict permanent damage?"

"Why not?" the duchess said. "That is what you have done to him, to Miss Marsh, to all of us."

"I'm prepared to swallow my punishment, Your Grace, all the last bitter dregs of it. But later, perhaps? Please, go to Anne now. I left her on a bench by the fountain."

"Very well." The duchess looked away, her back upright, her hair gleaming gilt in the sun. "After all, she is about to become a member of this family."

"I did not intend to come home like this," Jack said. "I never wished to wound you."

She glanced back at him, the green eyes soft with tears. "Nor I you. Yet you are more hurt than you know, Jonathan, and more deeply than I can fathom. As Miss Marsh was hurt to discover that her fiancé would give her up so easily."

He stared at her, the mystery of his life. "She doesn't love him."

"Perhaps not. So, both wounded, you took comfort in each other's arms. It's understandable, but it's no basis for a marriage."

"What would be?"

She brushed her fingers over another rose, a soft peach-and-primrose bud, still crisp, barely open.

"Brilliant social consequence," she said. "Or, without that, true love. Take one or the other."

"True love?" He repressed the impulse to touch her, to offer—or seek?—some kind of tactile comfort. To offer it and be rejected? "An unexpected admission from the Duchess of Blackdown, surely?"

"God knows," the duchess snapped, "there's no other acceptable reason for a son of mine to marry a nobody!"

Jack stared after his mother as she walked away, her skirts swaying.

His normal alertness felt blurred, as if he had been staring at the sun. *True love?* He did not even know what that meant. He understood carnal desire. He knew, even if he did not quite understand it, the deep, inchoate love he felt for his family. He had known admiration and desire for the women in his life. He felt an aching tenderness, in spite of everything, for Anne. *True love?* The words sounded absurd, fantastic.

He turned to leave and met his brother's fist, striking hard and fast toward his jaw.

Unlike the blows that he had—with such painstaking care—partially deflected from Arthur Trent, Ryder's punch was about to find him entirely undefended for the first time in his life. With only a split second to realize what was happening, Jack's reflexes reacted before he could prevent them. His mind opened onto blankness as he spun away, chopped hard with the side of his hand, and kicked out.

Ryder went down like a felled tree.

* * *

"MY DEAR CHILD," A WOMAN'S VOICE SAID. "TAKE MINE. It's dry."

Jack's mother, the sun at her back, the fountain weeping behind her, stood gazing down at Anne. She was holding out a handkerchief.

Anne dropped her feet back to the ground and smoothed both hands over her disordered hair. She knew how she must look. Shame inundated her bones, hot and relentless. Yet a stubborn pride made her sit up with her back straight. She met the older woman's gaze with something of defiance, though it seemed only a further humiliation that her face must be stained with tears.

The duchess sat down. With deft, gentle dabs of her handkerchief, she dried Anne's cheeks.

"Hush, now! It's all right."

"No, Your Grace," Anne said. "It isn't. Your sons are becoming enemies because of me."

"I also have daughters and I am very pleased to welcome a new one into my family."

"But I don't understand how I could be so—"

"Wanton?" the duchess asked dryly. "A flaw, I would say, in how we raise our daughters. We warn them to reject importunate male desire, but never teach them how to handle their own. You will have to marry Jonathan now, of course. As for my sons, they love each other. In spite of what Ryderbourne just witnessed here, you are not what comes between them. In fact, it will do them good to face this together."

Anne bit her lip and looked away. "Lord Jonathan doesn't love me. I did not mean . . . There must be a way to free him from this!"

"He doesn't know what he loves, nor what he wants. What makes you think that you have bound him?"

"I have not," Anne said. "But he's becoming bound by his own honor."

"I am very glad to hear that you think he still possesses any," the duchess said. "Though I was reassured a little when he did not take the escape he was offered in the Fortune Tower. Now hush! Sexual passion isn't only a man's prerogative. You will not solve anything by tormenting yourself over what cannot be changed. It will not hurt Jonathan to marry, though at the moment I don't think he takes heed one way or another whether he lives or dies."

"He would take his own life?" Anne asked, appalled.

"No, I am sure he would not. Yet somewhere I think he has lost the will to really care about his own existence. Thus you have done my sons no harm, though the opposite is not the case."

"Then you would not have me weep for any of the St. Georges?" Anne asked. "I'm sorry, Your Grace. I do not wish to cause you discomfort, but I think I'm about to torment myself a little more—"

"My dear! What else are mothers for?"

Without another word the duchess gathered Anne into her embrace. From sheer surprise Anne let her head drop to the duchess's shoulder, then closed her eyes against newly seeping tears: the grief of anger, or of shame? She wasn't sure, but she felt tired enough to sleep for a thousand years.

Jack's mother began to sing very softly. It was strangely comforting, as if a faraway nurse were singing reassurance to a changeling. The tune was as soothing and sweet as a lullaby.

Sigh no more, ladies, sigh no more; Men were deceivers ever:
One foot in sea and one on shore, To one thing constant never:
Then sigh not so, But let them go, And be you blithe and bonny;
Converting all your sounds of woe into hey nonny, nonny.

"GOD, JACK!" RYDER SAID THICKLY. "WHAT THE DEVIL *have* you become?"

"Not someone you should try to punch in the jaw when he's least expecting it," Jack said. "I'm sorry about that, but very glad to welcome you back to consciousness."

"How the hell did I get in here?" Ryder lay sprawled on a couch in his bedroom in the Whitchurch Wing.

Jack dipped a cloth back into the ice water he'd ordered from the kitchen. He wrung out the cloth and held it once again to the bruise blooming on his brother's jaw.

"I carried you. You weigh a ton. No, two tons."

Ryder felt gingerly about his mouth with his tongue. "No teeth missing, but I admit I feel a little strangled."

"If I hadn't realized it was you just in time, I might be ordering your coffin, not worrying about whether I'd damaged your bloody teeth."

"Why are you dripping ice down my neck?"

"I'm attempting to salvage what's left of your windpipe. Or you may interpret my cold compresses as just a nice Oriental torture, if you like."

Ryder pushed himself up against the curved back of the seat. He clasped one hand to his throat and swallowed, then grinned a little unsteadily. Jack had already removed his cravat and opened his shirt.

"If you were to order hot brandy and honey, would I be able to drink it?"

Jack handed him the cold cloth so his brother could hold it to his own jaw. "It's already on its way. You're only bruised, I think."

Ryder's laugh was strangled by an uncomfortable cough. "Then that makes two of us! Have you looked at yourself in the mirror?"

"Rather splendid, isn't it?" Jack stood up to face the glass over the mantel. "Mr. Trent was moderately thorough. I'm delighted that you thought you could add anything more to his thrashing."

"It wasn't exactly honorable for me to try to hit you without warning—"

Jack turned to gaze down at his brother. "If you apologize for that, I *will* kill you. You were in shock at what you'd witnessed in the rose garden. Then I assume you met Mother, who of course read in your face exactly what had happened."

"Yes," Ryder said. A shadow stained his green eyes.

"If our positions had been reversed, I'd have done the same thing. In fact, I might have gone to fetch a horsewhip first."

"No, you wouldn't. You may have the sexual morals of an alley cat, but no man with your fighting skills would ever strike an undefended man unless he meant to slay him. I don't believe—yet—that you're a cold-blooded murderer, or that you're intent on fratricide."

"Yet? Then you might believe it with more evidence?"

"God, Jack!" Ryder winced as he tried to turn his head. "What the devil am I supposed to believe? You're gone from England for all these years. Your letters are filled with nothing but amusing anecdotes about travel in Persia or India. Your sisters begin to weave fantasies about your exploits, tales better suited to *The Arabian Nights*. And a legend begins to grow."

Jack walked away to gaze from the window. The bright spring afternoon beat down on a small courtyard, another odd corner formed by the endless building and rebuilding of Wyldshay over the ages.

"Meanwhile, you hear something quite different," he said. "Other tales start to circulate in the London clubs. Your brother has become depraved: Wild Lord Jack, for whom no sensual adventure is too base, no vice too extreme. He's lost to honor and decency. Perhaps the hints of it even haunt my letters. You don't want to believe it, yet deep in the bone you're afraid it might be true—and so is Mother."

Ryder lay back and closed his eyes. "I did *not* believe it, until you dishonored an innocent Englishwoman—"

"Only to ravish her again just now in the rose garden?" Jack turned from the window and strode back to him. "Yes. That is what I have done. There's no need to mince words."

His brother said nothing. Jack took the compress, dipped it into the ice water and wrung it, then pressed the cold cloth once again to Ryder's throat.

"I cannot explain Miss Marsh," he said quietly. "I don't understand it myself. Objectively I can see that she's not a raving beauty, nor a vision of seductiveness. It's like a kind of madness, as if she alone had the power to strip me to the bone—"

"You're not in love with her?"

"No," Jack said. "How could I be? Yet I shall marry her, even though I must leave England again right away."

"Why?" Ryder asked, gripping Jack's wrist in strong fingers. "Why must you return to Asia? You owe me the truth, Jack. 'You gave birth to a wanderer, madam. Let him go!' Father knows your real reasons, of course?"

Jack stared at Ryder's hand. He could break the grip easily. Instead he relaxed and surrendered to the contact, though it hurt.

"Yes. Most of them. The duke also knows that my work will be useless if any of it becomes known."

Ryder released Jack's wrist and swallowed. "You don't think you can trust me?"

"I would trust you with my life."

His brother glanced up into Jack's face. "I suppose we might say that I just trusted you with mine. You're a damned lethal machine, aren't you? How the devil did you learn to fight like that?"

"In bits and pieces. There are several fighting arts current in the East. This one was originally developed by monks. They've had millennia in which to perfect the training of both mind and body."

"Not Christian monks, I assume?"

Jack grinned. "There are older religions than Christianity, Ryder. These monks must sometimes travel through regions infested with bandits. They created a way to defend themselves without carrying weapons. The practice is also a spiritual exercise."

"Do such holy men kill?"

"No, almost never. I learned that later."

"If it kept you alive, I'm glad. Your work, you said. Can you tell me?"

Jack didn't know why he was reluctant to give details. He did trust his brother's integrity absolutely. Nothing he told Ryder would ever leave this room. Yet he felt as if he might have to peel away his own flesh to reveal the pattern of his bones—though of course any more pain to himself was now entirely irrelevant.

"There's not much to tell," he said. "You're aware that Russia and Britain fight a secret, weaponless war over influence in Central Asia? Russia wishes to subdue the tribes that threaten her borders, yet Britain cannot let Russia gain access to the passes that could be used for an invasion of India."

"Is that likely?"

Jack paced restlessly about the room. "It's our single greatest fear: that hordes of warriors—with or without Russian encouragement or help—may sweep down from the north to devastate the jewel of our empire. Yet we know almost nothing about possible routes of attack. All of that disputed, though coveted, land lies in a great white space on the map."

"Another edge to the known world," Ryder said. " 'Here there be dragons?' "

"We're talking about the highest mountains in the world, and beyond them deserts that strike terror to the soul. Every inch that's even remotely inhabitable is fought over by warring tribes, none of whom look very kindly on trespassing strangers, especially Englishmen."

"Yet British India is desperate to gain access to these countries and control them?"

"If we don't, Russia will. But first we need maps. We must know what all that country is like and how easily a modern army could cross it."

"Alexander the Great did it," Ryder said.

"Exactly."

"So how did you get involved?"

There was a discreet knock. Jack strode to the door to relieve a footman of a tray. He came back to prepare a soothing drink for his brother: honey and fresh lemon juice stirred into hot water, plus a liberal dose of brandy. Jack then added one other ingredient that Ryder didn't know about.

"I'd rattled about in Greece, then wandered to Aleppo and Baghdad. I learned a smattering of languages as I went and discovered that I also had a gift for disguises, a useful attribute if one wishes to travel freely in the East. Meanwhile, I'd read Marco Polo and I made a hobby of studying obscure ancient Greek texts wherever I found them."

"What the devil does Marco Polo have to do with the classical Greeks?"

"They both traveled the Silk Road," Jack said. "One Aristeas rode all the way from Athens to the borders of China some twenty-five hundred years ago. Only fragments of his writings survive, but other accounts confirm the tale. He went to find griffins."

"*Griffins!* For God's sake, Jack!"

"But these griffins were rumored to make their lairs in vast fields of gold, like dragons nesting on treasure. There were reports of dragons in India, as well: their skulls covered with gems. We may dismiss it all as myth, yet the ancient Scythians crafted solid gold ornaments featuring the griffin and tattooed replicas of the creature on their skin. When these tales reached the ears of the Greeks, Aristeas decided to go for himself."

"Don't tell me," Ryder said, his voice beginning to drift. "You traveled in his footsteps and found gold?"

"No," Jack said, taking the empty glass from his brother's slack fingers. "I found bones."

* * *

*J*ACK WALKED SLOWLY OUT OF THE BEDROOM. RYDER SLEPT now in the deep oblivion of the opium drinker. He would wake, perhaps, without pain and—if the ice compresses had done their job—without visible swelling.

I almost killed my brother! A little closer to the jugular . . . If I had not pulled back in time!

With anguish like a burn in his heart, he closed the bedroom door, then paused for a second in Ryder's study. Something lay shattered in the grate. Jack strode to the fireplace and bent to pick up the pieces. He turned them over in his hands—the curve of green mane like jade spume on a wave; the dainty, ferocious little hooves—

A small noise made him look up. Anne was standing in the shadows by the bookshelves, her face white.

"My mother sent you up here to see Ryder," Jack said. "You've been here all along. You've just overheard everything that we said."

Chapter Thirteen

UTTERFLIES LAUNCHED INTO FLIGHT IN HER STOMACH. *You are not in love with her? . . . No. How could I be?*

"I didn't mean to," Anne said. "I was shown in here by the footman. . . ."

"It's all right." Jack's eyes seemed very dark. His expression was unreadable.

"Well," Anne said. "Hardly all right. Yet when I heard your talking, I was afraid to disturb it— No, it was grossly dishonorable of me not to leave right away, even if I had interrupted what was happening."

To her surprise, he smiled: a smile of genuine humor, colored by that rich appreciation for the absurd. "My dear Miss Marsh, it's a bit late now for you and I to stand upon *honor*."

In spite of all the emotions she had felt in the previous few hours, Anne found herself biting her lip to keep from grinning like a fool. "Yes," she said. "I suppose it is."

Jack strode to the door to the hallway and held it open for her. "I imagine you're beginning to think that gaining whatever knowledge you can about me and my family is now very much a matter of survival, which is almost always more important than honor, whatever schoolboys may claim."

"If you like," Anne said, walking forward while the butterflies circled beneath her corset. "I certainly believe that I felt rather pinned, like a rabbit in a trap, in case any movement I made might interfere and prevent your talking to your brother like that."

"Like what?"

She looked down, filled with awkward self-awareness. "With love, I suppose."

"That's not what you would have expected?"

"Even after what you showed me on the rooftops, I thought you were at daggers drawn. Though the duchess didn't send me here. I came on my own."

"Because you thought it might help if you were to explain to Ryder what happened at the fountain?"

"I wanted to try to heal what I thought was a breach between you. I see now that was presumptuous."

"No, it was generous," he said. "And I don't think for one moment that you're a very natural rabbit, Miss Marsh, but then I never have. I'm already a stunned admirer of your courage."

She stopped in the doorway to look up at him. "I don't understand."

"You've shown an extraordinarily brave spirit ever since we met." He winked with real gaiety. "If you marry me, you'll be very brave indeed."

"I was glad that you and Lord Ryderbourne could talk together so calmly. I was afraid—"

"That we might murder each other?"

She avoided his gaze as she brushed past him into the corridor.

She could not escape the shiver of awareness, her body's flare of arousal, when he was standing so close. His scent was lovely, the wild masculine essence of open skies, carrying wicked promises from mysterious, unknown lands. Yet now it only deepened her shame, as if being seen at the fountain had brought home the enormity of her sin.

"Yes," she said. "I thought perhaps you might."

"Ryder is disappointed and confused, certainly. In fact, he's worried almost to death. But he doesn't hate me. He's my brother."

"Then perhaps you should have explained something of your life to him before this," Anne said, closing her mind against the onslaught of that heady wind and her own confused feelings. "It's that competition between Britain and Russia that's so important to you, isn't it?"

"This game between the great powers is all that really counts. But don't impute too much nobility to my motives. My first interest was simply adventure and wanderlust."

"Because you'd read those ancient tales and you traveled beyond the edge of the known world to hunt dragons?" Dust motes danced lazily in the sunbeams slanting across the hallway. She felt giddy, as if she must escape outside or she would fall headlong into his embrace once again. "I'm sure that the maps and the politics matter, yet your fossil will change mankind's view of his place in the universe."

Jack strode ahead of her to fling open a door that led into a courtyard. Walls soared away into brightness.

"Not this time," he said. "This fossil is going to be lost."

Anne stared at his profile. She would never be immune to the effect he had on her! Never! She leaned back against the wall, grateful for its cold support.

"Lost? How can it be lost?"

"I can see I'm going to have to explain a little more about our troublesome dragon. Come, join me out here in the sunshine."

She nodded and walked forward. It was very simple. First one foot, then the other. In spite of his casual smile, in spite of the careless way he held open the door for her, something in his expression filled her with dread.

"Someone's been murdering people, or trying to murder them, ever since you arrived back in England. Now we're locked up here in this fortress. It's not just for my protection, is it? It's for yours. Your life is at risk?"

"You would care about my wretched life?" he asked. "Ah, Miss Marsh, you have a benevolent heart."

Rooted in moss and a few straggling ferns, a statue dominated the center of the little courtyard. A dragon, of course. Dark shadows wrote mysteries in a looping script beneath each carved scale. Anne sat down on a stone block that projected from the base of a buttress. With one hand on the dragon's head, Jack stared down at it as if he might borrow its leathery wings to fly straight up into the sun.

"I will try to give you more than the shreds of a tale," he said. "I believe I owe you that much, at least. Where would you like me to start?"

"How did you travel? If all those places are so hostile to foreigners?"

"I became a horse trader, a holy man, whatever suited the moment. The fabled gold of the ancient Scythians was one excuse, but travel has a way of becoming its own purpose. I saw things that no European has seen for centuries, perhaps not since Alexander."

"What kinds of things?"

"Holy statues hundreds of feet high carved into cliffs. Deserts where towers of wind-scoured stone loom like monsters to guard the graveyards of their brothers. Abandoned cities lost in sand." He folded his arms and turned to lean back against the dragon. "Eventually in a desert near the Altai Mountains I found myself in a place where huge bones cover the ground like a pavement. Perhaps they weren't really griffins, but giant creatures with beaked faces certainly lived there once, along with even larger animals. There are entire skeletons. Complete families and their nests."

"*Nests?*"

"Stone eggs laid in nests on the ground, like enormous birds."

Her heart began to drum. "Did you take notes, make drawings?"

Restlessness haunted him, as if he might soon unfold wings of his own. "Another man did. I was sick almost to the death. If I hadn't been carried back to India, I'd have added my bones to those of the giant lizards. It wasn't an easy journey. Apart from anything else, I was haunted."

She stared at him in silence, as chilled as if a breeze blew over her heart.

Jack glanced back at her and smiled. "Marco Polo wrote that the Takla Makan was inhabited by evil spirits. They steal the souls of travelers, haunting them with music and drums, or the clashing sounds of battle."

"You heard that?"

"I tried to tell myself it was only a natural phenomenon caused by the wind, or by my fever and weakness. Yet I admit there were moments when I believed in demons. Yet my companion carried me safely through all of it and up over the snowbound mountain passes where the bones of travelers litter the path instead. The fossil tooth, the drawings, the notebooks—proof of everything I've been telling you—were all his."

"You made no records of your own?"

"Much of it was lost long before I met him. What I had managed to keep, he took care of for me. On that return journey he also transcribed whatever else I could remember. However, all of those papers fell into the hands of a fanatic named Uriah Thornton. Everything I've done since then has been designed only to recover them."

"This is a matter of life and death?"

Jack hesitated for only a moment. "It's my sole reason for existence. Those notes contain the vital information that Britain desperately needs to map of all that country north of India."

"But the tooth is evidence of a whole new creature," Anne insisted. "One that lived long before the Deluge. It may be the single most significant fossil ever found. And there are drawings and descriptions, as well? Even of their nests? If that's not equally important to you, it should be!"

Something moved in a doorway. A footman gazed impassively across the courtyard, his white wig ghostly in the shadows.

"My lord," the footman said. "A Mr. Marsh of Hawthorn Axbury is here. He has been shown up to the drawing room in Miss Marsh's guest suite and given tea."

Anne leaped to her feet. Leaving Jack standing by the dragon, she raced up to her rooms.

JACK WATCHED HER GO, THEN GAZED UP AT THE CIRCLE OF bright sky far above. He had known women in London, in Greece, in Aleppo, professionals. He had known the touch of an

Indian courtesan, soft with exotic potential and hazy with the smoke of hashish. He had known the slow torment of dark nights in the desert at the mercy of a lover's every erotic desire, where even a man's own ardor might become a cruel master, if he let it.

Yet something in him craved that cool, levelheaded English gaze—even if she couldn't really grasp the significance of his purpose—and that surprising intensity of passion that unfolded whenever he touched her. The madness of this craving terrified him more than anything he had ever known, even the threat of being blinded and flayed alive. At the heart it left him without control over anything, not even himself.

He had even found himself—with absolute faith in her integrity—confiding his real purpose to her. Did he trust her more than he trusted his own family? More than he trusted himself? Or was there simply safety in knowing that their lives would soon part and never touch again?

He would take ship for Asia and leave her his name and his fortune. With her English common sense, she'd soon know that she'd felt nothing for him but a passing infatuation. She'd be grateful for the aura of respectability resulting from their wedding. Then she would forget him. Once Anne was firmly established in society, his family's influence would be enough to undo their marriage: annulment or divorce, it didn't matter. Then she would be free to marry again—and better than her family would ever have imagined possible—with only an occasional fleeting smile at the memory of Wild Lord Jack.

So perhaps the scars of their encounter would mark him more deeply than they would mark her. She had learned simply that the body offers its own pleasures and that a passionless man like Arthur Trent could never have made her happy. Whatever the judgment of society or his family, or even her own accusing gaze, he couldn't regret that.

He regretted only that he'd been foolish enough to come home and been mad enough to make love again in the rose garden. It was proof, if he hadn't already known it by now, that—in spite of all of the harsh years of training—he might yet come unglued at the core. The irony was that the unraveling would not be from physical danger or pain. Perhaps it would only be because time had finally caught up with him? Or perhaps because Wyldshay was trying to claim with remarkable insistence that he really was someone else, after all.

Whatever the reason, if he didn't leave soon, Jack thought he might simply unfurl like a tossed bolt of silk.

Thank God he was sworn to return to Asia right away. Thank God her father was already here. Mr. Marsh must have left before any letter of Jack's arrived. So her family's love had simply reached directly into Wyldshay, where love was otherwise far too complex to understand.

"WELL, ANNIE, HERE'S A FINE TO-DO!"

Anne gazed up at her father. Beneath a silly little patter of nerves, her heart soared, as if the presence of a member of her own family could undo everything that had happened, as if her father could miraculously spin her life back into its old path. Though she knew that was impossible, a dance of happiness still cavorted in small, rhythmic steps beneath her bodice. Someone of her own was here. Someone who would be on her side. Someone who would understand.

Mr. Marsh patted the skirts of his crumpled old coat and

glanced down at his mud-splattered gaiters, almost as if he was embarrassed to face her. Wisps of graying hair stuck to his head where they'd been pressed down by his hat. His whiskers were ruffled at the edges.

"A fine to-do," he repeated.

Anne folded her hands in her lap. She had reached a strange kind of calm, where any future seemed equally impossible.

"Yes, Papa," she said. "Not what any of us expected when I left Hawthorn Axbury with Mr. Trent."

He took a chair opposite hers and ran one hand over his hair, leaving it sticking up at odd angles. "When your aunt Sayle brought the news of what had happened—with the tale thoroughly embellished by Edith, no doubt—I thought I'd better come after my girl right away. Old Bessie wasn't too pleased about being pulled out of her paddock at such short notice, but she came willingly enough once we started."

"It's all been rather sudden," she said, "like the time the ceiling fell down in our dining room. Yet the duke would have sent a carriage for you."

Mr. Marsh pursed his lips. "No doubt. No doubt. And a very grand carriage at that! But the road's still flooded in places, Annie. There are trees down. On horseback I could ride along the old ridge tracks and avoid all of that. So here I am. I've met the duchess."

"Then you know what has happened?"

"Yes. Though I cannot quite fathom it. But yes, Her Grace has told me everything. With a very fine delicacy of manner, I must say. Perhaps that's to be expected with duchesses?"

His voice was gentle, though colored by something of heartbreak. Yet his very real shock was all to be covered up with tolerance and good humor. No domestic disaster was so terrible that the Marsh family might not find a small, brave joke in it. A shiver passed down her spine. She almost wished that her father would be angry with her: that he would hold her to account for her sins, as Jack's family had held him.

"Then you know that I've disgraced myself, and you, and Mama, can never be suffered in decent society again."

"Disgrace. Yes." He sighed and glanced up. "Yet you're not the first innocent child to be ruined by a ruthless young man."

"Please don't say that, Papa! Everything that happened was my fault."

He made a face. "Maybe. Maybe not. Blame is neither here nor there now, is it? You cannot marry Arthur Trent, either way. Do you still wish to?"

"No! I . . . I believed that I did, but no. Our marriage would have been a mistake. And though Arthur's very hurt and angry at the moment, in his heart I think he believes now that he made a lucky escape."

"A lucky escape from marrying a daughter of mine? If Mr. Trent is so lost to good sense as to think that, I'll knock him down myself for his insolence!" His forced smile threatened to break her heart. "But what am I to think about this lad of the Blackdowns who's causing you so much grief? This Lord Jonathan Devoran St. George? Quite a catch—a duke's son—if it were not for who we are, along with all the other uncomfortable circumstances!"

Anne swallowed. Her father was here. He was on her side. Yet he couldn't save her.

"Then you think I must marry him?"

"He's not a member of our faith or our class, and in spite of his worldly position he's proved himself something less than a gentleman. Yet if he's willing to do the right thing by my girl—and the duchess says that he is—it may be the only answer, Annie."

"Then I cannot come home to live as I always have?"

"I'm not sure." His wise eyes searched her face. "Are you the same girl that you always were?"

Anne gazed at him in dismay. Had everyone else changed, or was it just her? Even her beloved father seemed to have become something of a stranger. Perhaps there was going to be an accounting, after all. A gentle, loving accounting, but still one that would force her to face the reality of what she had done.

"I don't know! Does it matter?"

"It's the only thing that matters."

"He doesn't love me, Papa."

"Perhaps not at the moment, but if His Lordship has a shred of good sense, he will come to love you in time. Any man worthy of the name would."

"You only say that because you're my papa. Lord Jonathan is going to leave for Asia immediately after our wedding. There won't be any real marriage."

Mr. Marsh thrust himself to his feet and marched to the window, where he stood gazing out. His shoulders looked stooped and fragile, as if he had aged overnight.

"Yet according to Edith and your aunt Sayle, this duke's son is a rather remarkable young man. Something of a romantic figure, I hear, larger than life and twice as compelling. I assume that is true, or this misadventure would never have happened?"

She closed her eyes. "Yes, that's true. But the duchess is prepared to cover up what happened, so no one would ever know."

"He would know, Annie. You would know. Honesty is the watchword of our faith. You know better, I think, than to try to live a lie for the rest of your life."

"I only ever wanted a marriage filled with contentment and peace, like yours and Mama's."

"Then I wish you'd thought of that before you welcomed this man's advances." His shoes trod heavily back across the room. "And yes, I do accept your protestations that you might have done so, Annie, though the Lord knows it's a hard pill to swallow."

Anne forced herself to stand and face him. "I'm so sorry, Papa."

His face worked as if he choked down some unaccustomed emotion. "So am I, Annie. So am I! But there's no undoing what's been done. Alas, I think there's no hope for it, my girl, but for you to marry the man."

S OMEONE KNOCKED. MR. MARSH WALKED UP TO THE DOOR and flung it wide. Anne immediately dropped back into her chair, her heart hammering. Jack bowed and extended a hand. Her father gazed into the forest-shadowed eyes for a moment, then took the offered hand and shook it.

"Lord Jonathan, I presume? You wish to ask for my daughter's hand, my lord? Unfortunately, I believe I must take her home first."

"I cannot allow that, sir."

"*Cannot?*" Mr. Marsh sat down. "You *cannot* allow it? I'm her father!"

"It's still too dangerous for her to leave Wyldshay, Mr. Marsh." As if tracing the other man's footsteps, Jack walked to the window to gaze out. "We would be delighted to extend our hospitality to you, also, as long as you wish to remain here."

"A dangerous hospitality, my lord, if I understand correctly."

Jack spun about. "Not to you, sir."

"So you don't deny that you're dangerous to my Annie?"

A deadly quiet seemed to have settled about Jack's body, as if he stood in the eye of a gale. "That's for her to decide, sir. Not me."

"I have responsibilities to my community and family, Lord Jonathan. I cannot stay more than the night. And I don't know that I can give you my blessing."

"I don't expect your blessing, sir. But you will not withhold your consent to the match?"

"I think none of us has much choice in the matter. You have stolen my child's innocence. Perhaps you would arrange for me to speak to the duke about settlements?"

"You may speak directly to me, sir. My affairs are my own and I'm prepared to be very generous. Shall we discuss it tonight after dinner?"

Mr. Marsh stood up, rotund and graying, but filled with quiet dignity. "Very well, my lord. After dinner."

Jack's forest-dark glance met Anne's gaze. The bruises on his jaw had flared into a multicolored quilt. He seemed as exotic and wild as any tattooed savage.

"Meanwhile, Miss Marsh, Mr. Trent is about to return to London with my cousin. I thought you might wish to speak with him before he leaves. In my study in the Docent Tower in ten minutes, shall we say?" He strode to the door, then bowed to Anne's father. "Please come, too, sir, if you wish to speak with Mr. Trent—"

"Or if I would like to shield my daughter from your perilous proximity?"

Jack's brows lifted as if in surprise at—or perhaps just in appreciation of—such plain speaking. "Other perils are more immediate, sir."

"So I understand. Thus you're going to have to explain to me exactly why my little girl is in physical danger and from whom. My sister tells me that it's all to do with a fossil tooth. This single piece of the Lord's creation has cast such deadly peril about Wyldshay?"

"Yes, sir." The arched doorway cast shadows over Jack's dark skin. "We're not the only people, Mr. Marsh, who have wondered if such objects aren't simply the work of the devil."

Anne's father watched his future son-in-law stride away down the hall. He walked thoughtfully back to Anne and sat down again, his expression bemused.

"Well, my dear," he said at last. "A most remarkable young man!"

HAMMERS POUNDED IN HER BREAST AS ANNE APPROACHED the Docent Tower, although her father held her hand tucked into his elbow. Jack's rooms.

A footman opened the door. Jack and Arthur Trent stood talking together beside the fireplace. It appeared to be a perfectly amicable conversation. Arthur looked around as they came in, then strode over to shake Anne's father by the hand. The two men exchanged pleasantries, followed by a remarkably unembarrassed acknowledgment of their changed relationship, before Arthur turned to Anne. Jack immediately took her father by the elbow and led him away.

Anne was left facing her ex-fiancé. He was sporting a grand bruise on his jaw and had the beginnings of a black eye, but he seemed happy, even exhilarated.

"The most extraordinary thing, Miss Marsh," Arthur said. "That huge tooth really is just a curiosity, after all."

"But I thought it was a find of great significance, sir."

"No, no. Without solid provenance it's anyway meaningless to science. I had assumed that His Lordship had collected it himself and could explain all the circumstances of the find. Yet Lord Jonathan tells me it's most likely a forgery, carved with great skill by native artisans. So it's just a memento of His Lordship's travels, after all."

Anne glanced at Jack. He met her gaze and winked, a tiny smile lingering on his bruised lips. She felt a little lost, but perhaps this falsehood was only for Arthur's protection?

"Then I am disappointed," she said.

"Yes, of course. I am, too. Yet by the remarkable coincidence of that curiosity falling into thy hands, Miss Marsh, and then mine, I am now to receive a duke's patronage. His Lordship took me to see the duke himself. His Grace was happy to assist and will not find my religious convictions any impediment."

"You didn't have to explain your work?"

"Lord Jonathan did so and with great eloquence." He looked away and chewed his lip for a moment. "My first assessment of him was correct, I think. I certainly don't blame thee for what happened, though I'm sorry that it's proved that thou and I should not suit. I hope we may remain friends?"

"Of course," she said.

"Then we part with no hard feelings," he said. "I am glad."

The other men joined them. The farewells were done. Jack escorted Arthur Trent from the room, leaving Anne alone with her father.

Anne sat down. She felt a little faint. She might never see Arthur again, except in a crowd at some social or scientific gathering, perhaps. If she hadn't found the fossil in her basket, she'd be marrying him. It was as if on that day in the High Street in front of Aunt Sayle's house, her life had split into two paths. Without even seeing the enormity of the divide, she had blindly marched off down the most perilous, and not discovered in time that it was too late to turn back.

"No broken heart there, Annie," Mr. Marsh said as the door closed. "Arthur Trent is a good enough fellow, my dear. Yet you've lost nothing by breaking your engagement to him, and perhaps gained the world."

She looked up at her father. "Gained the world?"

"I don't know," he said. "I don't know. The Good Lord sometimes hides his purposes from us, Annie, in ways that we can't quite understand. You have sinned, my dear. I know that. You know that. Actions have consequences. Sins must be paid for. Yet against my better judgment, I believe I can trust my daughter's future to Lord Jonathan, after all, for all of his charm and his vices."

"Vices?"

"Oh, yes. I think so. No, I'm sure of it. Yet a good woman can be the salvation of a wicked man, as long as he's not cruel at the heart."

She closed her eyes to block a mysterious prickle of tears.

"No," she said at last. "You have it wrong. He's not a wicked man."

"Because you think him a wicked angel?" Mr. Marsh said.

Something clicked. Jack stood with the closed door at his back.

"We're entering the endgame," he said. "I'm sorry that I couldn't take you into my confidence before now, Mr. Marsh. You have the right to know what is happening, of course."

"What, my lord? The endgame?" Mr. Marsh dropped into a chair. "Whatever do you mean?"

"That I have not been allowing affairs to drift." Jack strode to a cabinet to pour Anne's father a glass of wine. "I've just received a message from my enemy: his response to one of my own. As soon as our business together is concluded, you may take your daughter home without danger."

Mr. Marsh took the wine. Jack paced back to the bookcase. Restless energy seemed to surge through him, as if he might spark his own lightning.

"As your daughter already knows, sir, I've traveled extensively in Central Asia. I had no particular interest in fossils. However, in one of the remotest deserts in the world I met a man whose passion was bones. He had uncovered the remains of a huge ancient carnivore, far too large to move. He was able to bring away just one tooth—through some of the most hostile terrain in the world. I cannot begin to explain to you the splendor of that achievement."

"And this fossil tooth was a murdered sailor's unwelcome gift to my daughter?"

"Yes, sir," Jack said. "The man who first discovered it was Toby Thornton. He became a friend."

"Thornton?" Anne asked. "But I thought your enemy was a Mr. Thornton?"

"Mr. Uriah Thornton is Toby's cousin."

"I should like some fresh air," Mr. Marsh said. "Is there some-where outside we might sit?"

Anne leaped up to go to her father. Jack flung open the door and led them out into another of those small, hidden courtyards. The walls were soft with mosses, but a single cherry tree in full, glorious blossom scattered petals across the flagstones.

Jack helped Mr. Marsh to a bench beneath the tree.

"So the fossil is indeed genuine," Anne said. "Why did you lie to Arthur about that?"

He turned, storm clouds massed in his eyes. "I thought perhaps I'd already broken his heart enough for one day."

"Broken his heart?" Anne asked. "Why would the truth do that?"

"Because as soon as Mr. Trent brought the fossil here to Wyld-shay, I sent Uriah a message that he may now come to fetch it."

"Fetch it?" Anne asked. "But I thought it was important to stop him getting it?"

"No," Jack said. "I shall give the Dragon's Fang to my enemy."

Shock sank straight down to her toes. "What will he do with it?"

Jack gazed thoughtfully at the cascades of blossom, some of the petals already a little brown at the edges. "Destroy it."

"Then how can you?" She felt prim and upright, as awkward as if her father's presence had undone any other feelings, even though an unaccustomed anger surged up her spine to mock her image of herself. "How can you? You said there were drawings, notebooks. There's a solid fossil that one can hold in one's hand. Proof of a carnivore larger than anything that's ever been discov-ered before. All that evidence must be taken to London, presented to the Royal Society. Arthur can do it, if you will not."

"Of course," Jack said. "That's why I had to lie to him. Now that he believes the Dragon's Fang is only a forgery, Mr. Trent can forget it and pursue his future with untrammeled courage."

"I am to trust my daughter to a man who willfully tells falsehoods?"

"Yes, sir, even though you Dissenters place such a premium on telling the truth, with the result that you're England's most trusted bankers and scientists and pharmacists." Jack brushed one hand over a branch. Petals scattered. "However, I'm not involved simply in a matter of commerce or personal honor."

"But what about the sanctity of friendship?" Anne said. "What about your friend Toby Thornton who went to such lengths to retrieve the fossil? Didn't he suffer, too, in those terrible deserts? Does his effort count for nothing?"

"He risked his life to collect the fossil. In the end it killed him."

"It *killed* him!" Tears of shock burned her eyes and throat. "Surely you care about that?"

His storm crackled about him, as if he might have the power to darken the sun. "For a long time it was the only thing that mattered."

"But now he's dead, you won't even protect his work to honor his memory?"

"*Honor* it?" Silent thunder rolled directly into her heart from his gaze. "Of course I honor it. Toby saved my wretched life at the expense of his own."

Her feet slid through eddies of blossom. As if battered by a storm surge, Anne stepped back, though she lifted her chin and still faced him.

"I'm sorry, but if you let his work be destroyed, what kind of respect for his memory is that? Don't you see that your friend's fossil is more important than anything? Nothing would have meant more to him than to know that his discoveries would outlive him."

"Yes," Jack said. "I know that. Toby lived only for truth and knowledge. He was a Dissenter, like you."

"My lord?" asked a new voice. "I was asked to bring this directly to you."

Anne looked around to see a footman. The man held out a small silver tray. Jack took the proffered card, turned it over, and read something scrawled on the back. His nostrils flared.

"When did this arrive?"

The footman was pale, his mouth set. "This person is waiting at the bridge, my lord. He and his companions have been asked to remain there until we receive your instructions."

Jack dropped the card back onto the tray. "I have invited this gentleman to Wyldshay, Graham. You will allow him access into the castle. You will also welcome anyone he brings with him, however outlandish such people may seem. I will join them in the Great Hall in five minutes. Some of our men may first be brought from their posts to make sure that none of these visitors stray any deeper into Wyldshay." He glanced up at the light pouring down into the courtyard, then smiled at the footman. "After all, we don't want any of the family trinkets to go missing."

"Trinkets, my lord?" Graham said, his voice choked. "Very good, my lord."

"And you will also convey this message to the duke and duchess."

Jack leaned forward to whisper into the footman's ear. A slightly green tinge suffused the man's face, but he bowed his head and left.

"This is the endgame?" Mr. Marsh asked, his voice sober.

"All danger to your daughter will be over very soon now," Jack said. "My enemy comes to entreat, not to threaten, though he may not know that as yet. If you wish to attend our meeting, sir, you'll be perfectly safe."

"Thank you, my lord. However, I think I'll remain here beneath this beneficent cherry tree. Even though, as I believe I just learned, your audience chamber will be surrounded by armed servants?"

Jack smiled as if the sun had just broken through clouds. "They won't be necessary, but yes."

"Then I believe Anne may bear witness instead, if she wishes to do so." Grimly determined, Mr. Marsh settled back on the bench and closed his eyes. Silver wisps of hair shimmered against the dark tree trunk. "This is, after all, her adventure, not mine."

A RAGGED GROUP STOOD WAITING, MANY OF THEM IN bare feet: brown-skinned men with turbans or tarred queues above their rough sailor's garb. The ceiling of the Great Hall soared above their heads. Hammered beams disappeared into darkness. Weapons decorated the walls: swords, hackbuts, daggers, pikes—all arranged in wheels or glittering ranks—a complete antique armory.

The visitors' eyes swept from the fireplace—where monstrous dragons were impaled by stone spears—to a painting of St. George on a white horse that hung on the opposite wall. A nervous, hostile tension kept them herded together like wolves.

With the arrogance of a family that had once commanded its own private army, Jack strode forward. His heels rang on the flagstones. Every pair of eyes swiveled toward him, as if those dark glances could strike him to the floor.

Anne hesitated in the doorway, wondering which of these men had broken into her bedroom at Aunt Sayle's, and who had murdered that sailor in the High Street. She felt as if she'd been dipped in ice water and was shivering at the core, yet she folded her hands and sent a quick thought to her father. His prayers seemed to wing straight back to her heart: *See it through, Annie!*

Several stalwart Wyldshay servants waited in the hallway behind her, grim-faced and openly armed, but they could never intervene in time if Jack was attacked at close quarters.

About ten feet in front of the sailors Jack stopped and bowed. The group sucked together. Something else now marked the brown faces: a reluctant but deep-seated awe, perhaps. A few heads swiveled to glance again at the impaled dragons on the fireplace.

The ice water congealed in Anne's veins. The shivering attacked her stomach, making her feel ill.

She forced herself to step forward to take a chair near the door.

Alight with leashed power, Jack waited as a tiger might wait when facing a wolf pack. Several of the sailors starting speaking in a language she'd never heard before. Jack listened. Just as the voices began to reach a cacophony, he answered in the same tongue. Silence descended immediately.

A man in a blue turban broke away from the rest and stalked forward. He and Jack held a rapid conversation, low-voiced, hissing. At last the man snapped down with one hand. The gang of sailors parted as if split by a sword.

"Mr. Uriah Thornton," Jack said. "You wish to speak to me?"

Impeccably dressed in the dull garb of a Dissenter, an Englishman stood revealed in the midst of the sailors. He bowed and walked forward, leaving his ragged escort behind. He did not look happy.

It was the rider Anne had glimpsed at the ferry, the man with the shielded gaze of a blue-eyed dog.

CHAPTER FOURTEEN

URIAH THORNTON STOPPED WITHIN A KNIFE'S THRUST OF Jack and stared up at his face.

"What are you saying to them?" Thornton asked. "You think a secret conversation with my servants will help you?"

Jack smiled down at him. "Servants? I'm not sure that's the way these men view your relationship, sir."

"If I give them the signal, they will demonstrate where their loyalty lies."

Still smiling, Jack removed an imaginary speck of dust from the shorter man's shoulder. Thornton tensed, but voiced no objection.

"Unfortunately their loyalty is to neither of us. It's to the beast they hold sacred. Haven't you looked about yourself yet? This room is a stronghold of dragon lore. It's also a nice display of weaponry. Your friend is impressed. In fact, he's overawed."

"An entire army at your call would make no difference," Thornton said.

"Ah, but your friend and I have been exchanging pleasantries in one of the languages that he and I share, but you don't. However, if you talk to him yourself in the one tongue that you and he have in common, I shall be able to follow every word. That gives me a certain advantage, don't you think?"

"Pleasantries?"

"About dragons," Jack said. "Toby's fossil has come home."

Thornton leaned forward like a dog scenting game. "Then you do have it?"

"Yes, I have it. We have both chased it across the world, but the Dragon's Fang has finally fallen into my hands, not yours."

Sweat glistened like a fringe of lace above the blue eyes. "It's mine."

"If you don't recover it, they will kill you, won't they?" Jack asked gently. "When you told them it was sacred, when you spun tales of its mystical power, your only thought was to win the prize and destroy your cousin's work. So his discoveries would disappear without trace. So he would disappear without trace."

"It was the Devil's work," Thornton said. "My cousin wanted to undermine God's sacred truth, His word as revealed in the Holy Bible."

"Alas," Jack said. "The Devil spread his handiwork over the globe a long time ago. Bones of other giant reptiles have already been found in England."

Thornton stepped back, his spine rigid. *"England?"*

The foreign sailors looked from him to Jack, their faces suspicious. Presumably none of them could follow this conversation.

"While you and I warred over your cousin's Asian finds, sir, Englishmen were also busy digging at home. Science has uncovered and named several new creatures recently: *Iguanodon, Megalosaurus—*"

"All fiends!" Thornton hissed.

"The beasts or the scientists? Such fossils will continue to be dug from the earth until the evidence is overwhelming. You're too late, sir. Your beliefs are irrelevant."

"My faith is certain," Thornton said, clenching his hands. "Without error."

"Whether you suppress your cousin's work or not, the bones will still be there for future seekers to find."

"Then you'll keep the fossil? You'll publish all this falsehood to lead ignorant fools to damnation?"

"It would be unfortunate for you, if I did. If you don't get the fossil back, one of this motley crew will slip up behind you one night with a wire. You promised them. Your only thought when you enlisted such help was to retrieve the Dragon's Fang and destroy it, but your tales took on a life of their own. Your hired assassins have become your masters."

Thornton was green, the sweat breaking and sliding in small runnels down his temples. "So you won't let me have it?"

"On the contrary, I asked you to come here for that express purpose."

"But you want something in exchange. What?"

"Your cousin's notebooks."

"I burned them."

"How unfortunate," Jack said. "Then I hope you're at peace with your God, because you'll be meeting Him very soon. Good day, sir."

"You cannot let me leave without at least a promise of the fossil!"

Jack smiled, as if dismissing the other man. "Of course I can. I can tell your friends that you never intended to recover the Dragon's Fang for them, that they've been misled, double-crossed, and come halfway across the world into this cold, wet country for nothing. I don't imagine they'll be very understanding."

"They will kill me," Thornton said.

"The world may be a better place without you, sir."

The dog-eyed man grabbed Jack's sleeve. "I have some of them, the notebooks, but I've already destroyed the descriptions and drawings of the bone fields—"

Jack shook him off. "Then you might have been less industrious, sir." He walked away to the fireplace, tossing his words over one shoulder. "We'll see, shall we, whether what you have left will be enough to save your wretched neck?"

The man in the blue turban, who had been staring at the carved dragons, turned. His stance promised action. Jack stopped and spoke to him. The man hissed an answer in the same foreign tongue. A rapid conversation followed, before the sailor bowed deeply, touched his forehead with both hands, then addressed the other seamen. Some of the sailors fell to their knees and pressed their foreheads to the floor.

"What are you doing?" Thornton asked.

"Giving you back your wretched length of days."

Jack tugged the bellpull. A footman walked in: Graham, the man who had first fetched them from the blossom-bedecked courtyard. He was still white-faced.

"You rang, my lord?"

"These men are to be escorted back across the bridge and allowed to leave freely. Mr. Thornton will return later by himself. He is to be brought up to my study in the Docent Tower. I shall receive him alone. We're not to be disturbed."

"Very good, my lord."

Jack nodded to the man in the blue head cloth, who signaled the others. They followed Graham from the room. With the pale gaze of a winter moon Uriah Thornton watched them leave.

"You and I shall meet at nine o'clock tonight to make our

exchange," Jack said. "You will bring me your cousin's notes, then perhaps you may have the fossil."

The dog eyes shot Jack a glance of pure hatred before the man turned away. His shoes clunked on stone as Uriah Thornton marched from the room after his hired assassins.

A NNE STOOD UP. EVERY MUSCLE FELT TAUT, LIKE A tightly tuned violin. With a strange, dark quietness in his eyes, Jack turned to face her.

"You're all right?" he asked. "You weren't afraid?"

"No. Yes. I don't understand anything," she said, "except that you would give up our fossil to save your enemy?"

Limber, apparently relaxed, Jack ran one finger over the lashing tail of a carved stone dragon.

"The one thing that's more valuable than knowledge, perhaps?" He smiled at her. "If I can still save a life—even one as worthless as Uriah Thornton's—and gain other vital information, why not?"

She looked away to hide the frantic squeal of her nerves. *I don't think he cares one way or another whether he lives or dies—*

"But what if the trade is your life for his? This man already tried to harm you, but you plan to meet him alone?"

"Yes."

Swallowing her pang of panic, Anne waved one hand to indicate the room, as if their visitors still stood there in all their outlandish glory. "Why did you want me to witness all this?"

"I don't know. Perhaps part of me would like you to understand. Perhaps I felt, as your father evidently did, that you have a right to be present at the conclusion of your own adventure."

"But this isn't the conclusion," she said. "It's only the beginning." She tried to smile, to lighten the grim shadow that seemed to be lurking in his eyes. "I believe we're still obliged to marry each other, my lord."

"And you think that marriage to me is more dangerous than facing down a madman and his lackeys?"

"Oh, I know that it is."

"I do believe that you mean that, Miss Marsh. Will you allow me some of that plain Dissenter honesty and tell me why?"

Her eye recognized the bruises and the shadows. Her heart saw only the loveliness of bone and the sweet curve of masculine lips. Her pulse began to thud heavily.

"Thanks to you, my lord, I don't even know who I am any longer. I can't find my bearings. All the things I've relied on in the past—a quiet reason, the still light at the center of my being—have collapsed like so much wheat in a storm."

"Ah!" He reached out to outline her cheek with his fingertips. "Yes. And you're sorry."

The caress was cool, firm and cool, as if her face became suddenly fevered beneath his serene touch. Fire sparked beneath her corset to spread flames through her blood.

Anne pulled away. "You mustn't," she said. "That's exactly what I mean. It's not fair."

His fingers dropped as if scalded. "Of course," he said.

His boots struck the flagstones like a death knell as he strode from the room, his storm following him like an albatross.

*L*IKE A COWARD, JACK THOUGHT. *I WANT HER AND I CAN-not face her. So I flee, like a coward!*

He felt desperate to fence, or box, or take out a fast horse.

Instead Jack raced up through the labyrinth of Wyldshay to the battlements at the top of the curtain wall. He strode around to the front of the castle, where the arched bridge spanned its branch of the River Wyld.

With the wind in his hair and the swallows beating above his head, Jack watched his enemy ride away on a Roman-nosed bay. The sailors ran at Thornton's heels, bunched like foxhounds. A lone footman sat on the stone wall that bordered the bridge, staring after them.

Jack dropped his forehead onto both fists where they rested on the merlon. *Anne Marsh!*

She was remarkable. She didn't pry. Her questions never reflected random curiosity or foolishness. With that pure, honest directness, she simply dived into the heart of a problem.

Why had he allowed her to watch that encounter with Thornton? Did he want her silent witness at each stage of this nonsensical drama? And how did he expect her to react, if he did?

He was going to marry her. He was never going to make love to her again. He had deflowered her in a moment of madness and then—like a lunatic—repeated his crime in the rose garden.

Those three facts summed up all the ironic absurdity of his existence.

He didn't want her in his life, or in his future. Yet he craved her slender body and her innocent, passionate surrender with every fiber of his being.

TWILIGHT CAST ITS SOFT SHADOWS ACROSS THE CARPET. HER father was ensconced somewhere with the duchess. Later he and Jack would be discussing settlements to decide Anne's future.

Whatever the results of that conversation, she would be married before her bridegroom left for Asia. She would probably never see him again.

Anne closed her eyes and sought for quiet. Instead she seemed to be in Lyme Regis. Gulls screamed overhead. Wind tugged at her cloak and battered her skirts against her legs. Surf pounded as if she stood at the end of the Cobb—the ancient stone jetty that jutted out from the beach—while boats tossed on the fretful ocean.

The place was exactly as she remembered, its slick, fossil-strewn stones hard beneath her feet. The boats, the gulls, the surf, everything remained unchanged. Only she was different.

Yes. And you are sorry.

Why not? What had she gained from this adventure? This deep-seated restlessness? This shameful craving for a man's touch?

If I learned one thing from the Takla Makan, Miss Marsh, it is this: When there's no going back, you must go forward. It's too late to retreat now, don't you think? You have nothing at all to lose.

Didn't he understand? She'd lost everything: her self-respect, her planned future, her father's trust, even the promise of study-ing the fossil. Humiliation sank to the bone.

Something rubbed against her hand. Anne opened her eyes. Sitting on the table at her elbow, the gray-and-white kitten gazed at her with bright yellow intensity.

"Well, puss," Anne said, reaching for the kitten with both hands. "I've been moping like a ninny. What do you have to say for yourself?"

The kitten purred and butted, then leaped onto her lap to knead her legs with tiny pink paws.

She rubbed under the soft chin. "You live only for the moment, don't you?" she asked. "No fretting for the future?"

Golden eyes closed into contented little slits as the kitten settled onto her skirts.

"You see," she said. "I can only go forward, puss. I couldn't retreat, even if I wanted to. Yet I think I may be wallowing in a little miserable self-pity. After all, I'm destined either way to discontent."

"Are you?" a man's voice said. "Why?"

The kitten leaped to the floor as Anne jerked and spun about. "Jack!"

His lean shadow stretched from the open doorway.

"I knocked without success," he said. "I didn't mean to startle you. Do you wish me to leave?"

Anne stood awkwardly by her chair. "No," she said, folding her hands. "No. Pray come in."

Jack closed the door behind him and strode into the room, then crouched to tap his fingers on the carpet. Whiskers alert, the kitten rushed out at his hand.

"I see you've found a friend," Jack said.

She sat down again. "No. He found me."

"Yet I think you are friends?" He scooped up the kitten. "This little fellow is old enough to leave his mother. What will you call him?"

"Call him?"

"Even a cat must have a name," Jack said. "He looks rather like a Cicero to me."

"Oh, no! I think he's far more of a Horace."

"Then Horace it is," he said, handing the kitten back to Anne. "Yours, if you want it."

Ears alert, Horace began to bat at her fingers. "You're very cavalier with the lives of free creatures, aren't you?" she said. "Is everyone your slave to dispose of as you wish?"

A little tremor passed over his back. Still on his haunches, his hands hanging relaxed between his bent knees, Jack seemed to freeze in place for a moment.

"No," he said. "I command no one's life, Anne. I have no sympathy for slavery. Of course, cats don't belong to us. We're chosen by them, if we're lucky, and I believe you've been chosen. This little fellow came a long way from the stables to find you."

The kitten skittered to the edge of Anne's lap. She caught it and lifted the furry creature up to her cheek for a moment. She felt oddly dreamy, as if she were truly out on the Cobb, feeling the breeze in her face.

"I'm not sure I've ever belonged entirely to myself," she said. "I've always belonged to others: parents, brothers, sisters, the community of expectations represented by our faith—"

He lifted his head to meet her gaze. A little ripple of apprehension traced down her spine at the blank void in his eyes.

"Don't say that! Don't say that you've ever belonged to others! It's nonsense. You may have felt duty, obligation, love. You may have felt hedged about by social convention. You've never been another person's possession."

"No, but I will be, won't I," she said, "when I wed you?"

In one limber movement Jack pushed himself to his feet and paced away. "If I thought that, I would never have agreed to marry you, whatever the world might say."

"A wife is her husband's to command."

"In your world, perhaps. Not in mine." His voice burned. "Once I'm overseas you'll be completely independent. As the wife of a duke's son, you'll command both wealth and social standing. You may order your days as you wish. Would you like to be a patron of science? Or of charity, perhaps? Become the benefactor of young scientists like Arthur Trent? Or would you prefer to turn the entire house into a geology museum?"

Anne bent forward to allow Horace to run away across the carpet in pursuit of Jack's moving shadow. "What house?"

"I have a house not far from the village of Withymouth," Jack said. "It's yours."

"Withymouth? But that's—"

"Just down the coast from Lyme, yes." He spun about and smiled. "So you see, you'll still be within easy reach of your family. The shoreline there is also filled with fossils. Find your own happiness, Anne. Take a lover—"

"*No!*"

"You sound very sure of that."

"You don't think I've learned my lesson?" she asked. "I shall not take a lover."

He dropped to one knee to tease Horace with a corner of his handkerchief. "So you intend to deny the life of the body?"

"I don't deny it, but the life of the mind is more important."

"Yes, but without the body there's neither mind nor spirit," Jack said.

Anne stood up. The kitten raced off, tail in the air. "Then you deny the existence of the soul?"

"Ah," he said, glancing up at her beneath his lashes. "Now I have shocked you."

"You don't answer."

He pushed himself to his feet and walked up to her. "I don't know the answer, Miss Marsh. I came to tell you that we'll be married by special license in the morning. Your father has agreed to the settlements, and the duke and duchess have approved all our arrangements. You may go home tomorrow."

"Home?" she said. "To Hawthorn Axbury?"

"To Withycombe Court, Miss Marsh, one of the loveliest old houses in Dorset: a place of walled gardens and mellow fruit trees and flowers. Two hundred acres of farmland, including cliffs, and hills, and a stream or two. There's even a secret dell where my great-aunt, who left me the house, once planted eight thousand spring bulbs. They've multiplied since then. You won't have to travel alone. I've ordered a carriage to be sent up. Your father will go with you, and the rest of your family will be fetched from Hawthorn Axbury. I'll even join you later to help greet your well-wishers, if you like."

The kitten raced out across the carpet to leap up onto Anne's skirt. She reached down to extricate its needle-sharp claws from the fabric and lifted Horace back onto her lap.

"You're the soul of consideration, my lord."

Jack walked to the door and bowed. "How do you expect me to answer that?" he said with an equally sardonic bite to his voice. "By telling you that I have no soul at all?"

*H*ORACE WAS CURLED UP ON THE BED, A SOFTLY MOTTLED shadow against the pillow. Anne stroked his soft fur. Uriah Thornton would arrive in the Docent Tower in a few minutes to visit Jack. That would be the end of her adventure with the fossil.

Her wicked angel would marry her in the morning. That would be the end of her adventure with him. She was to make a new life by herself in a house called Withycombe Court, where daffodils outnumbered the stars. She had eaten and paced and prayed, though her prayers were only incoherent offerings of shame, and her thoughts were still colored by a confusion of longing.

Yet it never paid to mope and worry. So she had been given a future different from all of her life's expectations! The only answer was to embrace it with all the courage she could muster. She would at least have a bundle of gray-and-white comfort and amusement: a noble kitten from Wyldshay—with all of its ducal connections!

Anne laughed at herself and tugged at the bellpull. If she was going to keep Horace, he would need food and a soil box.

This time when Anne sought the quiet place, a clear white light enveloped her in silence. There was no reason for peace and every reason for apprehension, yet tranquility filled her heart as if to mend the sore places where it had come so close to breaking.

> *Then sigh not so, But let them go, And be you blithe and bonny;*
> *Converting all your sounds of woe into hey nonny, nonny.*

Someone rapped at the door: no doubt in answer to her summons. The kitten leaped from the bed. Skittering like a blown leaf, Horace danced stiff-legged after an imaginary mouse, then disappeared under a dresser. Anne crouched down to retrieve her new pet.

The knock sounded again.

"Come," she called over her shoulder.

Horace had retreated to a dark corner, forcing Anne to bend her head almost to the floor to peer after him. Yellow eyes gazed back at her for a moment, before the kitten made a little rush at her tapping fingers. Heavy footsteps clunked across the room. Anne looked up. A footman's stout legs blocked her view of the room.

"I was expecting Roberts," Anne said. "I need food for a cat and a box of earth."

Struggling with her skirts, she tried to stand. The footman stepped aside. She caught a glimpse of a turban and a greased queue as two barefoot sailors dashed at her. Stepping on her skirts, she stumbled against the dresser. A wire flashed. Anne was still on her knees with Horace leaping at her hem when the garrote slid about her neck.

She froze in place, looking up at the footman's white face. It was Graham.

"If you'll come quietly with us, miss," he said. "You'll come to no harm."

The wire choked, hurting. Anne couldn't speak or even nod, so she gestured her assent with one hand. The pressure eased just a little. Though her legs had the consistency of dust, she managed to stand. She felt Horace claw his way up to the slit in her skirts and dive into her pocket, where he curled up in a silent ball of fear.

Anne couldn't see it, but she knew it, because her heart had done the same thing.

Her thoughts winged to the little cat: *It's all right, puss! No one's going to hurt you! Though they are, perhaps, going to murder me, after all—*

One part of her mind accepted that with quiet calmness. Another part filled with indignant rage. Yet deeper than thought, a primeval terror paralyzed her heart. Not because she thought that the sailors really meant harm to her. Why would they? She was irrelevant to their drama and always had been.

But Jack's enemy must be in the Docent Tower by now. These were his men. Thornton must believe he could use her against Jack. He'd not know, of course, that Jack was entirely indifferent to the fate of Miss Anne Marsh of Hawthorn Axbury and always had been.

JACK SAT BACK AND SURVEYED HIS VISITOR. THORNTON'S eyes darted about the study, sweeping over books and papers and the small Buddha on the desk. His hands clutched the neck of a leather bag. Sitting close to the fireplace, he was sweating visibly.

"You have the notebooks," Jack said. "I have the fossil. You see how simple this is? We don't need to suffer each other's company for more than a minute or two."

"I hope never to lay eyes on you again." Thornton lifted the leather bag onto the desk, opened the neck, and tipped out a jumble of tiny notebooks and scrolls of yellow paper.

Jack's heart began to beat hard as he leafed through them—the vital records that he and Toby had sacrificed so much to collect. He didn't bother trying to control his pulse. Excitement thrummed through his veins.

"That's all I have," Thornton said. Beads of moisture gleamed on his forehead.

Jack scanned a few of the papers at random: the minute script, the sets of numbers, the crabbed shorthand he'd invented so that he could make rapid notes in the dark—or when his life would be forfeit, if he were seen writing. Even more important were Toby's scratched observations, like spider tracks on silk. A few of his larger drawings, folded and refolded, had also been brought back from the end of the world.

Not everything, but enough. Enough to have made this entire mad quest worthwhile, though most of it would be meaningless to anyone but him. Relief flooded, like a torrent beneath his skin. He looked up.

"I'm amazed that you didn't destroy all of this before now," Jack said. "Especially these scientific drawings, containing, as they do, proof of the Devil's wicked handiwork?"

"You call it science. I call it blasphemy."

"Yet you would allow me to have this ungodly evidence, which you believe will only plunge mankind into an abyss of sin, just to retrieve the fossil and save your own life?"

"I've not had the stuff very long," Thornton said. "You know that. You almost got to it first."

Jack strode over to the cabinet where he had hidden the fossil tooth. "Yes. Yet if I believed as you do, I'd have burned the lot and damned the consequences."

Thornton looked uncomfortable. "The tooth is more important. The papers are nothing without it."

"That's where we differ, sir, which is fortunate, or else this exchange couldn't have taken place."

Shadows lay deep in the room. Without lighting the lamp, Jack set the fossil on the desk—evidence of extinct monsters of unimaginable ferocity—and thought that Anne might not agree.

"Here you are, sir: the Dragon's Fang. Your passport to a few more years of miserable existence."

Uriah stared at it as if pinned in his chair, while the firelight danced over his moist face.

Someone knocked at the door.

Vigilance instantly roared to full alert. Every muscle tightened in a warrior's readiness. Jack slipped the fossil back into his pocket. *Uriah had been expecting this!*

"If you move," Jack said, "I will kill you. Don't think I can't do it, whether I am five feet from your stinking carcass, or fifty."

Thornton remained in his chair, his eyes bulging. "Probably just a maid," he mumbled.

"There's not a servant in this whole damned place who would interrupt us now, sir, and you know it."

Prepared to deal death if necessary, Jack flung open the door. A gray turban. A greased queue. One of the footmen—Graham?

And Anne!

Proud, upright, brave, terrified. Her eyes reflected his shock, though she held her head high. A thin dark seam marked the column of her neck: the crushing grip of a garrote. An impact like a cannonball struck straight to Jack's gut. *Anne!*

The wire tightened. The reverberations from the cannonball threatened to shatter him limb from limb. *I allowed for everything except treachery from one of Wyldshay's own. They are using Anne as a hostage.*

Jack took a deep breath to calm his heart, then smiled at Anne with all the reassurance he could muster. She met his gaze as if her faith in him was absolute.

You're my hero, her eyes said. *I know you can slay dragons and defeat legions of demons, and so you will save me.*

He could not. Not from the instant retribution of that wire. It would seem that he was about to fail in the very first test of a hero. He could not rescue the maiden.

She managed to smile back at him, with a wry little quirk at the corner of her mouth. Behind that superficial sheen of blind trust, intelligence and determination lay deeper—as if she recognized her own unspoken message and rejected it out of hand? Did that mean that she also saw the deceit in his gaze and knew that his attempt at comfort was empty?

"You have come for the Dragon's Fang," he said in one of the languages he was sure her captor would understand. "Release this woman and you may have it."

The man glanced a question at Thornton.

Uriah Thornton waved his hand. "You're hardly in a position to bargain, my lord. Don't try to make independent deals with my men."

With deliberate dispassion, Jack turned and walked back to the fireplace.

"As you claim to be an Englishman," he said, "you will order your lackey to release the tension on the wire. And allow the lady to sit down before she faints. It's offensive to my more noble sensibilities to try to cooperate with you while a female is choking behind me."

Thornton signaled. With the garrote still at her throat, but less snug, the sailor thrust Anne farther into the room. The man with the queue entered right behind them. His face as blank as if he'd seen a ghost, Graham closed the door and placed a chair for Anne. Though still in the hands of her assassin she was able to sit down.

Jack glanced across the room into the footman's face. Graham had been at Wyldshay most of his life. His betrayal seemed inconceivable.

"Graham will do as I say," Thornton said. "He has already allowed my friends inside the walls of this castle and taken them to this woman's room. Having thus forfeited any future he may have had with the St. Georges, I now count him as one of my own."

"I thought you might try coercion of a member of the staff," Jack said with a forced shrug. "I didn't think it would work."

"We have his brother," Thornton said.

"He said they'd kill James, my lord." Graham looked ill. "He said my brother would be safe only if I helped him."

"I understand," Jack said. "You're not to blame."

"They said nothing bad would happen to the lady."

"Then they lied."

"But you promised," Graham said, looking across at Thornton. "You promised. If I allowed these men inside and helped them bring the lady here, you said you'd free James and no one would get hurt."

"No one will get hurt, if His Lordship obeys my demands," Thornton said. "But the duke will never take you back either way. You've thrown in your lot with me, sir, whether you wished to or not."

Jack watched them, his arms folded over his chest. "I am trumped, I see. Two hostages. This man's brother and this lady. With Graham's assistance, your men were no doubt able to fell the guards I had set about her room. Yet if he had come to me for help instead, his brother would already be free by now."

"Why should he trust you? What does a footman owe to the prodigal son?"

"Not much, obviously," Jack said.

Graham stared off into space. A muscle twitched in his jaw.

"Set the fossil back on the desk," Thornton said.

Jack obliged, letting it clatter on the wooden surface. The sailors' attention immediately locked on to it. The man with the queue stepped forward, then dropped to his haunches against the wall at a signal from Thornton.

"There's your Dragon's Fang," Jack said. "But you were promised that anyway. What else do you want?"

Thornton leaned forward, his eyes glassy. "These writings are all that you really care about, aren't they? What's so important? A sentimental diary of your travels with Toby? The wretched lies he told about the bones?"

"Something like that."

"I don't actually give a damn why you want them," Thornton said. "Only that you care about them so passionately. You'd have given your life to get your hands on these papers long before now, wouldn't you?"

"Do you wish for my life?" Jack asked. "How melodramatic!"

"I want only to watch your face as you destroy everything you've striven for. All these papers. Burn them!"

"With my own hands? Isn't that just a little sadistic, even for you?"

"I want to see you do it! Right there in your own fireplace. I could have destroyed them myself as soon as I found them. I kept them only for this moment: to see you burn the Devil's work, your work—"

"And your cousin's. Very well. Remove the garrote from the lady's neck and I'll do it."

"Oh, no!" The strange light of insanity shone from Thornton's face. "We all know how fast you can move. One wrong step from you and she dies. The wire remains. If you obey me, maybe she won't suffocate."

"And the unfortunate James?"

"Goes free. Unless this footman interferes now. Burn them!"

Jack began with the larger pieces, the loving drawings of the fossil skeletons, the strange bones jutting from the red earth, the skulls staring up from their blank sockets at the punishing sky. So a St. George once again cast terrible creatures into darkness. There was a certain black irony to it. Writhing and dying, the dragons breathed flame for the last time.

Meanwhile, his mind searched for any possible solution, any way out of this impasse, and found none. For even if he complied with every demand, even if he immolated every last shred of paper, there was nothing to prevent the man in the turban from breaking Anne's neck as a last farewell gesture.

In which case, even if Jack reacted with every fighting skill he possessed, it would still be too late.

Graham had leaned his head back against the wall and closed his eyes, but the sailor in the gray turban gazed with uneasy intensity at the fossil on the desk. The man had relaxed just a little. Though tears brimmed in her eyes, Anne took a deep breath, then another. Yet one hard jerk, one twist, and her throat would be crushed before Jack could reach her.

So he could do nothing except try to buy a little time during which to create as much complacency in his enemies' minds as possible, and be ready to take advantage of any distraction, however slight.

"You think," he said to Thornton, "that the loss of this evidence will change reality? Is your God so small that he cannot encompass the truth of His own creation?"

"Be quiet!" Thornton's eyes glittered, flames flaring in their black depths. "All that your science has created, all that it led Toby to, is nothing but blasphemy!"

" 'But ask now the beasts, and they shall teach thee. . . . ' " Jack quoted softly as more paper curled and flamed. " 'Or speak to the

earth, and it shall teach thee. . . . Who knoweth not in all these
that the hand of the Lord hath wrought this?' "

"Don't you dare quote Holy Scripture to me!"

"Especially not the Book of Job? After all, it is a tale full of
doubt—"

"You'll not distract me," Thornton said. "You'll not trick me.
I've waited a long time for this. I want to see your hand shake."

With grim determination Jack turned back to the task at hand:
the destruction of everything he'd worked so bloody hard to save
throughout the bitterest year of his life. Words curled and blackened. Numbers dissolved into ash. Pages of painstaking notes,
scratched by moonlight, hurriedly scrawled whenever he had the
chance, spiraling away into smoke to be drawn up the chimney.
Toby's calculations and observations, the brilliant focus of that
brilliant mind, all absorbed into oblivion by the flames.

And when it was done, when Thornton was satisfied that nothing remained, what was to stop him from killing Anne before he
and his men took the fossil and disappeared?

Jack held another of Toby's precious scrolls over the fire, and
his hand shook.

*A*NNE THOUGHT SHE HAD BEEN TERRIFIED ENOUGH WHEN
the sailors first forced her from her room with the wire
about her neck. But now the fear reached deeper, into black
depths she had never imagined existed. Jack stood quietly beside
the fireplace, taking the notebooks and slips of paper and casting
them into the flames. A red glow lit his skin as if he burned from
within.

Surely, surely, he had a plan? He must have foreseen that something like this might happen, that there might be treachery?

Yet he destroyed the papers, one by one, and at last his hand shook: that lovely masculine hand with the elegant fingers that knew how to deal death, now vibrating as if her terror had overwhelmed him, too.

If Jack was afraid, then there was no hope, at all.

A handful of papers skittered through his fingers to the floor.

"I'm sorry," he said. He leaned his head onto the side of the mantel. "You must give me a moment. I am, as you may imagine, not enjoying this."

"Take all the time you like, my lord. But the longer you take, the longer this lady must sit and watch, while she wonders how many more minutes she has left in this world."

"Devil take it!" Jack whirled about, his voice ferocious. "Does it matter? Kill her! Surely by your philosophy, as an innocent, she is assured a direct path to heaven?"

"You won't convince me that you don't care," Thornton said, smiling. "Try any ruse that you like, it's a bit late now to pretend that you don't mind if she dies."

Jack bent to retrieve some papers and tossed another handful into the fire. His face was stark, as if he knew agony, though he smiled. "The duchess would never forgive me if I littered the rugs with the corpses of her guests."

"But Anne Marsh is not just a guest, is she? You and this creature from nowhere are to marry in the morning. A charming idea. Too bad that the promise of those very nuptials might sign her death warrant. Have you not recognized yet, my lord, that my revenge on you has only just begun?"

CHAPTER FIFTEEN

APERS FELL FROM JACK'S HAND INTO THE DEVOURING flames like leaves from a tree.

Anne watched him carefully. Beneath his obvious distress, he seemed almost inhumanly alert. Was he waiting for something?

"Our troubled footman Graham told you that, I assume," he said. "Did he also tell you that our wedding is merely a social convenience? However, for your purposes it's all one and the same. I would wish to protect this lady and the hapless James, whether they were personally dear to me or not. That concept might be a little hard for you to grasp—"

"Yes," Thornton said. "You and Toby were alike in that: mewling remorse about the suffering of innocents. There are no innocents, my lord. Not me, not this woman, and certainly not you. We're all sinners."

"Yet perhaps some failings are more sinful than others," Jack said.

As he picked out another paper to burn, Jack glanced once at Anne, then spoke one sentence in a language she didn't know. The sailor with the queue stepped forward and replied. Her captor interrupted, the men entering into a rapid three-way exchange.

"What are you saying to them?" Thornton asked. "You'll not suborn these two!"

Jack glanced at him and laughed—laughed! "No," he said. "But I can try."

Thornton leaped to his feet. "I'll have you gagged."

Something tickled. Anne looked down. Whiskers alert, Horace was peering from her pocket. The wire about her throat was loose now, cool against her skin, as her assailant concentrated on Jack.

"Very well," Jack said. "I promise to be good. Why don't you explain to them? These sailors care about the fossil, but they're still mystified by the rest of your behavior. They want to go home."

The kitten jumped to the floor. Jack's glance instantly flickered away. No one else seemed to notice.

One of the sailors spoke again. This time Thornton replied. The sailor looked questioningly at Jack.

Horace scampered over to the side of the room and raced up a curtain onto the bookcase. Ignoring her pounding heart, Anne tried to decide what had attracted the kitten's attention. The tasseled end of what looked like a small roll of silk hung from a shelf.

"You've made them promises you can't keep," Thornton said, turning back to Jack. "You've promised them—"

Horace tiptoed up to the tassels, then leaped. Sharp claws grabbed the end. The silk roll unfurled, carrying the clinging kitten to the floor. Writhing like a dervish, a dragon hung from the bookcase. Embroidered in red and green and gold, the beast clawed and grinned on a sky-blue background. The fabric leaped as if alive, the cloud-breathing jaws gaping silent laughter as the invisible kitten battled the tassels.

Jack spun about and shouted. Anne's captor dropped to his knees alongside the other sailor, their foreheads pressed to the floor. Uriah Thornton leaped to his feet, then slowly sat down again. The door had crashed open.

Framed in the archway, Lord Ryderbourne held his pistol pointed at Thornton's head.

Anne snatched the loose wire from her neck and retreated to a corner, shaking as if she were possessed. Yet Jack still stood next to the fireplace, both hands pressed onto the plaster behind him.

"Thank you, Ryder," he said. "I couldn't call you in before." Deep shudders racked his body. "Please escort all this flotsam from Wyldshay and see that Graham's brother James is recovered unharmed."

"Miss Marsh?" Ryder said, looking at her.

"I'm all right." Anne thrust the wire behind her skirts. "Thank you, Lord Ryderbourne."

"With discretion," Jack added, his eyes focusing on her. "So that no one else in the castle is alarmed—"

"Especially Mother?"

Still without moving, Jack spoke to the sailors in their own tongue. The man in the turban looked up. Jack said something more. With one eye on the silk dragon, the sailor rose to his feet and reached for the fossil. Ryder stepped forward.

"No," Jack said. "Let him have it. I promised him retribution from heaven, if he didn't do as I asked." He flung out one hand toward the silk. "And all the power for good fortune of the dragon, if he did. He will grind up the tooth and destroy it, but I gave him my word—as an English gentleman, you understand."

The sailor slipped the tooth into his clothes. Ryder hesitated.

"Please, Ryder." Jack sounded almost desperate. "Go! Graham will help you."

A chill touched Anne's heart. Jack's nostrils were flared like those of a running horse. Beneath the deep tan, his skin seemed glassy. He vibrated with small tremors as if he had a fever.

"It's all right," Ryder said gently. "I'll take care of it from here. No one else need ever know that anything has happened. Miss Marsh, you're sure you wish to stay here?"

"Yes," Anne said. "Quite sure."

The sailors hurried out. Ryder marched Thornton and the footman from the room.

"But one last thing," Thornton said from the doorway, gazing back at Jack, his dog eyes bright with triumph. "You think he's dead. He's not. But he is in hell, where he belongs."

The door banged shut.

Anne was alone with Jack.

𝓗E THOUGHT HE MIGHT FALL. SHUDDERS RACED UP HIS spine. Her face white, Miss Anne Marsh—the lady he was to marry in the morning—stared at him with that solemn blue gaze. Color was seeping slowly back into her cheeks. He ought to go to her. He ought to offer comfort, explanations. Instead, Jack was paralyzed.

"They've gone," she said.

"Yes." It was all he could muster.

"You're ill?"

Jack shook his head.

The kitten abandoned the silk hanging with its embroidered

dragon and skittered across the floor. A few of Toby's scrolls still lay on the rug. Horace pounced and scattered them, then jumped into a chair where he began to lick at a paw.

Anne bit her lip. Tears glittered in her eyes. She ducked her head like the kitten, hiding her face.

"You lost the notebooks because of me," she said.

"No." Jack unpinned his fingers from the wall one by one. From the sheer effort of holding on to his self-control, he still trembled deep in the bone. *I refrained from killing because of you!*

"But if I hadn't been here, you'd never have had to burn them, would you? Is that what's made you so ill?"

Jack thrust both hands over his hair. "Yes. However, that was not the cause of my little tantrum just now."

"Tantrum?"

"The indulgence of some of my less noble emotions kept me pinned to the wall for a moment. I regret my momentary loss of good manners."

She sat down with a thump, her face ravaged. "Because you burned all of those papers and still gave away the fossil? I don't know how you could have done that. I don't know why you didn't foresee what would happen, why you didn't try to prevent it."

"I misjudged. I didn't think they could reach you. I expected a more deliberate violence, directed only at myself."

"Then you were wrong. And now all of the evidence of that giant reptile is gone. Don't you care about that?"

"No, not really." *You think he's dead. He's not.*

"Thanks to you, what may be the most important discovery of the century has been lost to science." She was crying. "History will never forgive you! Civilization will never forgive you!"

"No," he said.

She knelt to gather the remaining scraps of paper from the floor. Her tears fell like rain. Miss Anne Marsh obviously didn't know how to weep prettily, with dainty dabs of a handkerchief. Instead she gasped out heartrending little noises of distress, while her nose turned red and her eyelids became shiny.

"I can't make any excuse, but the bones are still there in Asia," he said. "It may take ten years, or fifty, or a hundred, but eventually someone will penetrate those wastelands again."

"You won't mount an expedition to find them?" She blew her nose.

"No."

"Why not?" Her eyelids were crimson, her cheeks splotchy, yet his bones melted at the sight of her bent back, her tender white neck.

"Circumstances have changed. No one from the West could survive there. Not for an instant. Not even in disguise."

She stood to face him, her gaze inflamed with accusation. "Then you have done something horrendous!"

"Yes," he said. "Yet this one setback won't change the truth, and perhaps no society can absorb too much revolutionary information too quickly. Meanwhile—"

"Meanwhile, what? You still have no idea of the importance of this, do you? It's all just an abstraction to you. I wish I could show you the creatures men have dug from the earth right here in England. I wish I could make you understand."

"You're the one who doesn't understand—"

Anne walked to his desk, her hands full of paper scraps, her cheeks ruined by tears. "How can I, when you explain nothing?"

"Then understand this: What if Uriah was telling me the truth and he's not dead, after all?"

"Who?"

"Toby Thornton!" He strode up to her and grasped her by both upper arms, shaking her. "*What if he's still alive!* Living flesh is more important than dead bones! I'm trying to choose life, Anne!"

She gazed up at him from uncomprehending eyes, the blue soaked like a Monday morning wash. Her lips parted, trembling. Without knowing what possessed him, Jack bent his head and kissed her.

She struggled for a moment, then she was kissing him back, her mouth drenched with tears. Her muslin dress crushed beneath his palms. The back of her corset was stiff and unyielding; laces ran in a little ridge up the spine. Anne Marsh, the upright Dissenter, still unable to reject the strictures of fashion, yet too compassionate to refuse him now.

Fierce, desperate, he plundered her mouth with lips and tongue, searching for her honesty and kindness, searching for the purity of her innocent passion. She tasted of salt and woman, erotic as sin. Sensations flared, spiraling down to the groin, scorching through his blood to fire his erection. He wanted to bend her back over his desk, throw up her skirts and take her, here and now, in an orgy of undisciplined lust.

Instead he broke the kiss, laid his cheek on the top of her head, closed his eyes, and sinew by sinew, forced himself to relax.

"Those papers that I burned," he said. "All those tiny scrolls and little scraps. They were the records of all my travels and all of Toby's travels. Without them I can't create the maps that Britain needs. If Russian spies reach that goal first, India might be facing invasion. That's why I had to secure the fossil to begin with, since nothing else was valuable enough to Uriah to make him save his cousin's papers."

She shivered in his arms, tender and angry and listening. "You can't reconstruct them from memory?"

"Maps need accurate measurements, figures, directions. During many of those journeys I was blindfolded or sick. We sometimes traveled at night. The Himalayas are a labyrinth and I was too often a sightless wanderer. Toby's notes made up for all of that. Now I have nothing. And worse, now I cannot track the place where Toby is being held, unless I go once again in disguise into that living hell of mountains and desert, and search, league by league, foot by foot, inch by inch, for his prison."

She pulled away to wipe her eyes and blow her nose, her mouth rosy and bruised. Her hair gleamed in a fuzzy, soft mass as she smoothed out the few remaining shreds of paper on his desk.

"You didn't expect to have to burn them, of course."

"No, I had even asked Ryder to wait for my signal, in case I needed help. Your arrival disrupted my plans a little."

"And so you lost everything. It was only human to want to take revenge," she said. "It's all right to be human."

"What do you mean?"

"You wanted to kill them all, didn't you? But you didn't." She glanced up at him and smiled with sudden radiance. "Because you might have disturbed the duchess with their corpses?"

Shocked into mirth, he began to laugh. She couldn't possibly understand. She couldn't conceive of what it would mean to him to have to go in search of Toby. All the time knowing that when he got there, if he got there, it would probably only be to find that Uriah was lying and that Toby really was dead, after all.

Yet she had faced death by strangulation, seen the loss of a fossil she valued like a jewel, and still she saw the truth. Then instead of being horrified by it, she tried to offer a little joke to rescue him from some of his pain? It made him feel as humble as if he had uncovered a miracle and wasn't pure enough to approach it. It made him feel almost sane.

"I would seem to be disintegrating," he said, once he had caught his breath. "I'm sorry."

"I think . . . I think I feel the same way," she replied, "as if I might simply come apart at the seams."

"Anne, I would like—"

She looked up at him with her heart in her eyes. "What?"

His courage faltered. "Whatever you would like," he said. He could not put it into words, this fragile need.

"Then I wish," she replied, answering it, "I wish you would hold me again. Just hold me. Perhaps then neither of us would disintegrate?"

In two strides he had caught her around the waist. Longing beat at him, simply to immerse himself in her warmth and wry common sense.

"Then come to bed with me, Anne," he murmured against her hair. "Just to cuddle together. Just to sleep. If it would soothe you, if it might help to stitch you back together, whatever I can give you in simple bodily comfort, I would be honored to offer it."

Her eyes filled with new tears as Anne laid her head on his shoulder. Her mind still felt buffeted by terror: the sensation of the wire about her throat, the cruel fanaticism in Uriah Thornton's dog-blue gaze. The prison where Toby Thornton might be held must be a terrible place. She had heard the desperation in Jack's voice. She had seen his face when he burned the papers—because of her!—and known then that something in him had shattered.

He would leave. Now that he had an even more urgent purpose, he would leave for Asia right away. She was irrelevant to all of his interests. They had nothing in common, not the fossils, not the excitement of science, nothing. He had flinched from sacrificing her only from exactly the same sense of responsibility that had made him flinch from sacrificing the footman's brother—no more, no less.

Yet she felt his arms about her shoulders, his steady breath warm on her ear, the lithe strength hidden beneath his clothes, and knew exactly what she wanted.

"Yes," she said. "Yes. I should like that."

Horace followed them, wobbling toward the stairs as Jack led her by the hand. Jack stopped and scooped up the kitten, carrying it the rest of the way.

His bedroom was small and round, the walls pierced by narrow windows. In one corner Jack created a nest of folded shirts for the kitten, then yanked a plant from its pot to make a soil box. Cold coffee and a small jug of cream stood on a side table. Purring like a hive of bees, Horace lapped up the cream, then curled up and promptly fell asleep.

Anne stood awkwardly for a moment, aware of her blotched face and damp cheeks. If he had ever desired her, it was not for herself, only for some random female comfort when she had been the only woman available. He had known exotic, beautiful women—*from Greece to Asia*—who indulged in esoteric practices she couldn't even imagine. Better not to try to compete. Better to accept her limitations and keep her dignity.

"Here's a clean nightshirt for you," he said, pulling a folded linen garment from a dresser. "I'll change in the dressing room next door."

Now that her mind was made up, she felt nothing of shame or

anger as she slipped out of her clothes. They would marry in the morning. Her father wished it. The world demanded it. Then he would leave for Asia, where very probably he would die in a doomed search for his friend. And if he did not die, then all those lovelier, more experienced women were waiting for him.

Lit by a single oil lamp, Jack's bed beckoned. With his night-shirt trailing about her ankles, Anne padded over to it. She lay down to discover that the inside of the canopy was painted with stars. Silver and gold on a background of deep blue.

At night, if you cast up a net, you'd catch millions of stars. You could wash your face in them.

He would leave her for those cold deserts. Return to the world's highest mountains, wrapped in the death of their eternal snow. She would pray that he survived to return safely to the arms of those foreign women. She could not in good conscience ask other-wise. Yet she knew that she wanted him to stay with her forever.

My beloved Lord Jonathan, I think for me you represent the mystery at the heart of it all. I must try to fathom it, even if only for a little while, even if I fail, even if it makes me unhappy.

Can you understand?

JACK WASHED HIMSELF FROM HEAD TO TOE, PUNISHED HIS flesh with the bitterness of cold water. His work and Toby's work, all of it destroyed by his own incompetence. *But he is in hell, where he belongs!* Was it true? Should he even hope for it, when—if he indeed still lived—Toby must be wishing for death every day? Whatever the truth, that one possibility had closed in on his life like a vice. His future now dived clear and straight on a single narrow line to perdition.

He strode back from his dressing room. The bed waited. He stopped and stared down at Anne for a moment. Her long plait snaked across the pillow. Her cheek was tucked against one folded hand. Her round shoulders were lost beneath the folds of his nightshirt. She was asleep.

An intensity of longing streamed in his blood, fired his bones, flooded him with awareness. He desired her as if he had never known desire. Light flickered over her fine skin, flamed in a tiny halo at her temples and along the curve of her eyebrows. Her eyelids were almost translucent, blue-veined like fine marble. She wasn't conventionally pretty. She wasn't exotic or obviously beautiful. Yet his body stirred for her, his skin burned, and he felt alight with tenderness.

Whenever she smiled and her nose made that little dip, his heart ached. Whenever she ducked her head, he wanted to enfold her, protect her, make love to her in a pure torrent of passion. This strange English creature had somehow become lovely to him, more lovely than life. How could she still trust him? Even now? Even after he had betrayed her, she still left herself vulnerable, once again helpless in his bed?

Jack turned out the lamp and slipped between the covers. The painted stars glimmered faintly, as if still retaining a gleam of lamplight. Blindly she turned in her sleep as he enfolded her in his arms. While his blood scorched with the immediacy of a man's hot desire, he cradled her head in the hollow of his shoulder and wondered about the true meaning of knowledge and innocence.

SOMETHING TICKLED HIS EAR. JACK WAS INSTANTLY AWAKE. Moonlight streamed faintly into his bedroom, casting webs of grayness and shadows. Anne lay curled into a ball beside him, breathing softly. He turned his head carefully. Fur brushed his cheek, then began to purr.

"Oh!" It was a breath, easing into the night. Anne opened her eyes, her pupils huge in the darkness.

Little claws sank into Jack's shoulder. A set of tiny eyes shone like mirrors.

He reached for his tinderbox and lit the lamp. Unblinking, Horace gazed up at him, before the feline pupils narrowed into slits. The kitten was curled into the curve of Anne's collar, whiskers arched as if Horace were smiling. Purrs rumbled in Jack's bed like thunder.

"We have company," he said.

Anne sat up carefully and extricated the claws from Jack's nightshirt. Cradling the kitten, she settled back against the pillows. "Horace obviously prefers our bed to his."

"I don't blame him. We all want warmth and companionship."

A faint flush fired over her cheeks. "I don't think this is wrong, is it?"

"Wrong? No. We'll be married in the morning."

She held the kitten to her neck to rub its head along her jaw. Jack dropped back to his pillow and gazed up at the shadows limning her cheek, the turn of her white hands as she stroked the soft fur. His pulse resounded in a hot river of pleasure. His cock stirred and hardened—

Jack closed his eyes to shut out the stars and concentrated on diffusing his desire, letting it breathe away into the cool night.

"You think it is sinful for you to be here with me like this?" he asked. "Even after what we have shared?"

"Perhaps. Perhaps especially . . ." Her voice trailed off.

"You want to go back to your own room? I will take you now, if you like."

"No. I don't want that."

"Then what is it?"

"I know you must leave for Asia," she said. "I know our marriage won't be real. Yet I would like to understand. Can you explain more things to me?"

He glanced up at her. "What things?"

She looked like a Madonna. She looked beautiful. "About Toby Thornton. About the fossil."

It was there first: the old reticence, the unwillingness to put any of it into words. Yet she seemed cocooned in peace, as if she alone might yet offer him a uniquely calm, quiet understanding. Jack took another breath and decided to trust her. Or perhaps, to trust himself.

"If you like," he said. "What do you wish to know?"

"I don't know. Everything, I suppose. When you first left India, did you travel alone?"

"Even when I had company, I was always alone."

She sat quietly, holding the kitten in her lap, where Horace tucked his front paws and closed his eyes. Purrs rumbled. "You could never really become close to anyone?"

He stared up at the gilt stars. "Even when I was apparently befriended, I couldn't make any genuine friendships. I was in disguise and living a deception. My life depended on it."

"Until Toby Thornton? Why was he different? Was he English?"

"Though his father had been an English trader in Canton, Toby's mother was Chinese. That explains the end of the story. The beginning was simply the tale of a wanderer."

She sat in silence for a moment as if allowing this to sink deep into her heart. "Then how did you learn to fight as you do?"

"I had made it through the Karakoram Mountains and come down into the desert. I was half dead, with sickness, with exhaustion. But before I became part of that last caravan, there was a year lost—or perhaps gained—when I lived with a man who'd seen through my disguise, but decided not to betray me. Neither did he befriend me. Instead, he made me his disciple."

Her fingers caressed the kitten's ears. He waited for her to ask questions that he couldn't answer, demand explanations of the unexplainable. Yet she seemed to digest what he had said with a gentle acceptance, as if she knew that he was already offering as much as he could.

"But you left him?" she asked at last.

"He died. I adopted a new disguise. If I'd been discovered, I would have been slain on the spot as a foreign spy."

"Where were you going? How did you discover the fossil fields?"

Where? He had been going nowhere! He had no longer been his own master by then.

"I was traveling toward one of those lost mountain realms somewhere between China and Russia," he said. "A little wind was just promising the scent of moisture and greenness from the foothills when our caravan was attacked by bandits."

"You fought them off?"

"Our guards were butchered without mercy. I couldn't stand very long alone against a troop of armed horsemen. I kept the bandits at bay just long enough to strike a bargain for my life, before I, too, was slaughtered. I saved our lives by promising infinite wealth to their chieftain."

"*Our* lives? You saved someone else, too?"

He took a deep breath. She had once again dived with exquisite clarity to the heart of the matter. Jack gazed at the bed canopy and said nothing. The stars shimmered in nights of musk and silk. His skin quaked beneath slender female hands tattooed with henna. Darkness hid both the sweetness and the bitterness of his surrender. None of that was relevant to the tale.

"Another traveler," he said. "It was the mad impulse of the moment. But that night I told the bandits the tales of the ancient Scythians, the griffin-guarded deposits of gold. So that's the direction we were taken."

"Which led you to the dragon bones?"

"No. Mistrust and violence broke out long before that. My . . . the other traveler was killed. I escaped alone into the desert. That's when I found the bones."

"And met Toby Thornton?"

"In a graveyard of fossils where I would have left my skeleton, too, if Toby Thornton hadn't found me. He'd learned fluent English from his father and felt himself partly an Englishman, but he looked entirely Chinese. Somehow Toby carried me through the lawless fringes of China and into the lands north of India. Alone I would have been killed instantly. I was anyway helpless much of the time. Meanwhile, he brought away the fossil tooth and his notes, and he was taking all my map readings for me, as well."

"How did Uriah get the papers?"

He could not keep the pain and distress from his voice. "Toby and I were attacked in a remote pass high in the mountains. I was stripped and left for dead. Toby and our packs were carried away, but his servant secretly followed. The man swore to me much later that Toby was executed. He couldn't save our baggage. He barely managed to rescue himself."

"But now Uriah says that Toby is a captive, instead?" She bit her lip. "Could he be? You don't think the servant might have lied?"

Jack allowed the tension to ease out of his muscles, then opened his hands to embrace the empty night. "No. I knew the man well. Yet perhaps he didn't see Toby die with his own eyes."

"So what happened to your packs?"

"A series of misadventures. The fossil and papers were of no interest to those tribesmen. Everything went missing. Toby's servant believed I was dead, too, but he'd discovered that his master's cousin was in India. He went to Uriah and told him everything. The man couldn't have known that Uriah wanted only to destroy all of Toby's work."

"Toby had told his cousin about the fossils? Why?"

"I've no idea. Perhaps Uriah had only become a fanatic since their last meeting in Canton several years before. Perhaps he'd promised to support Toby in his work, while planning to destroy it. I don't know. Whatever the reason, Uriah now knew about the missing evidence and he knew about me. When I turned up alive, he was desperate to recover everything before I did. As you may imagine, we didn't get along."

The nightshirt had fallen open at the collar, revealing the pure line of her neck. "So he put about the story that the missing fossil was sacred, the holy fang of a dragon?"

"Yes, and with a great reward waiting on its recovery. Such stories—especially when started by an extremist—have a way of growing into sacred truths in Asia. Soon the tale was controlling Uriah, rather than his controlling the tale. Although he had recovered most of the missing papers—found in a bazaar—he knew by then that he had to recover the tooth if he was to keep his life. Meanwhile, to force him to keep the papers safe, I planted other rumors that I had already recovered the fossil and would trade it for all of the notebooks."

She ducked her head, turning her face away. Her pulse beat hard. "Didn't that put your life in danger?"

He shrugged. "I was living and traveling in the shadows."

"So why was that sailor bringing the fossil back to England?"

"Because he heard the rumors and believed it was worth more money here. I, too, had quietly begun to offer a reward for it. The fossil had passed from hand to hand several times by then, sometimes with bloodshed. The hunt was threatening to become the focus of tribal rivalry. Chaos and massacre were a serious risk. The sailor didn't know whom to trust. Meanwhile, I discovered only that it was on the *Venture*."

"But Uriah knew that, too, so he had his assassin waiting? It's horrible!"

"Yes," Jack said.

"And now everything is lost."

"Yes, but Toby might still be alive."

"And you must try to find him."

"Yes."

A small ripple quivered over her white throat, before she looked back at him. What had he expected? Consternation? Fear? Reproach? Instead she looked grave, as if she was thinking deeply and making no judgments whatsoever.

Horace jumped to the floor. Anne said nothing as she sank down to snuggle back beneath the covers. Jack reached out to snuff the lamp. The room and the bed plunged into darkness. He did not reach for her, for her warmth and compassion. Instead he lay and stared at the shifting shadows. Horace was stalking the edges of the room, his kitten eyes open to the dark world.

Yet Anne turned and put her arms about Jack, tucking her head into the hollow of his shoulder.

"You must go," she said. "I see that. But what if you can't find him? What if you die in the attempt?"

"Then you'll be free," Jack said.

THE DORSET COUNTRYSIDE PASSED BY IN A BLUR, JUST AS the last twelve hours had passed in a blur. Anne had slept, encompassed in the warmth of Jack's arms, then woken in her own room, where the duchess had arrived with the dawn to prepare her for her wedding.

So Jack had carried her back, after all, while she slept: the bride he didn't want.

Later that morning Anne stood up with Lord Jonathan Devoran St. George to take vows to love, cherish, and obey him for the rest of her life, till death them did part. If she had married Arthur, all her friends and family would have been invited to a celebration in Hawthorn Axbury. But there were no friends and no family at Wyldshay—except her father—and she was married in the round room in the Fortune Tower. The room where she had witnessed Jack's family trying to force him not to marry her—then compel him to do so.

Did no one else realize that death might part them quite soon?

Jack took his leave immediately after the ceremony.

"Well, Your Grace," Anne heard him say to his mother. "Though I promised Anne I would put in an appearance at Withycombe—

just enough to allay gossip—I shall take ship for Asia directly, as you requested."

The duchess gazed at her son, her green eyes dry. "Even with a battering ram, I cannot breach the wall you have built, can I? Godspeed, Jonathan. Your bride will be in safe hands."

Jack looked away for a moment, his mouth set, then he bowed over his mother's fingers and smiled up into her eyes. "Yes," he said. "As I always was— Thank you, Your Grace."

"My door is open," the duchess said, her ribbons shimmering. "It has been all along."

"But now I can no longer walk through it," Jack said.

"Jack asked me to tell you that James is safe, Lady Jonathan," Ryder said quietly to Anne as he watched his brother next take leave of their father. "Uriah Thornton has gone, God knows where. Graham has been dismissed from this household, but a post has been found for him at one of the duchy's other properties. Jack told me everything. You should know that I was tempted to lie to him: tell him that one of the sailors showed me proof that this Toby Thornton is dead. Perhaps then he would stay in England."

"But you didn't?"

"No. For his sake and for my mother's sake, I'd have done it. For your sake, I could not."

"No," Anne said. "No, of course you could not tell a falsehood, even for your own sake. Thank you for telling me, my lord."

"You're better off without him," Ryder said.

Anne turned away, at a loss for words. Jack was lovely: lean and strong and ferociously good-looking in his wedding clothes. He clasped his father once more by the hand, then spun about and strode from the room.

"Damn him!" Ryder said, as if to no one in particular.

So it was over. All tied up and done with. Anne barely noticed the wedding breakfast, only her father's eyes as he helped her into their carriage. Another carriage followed with baggage and extra servants, including Roberts, who was carrying Horace in a basket. At home in Hawthorn Axbury, Mrs. Marsh would pack up all of Anne's possessions: her clothes—though the duchess had promised to send dressmakers to remake her entire wardrobe—and her personal things, even her fossil collection. The duke would send wagons and staff later for their transport.

Anne and her father talked of nothing but practicalities as they sped along the mud-spattered lanes, past gangs of men sawing up the trees that had fallen in the gale, to Jack's house, Withycombe Court. She was going to have more spending money than she had ever dreamed possible. She thought she might help endow a school, as well as create her museum. Meanwhile, she would arrive at Withycombe to be swept up in the well-wishing of her family. Her father had sent everyone a message, and the duke had sent carriages.

Of course she longed to see them. Of course she was happy about that.

But would Jack join them all there later that day, as he had promised? Whether he did or not, he would leave immediately for the nearest port to take ship for India.

She had married him. She might never speak to him privately again. Beneath her calm smile, unhappiness beat at her ribs like a caged bird.

WITHYCOMBE COURT, MISS MARSH, ONE OF THE LOVELI-est old houses in Dorset: a place of walled gardens and mellow *fruit trees and flowers* . . . Also a house of gracious proportions and tranquil walls, honey-sweet stone and ancient trees, tucked into a rolling blanket of hills. Everyone was there, gathered in the sun-filled porch to greet the new bride and her father: her mother, Aunt Sayle and Edith, her sisters Emily and Marianne, and her little brother, Andrew, awed for once into silence by his sister's sudden change in fortune.

And therefore take the present time, With a hey and a ho, and a hey nonny no . . .

Laughing and joking with her family, Anne hugged them all and was hugged back. Acting hostess to her own mother, she poured tea and saw that everyone was served with little cakes. Yet she performed the role of new bride as if she walked through a dream. She was safe once again with the people she loved, though panic still drummed insistently beneath her rigid bodice: *Are you the same girl that you always were?*

He had said he would come. He had said she wouldn't have to face this homecoming alone. He didn't come. The day began to ebb. Chill shadows formed in the corners of the room. Mrs. Marsh had just stood to begin gathering her brood, when the door swung open.

Everyone looked up as Jack strode into the room. Anne's heart bounded like a hare chased by hounds. Suddenly she saw her family through the eyes of his: a gaggle of humbly dressed Dissenters. Her mother in a dark gray dress that had never been in fashion. Her sisters, even in their best gowns, looking plain and provincial, with their simply dressed hair framing glowing, unsophisticated faces. Even her father seemed unkempt, his coat rumpled, his hair flying in wisps about his face.

Anne leaped to her feet, ready to defend all her sheep against the stalk of the tiger.

But Jack shook her father and Andrew by the hand, bowed to her mother and sisters, greeted Aunt Sayle and Edith with a little joke, and suddenly they were all sitting down again, laughing, as a maid brought fresh tea. Horace, who had been purring beside the fireplace, raced over to be picked up and petted.

An hour later as the carriages rolled away, Anne knew that every single member of her family, from her mother to Marianne, was as much in love as she was. Andrew had become completely enthralled. Even the kitten had never once taken his round eyes from Lord Jonathan Devoran St. George, who seemed to have the knack—when he wished it—of making friends with everyone.

"How did you do that?" she asked as quiet settled back over the drive.

"Do what?"

"Charm everyone? They like you!"

"I hope so," Jack said. "I like them."

Tears—of anger, of exhaustion, of stress—burned her eyelids. "How can you say that? I don't want you to condescend to my family!"

His gaze held the gilt severity of a heathen idol. "Damnation, Anne! I like them! Of course I wanted them to feel welcome and at ease, but why must you look for other motives? I *like* them! Your mother is kind and honest. Your aunt is warm-hearted and generous. Your little brother and sisters are clever and funny and charming. And your father . . ."

"What about my father?"

"Mr. Marsh is a remarkable man."

The tears spilled hotly down Anne's cheeks. "That's what he said about you," she said. "But if you like him so well, why were you so late?"

He took her arm to escort her into the house. "I'm sorry for that," he said. "My first errand took longer than I expected."

Anne pulled away to march through to the drawing room. The maids had already cleared away the tea things. "To arrange your passage?"

"Yes, but I also went after a certain fellow in a blue turban."

She collapsed into a chair. "That sailor? The man who tried to murder us?"

Jack crouched and twirled a paper spill from the mantel for Horace. The kitten pounced and batted.

"I had to know if Uriah has simply left me a trap."

"And has he?"

"I don't know. Perhaps it doesn't matter. I'll sail as soon as there's a suitable ship passing by."

"Passing by?"

"I'm a duke's son," he said. "When he's about to sail by, the captain will send a ship's boat to pick me up. It's just a matter of sending messages to the right people."

"Oh," she said. "Your father's influence, of course."

He looked up at her. "I don't want to impose on you, Anne. If you prefer that I leave—?"

She stood up. Horace raced over to attack her hem. She bent and picked him up. "No! If you must remain in England for a while longer, I should leave and you should have this house."

"You're my wife. My home is yours."

"I can go back to Hawthorn Axbury."

"If you do, people will gossip and speculate about our marriage. That will only make things harder for you in the long run."

"And you're my husband," she said. "We were married this morning. If you leave again now, the servants will talk. Word will still get about. You should stay."

He pushed himself to his feet and strode to the window, where he stood with his back to her. "If you wish it."

"Yes," she said, hugging the kitten to her chin. "Yes. I do wish it."

Chapter Sixteen

Jack stared blindly, not seeing beyond the ripples in the panes. She wanted him to stay?

I, Jonathan, take thee, Anne, to my wedded wife, to have and to hold . . .

Not to have. Not to hold. Only to long for.

Anne was right, of course. Until the ship's boat came for him, it would be better for her if he did not appear to spurn her. But could he trust himself to remain under the same roof and not lose himself entirely in that grave blue gaze?

"I should show you the house," he said.

"The housekeeper will do it, if you don't wish to."

He turned to look at her. She seemed calm, smiling at the kitten as it ran off, tail upright.

"No," he said. "I would like to."

The tip of her nose dipped as her smile washed over him in his turn. It riveted his attention, touched his heart.

"Then I would like that very much," she said.

Jack strode ahead of her, trying to concentrate on the house, negate the madness of his feelings. He had never paid much attention to Withycombe Court. He had known it would be his. He had spent some time here as a boy. Why had he never thought he would live here? Now, as the day wound down into a damp evening, the rooms welcomed as a warm fire welcomes the traveler returning after a storm. Stairs creaked like the jokes of old friends. Doors opened on peace and whispered promises of contentment.

And as they inspected room after room, his new bride began to glow as if a fire had been lit under her skin.

"This is your bedroom," he said at last.

His favorite, it spanned one end of the house from south to north, commanding views across the countryside from three sets of windows. There was a four-poster. A pair of settees sat on each side of a fireplace, where a log fire burned merrily. Other than the beauty of polished mahogany, everything in the room was painted or upholstered in shades of ivory and white. Except that—as unexpected as a sudden burst of song—an exquisite carpet filled the center of the floor. The carpet inspired lush, Oriental visions, colored by birdsong and the scent of flowering vines. As if a second fire burned there, the carpet cast warm color onto the plaster walls and velvet drapes, like the reflections of flames.

Anne stopped in the doorway and said nothing.

"I thought you might like it," Jack said, "though you may choose any room, of course."

She walked over to the bed and touched the white hangings. "I don't know what to say. When did you have time to think of what I might like?"

"I had to send orders to open the house. Let the staff know which beds, which fires—"

He felt oddly insecure, as if he might know real pain if she spurned his choice, but she glanced back at him, her eyes sparkling.

"I think its beauty comes from its simplicity," she said. "Yet that brilliant carpet charges the space like a heartbeat."

"You do like it?"

Her nose tip dipped as she smiled, melting his bones. "It's a room one could dance in," she said. "I do like it. Very much. Thank you, Jack."

Heart soaring, he spun about and flung open the door. "Then I hope you'll also like your presents!"

"Presents?"

"Wedding presents. Downstairs," he said. "Where a meal also awaits us."

She followed him down to a small parlor, paneled in oak, a room where he had spent many quiet and happy hours as a boy. A table for two had been set before the fire. Not the formal expanse of the dining room, just an intimate supper for a couple on their wedding night.

The efficiency of English servants would never cease to amaze him.

Two trunks sat at the side of the room. Anne sat down on a chaise longue as Jack tossed back the lid of the first. He reached inside and turned around with a handful of books and pamphlets.

"Just about everything that's ever been published about ancient lizards," he said. "Papers on the latest research. Books on anatomy, geology. Anything I could think of that might help your study of fossils."

Anne turned white, then flushed with color like a pink rose. "You thought of that? For me?"

She walked over and knelt beside the trunk, then exclaimed over title after title. Clutching several large tomes, she crossed back to the chaise longue.

"Oh, I've been wanting to read this—and this! But how could you put all this together so quickly?"

"I gave the order as soon as we arrived at Wyldshay—the power of the Blackdowns."

She smoothed her palm down the spine of an illustrated treatise and smiled at him. "Thank you, Jack."

"You don't want to know what's in the second trunk?"

She laughed. "Nothing could be better than these books!"

"For the mind," he said. "But what about the spirit?"

He wrenched open the second lid and tossed out a riot of color: blue silk, embroidered in silver thread with tiny flowers; a pale, whisper-soft jade with tiny golden birds; a pure, almost translucent white-on-white, where ghost dragons trailed their snow-burning breath beneath the fronds of ghost trees; then red, then cream, then yellow—

A kind of wildness filled his mind. He strode up to his bride and flung out bolt after bolt of colored silk, as if he would negate her plain dress and embroider it with sensuality.

"Here," he said, as blue and gold and green cascaded over her lap. "The duchess will send a dressmaker, but I brought these fabrics for you from the other side of the world."

Her fingers strayed over the tiny embroidery, as fine as spiderwebs, and her face flushed, beautiful, maddeningly desirable.

"Not for me," she said. "You didn't know about me then."

"Nonsense! They're all for you. They were for you when I bought them. I just didn't know it at the time." Jack draped a garden of tiny embroidered flowers about her shoulders. "This blue is just the color of your eyes when you're angry."

"Angry?"

He laughed. "Yes!"

Her fingers strayed over the silk. She lifted the ivory gauze to her face and stroked it along one cheek. "But I'm not angry now."

"Then you should be," Jack said. "I've married you, yet promised to abandon you. You should be angry."

She stood up. Silk slid away to pool like paint on the couch behind her. "Why should I be angry, when what happened was all my fault to begin with?"

He seized her by both hands. "Don't be so damned forbearing, Anne!"

"It's my wedding day," she said, gripping his fingers. "I'll be just as forbearing as I wish."

Scent spiraled from her hair: the innocence of lavender and rosemary, sweetly forbidden. A dark pulse began to pound in his groin, heavy and hot and not innocent at all. He wanted very desperately to kiss her, but he was balanced on a knife edge between desire and desire. His longing for her. His longing for—what? Freedom?

Yet consumed by the craving, he thought he might simply begin to peel at the core, layers of pain opening as if he were being flayed from the heart out. He dropped her hands.

"Was there something else you wanted for a wedding present?"

She shook her head. "No. This fabric is lovely. The books are even better. I didn't expect anything at all."

Jack stepped away from her as the door opened.

ANNE LOOKED AROUND. A LIVERIED SERVANT HELD A tray. Jack escorted her to the table. Servants brought a succession of delectable dishes, carefully prepared. She picked at them, eating just enough so that he wouldn't notice that she had no real appetite for food.

She had lost him. He would leave for Asia and never come back. Of course she could make a new life for herself alone in this wonderful house. She didn't regret losing Arthur, or even Hawthorn Axbury. Everything she had once taken for granted now seemed only confining and trivial. She was Lady Jonathan Devoran St. George. The world would offer her more opportunities than she had ever dreamed possible. Yet that future hadn't really begun and the present was still very much alive.

At last the cloth was removed and the servants left. Firelight danced over a silver dish of hothouse fruit and sparkled in the facets of a brandy decanter.

Anne played with a handful of grapes, pushing them about on her gold-rimmed plate. Jack was achingly handsome, telling stories, drinking the rich wine, entertaining her as if she were a stranger. His fingers were lovely, caressing the stem of his glass. His smile was lovely, wicked as a fallen angel's.

If she reached a hand across the table, she could touch him. As if shutting out the sun, she dropped her lids and sought for the inner voice.

See it through, Annie! Grasp life with both hands! Even if that means that when he leaves, he will break your heart.

She opened her eyes and clenched her fingers in her lap. His dark hair fell forward over his forehead as he gave her a quizzical smile, and her heart seemed to stop in her breast.

"I do know what I want," she said.

"For a wedding present? If it's within my power, I'll give it to you."

"You promise?"

"Yes, why?"

Her hands began to tremble, leaving a faint trace of moisture in the palm. "Because I want a child."

Jack seemed to freeze in place, as if he heard tigers stalking. His almost empty glass slipped from his fingers and tipped over. A runnel of brandy spilled across the polished table.

"I've no right to claim you as a wife. I will leave any day. You may never see me again."

She lifted her chin, fighting panic. *See it through!* "So you will leave me here alone. I accept that. I accept that you've taken my life and shaken it and spilled it into these new channels. Yet you don't think I have the right to claim the solace of a child?"

"You'll marry again," he said. "You'll bear another man's children."

"No. I shall not. Even if you die, I shall not marry again. Unless you get me with child now, I'll never have children, and that's too great a price for me to pay, Jack."

His empty glass rolled to the fruit dish. His fists clenched until the knuckles shone white. "I promised myself I would not—"

"Why? We are married."

"Yes," he said, suddenly dropping his head into both hands. "You're right. I wouldn't deprive you of children."

Her heart began to pound. A wave of heat washed treacherously over her skin. "I also want to learn more things I don't know. Unless I displease you—"

He dropped his hands and lifted his head. To her surprise, he smiled at her with the brilliant radiance of the archangel. "My dear girl, nothing about you displeases me. Indeed, you please me very well indeed."

"I do?"

"If I've hesitated, it was only because I told myself that such restraint was best for you. I was trying to be noble. Yet, God help me, Anne, I don't feel in the least noble. You said once I was a hero. I'm not a damned hero. I'm just a man and I want you with soul-shaking intensity. Don't you know that?"

The trickle of panic had grown into a thundering torrent. Fire burned and scorched up her neck. "I don't know why you would think restraint was noble in the first place. Was it because there really are wicked things, things I mustn't know?"

He raised a brow. "Wicked things?"

"That men and women can do together?" She began to chant from memory. Her voice rang in her ears in an odd little singsong. " 'Can you deny that you have studied esoteric techniques that would shock every idea of decency? That you have been a willing pupil of the most shameless of courtesans and concubines? That you consorted without limit with every lascivious, exotic female, from Greece to Asia, who offered you her tainted embraces?' Is it because of that?"

His mouth stiffened a little as he looked down. "God! And believing all that, you still risk asking me to show you?"

Anne leaned forward, feeling frantic, knowing her face flamed like a candle. "Why did your mother say those terrible things? Are they true, after all?"

He glanced back at her, his gaze forest dark, though lit now with a hint of hidden mirth. "Not as my mother implied. I would like to show you that with every fiber of my being, Anne." He bit his lip and tipped his head back, as if filled with wild amusement. "Alas, I don't know what 'tainted embraces' would mean."

The heat was burning deeper, down her belly, pooling

wickedly between her legs. "The duchess meant something by it," Anne said.

"Mother was playing a game. She wanted me to admit to sin, so she could forgive me and embrace her prodigal back into the family. I wouldn't play. That exchange wasn't about sensuality, it was about power."

"Power?"

"My mother wanted to know if she could control me. I showed her that she could not. I also tried to show her that we can still love each other."

"But Ryder agreed with her and so did Arthur."

"With all that babble about purity?" As if he'd just noticed it for the first time, Jack reached for his glass and set it back on its base. His fingers came away sticky. Still laughing into her eyes, he licked off the traces of wine. "What the devil is impure about the body? None of the ancient religions of the Orient teaches such nonsense."

"So you have become truly foreign? That's really what your mother is afraid of, isn't it?"

"It's as if a madness is gripping England. Everyone is mouthing this new philosophy of shame and ignorance. Prudery wasn't the way of the world when the Prince Regent ruled over a lascivious court. It certainly wasn't the bawdy, merry England of Shakespeare, or the witty, naughty England of George the Second. Yet now we must all indulge in the hypocrisy of demanding something called purity in women. Even though an English dinner dress reveals more female flesh to the male gaze than any woman in the East would consider decent."

Anne glanced down at her dress: one of Lady Elizabeth's, cut away from the neck. An invitation for him to look at her with desire?

"You're saying we're all hypocrites?"

"Why the devil must we demonize lovemaking? Unless one party isn't willing or cannot give true consent, what can lovers do together that could possibly be described as tainted?"

She wanted to believe him. Yet her pulse resounded like cannon fire and her skin flamed. "Then why did you think it was wrong to make love to me at the cottage, or later at the fountain?"

"Because you didn't know what you were agreeing to. You couldn't give informed consent."

"But I didn't ask you to stop, even after I started to understand. I'm not a child or an idiot. If you sinned then, I was an equal partner in it. Deny me that, and we have nowhere left to go."

"No, I don't deny it, though I don't think either of us was really thinking of the consequences."

"Well, I certainly wasn't," she said, gathering her courage and smiling at him. "Yet it happened and now I'd like to understand more."

Jack picked up the decanter and refilled his glass. "What exactly would you like to know, Lady Jonathan?"

"Whatever it was that all those exotic ladies taught you. Unless it would distress you to show me?"

He laughed, the sound filled with simple mirth: deep, rich, full of promise. "No," he said. "It would not distress me." Firelight danced in the twisted stem as he lifted his glass and swallowed brandy. "My dear Anne, right now I want very much to unbutton all those silly English buttons and ravish you in an orgy of lascivious pleasure. I only want to be sure that you mean exactly what you say."

"I trust you. Even in things your brother would think wicked."

"There is nothing wicked, though there are practices that Ryder might think inappropriate."

"And you don't?"

"Not if it's simply because they're ways to find pleasure, rather than ensure procreation."

"So nothing lovers can do is sinful?"

"Not unless you find you dislike something, or prefer not to try the experiment."

"Science is all about experimenting," Anne said, calling on a mad bravado. "If I don't like something, I'll tell you."

He set down his glass and ran one finger around the rim. "Yet I think you ought to feel just a little afraid, don't you?"

"Why?" she said. "Even if I'm stark with terror now, what is there to be afraid of?"

"Only this: I've been trying very hard not to complicate things between us. My ship to India will arrive any day. I will give you this, since you insist, but I can offer you nothing more, Anne."

"You can give me *now*," she said. "You are here *now*. The consequences, if there are any, will be mine to deal with. They are freely chosen."

"I will give you whatever I can for these last few days that we'll have together," he said. "If you say stop, I will stop."

She was shaking, deep in the bone, as terrified as if she were about to step off a cliff.

"I won't be the same afterward, will I?"

"No. You won't be the same. Yet you'll still risk it?"

"Yes, Jack. Though I know it's not what you wanted, though I know it won't solve anything in the long term, right now I'm still your wife. Anyway, I don't think I'll say stop."

He pushed away from the table, then turned so that he stood just behind her. Her skin prickled into alertness, alive with hot sensitivity. She loved him. She wanted him with a terrifying intensity. And yes, she would indeed like a baby. His baby. A child to give meaning and purpose to all the rest of her days without Lord Jonathan Devoran St. George, who had stolen her soul. A child to break her heart as it grew into another independent spirit who would leave her.

"Very well, then." His fingertips brushed the back her neck, firing sensations so acute that she gasped. "I have no arguments left. Let us make love without restraint."

Unable to speak, she simply nodded.

Jack peeled off his jacket, then leaned down to whisper in her ear. "But first we must invoke spells for good luck."

"Spells?"

"In China dragons toss giant pearls of happiness across the heavens. We most definitely should invoke the dragon of good fortune. Just here, I think, inside your elbow." Jack ran one hand down the sleeve of her dress.

Firelight warmed the fabric of his shirtsleeves and highlighted the delectable planes of his face. Anne watched his lean fingers as he began to unfasten the row of tiny buttons that ran from her wrist to her elbow. He peeled away her sleeve to trace his fingertips over her skin. His cleanly shaped, lovely fingers, gleaming warmly in the flickering light. Delight bloomed beneath his touch. Anne took a deep breath and surrendered to sensation.

Yet in spite of everything she thought she believed, she felt wicked. Wanton and wicked and abandoned. Her pulse beat heavily, spreading heat through her veins.

Jack moved to kneel beside her, resting her wrist on his knee, then he dipped his forefinger into the spilled brandy on the table and traced a line of careful symbols on her skin. Like ancient runes ground from rubies, the mysterious characters glowed against her white flesh.

"For good luck?" she asked.

"For good luck." His finger traced lightly, firing mad impulses as each character followed the next, from wrist to elbow. "This sign stands for wisdom and this one for grace." He blew gently on the lines of brandy. A surge of goose bumps ran exquisitely over her skin. "Here is fecundity, and here is the sign for long life and happiness."

"Oh," she said, all her attention focused on the torrent of sensations. "Will I wear them forever?"

"Yes," he said. "Even though now I shall lick them off."

His lips touched warmly on her wrist, then the tip of his tongue traced over a brandy rune, the one for long life. Pleasure exploded somewhere deep in her belly.

"Oh," Anne said. "Oh, my!"

Gilt and dark, gazing up beneath thick black lashes, his wild-forest gaze pinned her as if she were a sacrificial lamb, offering itself willingly to the god of tigers.

"Thus I share the good fortune and become potent and fertile. That will guarantee us a baby."

With his eyes still on hers his mouth moved higher, delicately licking away one brandy symbol at a time. Her wicked angel: amused, passionate, focused only on her pleasure.

"Now for grace," he said, kissing higher, almost to the bend of her elbow.

Shivers of delight rippled and rippled, as if his lips touched her all over, as if he kissed her in forbidden, unimaginable places.

"And now for wisdom."

His tongue touched gently inside the bend of her elbow, teasing, tantalizing. She was melting in her chair, limber as a candle left too close to a fire.

"There," he said. "Now we can do nothing unwise but perhaps we should paint more good luck symbols to be sure."

"Oh, yes," Anne said. "Yes, please."

Still gazing up at her, he sat back on his heels, his eyes filled with mirth and intelligence.

"Yes, please?" he said, grinning.

She covered her hot face with both hands. "I liked it," she said. "I don't think it's wrong to like that."

"Then we'll try something else you might like." He took her right foot and removed her shoe. She wriggled her toes at him. "Hmm, the very best silk stockings. It would never do to wet them with brandy." His hand slipped up her calf to the flesh of her thigh, firing tantalizing, wicked sensations. "Here," he said, sliding her skirt up over her knees. "We must ensure more good luck here."

She had been naked with him before. They had made love again at the fountain. Yet to let him lift up her skirts at the dining table! Though he allowed the drape of her hem to cover her most intimate places, his palm caressed her skin, as if he took infinite delight in the shape of the muscle and soft flesh just above her garter.

"What if the servants come in?" The question sounded breathy, excited.

"If they do, they'll beat a hasty retreat, but no one will come in."

Her cheeks could set forests alight. Her pulse drummed a primitive, sensual new rhythm.

He reached to dip a finger in the brandy, smoothing his other palm over her knee.

"Oh," she said. "Surely you won't write things there!"

Lines of merriment marked his cheeks and the corners of his eyes. "Oh, surely I will!"

Anne clung to her chair with both hands as he began to trace brandy runes on the inside of her thigh.

"The Duality of the Creative Heaven," he said.

Her skin prickled as the brandy dried. She was pulsing for him, somewhere deep inside, as if only this mystery existed in the world.

His forefinger created another set of lines. "The mountain remains while flames rise above it: the Traveler, whose only rest is within."

"I shan't be traveling," she said, her voice strangled. "But you will. I should paint that on you."

"Oh, you'll be traveling." A mad gaiety colored his voice. "I'm going to take you to all kinds of new places."

Her foot trembled on his leg.

"*Hsiao Ch'U,* the Taming Power of the Small. 'The gentle wind and the creative heaven, as clouds gather. Gentleness must temper determination.'" He spread her knees and wrote another message of pleasure on her hot skin.

She didn't want him to stop. Her breasts ached. Her skin flamed. She felt wanton and wicked. She didn't want him to stop.

He reached nearly to the top of her thigh. "*T'ai,* heaven and earth unite in harmony, creating peace. And now to share that with you."

A sigh like a benediction eased from her lips as the tip of his tongue swirled over the Duality of the Creative Heaven, licking away the trace of brandy. His lips kissed away the rune for the

Traveler. His mouth lingered over the Taming Power of the Small, then moved higher to suckle at Peace, his dark head close to the edge of her skirt.

Goose bumps rose all over her skin. She was liquid and heat and languid, pulsing pleasure.

"You want more?" he asked.

She nodded, speechless. His eyes were night, unreadable, as he swept her up into his arms and carried her to the couch.

The chaise longue was aflame with colored silk. Jack's arousal filled his mind: desire for this English girl who knew nothing but *yes*. His wife!

He glanced down at her flushed cheeks. She weighed almost nothing, her head pillowed on his shoulder, her feet dangling. She ducked her face into his collar and sighed. A terrible pain locked around his heart, as if it would break. Perhaps he would shatter like Ryder's jade horse, yet first he would teach her this one great lesson. Even if he must use all of his training to keep the brittle bounds of his soul in check.

The Clinging Fire, the Still Mountain, the Wanderer. Jack closed his eyes for a moment. *You won't be the same!*

He set her down on the couch. The riot of silk flamed in sensual color. Anne glowed like a paper lantern on a still night. His sense of self began to slip, as if merging into the sensations crowding his brain. The fire crackled, but the noise receded and receded into a distance echo. Smoke and wine and lavender dissolved into one single perfume that diffused into nothingness. His entire being had become a spear of desire.

The Traveler must always oblige others. If a stranger in a strange land ever forgets that he is a wanderer, he will find only tears.

He peeled away the fabric of her dress, then plucked one by one at her corset strings. Somewhere the universe played a symphony of pleasure. Slowly, slowly, her lovely white body emerged from its carapace, leaving her clad only in a thin shift. Silk caressed her. White dragon breath huffed onto her naked arms. Golden birds fluttered beneath her stockinged feet.

"This other thigh is jealous," he said. "It would like messages of its own."

"Yes," she said, covering her eyes with her hands. "Yes, Jack."

He strode to the table to fetch his glass, staring down into the bronze liquid for a moment as if he were a candle flame seeking its hot, wavering reflection.

The wanderer finds rest only deep within himself.

If I have hesitated, it was only because I told myself that such restraint was best for you.

Didn't she know that he was lying? That when he said he was no hero, he was telling her the simple truth? He hadn't held back for her sake. How could what they were about to share possibly harm her? No, he had held back because of his own craven weakness, because—if he made love to her with all of his skill and passion and knowledge—he didn't know what would happen to *him*.

You won't be the same. Yet you'll still risk it?

Yes, he would risk it, but only because he must. He would even risk giving her a child, though that would mean that he'd never see his own firstborn—a thought that threatened to tear his heart from his body. But he owed her whatever she asked for, and he was consumed by lust and ardor and madness. She had left him nowhere else to turn.

He smiled as he walked back to the couch. "Now to share these," he said.

He began to write more Chinese characters up the inside of her left thigh. His erection throbbed. His mind arrowed in on the urgency of his desire. Yet he kept himself carefully poised in the place between control and loss of self.

She sighed and burned, her skin hot beneath his tongue, hot beneath his palms cupping her hips. She was quivering like a violin string. Her nipples thrust hard against the fabric of her shift. He reached up to brush his fingertips over them, lightly, lightly. Anne bit her lip and arched her back. Silk slid sensuously over her flesh. Her breasts filled his palms. His kisses traced up her soft thigh, higher and higher still, as she trembled and gasped.

Duality. Gentleness. Peace. Yin and Yang circling forever in the cosmic dance.

With both hands he pushed her skirts up to her waist and stroked one finger over the soft down hiding her sex. She was already swollen and moist, her little nub peaked like a tiny penis. Jack smiled, one burning flame of male ardor, as he lowered his head to taste her. She barely tensed for a moment before she opened herself naturally to his questing tongue. Exquisite, enthralling.

He kissed her, savored her, taking and giving that infinite excitement. She moaned and whimpered, clutching her hands in his hair, clutching at the silk on the couch, writhing beneath him. Inundated by an intensity of pleasure, his body responded in kind. He was engorged and hot, his scrotum tight and heavy at the base of his penis. His hands stroked over softness and curves as he suckled with exquisite restraint at her hot, sleek flesh, then tantalized her with little flicks of his tongue.

"Oh," she breathed. "Oh . . . oh . . . oh!"

His mind caught fire. His very essence yearned for her pleasure, until at last she convulsed beneath his lips and her sex kissed him back, silky and smooth. She cried out like a woman stricken to the heart. He climaxed—not the final climax of ejaculation—but the less intense contractions of ecstasy at the knife edge of that release, a place he could now reach again and again, if he wanted to.

Her eyes opened slowly. Moisture sheened over her flushed cheeks. Her pupils were dilated like reflections of the night.

"Oh," she said, blushing like a dog rose. She bit her lip and giggled. Funny, relaxed, blissful little giggles. "Surely that was very wicked?'

"You think so?"

The dog rose pink deepened to the color of red campions. "I know so. No wonder the world has conspired to stop ladies from knowing about such things."

"No wonder?"

The tip of her nose dipped. She was lovely, as desirable, as desired—and perhaps as dangerous to the traveler—as the Sirens. Like Odysseus, he thought he might not be able to bear the piercing beauty of her song. Though, of course, she didn't sing, she only smiled and smiled, like a cat with cream.

"Because after that," she said gravely, "how can any female not want it all over again?"

"Then you forgive my sinful ways, Lady Jonathan? You would allow me to show you even more wickedness?"

She curled back against the silk-covered couch and gazed at him from beneath sleepy eyelids. "How can there be anything more—except for you?"

"The advantage of being female is that there is always more," he said.

"And there isn't for men?"

It wasn't something he could explain to her. Not because he felt any prudery or reticence, just because he didn't know how to express it in language that she could understand. Hot pleasure still suffused his groin and pulsed through his blood.

"Why don't we find out?" he asked instead.

"Yes," she said, her mouth smiling and ripe. "Yes, please."

CHAPTER SEVENTEEN

PIECE BY PIECE, KISSING AND CARESSING, THEY SHED THEIR clothes. Scooting back against the garden of silk on the couch, Anne watched Jack as he tossed away the last of his undergarments. Reflected flame licked over his muscles, reveled in the firm shape of shoulder and back, the lovely curve of buttock and thigh. As he turned, the warm light washed over the hard length of his shaft, standing upright in the caress of the firelight. Glorious.

All that power and beauty to be shared with her.

A pulse thrummed insistently through her body, as if she vibrated in a scorching, invisible wind.

He walked back to the couch and leaned down as if to kiss her. Anne shrieked as he swept her up into his arms instead. He sat down and deposited her on his lap. His erect privy member brushed against her belly. Her hot, satiated, intimate place fired little shocks of pleasure at the contact.

"We've made love before," he said. "Madly, in the cottage and at the fountain. Madly, because we didn't deliberately choose what we were about. This will be different. Now I want to show you that lovemaking can be exquisitely conscious and aware. Not hurried, not blindly seeking the end, but alert to every nuance of feeling. Will you take this risk, also?"

She draped her arms about his shoulders, reveling in his firmness, the exact delineation of every muscle. "Why is it a risk?"

"Because you'll be making a considered commitment at each stage, not only to pleasure, but to a communion of the flesh."

"You mean I cannot simply close my eyes, lie back, and do my duty to England?"

He smiled back. "Oh, that, too! Of course."

She was already keen for him, slick and prepared. Yet he caressed and lingered over each caress: her breasts, her arms, her hair. Playing almost casually with each nipple, he took her to the brink of a stiffening rapture, then eased away again. When Anne thought perhaps she couldn't bear any more pleasure, when she longed for that incredible release, he lifted her to straddle his thighs.

Her face flaming, she felt the smooth head slip between her intimate folds, the separation, the surrender. Slowly he eased himself deeper, sliding on her moisture. Waves of delight spread up like a sunrise through her belly.

She wanted to move. Surely she ought to move, to work for more pleasure, yet his sleepy, tiger gaze held hers, as if asking her to wait.

"Now," he said. "Now sit quietly, open and relaxed, and just feel me."

Anne dropped her head to his shoulder. "I do feel you. It's lovely."

"Can you feel the head? The rim where it touches the mouth of your womb?"

She closed her eyes, sitting quietly with a bent knee on each side of his hips. His hands rested gently on her waist. She was filled, but could she feel—?

"Ah, yes!" she said as her eyes flew open. "I felt that!"

"I'm caressing you inside," he said, his eyes dark with mysteries. "Can you caress me back?"

"I don't know. I don't know how."

"Never mind. Breathe. Just as I showed you before. Let your concentration sink deeper and deeper. Let the relaxation fill your belly, open and easy and receptive, and just feel me again."

She breathed. Deep and easy and open. With her head on his shoulder, she sat absolutely still and concentrated. A pulse ran up his penis, creating ripples of satisfaction deep inside. *Yes. Yes!*

"You're growing even bigger inside me," she whispered. "I feel the . . . the head caressing as if it kissed me. It's lovely, Jack. Lovely. Now you're doing it even deeper! Oh! Oh, my!"

Her mind filled with sunshine, hot and yellow. Her intimate places quivered with a sensitivity so acute that her eyes filled with tears. As she focused, his quiet caresses created waves of pleasure, spreading and spreading in her blood.

He kissed her temple, his lips feather soft. "Now see if you can follow my lead with your inner muscles."

Everything converged on the pulse of his movement. Then, as if her body already knew what to do, she found the way to embrace him back, rhythmically clenching, creating an ever deeper intensity of pleasure as if they dived together into a whirlpool.

He slid both hands into her hair and lifted her face so that he looked directly into her eyes as they communed with these silent, secret little shivers of bliss. His smile seemed sublime. His eyes shone tiger-wild, though the depths echoed strange whispers of compassion. A tiger haunted by the spirit of the forest god, recognizing that power and voluntarily possessed by it.

Her eyelids felt heavy, as if she were drugged, hazy. Her lips smiled. Thought had fled entirely. She was dissolved, one hot, molten crucible of intimate pleasure. With her hips and legs relaxed, all of her being concentrated on this exquisite joining with this one man. Pleasure built and spilled inside her like hidden breakers. At each surge she knew more: the veins on his shaft, the curve of the rim, the seep of moisture from the head. She knew everything, as if her inner spaces were lined with tiny fingertips.

She was still staring into his eyes, lost in that dark gaze, when the intensity imploded past the point of no return. A tidal wave surged and exploded into rapture. His face disappeared, lost to sunshine and darkness. Her own cries rang in her ears. Her open mouth tasted moisture and salt—the bittersweet ecstasy of tears.

"Hush, hush," someone said, supporting her limp body in firm arms. "Hush, beloved."

His lips kissed her cheeks and eyelids, feathering over skin as suddenly sensitive as a tongue tip. Anne was floating in an ocean of sensation, knowing everything at once: his member still erect inside her; the hard muscles of his thighs; the silk caressing her folded knees; the pressure of his arms at her back; her breasts crushed against his chest; every nuance of his glorious scent filling her nostrils.

Yet she also knew the crackle of the fire, the tiny crevices of the paneling, the dark gardens outside, trees and grass running with their own live ardor directly to the sea. Her mind expanded and expanded until her whole being flooded with awareness, as if of the entire universe, while her mind flitted among the stars and shadows of an ongoing bliss.

Pleasure on pleasure on pleasure, only ebbing finally into one still white light of pure happiness.

She folded against him to weep in earnest.

"Hush," he said. "It's all right. Sweetheart. It's all right."

"Oh, yes," she said, choking back sobs. "More than all right. Exquisite."

He stroked damp hair away from her forehead. He was still erect inside her.

"I don't know why I'm crying! I had no idea—I'm still waiting for my mind to return to my body."

His hands soothed and caressed a deep reassurance. "We have all night."

All night. And then he would leave, if not this morning, then the next. He would leave and he would never come back—except, perhaps, in a coffin—

As if drenched in cold water, Anne knew then what they had risked. To share something this profound with another human being forged a bond that might never be broken. Jack had invaded not only her body, but her soul. And perhaps, perhaps, she had done the same to him?

She licked away the salt still lingering at the corners of her mouth, and knew now what her weeping was for. She hadn't known what she had asked for when she had persuaded him, when she had asked him to show her just how wicked lovemaking could be. But Jack had known. He had known—and he had risked it anyway?

Anne gazed up into his eyes, determined to say nothing of this new revelation, determined not to add to his burdens. Now that they had gone this far, she wanted to give him everything. He was her husband. Nothing they could do would be wrong. And if they were bound, they were bound. If he could risk it, so could she. *When there's no going back, you must go forward—*

"Now it's my turn," she said.

"Your turn?"

"My turn to bring such pleasure to you."

His hands rested quietly on her waist. He dropped his head to the silk-covered couch and laughed. "You did. You do."

"I want to touch you."

His eyes closed. "God! You have touched me."

"No, with my hands and mouth. I want to please you."

"I'm already as pleased as I've ever been in my life."

"But there is more, isn't there?"

"There's always more," he said. "But perhaps now we should make you a child?"

$\mathcal{I}$T WAS A SLOW, LANGUOROUS LOVEMAKING, ENCLOSED IN silk. *All night.* Jack gave, then gave some more. He wanted to give her the world. She was sheened in bliss, his wife. She was velvet and heat and satin smooth, his wife. She refused nothing, bestowed everything, as he led her on a long dance into rapture, until at last, at last, he allowed his seed to spill deep at the mouth of her womb. A child he might never see.

She slept then, wrapped in gilt birds and dragons' breath. Jack dragged himself from the couch and walked naked to the fire. Hot ashes stirred beneath a touch of the poker. He added more fuel. The fire sulked for a moment, then blazed up to warm his cold skin.

He dropped his head into his hands and fought the imminent scald of tears.

"What is it?"

He looked up. A rainbow of silk clutched to her breasts, Anne swung her feet to the floor. The ease, the bliss he had given her had smoothed her forehead, laid contentment about her mouth, but now she frowned.

"Jack? What is it?"

With a wry smile he called on control. To declare that he loved her, then leave her, was impossible. As he stood and walked up to her, he made sure that he projected only quiet confidence.

"Nothing," he said. "It will get cold in here. Let me take you to bed."

He carried her up through the sleeping house. The staff were long abed. The corridors lay dark and quiet, home of mysteries. Yet moonlight flooded the gracious bedchamber he had chosen for her and a fire still burned merrily in the grate.

Jack removed the warming pan and tucked her into the shadows of the canopied white bed. Her hair trailed across the pillow. Her ripe mouth smiled at him from the darkness. He knew with absolute certainty that she had left no room in his heart for any other woman.

"You will leave now for India?" she asked.

"Hush," he said. "Go to sleep. I'll still be here in the morning."

*A*NNE DRIFTED UP TO CONSCIOUSNESS. SHE WAS WARM, satiated, satisfied in every pore. She felt like laughing. Morning eased into the room carrying the chill of dawn, but new logs had just been added to the fire. She sat up. Jack wasn't in the room. She hadn't really expected him to be there, had she?

She grabbed a robe and walked to one of the windows. White haze hugged the ground. Trees wept moisture. A gray-and-green landscape, where sea-tossed moisture covered everything. In spite of the cold and damp outside, she tugged up the sash and leaned out to breathe in the salt air. Breakers sounded not too far off, like a heartbeat.

A shadow flitted over the flagstone courtyard below the window. Jack strode out into the cold space. He stopped, facing east toward the rising sun. A little fringe of fire rimmed his dark hair. His naked back gleamed above loose trousers of white cotton. He stood perfectly still for several moments, then began to move. A slow, stately dance, as if his body wrote secret runes on the quiet air, almost as if he offered worship to the dawn.

Yet slowly, inexorably, his movements grew in intensity. The dance became faster. Strikes and punches blended into a rapid-fire blur. Sweating and panting, his face contorted, he leaped and kicked, again and again, as if fighting an invisible demon—while a drift of figures began to emerge from the mist.

Anne stared at them, her heart in her mouth, and almost cried out. But Jack stopped, his arms dropped as if completely relaxed, and turned to face them: two sailors. The three men began to talk. The few snatches that drifted up to her were spoken in a language she didn't know.

Feeling suddenly faint, Anne turned away from the window, her heart hammering. She staggered over to a chair by the fire and held her hands out to the blaze. They had come for him.

What had she done?

A whirlwind of thoughts and images spun behind her closed lids. Of Jack's body. Of his eyes. Of the ecstasy they had shared.

What had she done?

She had stumbled into a world she did not really understand. She had fallen in love with a man who was too strange, too terrible, and too lovely for her to fathom. She had momentarily entrapped a dragon and tried to tame it. Now the dragon would spread its great wings, splintering her little wicker cage into fragments, and fly away. She would never see him again.

Yet she had spent a night forging chains that would rip her heart from her body when he left.

And what had she done to him?

She forced herself to go to the washstand. She must wash and get dressed and prepare herself to bid him farewell. He would want her to put a brave face on it. He would want to think that he could leave her here content.

A jug held water that was still faintly warm. She didn't bother ringing for fresh. She felt a small trickle on her leg. A trace of blood smeared the washcloth. Anne stared at it, then went to her cases for the necessary supplies and thought that her heart would break.

She was sitting in the breakfast room when he came in.

"Anne?" he asked softly.

Jack stood in the doorway, a strange robe over the loose trousers. His hair fell forward over his forehead.

"You've received a message from the ship," she said. "Your passage to the East."

"Yes."

She looked down at her clenched hands. "It's all right. I know you're eager to go."

"Eager?"

"Yes." She was determined not to cry. Yet her throat hurt and tears scalded, and suddenly she didn't have the strength to be noble, even if she must be petty and mean, instead. "You must be longing to go back to all those exotic women. Women who don't need to be taught."

As if she had struck him, he turned his head away. "You don't understand," he said.

"If I don't, it's because you haven't told me the whole truth. This isn't only about the game with Russia or the need to find your friend. There are women waiting for you all over Asia, aren't there? Or . . . a woman."

"What women, Anne? What are you talking about?"

She hugged her arms about herself, as if to cradle her misery. "Why did you drape me in silk last night? Why did you really teach me all that? Did you try to make me into the woman you lost? That traveling companion you mentioned, the one whose life you saved when the bandits attacked you, but later was killed—that was a woman, wasn't it? She was your lover."

She waited for him to deny it, knowing he could not.

"Yes," he said.

"Did she teach you all those wicked things?"

"Many of them, yes."

"She wasn't an Englishwoman, was she?"

"God, no! She was part Turcoman, part Tartar, part Russian, perhaps. I don't know. We didn't talk about that."

"What did you talk about?"

"Nothing. We almost never talked." He strode away. "Listen, it doesn't matter. I met her. We became lovers. She died. In the meantime, we shared a bed and a journey, which isn't necessarily the same thing, especially when camels are involved."

"I'm sorry," she said.

"Sorry? Why?"

"That she died and broke your heart."

He spun about. "Broke my heart? Good God!"

"Then why are you ashamed?" she said. "That's what your mother saw in your eyes that she couldn't bear, isn't it? Shame! If it's not because of all those exotic females, then it must be because you failed to save the life of a woman you loved—"

"No! I didn't love her. I didn't choose her. She had purchased me in the market."

Anne jerked upright. "Purchased you?"

His eyes were stark. "Yes. Purchased me. I had been captured and sold into slavery like a beast." He turned and strode away. "Not quite the dashing image the world seems to hold of me."

She saw the enormity of the dark ocean lapping at him, the waves trying to enfold him. *He had been a slave?* Any grudging jealously, any sense of threat, dissolved in the face of it. Tears stung. Anne dropped her head and sought for the quiet place. A white light filled her vision as if a thousand bright suns shone over an ocean of love. A love that could even let him go, if necessary.

She opened her eyes, her heart seared by tenderness. "Jack, I'm sorry for what I said just now. It was wrong of me. I love you. You're a light and a miracle to me."

"You're not disgusted?"

"By something you could do nothing about? How could I be? Is this the shame that so contaminated your homecoming?"

"Perhaps. It wasn't something I thought anyone could understand. A degradation. Not of the mind or body—fate gave me a fortunate enough mistress—but of the soul, I suppose."

"Yet you longed to go back?"

"I had to go back only because my mission there remained

unfulfilled. It still does." He tipped back his head. "But now I'm afraid."

"You're the bravest soul I can imagine," she said.

"Foolhardy bravery is far easier when a man doesn't overly value his life. Alas, now I want to live." He gazed back at her with a strangely compassionate humor. "That was the risk that I took when we made love like that last night."

Tears built, then quietly streamed down her face. "I've made you want to live?"

He nodded. "Yet do you think that I want to spend the rest of my days with tribesmen who believe betrayal is a form of honor? Do you think I long for the desolation of deserts and mountains? Yes, it was splendid. Perhaps it was even worthwhile—or would have been, had I not failed so damned miserably to save Toby's papers. But those years robbed my soul piece by piece from my body. Last night you insisted on replacing it. I don't think I can bear to lose it again."

"But I've given you nothing," she said. "I'm plain and stubborn and ignorant about the world."

"You have the courage of dragons," he said. "You've given me freedom. You've given me yourself. I love you more than life, but you have indeed robbed me of that mad bravado, Anne. Your courage is far greater than mine."

"Any courage of mine is only what you've given me. Real courage is what you're showing now, to go back to Asia when you fear you have everything to lose. Real courage is what kept you alive when you were there. And only real heroism allows you to tell me now that you love me."

"God, yes, I love you! My brave wife, I love you. If there were any way to lay down this burden, I would do it. Yet if Toby lives, it's in conditions of unimaginable horror in one of the most sadistic places in the world. I'm the only man who has any idea of where to look or how to travel. If I can extricate him, I must do it."

"Yes," she said. "Yes, you must. I see that. If it were the only answer to our dilemma, I would be here waiting for you when you came back."

"I don't expect you to wait," he said. "Ours was a marriage of convenience. I don't expect anything from you at all."

"Then you should, because I shall love you forever, Wild Lord Jack, with all my heart, with all my soul, and with all my body. Didn't you realize that you risked that also last night? That you bound me to you for all eternity? So now our courage is only in each other."

"Yet I must leave you," he said.

"But I can come with you—not as far as Toby's prison, of course—but as far as I can. Why not?"

He looked incredulous. "You would leave England, leave your family, abandon all your work with the fossils?"

"Yes," she said. "Yes! It wouldn't be forever, but meanwhile we'd have all those months on the ship, and at least some of the overland travel after that. Perhaps, if we stay together, we'll create something strong enough to sustain both of us."

He quaked as if buffeted by a strong wind. "God, you don't know how tempted I am to agree, but you don't really know what you're asking, Anne."

"I've never known, have I? Yet I've insisted anyway. This is right. I know it, Jack. Keep me with you as long as I give you courage. Leave me behind when I become a burden. Why not?"

"And if I don't come back?" he asked. "If you're left alone in India?"

"Then I'll have had those months and those memories, and so will you."

"We might have already started a child."

She shook her head, filled with gratitude, though earlier the discovery had brought her nothing but grief. "My courses began this morning. We did not make a baby, after all, but perhaps if we journey together to Asia, your son or daughter will yet be born to inherit this place."

He strode away to stare from the window, where he stood in silence.

"There must be somewhere safe you could leave me," she said, "before you adopt your disguise and head up into the mountains?"

"Yes, of course. You could stay with the officers' wives in any town protected by British troops. Perhaps on the ship you could even teach me about fossils?"

"Then you'll let me come, Jack?"

He turned, his face streaked by tears. "I don't have the strength to refuse you. You're giving me everything I've longed for. Yet we must pack and be ready by morning."

IT WAS A FRANTIC DAY. ANNE THREW BELONGINGS HAPHAZardly onto the bed and let a bevy of maids pack them in cases. The books that Jack had given her could be loaded directly onto their ship. Clothes could be sent for. Supplies ordered and delivered instantly, thanks to the influence of the Blackdown name.

Yet Horace would have to stay behind. Anne kissed the kitten good-bye, her eyes damp, then laughed when he ran off, tail in the air, perfectly content to be the new kitchen pet. Withycombe Court was a paradise for cats, especially one that Her Ladyship had placed in the particular loving care of the housekeeper.

Later that afternoon Jack carried Anne back in the carriage to Hawthorn Axbury to take a tearful farewell of her family. Her mother wept as her sisters clung to her. Jack stood off to one side, his hands folded behind his back. Mr. Marsh walked up to him and the men shook hands.

As they climbed back into Jack's carriage, Anne's father grasped her hard by the hand. She leaned down to kiss his cheek.

"I'll come back to you, Papa," she said.

"Of course you will," he replied, gray wisps of hair blowing about his face. "In the meantime, whatever happens, see it through, Annie!"

Laughing through her tears, she waved good-bye until they were all out of sight.

"It's not too late to change your mind," Jack said.

She glanced about at the beloved countryside of her native land and shook her head. "No. Not unless you've changed yours."

"I'm not that foolish. Besides, I'm looking forward to my lessons about fossils. To pursue the truth about the history of the earth will be a compelling enough adventure."

"More so than our adventures in bed?"

"Ah, but those aren't adventures merely of the mind and body, beloved. They are adventures of the soul."

"Then 'whither thou goest, I will go.' Even to the ends of the earth, and most certainly to India. I want to see those giant skulls full of gems, the fossil dragons lurking in the foothills of the Himalayas."

"I only heard about them," he said. "I never saw them with my own eyes."

"Then when you must go alone after Toby, perhaps the thought of those eye sockets full of crystal, those stony nostrils framed in diamonds, will give you enough reason to come back to me alive."

His smile spoke louder than his words, though she knew she would always treasure them.

"I need no other reason than you," he said.

THEY BOWLED BACK UP THE DRIVE AT WITHYCOMBE TO find another carriage waiting in the forecourt. Erect, stiff, the Duke of Blackdown had just stepped down. The duchess joined him. Behind them, Lord Ryderbourne swung down from a black gelding. Anne invited them all inside, her formidable new family, and felt no trepidation at all.

"Lady Jonathan?" Ryder said quietly. "You look radiant! Not because Jack takes ship tomorrow?"

"But, yes," Anne said firmly. "Because I am going with him—"

"To *India*?" the duchess said.

Jack turned to face his mother. "We need to be together, even to the ends of the earth. Can you forgive me for that, Your Grace?"

She stepped up to him, ribbons fluttering, and laid her fingers on his sleeve. "There was never anything to forgive, my dear son, except this one thing: that I feared you had lost the will to live, that you had tried to negate love."

"You weren't wrong," Jack said, setting his hand over hers. "But you don't need to be afraid for me any longer. Anne will make sure I survive anything fate may throw in my path. Meanwhile, she's going to teach me how to understand the age of the earth and the terrible creatures that once made the ground shake. Together we shall reach for the mind of God with our paltry human understanding."

The goddess-green eyes filled with tears. "You won't shock me with blasphemy, Jonathan."

"I don't wish to," Jack said. "Come, let us stroll together."

They walked away, his dark head bent over her blond one as the duchess listened to her son or asked the occasional question. At the end of the room they stopped, facing each other. The duchess said something more. Jack leaned down to kiss his mother's forehead. When they came back to rejoin the others, his mother's cheeks were damp.

"So you and my son have found a new purpose," the duchess said to Anne, smiling. "You will go hunting for dragons together. Bless you, my dear! You have begun to heal him, I think. Yet my son will change you more than you will change him."

"I hope so," Anne said. "Jack is opening up the world to me. He's offering me the depth and splendor of his spirit. He could never damage or corrupt me. How could he? We love each other."

The duchess leaned forward to kiss Anne on both cheeks. "Then you are his salvation. And your love for each other will keep him alive until he is ready to come home."

There was little time for more. Their ship was beating up the Channel. The duke's coach waited. The duke and duchess bid farewell to their younger son and his new wife.

Anne stood with Jack and watched their carriage leave. Ryder walked up to stand beside them. A groom held his horse near the mounting block.

"My turn," Ryder said. "And I have a private message from Guy—he'll try to catch you to make his own farewells on your way to the ship. It's too complex for me to explain." Ryder held out a note. "Something to do with a woman—a Miss Rachel Wren? And there's other news."

Jack glanced over the note and looked back at his brother.

"Yes. Uriah Thornton has been killed," Ryder said. "Garroted. No one knows who did it. I'm sorry, Jack."

"That I didn't take his life myself? I'm not!" The brothers clasped each other in a bear hug. "Thank you for being you, Ryder," Jack said. "Don't change. And thanks for coming to say good-bye."

Lord Ryderbourne strode over to his mount and swung himself into the saddle. He leaned down and winked.

"I only came to ask you to bring me another jade horse," he said. "I was careless with the first one. I shall never be so foolish again."

CHAPTER EIGHTEEN

❧❧❦❧

THE CAVALCADE WOUND ALONG THE DUST-FILLED ROAD, then dropped down toward the river. The carriage horses pricked their ears. Shaded by her silk parasol, Mrs. Dilton-Smythe chattered on, complaining, gossiping, sometimes reaching out to pat the back of Anne's hand. Anne smiled and nodded and heard nothing that her companion was saying. Beyond the river a snowcapped range of mountains towered into the clouds: the great Himalayas.

She was in India, where a man could climb a rope into the sky and disappear. India, where dragon bones encrusted with gems lay waiting to be discovered.

Major Dilton-Smythe's redcoats marched behind the ladies' carriage. The officers and a small troop of cavalry rode ahead, their horses lashing their tails against flies. The rest of the soldiers stepped along smartly, sweating beneath their glittering gear and heavy uniforms. At the rear of the column, a ragged group of Muslim traders and a gaggle of native servants led a small caravan of camels.

The first soldiers reached the riverbank. The ladies' carriage pulled up. Major Dilton-Smythe had called a halt to water the horses.

"Don't be afraid, Lady Jonathan," Mrs. Dilton-Smythe said. "It's a shame that business calls Lord Jonathan away to the south, but this area is all solidly under British control. We're as safe as if we were in England."

"So I understand," Anne said. "I'm not afraid."

"Though I wish the major would not allow those native traders to tag along with the servants. They believe our military glory will reflect favorably on them, no doubt, but they're all filthy heathens. You shouldn't involve yourself with them."

"It seems a small thing," Anne said, "to offer the use of my compass to more accurately locate the direction of Mecca."

"So they can scrape their foreheads on the ground five times a day. We should insist that all these people become Christian."

"Then we must show them a little Christian charity," Anne said as solemnly as she was able. "How else can we demonstrate the superiority of our faith?"

Some hours later they reached their destination without incident: the last outpost of the East India Company that was suitable for officers' wives. Tea and cakes awaited the ladies. Anne was shown into an airy room, her bedroom for that night and for the next several months. It was as close as she could get to the mountains.

She lay awake long after dark, curled in her bed with her head on one arm, staring at her window. Mrs. Dilton-Smythe and the major snored in the next room. The sound rumbled through the thin walls. Insects chirped somewhere outside, saturating the night with a pulse of anticipation. Anne felt that promise echo in her blood, as clear as her own quiet breath.

A shadow moved at the window. A darker shape blocked the stars for a moment.

Her heart began to race.

Robes flowed as if a warm wind stirred a curtain. With the stealth of a robber a man crept over the sill and padded up to the bed. Her heart thundered, deafening her.

The man leaned down to press two fingers against Anne's neck, just beneath the jaw.

"Your pulse is a little rapid, my lady," he murmured in her ear. "Please tell me that some very wicked thoughts are already exciting you."

"*You* excite me," Anne whispered, pulling his hand down to kiss his palm.

Jack began to shed robes. Layers of fabric pooled at his feet until he stood entirely naked beside her bed. Faint starlight glimmered over sharply defined muscles, gleaming as if beaten from bronze. He was already erect for her.

Her pulse hammering, Anne sat up and tugged her nightdress off over her head. Her nipples puckered in the scented night breezes as if they were cold. He brushed his fingertips over them, and his intaken breath hissed into the quiet night.

Though her knees trembled and her blood burned in hot eddies, she knelt on the bed. Her breasts brushed his chest as she leaned forward to breathe into his ear.

"Hush, hush, beloved! You'll wake the major."

His hands slipped down to rest on the swell of her buttocks. He pulled her against his body, trapping his erection between their bellies.

"That's his snoring?"

"I think the loudest snores are Mrs. Dilton-Smythe's."

Silent laughter shook its way down his body. "What would the major's wife think if she rushed in to prevent your being ravished—"

"And found that the man doing the ravishing was a despised Muslim trader?"

"A filthy camel herder—"

"—who knows all the wicked erotic secrets of the Orient: my beloved husband, Wild Lord Jack?"

"Enough talk, my lady," he said, his voice husky, his arousal pulsing against her. "Shall we let the ravishment begin?"

$\mathcal{J}$ACK TORE HIMSELF AWAY BEFORE DAWN, LEAVING ANNE sleeping, her mouth curved into a smile of contentment. This was the last time! They had both known it and not spoken of it. They had hatched the plan together on the ship: that he would pretend to leave her in Major Dilton-Smythe's care. Anne had given away nothing, even when he had rejoined her party already disguised as a horse trader. She had simply opened her arms to him every night when he crept into her bed.

His robes fluttering behind him, Jack strode out to the edge of the town, then beyond into the vast darkness of the Indian night. Soon he must rejoin the others. In the morning the camels would head north and east, into territory that Anne couldn't visit. Then, as the caravan went on its way without him, he must travel alone into the white spaces on the map. There he must once again penetrate secrets no European had ever dared uncover—except him, because he had to.

He spun about and walked back. The dark shapes of the camels grumbled and shifted. One of the sleeping traders grunted, but none of them questioned either his identity or his devotion to Allah. After all, hadn't he been the one to persuade the young English lady to pull out her compass every day and show them all the true direction of Mecca? Yet the ruse had been entirely Anne's own idea: a way for them to speak—even if briefly—five times each day.

Jack rolled himself in his robes and went to sleep, knowing he would dream not of the exotic ladies of Asia, but of his passionate, lovely English wife, who was as brave and resourceful as an eagle.

Four days later he bid good-bye to his caravan and headed north with only one servant. The mountains reared up before them, mocking the two tiny figures riding up through the foothills. He was living entirely in character now, eating, sleeping, speaking as a devout student of the Koran who also knew horses. The servant had no idea that his master was really the son of an English duke.

They camped that night beneath an overhanging cliff. Jack crawled into his blanket and thought about Anne. At Withycombe—when he had first realized just how desperately he wanted to live and how absolutely he loved her—he had thought she had robbed him of the courage to do this. Now he knew that any courage he possessed was only because of her.

His mind filled with memories of their shared passion, yet also of her humor and her ardor for science. All three enthralled him. If he survived this last adventure, the study of the earth would intrigue him as much as it fascinated her for the rest of their days.

Something moved outside. A clopping of hooves, a vague shuffling, the arrival of two—perhaps three—horsemen in a place where no one traveled but bandits. The servant hissed an alarm.

Alertness seared Jack's blood as his pistol slipped into his hand.

He rolled from his blanket and spun into the shadow at the base of the cliff, where he could keep his back against solid rock and where his assailants would have to cross through the light of the campfire to reach him. He had two bullets, then he had his body and the long, hard years of training.

More than that, he had a wife to live for, to return to.

He felt no fear at all.

*J*ACK WAS GONE. HE HAD JOURNEYED ON WITH THE CARA-van that morning, leaving Anne to hide her grief and her hope.

I will come back to you, beloved, he had said. *Nothing can possibly prevent it.*

She stared up at the vast Himalayas bulked against the sky—where only the bones of travelers marked the high, snowbound trails—and sent a stream of silent prayers after him. Their British outpost seemed such a frail ornament tacked onto the hem of those huge, heartless peaks.

Nevertheless she would not let herself be afraid. If she allowed fear, Jack might sense it—winging straight from her heart to his—and be undermined by it. Soldiers all over the Empire were separated from their homes. All those wives and mothers and sisters waited with quiet courage for a homecoming that might never happen. She could surely do as much.

So Anne traveled into town that afternoon in an open carriage with Mrs. Dilton-Smythe as if nothing had changed. Their small escort of soldiers pushed a path for the English ladies through a jostle of pack animals and travelers, but a gaggle of men in filthy white robes blocked the road as they broke into a voluble argument.

"Make way!" The major's wife flailed at the men with her parasol. "Make way for Mrs. Dilton-Smythe and Lady Jonathan St. George!"

Anne doubted that any of the turban-clad traders either understood English—however loudly shouted—or cared who they were. Everyone was intent on his own business. Camels and donkeys eyed them with supreme indifference. The throng closed in about them like water piling up behind a dam. Their carriage jolted to a halt, caught in a tangle of animals and men with impassive faces.

A covered litter bumped into Anne's side of the carriage. The curtains parted for a moment to reveal a man's face, white and round beneath a shock of inky hair.

"Make way!" Mrs. Dilton-Smythe barked, exasperated.

The litter scraped. One of the soldiers turned his horse to force a way through, shouting at the crowd. Anne caught another glimpse of the man's intense black eyes, before the curtain swung closed. Yet as the ladies' carriage lurched forward, a hand reached from the litter to press something into Anne's open fingers.

Her heart beat as if she'd been running. Acting entirely on instinct, she palmed the slip of paper and hid it beneath her skirts. For a moment, in spite of all her resolutions, she felt the cold touch of fear. The stranger in the litter wasn't English. He was Chinese.

THREE MEN—NOT TWO—MATERIALIZED OUT OF THE DARK and dismounted. The horses shifted nervously. The night air breathed absolute silence, except for the slight jingle of bits. A small scrape and click betrayed weapons being drawn. Jack cocked his pistol. His servant had already pulled out a long, wicked knife.

Jack steadied his aim, his mind clear and cool. Bandits would not be interested in the niceties of hand-to-hand combat. If they rushed his hiding place, he could drop two of them in their tracks.

Yet one of the intruders stepped forward into the firelight. He was merely a boy, grimy and disheveled, white face ghostly beneath his turban. The hair rose on the back of Jack's neck as the boy turned with unerring instinct to stare directly at Jack— almost as if he could see straight through the dark to penetrate the other man's soul—and smiled.

With crushing strength Jack gripped his servant by the wrist, forcing the man to drop his knife. He glanced quickly at the other two horsemen: British cavalry officers—Pence and Lord Merton— also dressed like natives. No one else. No bandits. Relief flooded his heart.

"May wonders never cease," he said dryly, thrusting his pistol back into his belt and striding forward. His pulse still lurched wildly. "The British army has taken to bringing wives into the wilderness!"

Pence had the grace to look sheepish. Merton tugged at his mustache and grinned.

"Her Ladyship insisted on coming, Lord Jonathan," he said cheerfully. "Game's up, I'm afraid!"

His native servant spoke no English. He had retrieved his knife and backed up against the cliff.

"These crazy English are bringing news of my brother," Jack said in the man's own language. "It's all right. Make some tea."

The servant busied himself, still shooting suspicious glances at the newcomers.

Jack looked back at Anne and beckoned her to the fire. Pulling her down beside him, he squatted on his haunches and gestured for the two officers to do likewise.

"I'll have your hides, sirs," he hissed. "What the devil possessed you to bring Lady Jonathan?"

"It was my idea," Anne said.

"You're as lovely to me as pure water," Jack replied. "Even with a foul-looking turban covering your hair and your nose smeared with dirt. Nevertheless I intend to punish someone for letting you come out here."

"Then punish me," she said.

"We'd better leave you for a moment, my lord," Pence said. Gripping Merton by the sleeve, he walked off as if to see to the horses.

"So what possessed you?" Jack asked.

"It was fun," Anne replied. "Though I'm sure I would change my mind, if I were to meet with bad company."

"You *have* just met with bad company: If this is some kind of mad impulse, I'll murder you myself."

"You'd better not," she said. "I have news of Toby."

Her words drove straight into his heart. *"Toby?"*

Firelight washed over her face. The tip of her nose dipped as she tried to swallow her smile. "We might go up into the hills first, if you like, after dragons, but I think you might prefer to come back to town now instead." Her voice dropped as she gripped his hand, palm to palm, and looked directly into his eyes. "I didn't come on a whim, beloved. Toby survived. He was ill and mistreated, but he survived. He's weak, but mending fast."

Jack swallowed an odd kind of anguish, as though hope was almost too painful. "You have seen *Toby?*"

"He passed me a note in the street. I had to creep out to meet him secretly, of course. Mrs. Dilton-Smythe would never have countenanced my visit to a Chinese. When he's strong enough, Toby wants to rewrite all of your notes that were lost, but he's going to need your help." Her fingers tightened, sharing the warm pulse of her life. "You don't have to go back up into the mountains, Jack. The game with Russia can be played out by other men."

Elation beat at him. He cupped her face in both hands and kissed her with painstaking thoroughness. Anne kissed him back as if to kindle the universe. The native servant spilled tea with a hiss into the fire. Merton and Pence coughed and stared away into space.

Tension seeped away as the knot at the center of his being simply unraveled. Years of training, now irrelevant. Years of painstaking work soon to be recovered, then abandoned. *The game with Russia can be played out by other men.*

Jack pulled back at last to wipe the spilling tears from her filthy cheeks with his thumb. She pushed her turban back into place and laughed. God, how he loved her! His beautiful, resourceful, intrepid wife!

"So we'd better go back now," she said. "You may not have realized it, my dear Lord Jonathan, but it's not really safe out here. Unless you want to go look for those gem-studded skulls, after all?"

Hilarity caught him out. He threw back his head and roared with laughter.

Perhaps the tiger was melting away to become indistinguishable from the forest.

"Alas, the fossils of India must wait, beloved," he said as peace spread through his bones. "We have maps to make first."

* * *

$\mathcal{A}$NNE WAS BLISSFULLY, DEEPLY HAPPY. TO THE SHOCK OF Mrs. Dilton-Smythe, Lord and Lady Jonathan Devoran St. George rented a large, airy house in the foothills, a short distance from town, with not a British soldier in sight. Instead, several outlandish-looking men—in the eyes of the major's wife—had attached themselves to Lord Jonathan like a ferocious personal bodyguard.

The lady's shock deepened to learn that the once-admired cream of the English aristocracy—the son of the Duke of Blackdown, no less!—was socializing freely with both Indians and Chinese, and even some nameless tribal people from the north. But what could you expect when a scion of the English peerage married such an eccentric creature? One so far beneath him?

Mrs. Dilton-Smythe and her friends elected not to call.

Anne was too entranced to notice. The garden overflowed with exotic vines and trees. Cool, scented breezes blew through their rooms at night, as if the snowbound passes far above smiled in benediction, after all. Like their Indian hosts, she and Jack wore light robes of cotton and silk. The house smelled sweetly of flowers and aromatic wood. Their cook served meals wicked in spiced subtlety.

And Jack was with her, every day and every night, at peace in his heart and at one in their love.

Toby and some fellow travelers had been given a suite of rooms of their own. After a few weeks of private nursing, he was still thin and weak, but he was at last strong enough to really talk. The tale of his capture and escape was neither easy to tell, nor easy to hear, but Anne sat with her hand in Jack's and listened with an open heart.

When it was over, Jack once again offered to fetch Toby the best English doctors available.

"None of your barbarian doctors for me!" Toby said, smiling. "My faith still lies in the Chinese tradition, especially in the loving hands of my wife."

Anne looked up to see a woman standing shyly in the doorway. A tiny Chinese lady with the face of a pansy. Anne had no idea how she had arrived, but perhaps she had been in Toby's rooms all along. Jack, obviously, had already guessed or found out.

"My Flower of Peace." Toby held out one hand. "Though I escaped my prison alone, I would never have survived after that without her."

Toby's wife walked up to the bed and sat down. She was quiet, self-effacing, and obviously spoke no English.

"She had been recently widowed," Toby said. "She was being sent back to China, but to her shame discovered me instead."

Flower of Peace kept her head bent, though her face lit like a lantern with clear devotion as she smiled at her husband.

Then it was Toby's turn to listen as Jack told him the fate of the Dragon's Fang.

"So Uriah's madness killed him in the end." Toby leaned back on his pillows and gazed into his wife's black eyes. "As for our fossil tooth, it will have been ground into medicine by now. It doesn't matter. I will write a tale of our dragon to entertain old women and children."

"You won't re-create your scientific notes and drawings?" Anne asked gently.

Toby's black gaze met hers. "No, never! No one must ever be tempted to go into those deserts full of death again."

She closed her eyes for a moment. It was a disappointment, of course, but her heart anchored on more profound values.

"Then let the dragons sleep on undisturbed," she said. "Their bones will still be there for a future adventurer in another age. Meanwhile, there will be other fossils, other finds, and the world will have the time that it needs to catch up to the splendor of this new truth about Creation."

"So let us make maps, instead," Jack said. "Simple accounts of trails and villages."

Toby grinned as if a burden had been lifted from his heart. "That's what I came here to do, Jack. After that the rest of my life must be in China. None of us can belong forever to two cultures. I'm still a Christian and a freethinker and half-English, but I am also Chinese. I have made my choice: China is where my heart lies. I would be forever just a visitor anywhere else."

Anne glanced up to meet Jack's eyes. *Wherever I go,* he had said once, *I'm just a visitor in my own life.*

As if he read her thoughts, he smiled. "As long as you are with me, beloved," he said, "I am at peace."

WHILE TOBY AND JACK WORKED ON THE MAPS, BUNDLES of letters arrived from Wyldshay and Hawthorn Axbury. Every week Anne and Jack wrote back. Meanwhile, she helped to transcribe the notes that Toby dictated from memory.

Whenever they all needed a break, Toby and Flower of Peace spent quiet hours together in the gardens, while Anne and Jack rode out on little excursions after fossils. The Indian rocks were a mystery to her, a geology she couldn't place. Nevertheless, she made notes on their composition and stratification, with Jack's keen intelligence also harnessed to the cause. Every night they reveled in argument and laughter and conjecture about the nature of the earth and the history of the terrible ancient lizards—and then they made love.

"I despair," Anne said one day as they rode into a new area, "that we shall ever find anything new, after all."

A cliff disappeared above their heads into an entanglement of lush vegetation. Flowering trees overhung a little patch of grass at its foot, forming a sheltered, private dell.

Jack swung from his horse and lifted her down. Her pulse leaped like a hind springing across a meadow as he smiled lazily into her eyes.

"With you, my lady wife, every night is a new revelation."

Hot blood eddied in her veins, but she made a face at him before she walked over to study the rock face. No bones had eroded out of the cliff. Nothing promising at all, except for the beauty of plants and the rustle of exotic birds—and the duke's son who had married her, then given her the world.

"No jewel-encrusted skulls here either, alas," she said.

Jack leaned back against a tree trunk and watched her. "Your love is the only jewel that I care about," he said gravely.

"But you have adorned my life with brilliance, Lord Jonathan Devoran St. George," she replied instantly. "Even the stars pale in comparison."

"Don't, don't!" he said, laughing. He strode forward to catch her around the waist. "I'm robbed of words, Anne. You're my lover and the wife of my heart. I adore everything about you."

"If you're struck so dumb by that adoration," she said with mock solemnity, "there's only one way left to prove it."

"Out here?" he asked dryly. "Where anyone may discover us?"

"No one will," she said. "They wouldn't dare."

The horses stood quietly tethered to a tree, oblivious as Anne and Jack made love on his spread coat with exquisite, leisurely ingenuity. An absolute communion of body and soul. Tongues dumb to words but eloquent with each sensitive, moist caress.

Afterward she lay back on the grass and gazed up at the trees. Jack dozed beside her, long and lean, his head pillowed on one arm. Birds rustled. The horses lazily switched their tails. A small breeze whispered of Paradise.

As long as you are with me, beloved, I am at peace.

THE NEXT DAY JACK WALKED IN WAVING THE LATEST PACKET of letters from England. "I rode in to town to fetch the post. Believe it or not, we have a letter from your former fiancé."

Anne glanced up from the final map that Toby and Jack had just completed. There were still many gaps and white spaces, but there was also vital information for Britain.

"From Arthur?"

Her husband grinned down at her, more lovely, more perfect, more real, more dear to her heart than any fairy-tale hero. His forest-dark eyes shone with genuine excitement.

"Mr. Trent writes to say that a flying reptile has just been discovered in the cliffs of Dorset, an almost complete skeleton. A *flying reptile,* Anne! Fossils from the same species have turned up in equivalent strata in Bavaria. Shall we go to see them?"

Her heart lurched. "A flying *lizard*? With wings?"

"With wings!"

"But what about our search for the jewel-encrusted skulls of India?"

Jack perched on the edge of the table, booted feet crossed at the ankle. His eyes suddenly serious, he began to play idly with a lock of her hair.

"I'm done with chasing chimera, Anne. Toby and his wife plan to go home in a few days with the last Chinese caravan before winter closes the passes. Our work here is essentially finished. Meanwhile, world-shattering science is being done in England and Europe, and we're both longing to see our families."

"Even the formidable duchess?"

Jack leaned forward to kiss her. "Especially the formidable duchess."

She smiled up at him, the love of her life. "Then I hope she'll be pleased to welcome her first grandchild."

Silence filled her ears as if angels sang in inaudible choruses. Jack sat as if transfixed.

"Are you sure?" he said at last, his voice husky.

"I only knew for certain this morning. I'm going to bear our child in about seven months."

"Oh, God, Anne!" His voice broke. "Our baby!"

Anne grinned. "You didn't really think we could keep making love with such abandon without consequences, did you?"

Jack lifted her up into the safe circle of his arms, so she sat across his thighs with her head pillowed on his shoulder.

"Then this is the beginning of a very large family." He nuzzled her ear. "So I think we must allow our firstborn to get to know the fossil-studded cliffs of Dorset—"

"And fly the dragon tray down over the roofs of Wyldshay!"

"And be spoiled by a doting coterie of grandparents and aunts and uncles—"

"And learn to be a perfect English lady or gentleman?"

Laugh lines etched his cheeks. "Oh, not entirely English! Our children will be rooted securely in love and home and family, but I trust they'll also be citizens of the world?"

Anne wrapped her arms about his waist. "They'll be philosophers and artists and scientists, of course. With such disgraceful parents, how could they be otherwise?"

"Yet if we leave right now, our baby can still be born in England."

"Yes," she said. "Yes, Jack. I would like that."

His eyes bright, he stood and swung her up into his arms. Anne squealed a fake protest as he carried her up to their private rooms. He set her down by the window where they could gaze out at the beauty of the far Himalayas.

She snuggled back into his embrace as Jack laid both palms flat over her belly, where the child of their love was growing strongly beneath her heart.

Wisps of cloud trailed like pennants.

"The dragon of good fortune flies laughing across the sky," he said. "Tossed by a wind that blows to heaven from the ends of the earth."

Anne set her palms over his hands, over the keen pulse of new life. "Then that same wind will fill the sails of a fast ship to carry us wherever our hearts desire."

"The only desire of my life is to be with you," he said.

"I love you, Wild Lord Jack," Anne replied. "I always have and I always will."

Jack leaned down to kiss her.

"Then let's go home, beloved," he said. "To England. To Withycombe. Home."

ABOUT THE AUTHOR

JULIA ROSS was born and grew up in Britain. A graduate of the University of Edinburgh in Scotland, she has won numerous awards for her novels. Julia now lives in the Rocky Mountains. Visit her website at www.juliaross.net.